THE RARKYN'S FAMILIAR

NIKKY LEE

PARLIAMENT HOUSE PRESS

ISBN: 978-1-956136-18-0

Edited by Cindy Kilbourne, Alyssa Barber, Megan Hultberg, and Malorie Nilson

The Parliament House

www.parliamenthousepress.com

To Nanna,
For always believing in me.

The Steppes
Galieva
Gila
Iros Mountains
Barðas Post
Nilos
Talos Province
Torin
Memnon's Spine
Hannon
Eyrar Wilds
Finnafell
Skagi
Kalana Sea
Lecne
Kraw
Chalcai
Gesham Plains
Phaia Province
Lakhan
Illredan Province
Larthuza
Messia
Illredus
Alsinei
Rodon Province
Mata
Koseia
Udoni
Galcus Sea
Amatrae
Eyos Province
The Illredian Empire

PART I
BLOOD PACT

’Ware the skies when the rarkyns hunt,
Bodies of bird and man akin.
Woe the fool who meets their gaze,
And sees the Aether’s heart within.

—*Fragment from* The Epic of Asander.
c. 500 years before the Illredian Founding.

CHAPTER ONE

His feathers itched; bones ached.

He crouched atop the shattered planks of Archer's wagon, a chipped and ragged rock in his talons, poised to strike the manacle around his wrist. *Break this time.*

He swung the rock, smashing it into the metal. The rock shattered, crumbling in his hand, its grains bouncing down the mound of mud and splintered wood to the gully floor.

"Aether damn you," Skaar exploded, grabbing the chain and rattling it.

The runes carved into the metal flared, strange letters flashing fluorescent green—and *pulsed.*

Skaar froze. Pressure slithered up his arm and he gritted his teeth. Cold seeped through feathers into skin, threatening to stab deeper, right down to bone. He stood, quivering, sucking in one slow breath, then another. The glow faded. *Close call.*

His stomach growled again.

Reythr curse this place.

He kicked a half-buried axle and when the wood didn't give, he swore as pain bloomed in his toes. The chain rattled under him, iron manacle chafing his wrist as he hopped about, wings flared, tail whipping the underbrush, hissing curses under his breath.

No matter how he looked at it, the manacle was an ordinary piece of metal. He crouched over it again, wedging a talon into the lock, twisted, failed, and then tried to dislodge the pins for the hundredth time that morning. The problem wasn't the metal. Metal he could handle—except for silver. It was the galdar runes spelled on top of it. The glow in those cursed letters, scratched and scored into the iron, refused to die. Magic was annoyingly potent in the hands of humans—when they could use it.

As far as landslides went, this hadn't been a big one. But it had been big enough. The mound stretched from top to bottom of the narrow ravine. Archer's wagon lay overturned in the rubble, metal cage twisted, shattered wheels bared to the world like wooden ribs. Above, the cliffs loomed, threatening to dump another load of rubble on top of him.

That he'd survived the first slide at all was a miracle. Locked inside the wretched wagon, he'd bounced within its tumbling mass all the way to the bottom, the final impact turning his mind black. He was sure it had taken him at least a day just to summon the will to open his eyes again, skull throbbing as if someone had carved it open with a rusted knife. When he'd probed the raw lump on the back of his head, the world had swum, and he'd doubled over and retched into the dirt.

Now here I am. Skaar shot the chain a savage look as it lay coiled in the mud. Trapped and exposed in the middle of human territory. *A hare out in the open.*

A breeze wafted the scent of musty earth over him, along with something else, a thick sour stench he knew too well. Death. Something —*someone* Skaar hoped—was rotting somewhere in the mound. Probably the horse. With any luck, Archer too. *And good riddance.* If Skaar never saw that accursed mancer again, he'd die a happy rarkyn.

Which might not be far off if he couldn't get free. It was only a matter of time before the runes became too weak to bind him. Human galdar was like that. Their magic was strong but short-lived. If his captor was truly gone in the landslide, the runes' power would soon fade. But who knew how long that would take? A fine thing it would be to die of starvation or at the hands of some yokel one day, only for the sigiled manacle to break the next.

He reached for the talisman about his neck and held it up to the light. Aloft in the air, the jagged rock of quartz spun in a slow circle. The lifeless rune carved into it—a memento from happier times—sent dapples of light over the forest floor and reflected a mud-crusted face back at him.

Reythr, you look like something a ginndir chewed on and spat out.

Dirt clung to his wasted limbs like a crusted scab, getting under every feather, into every orifice. Skaar scratched the mud-clogged crest atop his head. Grit rained from the long plumage and stuck in the ridge of feathers along his nose and brow. He sneezed, teeth nearly taking off his tongue, and grimaced as a fresh throbbing started in his head, just under his horns. Wretched luck.

He ran a talon over the rune in the crystal talisman: an old habit unbroken. Unlike the manacle, this piece of galdar working had been made for his tampering, but he'd drained the rune's magic long ago.

He gave it a shake. "Useless thing."

The crystal gleamed back at him. Dead. A mirror was about all it was good for. He let it drop with a sigh.

Forcing his eyes closed, Skaar leaned on the mound, willing himself to rest. Rest, recuperate, then challenge the manacle again.

A cloud fell across the sun.

Eyes shut, all Skaar knew was the warmth seeping into his bones left. He scowled, impatient as he waited for the warmth to return. It didn't. A faint, rustling footstep triggered a warning in his head. He vaulted to his feet. Too late.

Not a cloud. Not a cloud at all.

A dart bit into his neck. His jaw dropped; a brief cry of surprise escaped him. His legs buckled.

Humans, was all he had time to think before the world teetered and turned black.

CHAPTER TWO

"Gods and ginndir, Hane, what have you done?" Lyss stared at the unconscious mass of feathers, blood humming in her ears, and tried not to vomit. *An aetherling.* By Sepp and all the gods, one of the Otherworld's monsters. *Here.*

This can't be happening. Not again.

She groped for her sword, only to find the bag of medicines on her belt. When Hane had run into camp and pulled her from her rune practice, she'd expected a hunting accident, a laceration from a wild boar or an ankle sprained on the mountain trail, but this?

The Eder Wilder boy beside her scuffed one boot, eyes darting to the small galdar ward scratched in the earth before them. Five runes marked the perimeter of a circle, lines and letters glowing green as its magic contained the creature within. Hane shoved his hands in the pockets of his tunic. "We, ah, shot it with a tinker's dart."

With a tinker's dart. The words rolled over Lyss. She drank them in, trying to drown out the thumping blood in her ears—and the memories flooding in. She forced her mind away, swallowing hard.

"We?" she asked, faintly, and searched the clearing. Trees, cliffs, a mound of rubble, and there, a tall lanky shadow stepping out of the shade. Darrin. A scowl crawled across her face.

I should have kratting known.

Hane pulled her off the trail, his thin, girlish fingers pale around her wrist. A head shorter and five years younger than Darrin, the fourteen-year-old looked more gangly than ever beside his brother.

"You *shot* it?" Lyss hissed at them. "Are you mad?"

The brothers exchanged a glance. Both shared the famous white, almost translucent skin of the Eder Wildner clan, but where Hane's eyes were bluer than the breast of a sky wren, Darrin's were dark—unusually so for a Wildner.

Darrin shrugged. "Looked like it was in trouble."

He stepped over the runes, shoving the creature's tail out of the way to reveal a heavy manacle clamped about its wrist. "See?" he said. "A sigil." He turned it over to reveal the runes embedded in the metal. "It's cutting him off from the Aether. At this rate, it'll kill him."

Him? Rage flared inside her. "It's an *aetherling*, Darrin!" she exploded, pointing at the creature. "Sepp almighty, it's a kratting monster." She took in the humanoid body, the feathers...the *claws*. Under her tunic, the old scar twanged as if a pair of fingers had reached into her chest and plucked it like a string. Cold rushed down her limbs. Suddenly, she was standing on the road to Caenis, soldiers on all sides, her father's screams beating in her ears as another monster sank its teeth into his—

No. She bit her tongue, hard. Pain swept through her mouth, drowning out the memory. *Save it for later. For when you find those bastards.* She wiped clammy hands on her tunic instead, forcing them into fists so Darrin and Hane wouldn't see them shake. *An aetherling.* She sucked in a breath, held it until her heart calmed. It was unconscious. *For now.*

Sepp help them once it woke.

Lyss studied the creature again. It was at least three heads taller than any of the Wildner, and over four heads taller than her. Thin too. A full set of ribs were visible beneath its mottled-red plumage and its limbs were knobbly and emaciated. Even the two black wings cocooned about it were dull and missing feathers. Under it, a long tail stretched, crooked feathers flaring from the end like the fletch of an old arrow. Lyss frowned, this was not an aetherling she recognized.

"It's a rarkyn," Darrin said.

Rar-kyn. She searched her memory for the name. And stopped, remembering the stories she'd heard. Songs of unwitting heroes dragged into the Otherworld by these creatures; rumored sightings of whole flocks winking in and out of the skies deep in the wilds. Curiosity flickered inside her, despite herself.

"Sepp be, what is it doing here?"

"I don't know, but it's not looking well." Darrin nudged the sigil around the rarkyn's wrist again. "And this isn't helping."

Lyss took in the starved creature. Aether was to them like water was to humans. They couldn't live without it. She blinked as the full implication hit her. *Kratting shit, he can't be serious.* "You want to *free* it?" she gawped. Her rage stirred again, hot and angry in her belly. "For Sepp's sake, Darrin, just let it die!"

"If it dies, what do you think will happen?" Darrin's voice remained steady, tone reasoning, as if explaining to a child. Lyss ground her teeth. Gods, she hated it when he did that. Never mind that they were the same age. She pursed her lips.

Truth was she had no idea what might happen. Aetherlings were Iga's wheelhouse, not hers. She hadn't got up to that bit in her mentor's lessons, nor did she plan to. Her grip tightened around her medicine bag. Not after what happened to Fa. She knew all she needed to: Aetherlings were dangerous.

Darrin scowled. "Gods be Lyss, haven't you heard the stories? When it dies, it'll tear a hole to the Otherworld as it goes."

"So?"

He released an exasperated huff. "*So?* It could pull *everyone* within a shout of here in with it. Of course, it might have enough self-control left not to, but do you want to bet on it while it's like that?" He pointed at the rarkyn's ribs.

A sinking sensation pooled inside Lyss' stomach. She recalled the rush of Hane's words back at camp: *I need help. Where's Iga?* Their mentor had been off tending the herds. Lyss was all there was.

"What about its mancer?" she asked. After all, where there was an aetherling, there was a mancer. There was never one without the other. She searched the clearing. Mancers summoned aetherlings from the Otherworld, bound them to their will, and by undoing their runes, could return them there just as easily.

Darrin pointed to the pile of rubble. A lopsided carriage lay crumpled within it. "They're dead. Probably. It'll be a while until we can clear it all to be sure."

If it's one of the Order, you're better off leaving them to die, Lyss thought, but didn't say. She shuffled closer to the circle, marveling at its stability. Hane's power was truly something. Envy twisted inside her. Not even a crease of concentration on his brow from holding the ward with his mind. He wasn't even panting as the magic burned through the Aether reserves in his body. It was then she noticed the odd shapes of the runes scored in the dirt. *Invented* runes.

She swore under her breath. *Gods and ginndir, Hane.* The Empire's laws of galdar use were absolute. Their runes or nothing. No deviation. No foreign magic. She'd told him, Iga had told him. So many times. Work unorthodox runes and you'll attract the notice of the Order. She shuddered, her scar pulling up her throat as she fought down the images again. Nothing good ever came from that.

Darrin stooped and put a hand to the rarkyn's head—between the short roping horns poking through its crest—and rolled the creature's head to one side. A gash and a patch of half-dried blood the size of Lyss' palm stained the rarkyn's feathers. "Can you tend to this?" he asked.

Lyss' gaze fell on the rarkyn's curled talons. Each one graced the end of a long digit, black as bear claws, and covered in grit. They could wrap around her throat with length to spare. A gurgling scream rose out of her memory and she pushed it down. If Darrin could walk around it like that, it must be safe.

Well, safe as it could be.

"Alright." She thumped her medicine bag down and shot Hane a glare. "We'll talk about *this* later." She indicated the runes. "You're sure it's unconscious?"

The two boys nodded. She stepped over the circle, hoping neither Wildner saw the tremble in her legs. *Breathe. It's fine.*

"Be careful of its blood, I hear it's potent," Darrin advised.

Lyss knelt, examining the blow to the rarkyn's skull. It had been a hard one. It was a wonder the creature was still breathing, despite its size.

Thanks to its Aether origins no doubt. The beast reeked of the Otherworld, even to her. She could practically taste the zing of it on her lips; hot, like the Krawan spices Fa used to covet. Her scar twisted across her chest again and she clenched a fist. *Stop it.*

Darrin leaned over her shoulder. "Have you seen a rarkyn before? When"—he hesitated—"when you travelled?"

Lyss cracked open a pot of salve, rubbed a bandage into it and dabbed at the wound.

"No, I've never seen one, at least not one that was alive. I saw bones in the markets once." She suppressed a shiver at the memory of a merchant handling a skull with teeth the size of her fingers. Her father had laughed and politely shaken his head at the offer: too expensive, as always. Another twinge.

"Is it true that mancers hunt them?" Hane's question to Darrin pulled her back.

Darrin shrugged. "They're aetherlings so it makes sense, I suppose."

Then why, by Sepp's divine balls, did you shoot one with a tinker's blowpipe?! Lyss bit down on her fury. They were lucky the dart had worked at all. She dug another lump of salve out and pressed it into the rarkyn's feathers.

"I heard you can gain second sight if you eat their eyes," Hane was saying. "Supposedly their blood brings back the dead—if they're fresh."

Lyss scowled. *No one comes back from the dead.* She held her tongue and said, without looking up, "You're better off putting your faith in something real than in silly superstitions."

Hane shrank back as if Lyss had bitten him. Darrin sighed. "That's our Lyss, ever the practical one." He turned for the ridge. "I'm going to find Iga, I want that sigil off."

Lyss glowered as his figure loped off through the trees, then returned her salve to her bag and hunted for a needle and thread. Her gaze drifted back to the rarkyn, taking the faded braies around its bony hips, the undergarment's drawcord tight with length to spare. She scowled. Clothes indicated some level of intelligence, which only made the aetherling more dangerous.

Thou shalt not summon above thy station.

Kallion's fourth law echoed in her head in Iga's rasping tones. It took more than a standard foot soldier to keep and control a rarkyn. The more intelligent the aetherling, the harder they were to control. Even Lyss knew that. She frowned and glanced at the sigiled manacle again, then to the pile of rubble beyond.

What kind of mancer could control a rarkyn even after they were dead?

Lyss eyed the splintered skeleton of a cart poking out from the mud. No matter. Whomever the mancer had been, he or she was gone. Just as well. Most trained mancers were affiliated with the Order, and the less of the Order in the north, the better.

She found a needle and worked a thread into it.

Next to the circle, Hane traced runes in the dirt with a finger, waiting for Darrin's return. He finished one, scrubbed it out, and began again with a new one. Lyss squashed her jealousy. Unlike her, Hane was gifted with the runes. He took to galdar like a goat to grass. Sensing her watching, Hane flashed a sheepish grin and rubbed out his latest bastardized rune.

"Just experimenting," he said.

Lyss glared at him. "Try and explain that to an Order soldier. I promise it won't go down nearly as well. One look at those illegal runes and they'll brand you as a krat, and that'll snuff your magic out for good."

Hane rolled his eyes. "The Order doesn't come—" He stopped, face falling; the pink in his cheeks leaching away.

Lyss heard it too. A hiss at her back; leaves crunching under a great weight.

"Lyss!" Hane's voice pitched upwards.

She spun and her gaze latched onto the rarkyn. Time slowed. Blood drained from her limbs. It was awake. *Oh gods and ginndir, how could it be awake?*

A feathered arm fell across her shoulders, dragged her back. Long fingers wrapped under her chin, tight. Lyss gasped and fought for air. Talons pricked her skin. A hot breath fell against her ear.

"Unbind."

She froze. It could talk? Her mind wavered. By Sepp, it could *talk*.

A red eye glared at her, pupil round, the iris a fierce blood-red sunrise.

"Unbind." The word hissed out through a set of teeth in a too-wide mouth.

Lyss stared; mind blank, unable to think.

The rarkyn shifted, revealing its left eye. Set in a pit of black, a brilliant iris sat within, round and silver as a moon in a night sky, a black prick of a pupil in its middle. The mismatched gaze bored into her and Lyss' insides shriveled. Oh gods, she was going to die here. Today. Now.

Another hot, sticky breath rolled across her face.

"Lyss!" Hane charged in, swinging a heavy stick like a broadsword. "Get off you bastard!" He lashed the branch at the aetherling's head. Its talons released, air flooded Lyss' lungs and her knees hit the ground.

No Hane. You mustn't—

The boy lunged in again, martial form terrible. "Stay off!" he yelled. The rarkyn hissed, lips peeling back, and intercepted. It pounced hard and fast, knocking Hane to the ground. For a heartbeat, Hane scrabbled. Flailing, grappling, kicking. Then the rarkyn's fist cracked into his head.

The boy crumpled and his ward around them dimmed as his eyes unfocused and head lolled.

Blood rushed to Lyss' limbs. *Move,* she screamed at her legs. *Fight! Or we both die here.*

The rarkyn rounded on her. Lyss scrambled up, groping for the knife in her belt. She snapped the weapon up. Pathetically small next to those talons. She swallowed. No disarming them either. The rarkyn sprang, claws scything down. Pain fired across her arm. She bit back a cry. *Block it out. Hold the knife. Stay alive.*

She spun away, heart thudding. The rarkyn followed. She dodged another swing, swept in and slashed at the rarkyn's throat. She got its cheek instead, nicking a red scratch under one eye. The aetherling hissed and grabbed for her, chain and manacle rattling around its wrist. Her eyes followed the links trailing through the dirt.

That's it. Lyss lunged, scooped up the chain and pulled. The rarkyn stumbled, thrown off balance, and rounded on her again. She sidestepped another strike and—

—went sprawling backwards over Hane.

Shit. Shit, shit, shit. She scrambled over on hand and knee, struggling to find her feet.

The rarkyn came like a charging bull. It dove, eight feet of feather, teeth and talon, and flattened her to the earth.

For a heartbeat the world hung, growing dark before Lyss coughed and sucked in a wheezing gasp. She opened her eyes and wriggled her fingers. Both arms pinned under her, her left an angry throb from where the rarkyn's talons had sliced into her flesh. *Kratting damn.*

The rarkyn's face loomed close, feathers bristled, eerie eyes inches from her face. It was huffing hard. *Of course, its head. With that injury it's a wonder it can see straight.*

"Unbind!"

"What?" Lyss glanced at the circle. "No!" Besides, she didn't know how. Not with Hane's invented runes.

Angry teeth flashed in the corner of her vision. Its talons found her neck and began to squeeze. "Let go," it spat.

"I can't."

Five pricks of pain dug into her skin. A dribble of warmth ran under her chin. Her scar twinged, its puckered length burning down her chest. *Helpless,* it berated. *You swore this would never happen again.* Lyss clenched her jaw. *Never again.* She worked her fingers under her, one fist coiling around the knife, the other closing tight on something cold, and tingling.

The chain. By Sepp, she still held it.

With a screech, the rarkyn shifted on her back. "Unbind!" it bellowed.

Now.

Lyss pressed her knuckles into the earth and heaved. Her arms shook, muscles burning under the weight of the rarkyn, and pain stabbed down her wounded forearm. An inch of space opened under her chest. Her knife-hand snapped out and stabbed blindly, striking flesh.

The rarkyn howled, clutched its leg and its weight fell away.

Lyss launched upwards.

"Get—" she roared, punching down at the rarkyn with the hilt of her knife, aiming for those gnashing teeth *"off!"* The pommel connected with the creature's face, and the crack of its nose breaking shuddered through the hilt. The aetherling reeled back.

Lyss dove across the dirt, grabbed the back of Hane's jerkin and hauled him up. Gods, he was heavier than he looked. A snarl boomed at her back. The rarkyn had recovered. Blood flowed unstaunched from its nose, red globules coalescing on its chin and plopping to the earth. Lyss dragged Hane to the edge of the ward. *You better have spelled this damn circle right,* she thought at him. If the rarkyn could cross the ward's lines, she didn't know what she'd do.

If I survive this, I'll never leave camp without my sword again.

The rarkyn surged forward. Lyss dropped Hane, planted herself between him and the charging aetherling and brandished her knife.

Then she saw it.

A flicker of runes in the manacle on the rarkyn's wrist. *The sigil.* Battered and weak, but a sigil nonetheless. If she could tap into its power, trigger it somehow, she could use it to subdue the rarkyn…

All she needed was enough time to get Hane over the lines of the ward. She switched her blade to her left hand and grabbed for the glowing runes. Her fingers closed around the shackle, cold and slicked in sweat and blood. Some of it hers, most of it the rarkyn's.

The rarkyn talons swung up to strike—

Sepp, Gods, Iga, let me do this just once. She reached for the magic inside her and *pushed.*

The sigil pulsed.

Before her, the rarkyn froze, Lyss forgotten as it sucked in a breath.

Heat lanced up Lyss' arm, down her ribs, deep into the base of her spine and then roared up her back like a striking serpent. She screamed, hands flying to her temples as a spark dug in.

Heat unfurled through her skull. The scent of blood crawled up her nose and over her tongue, its metallic taste gagging in her throat. Her eyes stung. Her vision went black.

Gods and ginndir, what had she done?

The world unhinged.

CHAPTER THREE

To let people use magic without the Conclave's safe and established runes will consign our Empire to ruin. Villages will burn where one untrained user sought to warm his hands. Farmlands will flood where one rogue thought to water his crop. It is a dangerous power. We must protect our people from it.

Those who refuse to accept this are a danger not just to their own, but to themselves. Brand them, for they have lost the right to wield this gift.

Those who resist are my enemy, and the people's enemy. Kill them. For they have lost the right to anything at all.

—Kallion's Decree, 892 years after the Founding.

LYSS WOKE TO PAIN. PAIN AND A HEADACHE KNUCKLING INTO her temples. *Sepp's balls,* she'd had her fair share of hangovers before but this...

Her muscles ached down to the bone. Even breathing hurt. She groaned and opened her eyes. Light and shadow played above her in a sea of fractured shapes and color.

"...lucky it was only interested in escape," a voice rasped from a dark blotch to her left. Lyss blinked, and Iga's stern nose and wrinkled face swam into focus, and a moment later, the tawny tarsie-wool walls of her mentor's hut. Lyss closed her eyes again and released a long, slow breath. *Here comes the lecture.*

"Have I taught you nothing?" Iga demanded.

Lyss pried open an eye—Gods and ginndir, even her eyeballs hurt—and faced her mentor hunched at the bedside. A fresh pipe smoked in Iga's fingers.

"The rarkyn?" Lyss asked.

"Gone." Iga lifted the pipe and took a draw. "Forced the ward open and took off. Not a difficult feat with Hane half-conscious and its sigil destroyed." Iga dropped a rust and mud-stained manacle onto the blankets. The runes scored across it were dull and lifeless. "This was lying next to you when we came upon the ward."

Lyss stared at the dead sigil. "It broke?"

"It did." Iga's wrinkles knotted together in a scowl. "Darrin and Hane told me most of the story. Fools the lot of you."

"Is Hane—"

"A good size egg on his temple, and he'll have headaches for the next week, but he'll live." Iga harrumphed. "Though the way he moans you'd think my grandson had lost a limb." She exhaled a cloud of smoke. For a moment, Lyss glimpsed, or thought she glimpsed, small figures dancing upwards in it, curling, and broiling in the haze as it climbed. She blinked, and the vision faded.

"How did you do it?" Iga tapped the broken sigil with her pipe. "That was quite the 'graving spelled on it."

Lyss opened her mouth, hesitated, and closed it again. How *had* she done it? She'd drawn on her little pool of Aether as always, but she hadn't felt the magic catch per se. There hadn't been that elusive spark Iga always described. No, it had been like having a keg of Kalana gunpowder go off in her face, and they both knew she didn't have that kind of power. It had been—she cast her mind back and her hairs prickled—raw somehow. *Fierce.* She swallowed.

"I don't know."

Iga sighed. "You got off lightly." She pointed to the bandage around Lyss' left forearm. "You'll have scars, but many mancers can't boast your kind of luck."

Lyss fingered the dressing. *What's one more scar at this point?* A throb rippled up her swollen arm at her touch. She parted her lips, heart quickening as a new thought occurred to her.

"Will I still be able to use a sword?"

Iga snorted. "Use a sword," she muttered. "Of course that's the first thing you ask. No thought at all for your ability to wield galdar." At Lyss' earnest look, she sighed. "Yes, you will. Just give it a week or two."

A few weeks? Her heart sank. Darrin had finally agreed to show her the Eder form too—she'd been looking forward to that. Undone by a kratting rarkyn. *I hope its Sepp damn nose mends crooked.* Lyss sank into her bedcovers and wiggled her puffy fingers.

"Guess that's the end of my rune wielding."

Iga huffed, her shoulders hunching towards the earth. "Perhaps it's better this way. I told you before, you have no talent for galdar."

Lyss stared at the wall of the hut. It still hurt to hear it. She picked at her bandages, rubbed the scabs on her good hand, anything to avoid her mentor's gaze. "There's really no hope for me?"

"A mancer must have control over their runes. You don't. You made a good student—despite your endless attraction to swordplay—but galdar was your father's gift, not yours."

Lyss gritted her teeth. At the mention of Fa, the scar on her chest had given a small twang, like a piece of string snapping. It wasn't like her mentor's words came as a shock. Months she'd practiced. And those months got her nowhere. She gripped her bandages, stared at the ceiling, and blinked back the sting in her eyes. *I'll never get into the Rose Brigade at this rate.*

Abruptly, she sat up and threw off the covers, aches be damned. Her boots stood at her bedside, still caked in mud and grass. Fighting her swollen fingers, Lyss pulled them on and struggled with the laces. She gave it up and left them loose. Room to breathe was all she wanted, she wouldn't go far.

"Don't leave camp, it's near sundown," Iga warned.

Lyss didn't move. Instead, her gaze fell on the shadows behind the mancer. Her mouth turned dry.

The shadows were *moving.* The longer she watched the more distinct they became. They were—Lyss' jaw dropped open—people? Gods and ginndir, tiny people moving in and out of the dark. Small white eyes glinted in featureless faces, like pinpricks in a blank canvas. None had any nose or mouth. They moved into one another, one suddenly here, the other there, as though they were vapor.

"Lyss!" Iga's voice snapped her attention back. Her mentor had risen and come close, brushy eyebrows furrowed. "What is it?"

"People. In the shadows."

An unreadable expression flashed across her mentor's face. Shock? Fear? Lyss couldn't tell. She shifted, uneasy. Nothing ever surprised Iga. Her mentor's voice dropped. "You see the smarokk?" Her gaze darted over Lyss. "That's not possible," she hissed. "Stay where you are."

Her tone sent a new stab of fear roiling through Lyss' belly. What were smarokk? Were they supposed to be seen? Gods damn, what the 'byss did it mean? "Iga—"

"Quiet!" Iga barked. She pulled a cold lantern from above the hut's fireplace. The mancer's gnarled fingers shaped a rune, forming a casting. Envy twinged inside Lyss and she pushed it down. *Accept it. You'll never wield galdar like that.* A sharp acidic scent hit her nose as the Aether surged to obey Iga's command. Green flame flared in the lantern.

"Be still." Iga held the lantern to Lyss' face. The mancer's gaze ran over her again, pausing to meet Lyss'. Her expression turned grim.

Lyss raised a hand to her cheek. "What's wrong?"

Iga shuffled to Lyss' trunk, flipped open the lid and pulled a small mirror from its depths. A feast-day present from Darrin. Lyss had tried to refuse it, but he'd insisted, placing it in her palm and wrapping her fingers around it. "It's rude to refuse a gift," he'd said. The sight of it in Iga's hands turned her chest tight.

One day, I'll leave them. A pang rose inside her. Must she? Really? The scar on her chest tingled. *You promised,* it whispered. *Swore on Fa's grave.*

Lyss rubbed it. *I know.*

Iga handed the mirror over. Lyss glanced into it. Nothing unusual.

"Look again with the light," Iga said, bringing the lantern closer.

Lyss' breath caught. Something was wrong with her eyes. Iga pulled the light away and the color in her irises faded to their natural, gold-flecked hazel. Iga brought the light in again: one of her eyes turned blood red, the other a glowing silver.

Lyss' mirror clattered to the floor. *Gods and ginndir.* She groped for her voice, managed to choke out the question. "What does it mean?"

"You've been bonded."

Lyss' world drained away. *Bonded? Like a familiar?* Panic spasmed through her. "That's old witching magic," she whispered. The kind of magic the Empire had gone to great pains to stamp out years ago. "Impossible. I'm no witch—I'm not even a mancer! And you need a circle. And runes—"

"You had a circle," Iga reminded.

Lyss shook her head. *It can't be.* "I can't get a familiar, I don't have enough Aether to bind it to me."

"You don't, but the rarkyn does."

Oh gods. Nausea churned her belly. It wasn't possible. It couldn't be. Iga was wrong. Lyss swallowed. *Iga is never wrong.*

"Sometimes the Aether has a will of its own." Iga stared at the sigil still lying on Lyss' bed. "Sometimes it defies runes and rules. Especially in the wake of something stronger."

"Like what?"

"Like blood."

Lyss took in the sigil and the rust and mud flaking off on her bedcovers. *Not rust,* she realized. She rubbed one of the red-brown smears; held her fingers up to her nose. Musky copper filled her lungs. Cold horror yawned in her belly. *Blood.* "We're in a *blood* pact?"

"It's possible."

Lyss' stomach dropped away from her, understanding sinking in.

"Control will fall to whoever has the stronger magic," Iga said from somewhere far off.

The rarkyn. Sepp help, the master is the rarkyn.

Lyss sank back onto her bedroll, staring at her stained fingers. This was not part of the plan. She shivered, cold spreading from her core. When she hugged herself, her skin was warm—hot even.

Iga pressed a palm to Lyss' neck. "'Byss curse it, we need to work quickly."

Lyss blinked. She'd never heard the old mancer swear. "Prepare for what?" she asked, but Iga was already shuffling away, cane clenched in one gnarled fist, her pipe in the other. She snuffed it out with a finger.

"Stay where you are," she snapped when Lyss made to follow. At the edge of the hut, she stopped, turned and scored the wooden tip of her cane along the ground, digging the arc of a circle into the dirt. Lyss stood still and tracked the mancer's full circuit, panic rising with every step Iga made. She dug her nails into her palms. *You're not helpless, not yet.* Lyss cleared her throat, stilled her quivering hands and faced her mentor. "Iga—"

"Hush!" The mancer silenced her with a hand. "I've not used this ward since Kallion's inquisition, let me think."

The words snagged in Lyss' throat. A ward from the *inquisition*? Sepp damn, that did not bear thinking about. Her mentor traced a galdar rune—a rune point—along the circle's edge, shuffled a step, then drew a second, and a third. Lyss tried to imagine a forty-year-younger Iga hunting down krats and rebel mancers for the Order, rifling out illegal galdar use in the provinces and fighting in the Emperor's armies against Kraw, but couldn't. The mancer might be a grouch, but she wasn't a killer. Lyss knew what killers looked like. They dressed in red cloaks and bore a rose and crown coat of arms on their sleeves.

Iga finished her twelfth rune point. Lyss swallowed, turning on the spot, taking the full ward in. Twelve points. Iga wasn't out for a lark. "What's it for?" she whispered.

"To stop you falling into the Otherworld."

Lyss' gut clenched. "That can happen?"

"Aye," Iga said. "A sorry end it would be for you too. If the raw power of the Aether there doesn't kill you, the ginndir will."

Lyss' heart thumped a little faster. Her eyes slid back to the whisp-like shadows hiding in the dim of the hut. The Otherworld, the Aether Realm, Home of the Aetherlings she'd heard it called many things. Only those with second sight could see into it; see those shadow folk dancing at the edge of Iga's hut. The mancer had tried to explain it once. *The Otherworld swaths our world,* she'd said. *"It's above us, below; all around. Some of its Aether seeps through to us here, on Terresmir."*

Everything on Terresmir had a little bit of the Aether inside them— trees, rocks, grass, people too—it was what allowed mankind to use galdar. Lyss had thought she'd understood until Iga had tapped the earth with her cane. *"The deeper you go in the Otherworld, the stranger, less like Terresmir it becomes. One theory is there is no end to it. The other is—"*

"The abyss," Lyss had guessed. *"Where the ginndir are."*

Every acolyte knew about the ginndir, even out here in the back-country.

"Aye, not every aetherling is sentient," Iga had lectured. *"Some are little more than embodied rage and magic. They are the ginndir. No one can control them, and if you are fool enough to summon one, it will be the death of you."*

Illredian mancers knew them by one other name. Flesh eaters. For that was what they sought. Flesh of any kind. Human, animal, aether-ling—they devoured all, and according to some, they grew with every kill, taking on the traits of those they'd consumed.

Back in the hut, a chill prickled in Lyss' gut. She shivered at the memory. You couldn't simply *fall* into the source of all magic from Terresmir. Could you? She wiped her sweaty hands on her bedclothes. "What aren't you telling me?"

Iga stilled at the edge of the ward. "Rarkyn were not used as familiars for good reason, Lyss." Her fingers rose, stretching like knobbed twigs. "Their magic is dangerous. Uncontrollable. Many witches tried, according to the histories. Each and every one lost their minds."

A tremble passed Lyss' lips as she parted them, fighting back the fear welling in her chest. "You mean I'll go—" she paused, unable to keep the waver out of her voice, "mad?"

"Insane, yes."

Gods help me. She swallowed down panic. Iga couldn't know for sure, could she? *She's never wrong,* the thought whispered through her. Was it her fate to become one of the empty shells she'd seen ranting and raving in the streets of Caenis?

Iga's fingers twitched, the only sign she made as she invoked the ward. A whiff of smoke, a hint of sulfur, and the runes flared green around Lyss. She clenched her jaw, gritting her teeth tight so she wouldn't scream, or worse, cry. One heartbeat passed. Then two. She took a breath and forced out her next question:

"How soon?"

"Some had a few hours lucidity. Some fought for months before the madness won, if the stories are to be believed."

"It can't be undone?"

"Unlikely." The mancer dug through her galdar supplies, shoving aside rune-graved stones and pre-traced summoning wards on paper. "Nobody knows precisely why; something to do with a rarkyn's magic. And no witch was ever fool enough to bind themselves with a blood-pact like yours."

Lyss shut her eyes, rubbed her forehead. She had a month. Probably less. Then she'd just *fade away,* her life's grime buffed off; polished clean. Part of her almost relished the thought—until Fa's face flittered out from her memory. Roping limbs, hard lines in a sun-tanned face, eyes so deep they drew her in at every bedtime story. What of her memories of him? She stiffened, clenched her fists. Not those. She wouldn't let it consume them. Not ever. It couldn't end. Not this way. She swayed inside the ward, muscles twitching as a fresh shiver ran over her. She itched to move, to do *something.* Anything. Clamminess chafed under her bedclothes; she put a hand to her cheek. Hot, feverously so. *Shit.*

"You're beginning to feel the effects of the bond." Iga returned from her supply case, an inkpot in her fingers. "That's good."

"*Good?*" Lyss repeated, incredulous.

The mancer nodded. "We cannot act until the pact is working through you. Quickly now. Give me your hand."

Lyss frowned but held her right arm out. Iga dunked a finger into the inkpot and scrawled a glyph on the inside of Lyss' wrist, a second followed next to it, then a third and fourth until a ring of six runes glistened cool and black on her olive skin.

"What are—?"

"Stay still," Iga commanded. She breathed over the runes, drying the ink. They prickled on Lyss' flesh, and a hot tingle fizzled into her muscles. She winced and Iga's index finger pressed into her forearm. "Brace yourself," her mentor warned.

Lyss opened her mouth to question—and gagged on air. Gods and ginndir, she couldn't breathe. Her heart slammed into her ribs. She gasped, then wheezed. Her hands flew to her throat, clawing at her skin.

"Stop that, silly girl!" Iga ripped her fingers away. Panic blooming inside her, Lyss struggled. *I can't breathe!* A croak escaped her. *Sepp help, she's suffocating me!*

Iga's grip held firm with a strength Lyss hadn't known her mentor had. She thrashed, jerking her hand free, arm burning as scabs tore open. She dug at Iga's fingers, trying to pry open her grip.

Cold washed over her.

Her arms went limp. She swayed, vision ebbing to black...

Iga's grip released and Lyss gasped, air rushing into her lungs. The world snapped back. Wrist throbbing, she shoved Iga away. "You're trying to kill me!" She would have screamed it, but she had no breath left.

Iga staggered, catching herself on her cane, and scowled. "Calm down," she snapped. "It takes much more than that to harm a rarkyn. *You* have nothing to worry about. I just bought you more time."

Lyss cradled her throbbing arm. "What do you mean?"

"The runes form a seal. They will protect your mind from the madness. They're blocking the effect of the pact—or some of it." Iga put a hand on her cheek and motioned Lyss to do the same. "See? Your fever is gone."

Lyss did so and blinked. Her skin was sweat-slicked but cool. Iga motioned to Lyss' wrist. "It's temporary, but it should give you a few extra months. Provided none of the Order see it. They're not fond of Krawan galdar."

Lyss' gaze snapped down. *Krawan* galdar? Six runes circled her wrist, strange letters still vivid but no longer ink black, instead they'd faded to an earthy green. She'd assumed Iga had fought with the Order in the inquisition, but perhaps she'd thought wrong. She turned her wrist over under her nose. It was almost a ward, not quite a sigil. And it was on *her flesh*. Her stomach clenched. Kallion had outlawed that long ago. Lyss gulped down the egg in her throat and whispered, "This is Kraw magic?"

"Aye, so keep it hidden or the blood pact will be the least of your worries."

"What happens when it breaks?"

"When the runes vanish, you will have a few hours left, days at most."

Lyss rubbed the runes. They didn't come off—they were printed in her skin. Like a tattoo. Or a birthmark. "Can't you make the seal stronger and block the pact completely?"

"It's as strong as I can make it." Iga busied herself with her pipe, shaping her fingers to spark a small fire casting into one end. With a practiced flick, she severed the spell, snuffing out the flame and placed the pipe between her teeth. She gave a long draw, her wrinkled jowls quivering as she sucked.

"What now?" Lyss asked.

Iga blew smoke into the ceiling. "We wait. I've done all I can." She wrapped her tarsie-wool shawl tighter, and sank to the edge of the ward, face grim like a city watchman resigned to their turn of the grave-yard shift. "You're in for a long night."

CHAPTER FOUR

THE FIRST TUG OF THE AETHER CAME LIKE A KICK TO THE
stomach. High in the air, Skaar's muscles twitched, then convulsed as
the Otherworld's power sank in. His wings snapped wide, his stomach
turned, and he retched. Bile splattered into his feathers, crusting over
the blood drying down his front.

"Reythr's fins," he swore under his breath, and pumped his wings to
stay aloft. His Aether was returning, ripping through him like a fire
through a dry thicket. He couldn't stay airborne; he needed a safe place
—a den, a hideaway, anything—to hunker down in. Somewhere to wait
out the flood of magic sinking back into his bones. A bolt of heat shot
up his spine, flared across his ribs. *Just a little longer.*

Ahead, the peaks of the Northern Steppes called, high and white
slopes impossibly steep, near unpassable for human caravans—but for
one road. Stay clear of that and he was safe. There, on the other side,
beyond that wall of rock and snow, so close he could almost smell it:
freedom.

Heat spiked down his back. His wings spasmed, strength falling
away. *No. Not now.* He flopped through the sky; the canopy rushed to
meet him. *The ground. Spot the ground!* One of Fengar's old lessons
sounded in his head.

A twitch of tail feathers and Skaar twisted, curled into a ball and crashed through the treetops. Branches clawed at him on the way down, like he'd got it into his head to roll in a thorn bush. He bounced twice, pain smarting under one rib as he crushed an air sack, then thudded to the earth in a shower of leaves and twigs. Agony lanced up his side, into his head, and the world teetered.

A picture of prowess, Fengar teased from his memory. Skaar groaned and shoved the errant thought aside. Now was not the time to listen to dead siblings. Wincing, he sat up and sucked in a wheezing breath. His nose gave an angry throb. *Reythr curse that girl.* Her face still glared at him, crisp in his mind. Hazel eyes flecked hawk yellow, bright against her skin. A set jaw, and strong, quick hands gripped around a blade dripping blood, *his* blood. A fresh throb. Damn her and her knife to the abyss and back.

His pain dulled and the Aether's burn returned. Almost as bad as Archer's sigil. But where the mancer's manacle had burned cold, the Aether burned hot, giddily so. Skaar rubbed the band of bald skin the sigil had left on his wrist. After years of swearing and cursing the thing, he felt oddly naked with the manacle gone, plucked like a pheasant before the fire. Yet now, without it—he allowed himself a grin—the Aether *seethed* back into him. At last.

It was both elating and terrifying.

Another flush of magic. Skaar held his breath, feeling heat and power rush into his bones; swirl in his marrow.

Wait.

Watch.

With a sigh, the Aether settled into him and steadied. His belly unknotted. Still in control. The Aether wouldn't claim him. He was still Skaar. Still a rarkyn; not one of the ginndir from the abyss. One day, but not yet. He closed his eyes and repeated the age-old mantra. *Not yet.*

"The Aether is like water. A little is good for us. But draw in too much and you will drown," Raska, the leader of his old pack, had said years ago, when Fengar was fresh out of ellirsott, the growing sickness. She gave the lesson to all young rarkyn once they recovered and were ready to begin drawing on the Otherworld's power on their own.

"How do you know when you've taken in too much?" Fengar had asked. Skaar had listened, trying to quell the jealousy his brother's awakening had caused. His brother was years older than he; he'd known Fengar would go through ellirsott first. But knowing was different from seeing.

"You feel it. A Fever all over. In your bones." Raska's talons had curled around Fengar's arm and shook it. *"In your body."* She patted his chest. *"In your lungs. It's like drowning in air."*

Where was the tipping point? Skaar wondered. How much was too much? Before the raid on his pack and Archer's sigil, seething in the Aether had been as natural as breathing. But now...now his bones burned but still felt empty. His muscles tingled but still they ached. His lungs...truth be told he couldn't tell. Not with a smashed nose and winded air sacks.

A fresh surge of power swept into his bones. Skaar grunted and doubled over, sucking in a breath until the heat subsided.

No sense swimming against the current. Another piece of brotherly wisdom from long ago. Time to find shelter and wait out whatever came next. And pray to Reythr for the strength to control it.

Skaar eased onto his feet. His vision swayed, his sight of Terresmir's physical plain and the Otherworld blurring into one another. Not good. He stumbled off, pushing through underbrush, heading for the tantalizing peaks in the distance.

A hook closed around his spine.

Or that was what it felt like. It dug deep into his navel, seizing him mid-step. His lungs emptied, mind blanked, arms flopped to his sides as something inside him *pinched*. Hard. Before he could blink, he was three steps back down the trail, feathers on end.

What in—

He took a tentative step forward, then another. The pinching grew in his chest, like a string winding tight around his sternum. Another step. The magic pulled taut, seared through his muscles. In his mind, his *hugrokar* unfurled; empathic mind magic waking and roaring at him to turn back. Skaar staggered to his knees. One shaky breath. Then two.

What in Reythr's name had that been? His found his talisman and squeezed. The rough quartz dug into the scaled pad of his palm and he curled his fingers around it, the familiar weight and shape calming in its way. *Breathe, you're fine. See?* The clench along his spine relaxed.

He eased forward, testing the trail again. Tension rose in his bones and the empathic link flared, buzzing inside his skull like a bee swarm.

As if warning him he was too far from a pack.

He snorted and pulled back. *Impossible. I would have felt them.* To prove it, he turned and blundered off the trail, shoving branches and bracken aside. In five strides, the iron grip seized his muscles and stopped him dead. He strained against it, gaining another half step before his legs locked with an unpleasant pull on the Aether inside him. Skaar backed up, the first traces of panic returning.

No rarkyn—no *pack*—had hugrokar this strong.

He stood still, mind churning. His people's empathic magic was supposed to keep them together in the Otherworld, help fortify their minds against the raw power of the Aether. The Otherworld was a dangerous place after all. Flesh eating ginndir were only the start of what lurked in its depths. That's why hugrokar overlapped their senses, mind bolstering mind, ready to respond together as one to the slightest stirring from the Deep.

But a rarkyn could ignore the link's warning pull if a hunt required it or if they joined another pack. Hugrokar had never physically stopped anyone. *Ever.*

Skaar leaned into the sensation. The mind magic fuzzed in his brain, snagged the Aether in his bones and locked him still. Teeth on edge, he pulled away again and glanced at his feet, just to be sure there wasn't a set of galdar runes scratched in the earth, barring his way.

No runes.

His snarl split the still morning. *How am I supposed to get to the mountains with this?* He paced back and forth, testing and retesting. The same every time.

It made no sense. The empathic link barred his way more effectively than a solid wall. Something was different—no, something was wrong.

It was all wrong.

Could it be this was not hugrokar at all?

Archer's face, scarred and red-tinted eyes, flitted across his mind. Had *he* done something?

A chill trickled down Skaar's back. No, Archer had been buried under a couple tons of earth. He was dead, his accursed human galdar magic undone.

But if anyone could survive that, it would be that bastard.

Skaar pushed the thought away. *No, he's gone.* Fear rippled through his gut. Wasn't he?

Again, he reached his mind out, searching for one of his own—for the clasp of another hugrokar meeting his and that elusive pull as he was brought into the fold. An ache rose inside him, longing turning his throat tight. What he wouldn't give to feel other rarkyn minds wink to life against his senses, like stars coming out one by one to fill an empty sky. Skaar's hugrokar twitched, the mind magic flexing out without his thinking, searching the surroundings for the empathic bond to a pack long gone.

Emptiness echoed back. His sky remained void and dark.

Skaar closed his eyes, pushing disappointment down. *Focus.* If no pack, what then? *Think.* Had years of wearing the sigil deadened his senses? Had it sapped his innate ability to recognize the presence of his own kind? Panic wormed into his gut. Had his mind snapped somewhere in those long years under Archer's spell without him even knowing it?

A grumble from his stomach interrupted his thoughts. *Soon,* he promised and ran his talons through his crest. *And sleep.* Once he found a way to put more space between him and the human settlements, he'd lie down under the trees and—

Something twanged at the back of his mind. Skaar froze, feather's quivering. Something, *someone,* in his hugrokar *was* there. Small and very, very faint, and on the outmost limit of his reach: another presence. He stretched his magic towards it, narrowing his focus as if squinting to make out a far-off figure on the horizon. The presence winked in and out, one moment there, the next gone. Stopping and then starting once more, flickering like an ember in the breeze.

Like a kit. Skaar focused again. Exactly like a kit. One going through ellirsott. But a kit going through the growing sickness here, of all places?

"Reythr damn." He turned in the direction he sensed it. If it had no pack, if no one stabilized the Aether as it worked through the kit for the first time, the magic could burn them up and... His feathers bristled, and a shiver rippled over him.

...And tear a hole to the Otherworld.

The kit would fall into the Aether's current and be swept away. Alone, without the protection of a pack's hugrokar, it would be at the Otherworld's mercy.

And you already know how that plays out.

Shadows leered out of Skaar's memories. He didn't remember much apart from the feeling of it. Fear and darkness, darkness and fear. No, he couldn't let that happen. Not to another kit.

He stretched out his hugrokar, skirting his mind closer, enough to let the kit detect him. No response. Its hugrokar flickered again, stronger, weaker, stronger, but it did not reach for him. Was it hurt?

Skaar hesitated and gave the kit a tentative nudge, the slightest brush of his hugrokar against the kit's, a long-distance equivalent of a tap on the shoulder. Nothing. Odd. He prodded, harder this time, a jab at the edge of its mind to get its attention.

The kit's hugrokar flared, rounding on him with the speed of a stoat, claws of power sinking in and tangling with his own. Heat from a campfire hit Skaar in the face. Dry leaves, smoke and herbs cloyed in his throat along with something else he was far too familiar with. *Human.*

A scream blasted through the air, into his head.

Skaar wrenched his mind away, spitting curses. The forest snapped back, grass damp under his talons, the stink of smoke and coals still raw in his throat. *What in Reythr's name was that?* That had never happened before. He had meant to nudge the presence, not slip right into them.

Unease settled into his stomach as if he'd swallowed a rock. He'd smelt human. Was the kit captive?

He chewed a talon and paced. Fear amplified hugrokar, he knew that well, and the kit could be Aether-turned, a *sigra*—one fated to be eaten by the Aether. Like him. The thought turned Skaar's feathers on end. Sometimes the changes the Otherworld wrought on a sigra went beyond physical things like a pale eye. Sometimes it turned their magic too, usually killing them in the process. If this kit had survived…that might, *might*, account for the unusual strength of its hugrokar.

Skaar gazed into his palms, tough pads of scaled skin, talons black and sharp, feathers on his long fingers still flecked with his and the girl's blood. Did the kit's mind affect him more because he was also turned? Was that what trapped him here? He shivered. There were too many unknowns.

At any rate, he couldn't break free. The thought chaffed like Archer's sigil. Skaar spat out a curse. No choice. He would have to fetch the kit. Snaffle it away from its captors and take it with him.

I must be mad. Trilling mad. To the abyss and back mad. With one last look at the Northern peaks, he gathered his strength, spied the gap in the canopy and spread his wings. He rose into the morning sun.

Unluck, unluck, what fate does fortune play?

A memory of kits chanting the words at him filled his head. Skaar swallowed a hiss. He wasn't dead yet. A prickle of heat washed down his spine, seethed into his muscles. The Aether again. Not as bad as before.

> *Was fortune who left you,*
> *Pale and broken,*
> *A feast for the Aether to pray.*
> Damn that song.

CHAPTER FIVE

Teeth. White, flashing canines. A growl that juddered into her bones.
Gurgling, and a sword lifting high, swinging, down, down, into her father's chest
with the finality of steel.

Screaming.

The shriek welled in Lyss' throat, jolting her from the nightmare. A
rough hand gripped her shoulder, shaking.

"It's over Lyss, it's over." Iga pushed the hair off Lyss' face, wiping
the sweat from her forehead with a cool cloth.

Lyss heaved a breath, then another, but it wasn't enough. Her head
turned light, her vision dotted with black. Panic burst inside her again,
flushing cold through her chest, careening her heart into her ribs as if
they were a door it was trying to break down. She shoved Iga's hands
away and sat up.

"I can't—" She clutched her chest, tried to suck in another breath,
but the tightness in her throat grew worse.

Iga's face loomed close. "Calm," her mentor instructed. She took
Lyss' uninjured wrist and squeezed. "Concentrate here," she said, tightening her hold. "Breathe, slowly. It will pass."

Lyss nodded, did at she said. She focused on Iga's fingers, the pressure of them around her wrist, power of their grip—surprising that. Her
heart eased and the dark spots faded; the cool dim of pre-dawn
returned, and her aches woke with a vengeance. She forced down bile.

Her thoughts felt fuzzy, worse than the time she and Darrin had discovered Wellan's hidden store of chara.

Iga held out her wet cloth. Lyss took it and rubbed it over her face with a groan. Cool seeped into her hot cheeks, easing her pounding temples. At the back of her mind, something, a pressure of sorts, pressed into her; a finger—no talon—digging at her thoughts, burrowing in like worm to eat her mind from the inside out. Her heart thudded into the back of her throat. *No, you kratting don't.* She rounded on the sensation and *shoved*, just as she might push her pool of Aether at a set of runes. *Skat!*

Pain twanged behind her temples. Lyss winced, caught a faint yelp, a flash of confusion, and the pressure jerked away. She sank into her covers, hands shaking, and wiped her forehead with the cloth again. Gods and ginndir, it was real. The pact, the rarkyn, all of it. Until now she'd held some small hope Iga had been mistaken. Maybe, just this once, the mancer had got it wrong.

She hadn't.

Gods damn her. Hot anger burned in Lyss for a heartbeat before reason sank in. Iga wasn't to blame for diagnosing the problem. No, this mess was the rarkyn's fault. It had worked its strange, aetherling magic on her. Turned her into its tool, its *plaything*. Hairs prickled on her arms and Lyss clenched her fists, an old anger stirring in her belly. *Let it try.*

"Here." Iga pushed a steaming cup of vile-smelling water into her hands. "Drink."

"What is it?"

"Tea. To keep your wits sharp."

Of course, because when dealing with the Aether, one couldn't afford to be distracted, one of Iga's first teachings. The mancer drank tea almost as much as she smoked.

Lyss' gaze dropped to the runes marked on her wrist. Months Iga had said. She shut her eyes, blotting out the smarokk moving about in the corners of the tent and sipped. Her throat closed the moment the scalding water touched her lips. All that training; months—*years*—of planning, searching for a mentor who would take her. Hundreds of hours hunched over Iga's books trying over and over to work the runes. All for nothing. Just like that.

Madness was all that lay in her future. In a few months she'd be nothing but an empty husk. An echo; a shadow; *nothing*. Fa's killers would get away. She would never reach the Order. Never put right what was done to him. To *her*.

She squeezed the teacup, half expecting to hear it crack in her bandaged hands. *Sepp damn it.* She forced another sip. Bitterness washed down her throat, not all of it tea. A couple of months and it would be over.

Then stop wallowing in pity and go. The thought came unbidden, surprising her with its intensity. If this was her end, why not go out with her sword in the gut of Fa's murderers? What had Fa once said? *Nothing is more dangerous than an adversary with nothing to lose.* She straightened, chin rising. Nothing to lose. That was the way it had to be now. The only way it could be. A smirk twisted her top lip. She'd do it.

Darrin's face flitted through her head, a lazy grin and quirking eyebrow crossing his features. That look meant trouble, she'd known it from their first meeting. Lyss' resolve wavered. To leave so suddenly. One day here, the next gone.

Face it, it's not like you ever intended to stay.

Even so, she *had* thought she'd have more time to say goodbye. Lyss looked down into her tea. Hard eyes stared back, accusing. *You promised.*

She cast inwards for her rage and stoked it. Blood thick on the cobbled road, Order soldiers laughing over her father's corpse, the thuds of their boots turning his broken body blue. Her scar twinged under her nightshirt. Yes, she'd promised. They would pay. Infiltrating the Rose Brigade had been the long play, to take them down from within, slow and insidious, as they deserved. Now, she'd have to expedite her plan. She'd find them in the capital, hunt them down one by one like the monsters they were and—

"I will gather your things."

Lyss started, visions of skulking down dark streets after her quarry evaporating like a dream. She blinked. "What?"

The mancer sighed. "You are in a blood pact with a rarkyn. You cannot stay here."

Lyss stared. Had she heard wrong? It was one thing to decide to strike out on her own, but to be—"You're kicking me out?" The words came out in a garble.

"The pact will draw the rarkyn to you, and you to it. You were lucky to escape your first encounter alive." Iga's gnarled hand rested on Lyss' bandages. "The Eder is no place for a rarkyn, or for someone bound to it."

Iga's voice was low and soft, as if trying to ease bad news to a child. Instead, her words smarted, and Lyss found herself gaping. Was Iga so keen to be rid of her? Was she *that* much of a burden?

So much for your sword is always welcome. The thought rose inside her like a sneer and Lyss beat it down. Iga clasped Lyss' bruised hands and gave them a small squeeze. "I am asking you to go before anyone else gets hurt," she said.

Lyss jerked free. "You want me gone. Before I go mad." Fresh anger simmered inside her, burning with something else that crept up her throat and turned her eyes hot. She threw off her blankets, shoved her feet into her cold boots and stood, then snatched up her coat and tugged it over her nightclothes. In three strides she was at the edge of Iga's galdar ward, the glyph of one rune point under her soles. Blow Iga, blow the lot of them. She stepped over the threshold, noting the odd pressure under her feet as she did, but too angry to care. She ripped open the canvas door—

"Lyss, wait," Iga's voice snapped across the tent like a whip. A command, not a request. Despite her anger, Lyss fell still, suddenly unsure. Iga didn't use a tone like that for no reason. And Iga *always* had a reason. She released the canvas and turned.

"What?" She almost cringed at the venom her voice carried. Why did that bother her? Iga was the one throwing her out. If the mancer noticed, she ignored it.

"We will give you a horse, and enough provisions to get to Bardas Post," Iga said. "From there, you can make your way to Illredus."

Lyss glared. "That's supposed to comfort me while I gradually lose my—" she stopped, heart flip-flopping in her chest. "You said Illredus?" *Did Iga know her plans?* Impossible, she'd never told anyone. Apart from Darrin, and he wouldn't betray her.

"Aye, Illredus." The mancer nodded. "To find a cure."

"But you said no one could help me."

"I have not been to the capital in many, many years. Times change. Discoveries made. Perhaps you'll find someone who can break the pact before it's too late. I have an old contact there. I will write you a letter of introduction."

"Then you think," Lyss stilled, hardly daring to hope, "there's a chance?"

"If there is, Illredus is where you will find it."

A chance of finding a chance is better than no chance at all. If not, well, there was always those dark streets and a quarry who needed to know the bite of her sword. She squared her shoulders. Yes, she would head to Illredus, the City of Mancers. Seat of the Order and Empire. She wouldn't go because she was told to, but because she *wanted* to.

"How soon can you have a horse ready?" she asked. A trip to Illredus was a two-month journey at best. With winter on the doorstep, perhaps even longer. Lyss rubbed the runes on her wrist; they tingled under her touch. That cut it fine, very fine indeed.

"Mid-morning tomorrow," Iga said.

Lyss nodded absently, already plotting the course in her mind. Bardas Post first, then join the King's Road down to the plains. From there it was a straight road to Illredus. Mind made up, she returned to her bedside, doing her best to hide the wobble in her legs. She pulled her coat and nightshirt off and slipped a fresh tunic over her head, easing it past her bandaged hands. Woolen leggings followed, then Fa's sword belted over the top. It took a moment to work the buckle, but dexterity had returned to her fingers overnight. Her hands no longer throbbed like before either, in fact, she paused, they didn't hurt at all.

Frowning, she turned her back on Iga and pinched the dressing on her left hand, enough to lift it free to peek at the raw wounds underneath. Her stomach dropped. *Gods and ginndir.*

Her hand was healed—or near as to it. Bruised yes, but the torn flesh had scabbed almost whole, the shallowest cuts fine white scars.

Sepp damn. Had Iga slipped something in her tea? Done a casting over her as she slept? There was no way…she couldn't have. Galdar healing took days, not hours. Galdar couldn't do this. *But rarkyn magic might.* Unease prickled across her neck and she pulled her fingers away. She'd seen enough.

"Is something wrong?" Iga watched her from across the hut.

"No, nothing." Lyss pushed the bandaging down and smoothed her tunic sleeves over it. The mancer's eyes narrowed, detecting the lie, but she pried no further.

"I'm going to collect my gear," Lyss said. Another lie. Everything she owned was in her trunk. But she needed air, a piss, and something stronger than tea—Wellan's store of chara might suffice. Lyss smirked. A last *"fuck you"* to the Bladekeeper. Oh yes, she'd take great pleasure in that.

"Don't go far," Iga warned. "The rarkyn is still out there."

Lyss patted her sword. "I'm ready for round two." She hoped she sounded more confident than she felt.

Her bravado evidently worked because Iga scowled, lips pursing and forehead knotting into ridges like the contours of a map. "I mean it Lyss. Remember your lessons. Don't underestimate—"

"The Aether, I know." She supposed aetherlings fell under that rule. "Seriously Iga, I'm not going looking for it. What do you take me for?"

Her mentor's answering silence said everything.

"IGA SAYS YOU'RE LEAVING." DARRIN SANK DOWN NEXT TO her at the edge of Wellan's training ground.

Lyss stared out at the Eder boys sparing in the practice rings: white paint marked out on the browning grass. Sweat hung heavy in the air. Where most Eder women wrinkled their noses here, Lyss basked in it. Sweat and steel. This was her place. Not the smoke and sulfur of a galdar filled tent. She took a swig from the flask she'd relieved from Wellan's not-so-secret stash. "Yeah."

"Little early to be on the drink, isn't it?"

"It's been a long day."

"It's barely past noon."

"Like I said, long day." Lyss held up the flask, sloshed it, and offered it to Darrin. Her friend grinned, took the bottle and gulped a mouthful. "Shouldn't you be training with the others?" She motioned to the grounds and the boys trading blows within it.

"I can afford to miss a session. Besides, Hane's using my training sword." He pointed to the skinny figure sparring against another boy his age on the far side of the grounds, next to the Bladekeeper's hut. The Bladekeeper in question watched their fight, glowering.

Lyss grimaced. Hane waved his sword around as if wielding a broom at a flock of crows. *Hopeless as ever.* She wondered if Hane thought the same about her every time he watched her try to work galdar.

Darrin followed her gaze and sighed. "I don't know why he persists at it."

Lyss smirked. "I do."

"You do?" Darrin frowned.

She turned on him. "You're really going to make me say it?" At his expectant silence, she rolled her eyes. "God and ginndir, Darrin, Hane idolizes you."

She thought he might argue, deny it straight away, and for a heartbeat he seemed to consider it. His gaze fell back on his brother as the boy lunged at his opponent, overreached and caught a wooden training sword in the gut for his troubles. Darrin's frown deepened.

"What about Grandmere's lessons?" he asked.

Lyss snorted. "He doesn't even need to try. Always gets it the first time." *Damn him.* She sighed. "The word prodigy comes to mind."

"I meant you. What about your galdar lessons?"

Lyss pulled at the sleeves of her tunic. "I'm quitting. Have quit. This morning actually."

Darrin stared at her. "I thought you were making progress."

"Sure, progress in the theory," Lyss tapped her head. "But all the theory in the Empire is no use if you can't wield so much as a single rune. And I *can't.*"

Silence as Darrin processed. "So, when are you leaving?" he asked at last, voice soft and low. He was still as air before a storm. Nothing of him moved, but for his eyes as they met hers.

Lyss shifted, not liking the weight of his gaze. She opened her mouth and hesitated, fighting the chara-induced fog in her head that, until minutes ago, had been a pleasant buzz. Now she felt slow and dull witted, and not at all ready for this conversation. *Sepp's balls, just spit it out.* She took a breath. "Tomorrow," she said, hating how small her voice sounded and the way her stomach twisted.

"It's nearly winter, where will you go?"

"To Illredus."

Darrin stiffened. Lyss sensed it as much as saw it—something in the way his shoulders tensed, how his jaw clenched. "Tell me this isn't about what happened yesterday."

"It's about what happened yesterday."

Darrin cussed under his breath. "Lyss, I'm sorry. I know Grandmere was angry at Hane and I." He ran a hand through his white hair, fidgeted, swore again. "But I never thought she'd take it out on you. I'll talk to her tonight, I will. I'll make it right. If anyone should be punished, it's—"

"This is not something words can fix!" It came out harder than she intended. Lyss took a breath. "Iga didn't throw me out. Well, she did, but I'd already made up my mind to go."

Confusion flicked over Darrin's features, the thin knotwork tattoo on his forehead shifting and moving like shadows in firelight. *Like smarokk.* She punched the thought away and swallowed, tongue thick in her mouth. *Damn chara.* "I'm going after *him*," she said.

Darrin stilled beside her. "I thought you needed, you know," he hesitated as if worried he might be prodding a raw wound, "galdar to get into the Rose. They're the Order's elite. Swordplay, no matter how good, isn't enough."

Lyss forced a laugh. "I'm not joining the Rose. I'm going straight for the throat. The man himself."

Darrin gawked at her, brown eyes searching her face, as if waiting for her to grin and call out the joke. She didn't, and his expression darkened.

"Don't be daft, Lyss," he said. "That's suicide."

Lyss squared her jaw and met his gaze with a fierce one of her own. Her friend's face slackened as he realized she was serious.

"Gods and ginndir, think it though Lyss! They're the best soldiers the Empire has. You can't." He folded his arms. "I won't let you do it."

"You can't stop me Darrin." She sighed and let her voice turn softer. "I'm telling you because you're my friend. Not because I need you to talk me out of it."

Darrin threw his hands up in the air. "This is madness Lyss, surely you see that."

Madness, ha, good one. Just wait a couple months.

At the thought, her gut clenched, panic lancing through her limbs. Her throat turned tight; the air hard to breathe. Lyss coughed, sucked in one lungful, then another, and fought off the rising horror. *Calm down. You're still you.* The thought didn't help.

A warm hand brushed her elbow. "Are you all right?" Darrin leaned over, peering into her face, concern all over his features. Lyss suddenly wished she was anywhere else but next to him. Heat rose in her cheeks. She was a student of the sword, damn it, not some queasy ninny. *Get it together.* She forced a deep breath, then another. Her heart eased; the air lightened. She coughed again. *Quivering like a frightened farm girl.* She'd sworn never to do that again. *Never.*

Darrin gave her back an awkward pat. She pushed him off. "I'm fine," she said, and scowled, recalling his last comment that had set the panic off. "I'm going. You can't stop me."

Darrin answered her scowl with one of his own. "What's the plan then? Barge into their barracks like a tarsie bull? I'm sure *that* will end well."

"I hadn't really thought," Lyss admitted. She shrugged. "I'll come up with something." She had a hundred other things to think through first. Namely, how to lure the rarkyn out and get it to follow her across the Empire.

But one step at a time.

Darrin let out an exasperated curse. "But *why*? You have something good here. You might not be Iga's acolyte, but you don't have to leave. You could join the Bladekeepers."

Wellan would never take me, even if I could stay, Lyss thought but didn't say. She shook her head. "I've got nothing else left."

Darrin swallowed. His gaze dropped to his hands, and he clasped and re-clasped them in his lap. "You have brothers here, if you wanted." His mouth cracked into a grin. "And a cranky old grandmere."

Lyss snorted. "You forgot chain smoking and tea-addicted."

"Oh yes, those too."

Quiet settled between them like snowfall, soft and still. Lyss stared into the trees. Growing up, she'd wondered what having a sibling was like. It had always been just Fa and her. Now, after two years with the Eder, she had an inkling. Infuriating, the both of them, what with Hane's infernal galdar talent showing her up at every turn and Darrin's position in the Bladekeepers. Gods, she'd been so mad after he'd been asked to join. All those months spent trying to convince Wellan to let her attend the trainings, only to have him turn around and invite Darrin instead.

Despite all that, Darrin and Hane had never been far from her side. When she was with them, she could forget for a while, let the memories recede. In two years, her heart had begun to beat again, even if it was a dull, hollowed out drumming.

But it wasn't enough. Not to sate the rage that simmered inside her. Lyss steeled her will and spoke.

"The rarkyn did something to me."

Darrin's head snapped up, then down at her bandaged wrist.

"More than this," Lyss said, squeezing her injured hand. "It's magic," she paused not sure the best way to explain it, "got into me. It wasn't Hane's fault—" she added when Darrin's gaze flashed to his brother across the training grounds. "I don't know how it happened."

"But it has," Darrin prompted.

"It's dangerous magic. Iga thinks if I go to Illredus, I might find someone to cure it."

Darrin's expression brightened, and Lyss was reminded vividly of Hane. They were so much alike. Two branches from the same tree. Only, where Hane saw roses, Darrin saw thorns. He knew how cruel the world could be. But every now and then, he surprised her. Like now. A smile quirked his lips. "I'll come with you."

Lyss stiffened. Gods, the thought of losing herself with him watching... She couldn't let him see that.

"No."

Darrin opened his mouth and she cut him off.

"There's no knowing if I'll find a cure," she said. "And if not, well, it's like I said, I have nothing to lose."

Darrin stared at her as if she'd slapped him. "You mean," he started, "it'll kill you?"

Lyss shifted, a fresh blade of fear pricking in her belly. *Don't think about it.* "As good as kill..."

At the edge of her thoughts, her awareness twisted. Red-silver eyes turned on her. Her words failed, snared in mid-air as she *felt* the rarkyn's attention fix and stay. Lyss' breath caught in her throat. She could sense it. Sense the magic thrumming through it. And it could sense *her.* Fear's blade stabbed into her stomach and sawed.

"Lyss?"

Darrin's face loomed at her. Lyss' hand shot out, grabbed his arm, her nails digging into his skin. "Get Iga." She rose, pulling him to his feet with her. "Now."

Her friend studied her, worry turning his face tight. He looked as if he wanted to ask something, to argue perhaps. "Lyss—"

"It's close."

His face fell. Understanding.

Before someone else gets hurt. Iga's words came to her, along with the memory of Hane helplessly trying to fight off the rarkyn in the ward. That could be any one of them, even Darrin. Her lungs constricted. Especially Darrin, *if he stayed.* She spun on him. Somewhere above, she sensed the rarkyn closing in, wind in its feathers.

"Go, run, tell Iga to ward the camp." When he hesitated, she shoved him, panic rising into her voice. "*Go!*"

Darrin lingered a heartbeat longer, then nodded, turned and ran.

Lyss swallowed, thinking fast. *Draw it away. Distract it until Iga sets a ward.* She unsheathed the blade on her belt. A faint ring to the ear and whiff of oil came out with it. She put the training rings behind her and crept beyond the tents. The trees were menacing, towering upwards over her head in utter silence. A predator was about, the forest knew. She closed her eyes, listening for the swish of wings, the crack of branches snapping if it landed. The pressure at the edge of her thoughts twitched, then *pulled*, as if tugging a cord attached to her. *That way.* She knew it as sure as she knew her own hands.

Fingers white around her sword grip, she pushed further into the trees. Gnarled branches blotted out the sky, their giant interlocking branches caging her against the earth. Grounded. Trapped. The sight of them set her heart thumping. She sucked in a breath. *Not trapped.* The ground was exactly where she wanted to be.

Wading through the ferns, she held her sword high and at the ready. Let the rarkyn see it and know she was armed. This encounter would not be like the last.

The pressure in her head cut off, stilling to nothing. It was here, and it knew she was too. She cleared her throat, opened her mouth.

"Hello?" Her voice rose as a whisper. A far cry from striking fear into the heart of the enemy. She blew through her cheeks, mustered her nerve and barked: "Come out!"

Silence.

Lyss stole forward, brushing past ferns and scrub. "You can hear me, can't you?" She peered back at the path she'd taken. No sight of camp. Good. But that meant she was on her own. *Fuck.* She adjusted her hold on her blade. *Focus.* She snapped her attention ahead—and her heart hit the roof of her mouth.

She hadn't seen, hadn't *heard* it move. Was it possible for it to just materialize out of thin air?

The rarkyn looked far from happy. Its ears were flat against its skull. Mismatched eyes glaring.

Lyss swallowed and gripped her sword tight.

CHAPTER SIX

"I KNOW YOU UNDERSTAND."

Understand? Skaar's thoughts churned. He stared into the hawk-yellow eyes and his hugrokar recoiled into a ball. *The* girl. Human. A human with hugrokar.

Impossible. Something was wrong with him. His senses were addled. Yet he'd been so sure. He'd felt a kit on the other side of the empathic link. Was it a trick? But *how?* His feathers prickled. *Why?* He circled, ears pricked and listening. No creak of a drawing bowstring or faint ring of swords being drawn. They were alone.

The girl bared the sword at him, blade tip tracking him as he prowled. She was small—smaller than most humans he'd seen at any rate—thin too, but her loose clothes belied a frame as lithe as a civet's. Fear rolled off her sweat, sweet and musky, but there was something in the way she stood, shoulders lax, weight even; how she held her weapon, light but firm in her grip. She could fight—*would* fight, if he pushed her. His nose gave a warning throb. *Do not underestimate her.*

His thoughts circled as he doubled back on his tracks. Had he imagined the kit's hugrokar? He unwound his magic and reached out to the presence tangled like a burr at the edge of his mind. He prodded: a light touch, just in case he was wrong. No sense harming the kit if it was really there.

Opposite, the girl stiffened, sucked in a breath. Her sword snapped for him. Skaar hopped back a step, but there was no murderous intent behind it. Instead, she glared. "Stop it."

Skaar stared. Somewhere far off, a croak rose in his throat. He hadn't imagined it. Reythr be, this human had hugrokar. An icy ribbon of horror wormed through his gut. *And you're trapped in her hold.*

This was bad. Very, *very* bad. He shifted, fanning his tail feathers, pinions ruffling. It was *wrong*. The thought of Archer flashed though his mind again. Skaar pushed it away.

The girl cleared her throat. "As you can see, we have a problem." Her voice quavered a heartbeat, then firmed.

A rumble started in Skaar's chest and worked up his throat. His teeth gnashed. A *problem*? This was a Reythr-damn nightmare. Kill her and be done with it. Freedom waited over the northern peaks. A day's flight, maybe two, and it would all be over. *All* of it. He could find his people, find a pack, see the stars in his sky once more.

But if her hugrokar trapped him close, what else could it do? He swallowed. Hugrokar shared more than feelings. A shiver ran over his feathers. It shared many things. Many. The killing blow of an arrow, the teeth of a ginndir, the sear of a mancer's spell—he'd felt it all; coiled his hugrokar tight to block it out. Would that work here? He curled his talons into fists. Or would he feel every blow? He shuddered.

A *human*. Panic trilled inside him. *Human*. Reythr, what was wrong with him? Nausea rose in his stomach. His mind spiraled. How could he find a pack with this girl tethering him? If his senses were muddled, how would he know man from rarkyn? Rarkyn from man? This could get him killed. Or worse, imprisoned again. The knot in his stomach hardened, resolve settling in. Anything but that. He'd die before he became a mancer's pet again.

Before him the girl frowned, her eyes glazing over.

Feathers rose around Skaar's throat and down his shoulders. That look. He knew that look. Little swine was picking at his hugrokar, pulling it this way and that, twisting and tugging as if trying to pop a loose tooth. He rounded on her presence, a snarl thundering through the air, tail whipped over the ferns, wings flaring open. He gathered the mind magic, coiled it tight and shoved. Hard.

The girl gasped, staggered back, one foot behind the other, arms groping at the air before her knees buckled and she landed flat on her backside.

Skaar blinked. The blow shouldn't have worked so well. A physical attack couldn't have been more successful. *Remember that.*

She was on her feet again in a heartbeat. Shaken, but fright wearing off and Skaar sensed anger underneath.

"Answer me this if nothing else." She spoke through gritted teeth. "How do I undo it?"

Skaar's crest bristled into a frown. Did she mean hugrokar? There was no undoing it. It was there, always. His heart sank as he took her in again. The wrongness of it settling like a stone in his gut. *How?* he wondered again. His mind raced, panic hounding reasoning.

"Well?" the girl asked, growing impatient.

Skaar hesitated. In the silence, a chorus of heightened voices rose from the direction of the human camp.

His heart smacked against his ribs. The rest of the clan was coming. Skaar spat out a curse. He plunged into the trees. A shout went up behind. Adrenalin hit him hard and fast, flooding his limbs cold then hot. They were close! *Run. Fly. Get away.* Feet thumped at his back. Branches bowed and snapped as the humans crashed after his trail. Very close.

Trees barred his path to the sky. He darted through the trunks, searching for a break large enough to let him through. A howl sounded from further down the valley. Dogs? His gaze snapped back the way he had come. They had dogs!

Aether-addled idiot. Why did you come?

He switched directions, turning a sharp right, heading south. *Confuse the trail,* Raska had taught him. He did it again, and once more in a new direction, heart hammering and mouth dry. The baying eased and Skaar leapt up the steep crag of the valley rim. Jumping three paces at a time, boulder to boulder, he scrambled up across the rocky pebbles and over the ridge. The sound of his pursuers faded. Clear sky greeted him. *Thank Reythr.* He threw his wings open—

A shout from the bottom of the crag snapped Skaar's attention down. He'd dawdled too long. Too late to fly to safety. He'd be shot in a heartbeat from up here. He bolted into the trees, just as a howl resonated through the trunks. Fear rose like bile in his throat. He leapt down the gully, skidding across bare rocks of the hillside, heading for the cover of thicker forest.

"There it is!" The shout from the ridge made Skaar twist, glimpsing the party of men and dogs racing down the way he'd come. An arrow snapped against the ground at his feet—he'd paused too long. Stumbling, he spun and fled deeper into the trees.

Dogs closed the distance behind him. Shoving twigs and branches out of the way, Skaar crashed through the undergrowth, squashing the rising gorge in his mouth.

Reythr guide the currents. Give me a way to the sky. The memory came unbidden, along with a pang. *Fengar.* He staggered onto a rocky shoreline and spat out a curse. *Useless prayer.* He should've risked the ridge.

The water looked deep and cold. Skaar glanced at the far shore. *Too wide to jump.* A dog's bark set him moving again. He raced upstream, just as the first beast burst through the trees. *Now or never!* He leapt up, snapping his wings open.

The dog's jaw closed around his heel, teeth sinking through feather and skin. Skaar shrieked, the weight and force of the dog's attack dropping him several feet. Gritting his teeth, he pulled upwards. The dog thrashed its head, teeth sinking deeper into his heel, oblivious to the drop below it.

With a snarl, Skaar rounded on it, kicking at the beast's muzzle as he struggled upwards.

A shout below. Humans stood on the bank, two of their number looking up at him through the nook of a pair of crossbows. The world wavered. *No! This couldn't be happening! Not now. Not this way—*

"Darrin no!" The shout rose from further off. Skaar glimpsed the girl lunge at one nomad, wrestling the crossbow away.

The Aether twitched and cold rolled over his feathers. Skaar's gaze snapped to an elderly nomad hobbling along the bank. Her cane clacked on the river stones, her free hand tracing the end of a rune in the air—

Pain slammed into him, the freezing grip of a galdar casting seizing his body. White exploded behind his eyes. His wings locked; vision fled. The world fell silent, blood roaring in his ears.

Reythr save me.

He dropped.

Water consumed him. Pins and needles gripped his muscles. Cold. Wet. Down. His head reeled and he clutched at consciousness. The water pressed in and his lungs burned. Panic returned in a wave. He couldn't breathe. Couldn't move. The spell tangled his limbs; snuffed the magic out in his bones.

Skaar opened his mouth, water rushed in and down his throat. Horror yawned inside him. He was sinking. Down, down. *Down into the abyss, where not even the light could reach him. To where the ginndir were. Waiting. Hungry. Misshapen bodies skulking in the darkness.* He wrenched his mind away. *Not that. Dear Reythr no, not that.*

Thump, thump…

The throb in his skull slowed. The odds had caught up with him. *I tried Fengar. I really did.*

His brother's face swam into his mind's eye, teeth quick to grin, sharp red eyes that missed nothing. He was ten summers old and half-fevered with the beginnings of ellirsott. Skaar had refused to leave his side, choosing instead to cling to his brother's feathers.

Fengar had laughed at him. *"I'm not going anywhere Skaar."*

"You might fall into the Otherworld. Then the ginndir will get you." As he'd imagined those mad, silver eyes coming out of the darkness for his brother, his heart had thudded into his gut.

Fengar had squeezed his hand. *"I won't. Promise."*

Thump…

Skaar struggled in the water. It was like trying to climb the sky without wings. His thoughts spun again, and he was back in Raska's shelter, standing vigil over Fengar as ellirsott ravaged his body. *"Let him rest Skaar,"* Raska had scolded. *"You cannot help him."*

Thump… The water pressed in. Time slowed.

Back with Fengar again; sweat-lathered and feeble as a mewling pup on a bed of feather and bracken. Ellirsott had burned away fat and muscle to allow his magic and bones to grow. The sight of Fengar struck down had shocked Skaar to the core. Brave, kind, fierce Fengar was not infallible. Strong as he was, he could break—and very nearly did.

Back then, he'd know the chances of either of them surviving into adulthood was slim. Mancer raids stole as many of their pack as the Otherworld did. This he'd known, but not understood. Until he'd realized Fengar was just like him: a rarkyn. No matter in which world they walked, there were creatures that sought to kill them.

That night he made his promise: Together, they'd beat the odds. Together they'd survive. If only that had been enough.

Thump…

I'm sorry Fengar.

Fight! A voice rocked through him, slamming into him so hard his limbs twitched in the water.

He was lying on the shore, rocks digging into his back. Hands, his hands, clawed at his chest as his lungs burned.

"Lyss!" An old nomad shook him. *"Pull your mind away! The rarkyn's drowning, not you."* The nomad uttered a curse and turned from him. *"Darrin, get it out!"*

Fight damn it! The girl's voice snapped him back to the water.

The world spiraled, washing over him in giddying waves. He tried to move. No good, he couldn't tell arm from leg, wing from foot. Nothing but the throb in his head and the chill creeping into his bones.

No! The girl's angry thought snarled across the link.

Skaar's thoughts spun into the dark. Perhaps it was better this way. He was tired of fighting, tired of surviving. Bitterness burned up his throat. He'd been so close. But his sky had been robbed; the chance to seek a pack somewhere out there again, gone.

Thank Reythr it's over.

A pair of hands wrapped about his chest, hooked under his arms and dragged him upwards. The grip was tight, crushing as it pulled him through the water. Cold jolted through his bones. His head swam. Thoughts dimmed.

Reythr, please let it be over, was his last thought before the dark swept in.

CHAPTER SEVEN

"Your horse is almost ready." Iga came to sit by the edge of the circle. In the distance, the telltale stamp of an impatient hoof carried from the Eder camp.

"I'm sorry it turned out as it did," the mancer said, turning her gaze to the unconscious aetherling trapped within the ten-point ward on the riverbank. The runes and circle glowed vivid green in the brown grass.

"You don't need to explain." Lyss had felt the power inside the beast—the Aether pulsing through its muscles. A growing burn of heat and magic before Iga's galdar had snuffed it out. What would have happened if Iga hadn't been there? Lyss shuddered, pushing down a gurgle from her memory. Best not dwell on that too long.

"It was still weak. A different story might have been told if its magic had recovered more," Iga said.

Lyss nodded and rubbed her hands together. Bandages gone, her fingers chafed over livid red scars. *More for the collection.* The friction warmed her cold digits for a heartbeat before a twinge in her left wrist made her wince. She thrust her hands under her armpits instead.

Iga's spell still lingered. She had not been subjected to the runes herself, but the rarkyn's terror had engulfed her senses as though she had. The shock of it had knocked the wind from her lungs. Cold had coursed through the rarkyn and stabbed across the link to her, seizing her muscles in its horrifying grip. She'd known galdar was powerful, even more so when Iga wielded it, but she'd never thought to fear the runes themselves. A shiver ran over her.

"*Tch!*" Iga said. "Your lips are still blue."

"I'm fine, really."

The old woman's eyes narrowed. "If time were not of the essence, I would have you stay and recover properly."

Lyss managed a small smile. "I imagine that would make you popular with the elders. You saw how they reacted earlier."

Iga scowled. "Don't listen to what they say. Your circumstances do not make you any less human than they. They'd do well to remember it." Lyss sensed the lingering heat of an argument behind those words.

"What about…" Lyss hesitated. "Darrin and Hane?"

"Forbidden to see you."

Guilty by association, was it? The elders had likely thought up a punishment for them already. Tanning tarsie hides perhaps. Or shoeing colts for the spring muster. Whatever it was, it would keep them busy until she and the rarkyn were gone. Her heart sank. Darrin, Hane and Iga were the closest thing to family she had left, and the kratting elders wouldn't even let her say goodbye.

"Don't you worry. They'll be here." Iga flashed a crooked smile. "I know my grandsons. Give it until dusk, they'll come. Here." Iga pushed a coiled parchment tied off with a piece of string into Lyss' hand. Lyss turned it over in her hands, inspecting the address Iga had scrawled on the outside. "When you reach Illredus, take this to the Conclave Quarter. An old friend of mine lives there. With any luck, she can cure you. If not, she'll help you find someone who can."

Luck? Lyss bit down on a haw of laughter. Luck had clean deserted her. Nevertheless, she tucked the letter in the inside pocket of her coat and thanked her old mentor.

A hoof-beat at her back and Darrin arrived, leading a pinto mare up the rocky trail.

Iga eased onto a boulder and gestured her cane at him. "What did I tell you?"

Hane followed behind Darrin, eyes fixed on the mare as it pulled on the reins. At the sight of the horse's mottled coat of chestnut and white, Lyss' mood soured. *Titch.* She hadn't expected the Eder's best horse, but this…

Spirited, Darrin had called the mare last week when she'd thrown him. Lyss scowled. Cantankerous seemed a better fit. She'd be lucky if she didn't break her neck riding the animal.

She approached and the mare's nostrils flared; it tossed its head, ears pinning flat and teeth snapping on the air. When Lyss reached for the reins, it jerked away with an impertinent nicker. She bit back an oath at the elders.

"She's the only one we can afford to lose before spring," Darrin said, wrestling to keep the pinto still.

"Better than no horse," Lyss said. *But not by much.* Darrin handed the reins over and his hand caught hers, gentle, but firm.

"You don't have to do this alone," he said. A furtive glance at Iga and he stepped closer. "I'll come with you. Meet me at Kith Brook, same time. I'll sneak off when night—"

Lyss jerked her hand free. "*No!*" She shook her head, swallowed and said it again, forcing her voice to a knife's edge. "No. I forbid it."

Darrin stared at her, shocked. Hurt plain on his face, a wrinkle in his brow. "But—"

"No, Darrin. I already told you." She'd always known it would come to this. Well, not quite like this. She glanced at Iga, then at Hane hovering awkward at the pinto's shoulder. Lyss would not break this family apart. She steeled herself. "This is my problem. I'll deal with it my way. I don't need someone to hold my hand."

A slap might have been kinder. Dismay flashed across Darrin's face and his jaw clenched. *Damn it to pieces.* She'd known not to get too close. She put a hand on Darrin's arm.

"Iga's sealed the pact. For now, I'm safe. There is nothing more you can do. Your place is here. With Hane and Iga. They are your family. You cannot abandon them, not for me."

Darrin swallowed.

Not with what I plan to do. Her words hung unspoken between them. She tried to meet his gaze, but his eyes slid to the ground. Disappointment stabbed her gut and she squashed it. This was not how she wanted to remember her last day with the Eder Wildner.

With the family who had taken her in.

Who had welcomed her as one of their own.

Her chest tightened at the sight of the three of them standing there, ragged and exhausted.

Still, she was an outsider. Look at how quickly the elders had turned on her. Lyss glanced at the slumbering rarkyn. Sepp pray it would not spook Titch when it woke.

"We packed as much as we can afford to spare," Iga said, indicating the saddlebags. "It'll get you to Bardas Post. Perhaps further if you're sparing." She scooped up Lyss' hand. "Take this as well." A coin pouch fell into Lyss' palm, full and heavy. She recognized it with a guilty start.

"Iga, I paid you this so you would train me."

"In that I failed," the mancer replied. "This is your coin back for a job not done, minus the cost of the horse." She nodded at the mare.

Lyss opened her mouth, several arguments springing to mind, but stopped herself before the first words could escape. The Eder drove a hard bargain and she could hazard a guess for such an act of charity. They wanted her gone. The thought burned holes in her heart. *Damn it.*

"When the rarkyn wakes take it far from here," Iga said. "The elders' patience is at its limit with it so close to camp."

Lyss wrapped her fingers around Titch's reins and led the mare to the rune-circle, tethering the horse to the low-lying scrub to graze. When she faced her mentor again, all three Wildners were watching her.

"I'll leave as soon as I can," she promised.

A smile flitted across Iga's face, but it never reached her eyes. They remained dark and heavy with the weight of knowledge. She knew Lyss' chances. Slim to none. "Sepp watch over you." There was a finality in her words and Lyss knew she would not see her mentor again. With a short nod, Iga turned, and hobbled back down the trail. Lyss' eyes grew hot, and she bit the inside of her cheek.

Darrin cleared his throat. His face was pale and drawn. The longsword still rested at his side, but the confident youth she'd spent two years trading blows with was gone. Instead, he hung there, small and deflated. Younger than she'd ever seen him.

You did this. The thought stabbed into her. She shoved it away. "You didn't have to see me off."

Her friend swallowed. "Yes, I do." He took a breath, and Lyss sensed him steady himself. "I wish," he began, and faltered. His shoulders hunched, and his fists shook at his sides. "If I had known what would happen—"

Before he could say any more, Lyss stepped in and drew Darrin close. He tensed under her embrace, then stilled, relaxing into her arms. "It's not your fault," she said.

Darrin gave a sharp intake, not quite a sob. "I'm sorry."

Before Lyss could reply he pushed free. "I can't—" He shook his head and rounded on the spot and hurried after Iga.

Lyss watched him go, gritting her teeth against the guilt. *You knew this day would come,* she counselled herself again. She turned on Hane. "Don't let him blame himself."

The young nomad nodded. "You forgive him, don't you?" His voice shrank. "Forgive us?"

She sighed. "You were trying to do the right thing. I wouldn't blame anyone for that." She bumped her knuckles into his shoulder. "But next time, maybe get Iga, eh?"

A smile flickered over Hane's face. For a moment Lyss glimpsed the energetic boy she knew, then it was buried. "He wanted to go with you, to make it right. We both did, but Gran forbade it." He swallowed. "You should have heard them row."

"You've done enough, Hane, I can take care of myself from here." She hoped she sounded more confident than she felt.

Hane chewed his lip. "I never got to thank you."

"For what?"

"You pulled me out of the circle." Hane's eyes darted to the rarkyn behind her. "You saved my life."

But not myself. Lyss rubbed the scabs on her hands, but her lips quirked as she recalled Hane lunging at the rarkyn with a stick. "You did the same for me remember? I'd say we're even."

She expected him to grin, perhaps even laugh. Instead, his blue eyes stared back at her, expression too serious for his fourteen years. "I don't like it," he said. "I can sense it, you know, when it's close like this. It feels wrong."

Lyss turned. The rarkyn still slept. *I thought it was just me.* Its silver eye flitted through her memory, along with those teeth. Her heart thudded into her ribs and her fingers found Iga's runes on her wrist and squeezed. *Focus here. Breathe.* She let the panic pass and swallowed. "I know. I don't like it either, but it is the way it is."

Hane's gaze fixed on hers. "If I know one thing about magic of any kind it's this: *it's devious.* Gran says it's drawn to people with a strong will." He scuffed a boot in the dirt. "If your will is stronger than the rarkyn's it will side with you, even if you can't use runes."

He made it sound so simple. Of course, for him it was. He was gifted that way, while she... Lyss drew a breath. *Get to Illredus. Break the pact.*

She lay a hand on the pommel of her sword. *Find Fa's killer.* Just contemplating the task ahead made her legs turn to water. It was too big. Too much.

One thing at a time. Isn't that what Fa used to say? Small steps. For now, she needed to be gone, the Eder Wildner could not get involved any further. She drew Hane into an embrace. "Thank you. I won't forget."

The Wildner boy stood still for a heartbeat, taken aback, then his arms wrapped about her shoulders. "I'm sorry too," he said.

A hot tingle ran up Lyss' throat. "Don't be."

"I'll miss our lessons. Darrin will too."

"I'll come back someday."

Hane withdrew and shook his head. "I don't think so." He gave a small smile. "You can't go back. But I hope we'll meet again."

Of course, the Eder Wildner believed in the seasons; in change. There was no returning to how it had been before. They accepted that and lived on. If only it were so easy.

Teeth, blood, and a falling sword flashed through her mind's eye, then red cloaks rippling in the breeze. Fresh rage prickled her gut. *I will never accept it.*

She pushed the memory away. Live on. That she agreed with. There was no going back, but she would survive this, rarkyn be damned. *I swear it,* she thought as Hane's back vanished from sight.

CHAPTER EIGHT

The first thing Skaar knew was hunger. His stomach turned over itself, dismaying in its emptiness. The ache came next. It was all he could do not to groan as he opened his eyes. Dewed grass met his vision, blurred brown stalks blocking his sight of the circle. He didn't need to see it to know it was there. The galdar runes twisted the Aether around one, two, three—he counted—ten points. *A strong one. Reythr be.*

A footstep snapped his attention to the edge of the circle. Hugrokar had alerted the girl to his waking. Hiding how much effort it really took, Skaar rose to his feet. He swayed, planted a foot down to stabilize himself and his knees wobbled. Damn that mancer's galdar. His eyes traced the runes of the circle. *More powerful than the last.*

"Are you hungry?"

He studied her, trying to discern her intentions through hugrokar. The human's face paled, and panic flashed through the link.

"Stop that!"

Her hugrokar pushed him away. *Hard.* The shove buffeting what little Aether he had in his bones. He recoiled with a snarl, head ringing from the mental strike. He hadn't expected her to learn to use the mind-link's power so quickly.

"I see your nose is healing well."

At the mention of it, his broken nose gave a throb. Skaar ground his teeth, recalling the pain of a dagger hilt smashing into it. The impact and the crack reverberating through his skull; the first head-spinning throb. He shoved the sensations down the link. See how she liked that.

The human rocked on her feet. Stunned, then her jaw clenched and her eyes flashed.

The memory hit him fast. Pain seared down his arm; talons ripping through flesh. He bit his tongue to stop the yelp. *She's strong.* Aether damn them all.

"That's enough," the girl snapped. She shut her eyes, sucked in a breath and held it, but he felt her heart thumping underneath, mirroring his own. "This is not helping anyone."

Skaar fixed her with a cold stare. Across hugrokar he sensed fear. And frustration. Good. Frustration led to mistakes, like accidently unbinding the circle. He swished his tail, fanning the feathers in a show of defiance.

The girl huffed, shoulders sinking a few inches. Across the link, her frustration ebbed, replaced with exhaustion. Skaar shook it away and frowned. Her emotions were leaking all over the place. *She must not realize she's doing it.*

Knowing made it worse too. One more distraction jangling about in his head. His stomach gurgled.

The human's lip twitched, amusement tickling Skaar's thoughts. The girl produced a satchel and threw it into the circle, along with a waterskin.

"Eat."

The satchel and skin landed at Skaar's feet and he caught the whiff of salted venison. His mouth filled with saliva. *Reythr it smelled good.* He didn't move.

"It's not poisoned."

Skaar snuffed. If they wanted him dead, they'd had ample time to do it. The girl's unguarded mind confirmed the food was safe. But why feed him? Why care at all? He pushed the questions away and pulled the bag open. The taste of the first bite was so strong it sent pangs to his stomach and he nearly gagged. Choking, he swallowed, coughed until it went down. He uncorked the skin; gulped water, then sawed off another bite, this time forcing himself to chew.

"My name is Lyss."

Skaar glanced at her, expecting her to say more but instead she fell silent, waiting. He ground a deer bone over his teeth, breaking it with his molars, rich marrow oozed over his tongue.

"What's yours? Your name."

Skaar spat out the two halves of bone and bared his teeth. "You take me for a fool?"

The girl blinked. *Drat it*, he'd forgotten to speak the human tongue. He muttered a curse and searched for a way to phrase it in his limited vocabulary.

"That's right, a name holds power over you," the girl, *Lyss* he supposed, said. Unease flickered inside her. "I'd forgotten that."

She was partly right. A name didn't hold total power, that only applied to the true Aether-born, to the aetherlings who needed galdar to summon and anchor them in this world. That was too difficult to explain, and he wasn't in the mood to try. He took another piece of venison from the bag and chomped at it.

A thump of a hoof outside the circle caused him to start—a horse tethered to a tree a few feet away. It pawed the ground, impatient. Saddlebags lay on the grass beside the animal. Skaar's eyes narrowed.

She's leaving. But where?

His stomach knotted. What if she travelled to one of the cities? Reythr save him, he'd be a mouse in a snake nest. The satchel of food before him lost all appeal, and he forced down his latest mouthful.

"Where you go?" he asked, grappling for the right words in the human tongue.

Lyss opened her mouth, began to speak, then apparently changed her mind. "Away," she amended. "You are coming too."

Skaar swallowed, taking in the circle again. It smelled like the old nomad's galdar, but he detected nothing resembling a sigil. Still, he couldn't be sure. He licked his lips, salt prickling his tongue. Reythr it was good. Good to distraction. He hawked and spat on the ground to get rid of the flavor. *Clear your head, Skaar.*

"Where?" he asked again.

"To Illredus, to find a way to undo whatever *this* is." She jerked a hand between them.

Skaar snarled. *Curse her, curse the lot of them! Illredus?* Even *he* had heard of the City of Mancers. It was the human city Archer had hailed from. The wretched mancer had spoken of it often, usually when drunk. Skaar would be damned before he went to the place that had spawned the likes of that man.

"No." He shook his head. "Illredus is bad. Mancers."

Lyss started, surprise resonating through the link. Had she thought he would not know the name? The girl folded her arms. "Who is going to remove this bond then? *You?* I think you would have already if you could."

Skaar gritted his teeth. She was right about that. He had no idea how or why they shared such a strong link, let alone how to undo it. Could it be done? Sharing hugrokar with a human was unheard of. Hugrokar wasn't like galdar. There were no runes to cancel any of it out. Hugrokar just *was*. Constant. Part of him. It wasn't a tool; it was a sense. A sigil might mute it, but it still existed, even if no rarkyn were within his range.

He paced about the circle, feathers on end, tail whipping about his feet as he gnashed his teeth. But Illredus? Panic stabbed though him at the thought of crossing that city's gates. His bones turned cold. *Bind him in sigils, he would not go. Could not.*

Opposite, he sensed Lyss' confusion. "I didn't think rarkyn feared mancers."

Skaar jerked his head up. His panic had crept across hugrokar without his realizing. He focused his mind again, tightening his hold on the magic to block her out. A pack might not fear a mancer, if it was only one, but Illredus had more than one mancer and he had no pack. His fingers curled about the bare patch of skin where Archer's sigil had chafed feather away.

"What about—" he stopped not knowing how to refer to the old nomad woman "—your friend. Old one," he amended.

"Iga? This is beyond her skill. Illredus is the only place where someone might know how to reverse the bond."

"Can't. Mancers will kill." He motioned at himself. *Then they would steal his eyes and draw his blood for their own perverted magic.* He flexed a talon and struck it down his palm, scoring a red line into his flesh. Lyss winced, one hand jolting to the other. "We share pain. I die, you die," he told her. Technically not true, hugrokar shared pain but never killed. Skaar doubted she knew otherwise—or would dare to test it.

The girl flexed her fingers, shook her hand and scowled. "Do you know of another way then?"

"Find rarkyn. Find a pack." If he could find his own people again, it might be possible. Though, not many rarkyn possessed that sort of knowledge. Not anymore. Mancer hunters, the mordkyn, had seen to that. However, it was better than Illredus, surely.

A jolt of panic across the link made him pause and look at the girl. Her chin gave a wobble. "Absolutely not."

Skaar's ears flattened.

"Your kind will be deep in the wilds. Impossible to find. And I—*we*—don't have time."

Her hugrokar fluttered, a dark snake of terror twisting inside her. Skaar's gaze fixed on her.

"What you mean?"

He sensed her shy away from the question. "Illredus is closer. I have connections there."

Skaar wasn't fooled. "What you mean?" he pressed.

The girl swallowed, glanced down at her hands, then to the runes of the circle. "Rarkyn and humans are not supposed to be bonded like familiars. It's not natural. Your magic will make me to lose my sanity." An edge of fury rose in her hugrokar as she spoke. "Understand? I will go mad."

Reythr be. Skaar shifted in the circle. "When?"

She held up her hand, revealing the runes around her wrist. "When these marks fade. Iga estimated two months."

Not good. Skaar fanned the feathers of his tail again, unease spreading through him. Being bonded to a human was bad enough. Being bonded to one who was insane would be... He shuddered. What was to say he might not lose his mind along with hers?

But to go to Illredus? All those humans, all that galdar. And that was just the city. What about getting there? Panic gnawed at his gut. *There had to be another way.*

"It will be hard going during winter," Lyss was saying. "But it can be done. In Illredus I will request an audience with one of the mancers."

Skaar half listened. The wilds were too far for a human to go on horseback. Had he been on his own, he could have covered the distance in half the time, even without the aid of *rasvenger,* the Aether flight his people were famed for. But his magic was still too weak to attempt that, and it was too dangerous for him to brave such distances in the Otherworld alone without the hugrokar of a pack to keep the magic focused. He muttered a curse under his breath. Illredus seemed like suicide, but if he did nothing, he ran the risk of losing himself along with the human. He glared up at the sky, grinding his teeth. The Great

Spirits really hated him. He drew in a breath. Perhaps he was already mad.

"Fine." He rose to his feet and hated how his legs almost gave out under his own weight. "But if humans try to kill in Illredus," he pointed to himself. "I make a Fever."

By the look of horror on her face Skaar guessed Lyss knew what a Fever was. Never mind that loosing control of the Aether inside him was as dangerous to him as it was to her, the threat of it was what mattered. Her mouth opened once, shut, then her jaw clenched. "I will make sure that doesn't happen."

Skaar nodded. "Good." He pointed a talon at the runes of the circle. "Unbind."

Lyss shifted, planted the sheath of her sword into the ground and used it to push herself onto her feet. Skaar's ears picked up a huff of exertion as she straightened. His eyes narrowed again. She too felt the aftermath of the galdar exposure? Most humans were immune to it. Even if her sensitivity to the runes had come from him and through hugrokar, she should not have been affected so much. Something was amiss. Curse Archer. Had he really done something after all?

Skaar's ears popped. The pressure of the circle released. Lyss had scuffed one of the galdar rune points out with a foot. She re-buckled the leather belt of her sword sheath about her waist and rested her hand on the pommel of the weapon.

"Last time we exchanged blows I didn't have a sword. Strike at me again and the outcome will be different."

Skaar didn't doubt she believed it. Rarkyn magic didn't do well going head on against the steel of man-made weapons. He couldn't afford to have Lyss discover that. He scowled. "I not want more broken bones."

He stepped out of the circle, giving the girl a wide berth. Her eyes followed him.

"Can you travel?"

Skaar gave a slow nod. Lyss turned to the half-packed saddlebags at her back, bundling them together in a few minutes to strap them down on the horse waiting under the trees. The animal tugged on the tether, head nodding up and down in impatience. Lyss untied the reins and threw them over the horse's neck, then swung into the saddle with a practiced ease. With a click of her tongue, she guided the horse from the foliage.

Skaar unfurled a wing.

The horse skittered sideways, hoofs stamping and nostrils flaring. Lyss hands clenched around the reins. Skaar caught the flash of panic through hugrokar before the girl's mind refocused and she pulled the horse's head to the right, forcing it to circle rather than letting it rear. Then she put a hand to the horse's neck and stroked it. The animal calmed.

"Don't do that again," she warned.

Skaar scowled. It was not his fault the horse spooked worse than a rabbit hearing the kee of a hawk. Did she expect him to *walk* the whole way to Illredus?

"Let me go ahead," she said, "and watch where you land."

She nudged the horse with her heels, directing it through the trees. Skaar huffed, waited until the trunks hid the horse from view, then lifted into the air.

PART II
OUTLAW

"Hark sky-kin, rarkyns red,
A drop of blood I seek
Save my Queen from sickness
That saps her body weak."

One rarkyn answered, legends say
A bargain struck and wrought
Yet, unknown to he, his Queen was cold,
Her spirit trapped in Baer's hold.

—Fragment from The Epic of Asander.
c. 500 years before the Illredian Founding.

CHAPTER NINE

She was back on the road again. The air dry; wind carrying the heat of the inland plains through the spinifex. Sweat ran into her eyes and she wiped her forehead and focused on her father's back. His strong, confident shoulders swayed as he walked, and a faint tune hummed on the breeze in his wake. Beside him their mule plodded, cargo listing to one side, then the other on its back.

"How much further?" Yes, she remembered asking that. *Her father turned, lips cracked from the heat. He pointed to the horizon. Lyss strained her eyes after his finger and made out a fleck of white across the plain.*

"The walls of Caenis. Not far now." He grinned. "Soft beds for us tonight."

Lyss pursed her lips. "We can't afford another inn."

"Where there's people—"

Lyss sighed. "There's opportunity." She squinted at the white walls. By that reasoning, wouldn't it pay to settle permanently? She was tired of the walking, tired of calluses and worn-out boots, tired of the never-ending loading and unloading of their cart, tired of never spending more than a week in one place. She huffed. "Can we at least stay for the Midsummer Festival?" Hope swelled inside her. She would eat roast pig, dance in the square, listen to a tune from a proper bard rather than the drunken ramble from a roadside inn. And maybe, just maybe, she could test her sword in the city tournament—there was sure to be one this time of year…

Her father shook his head.

"*There will be ten times the people! We'd make more in one day than we do in a month.*"

"*No.*"

"*But—*"

"*We leave on Fifth-day.*" His tone was final, and Lyss clenched her jaw to stop the exasperated sigh. Another year of looking back down the road at the lights behind them and listening to the drums and the cheering crowd on the wind. She shifted the weight of her pack on her shoulders and stomped ahead of the cart, muttering oaths under her breath. Once, just once, one festival, what was the harm in that?

"*Lyss!*" Her father called. She ignored him, picking up her pace to put more distance between them. His call came again, more urgent. Lyss turned. His eyes were fixed over her shoulder. Something in his expression screamed alarm. She followed his gaze and spotted the dust cloud in the distance. Horses. They were too far away to make out individuals riders, but a cloud billowed in their wake. And they were coming fast.

An indignant ee-haw was her father pulling their mule and cart off the road.

"*Lyss!*" he shouted, waving at her to follow. She stepped off the track, pushing through thick spinifex to reach him. She was almost at the cart when his posture shifted, a subtle tensing of shoulders, a hand twitching closer to the sword on his hip.

"*Fa?*"

"*Hide.*" He pointed to the grass.

"*No, let me—*"

"*It's the Order.*"

Lyss squinted. She spotted the telltale flash of red. Her breath caught and she searched again. Real Order soldiers? She'd heard stories of them in the villages they visited, but to see them in the flesh...

She stood her ground. "*We've done nothing wrong. They are probably just passing.*"

"*No. Get out of sight.*"

Lyss pulled her eyes from the road and opened her mouth. Her father locked her in his gaze.

"*Now!*"

Lyss swallowed. That expression wasn't to be argued with. She darted off the road and flattened to her stomach in the spinifex, long stalks folding around her. The hooves thudded closer, reduced in speed... Lyss peered through the stalks at Fa, his head bowed low beside their cart on the side of the road.

There were four of them. Their horses were purebred; long legs and sleek bodies *honed to run. Only the wealthy could afford those. Each soldier bore a red cloak with gold lace inlaid on the hem and an emblem on their left sleeve—a white rose and a crown. She stared. Rose Brigade. King Therrin's elite. What were they doing out here?*

The lead soldier dismounted. He was older than the rest by a score of years, his thick gray hair matching the gray in her father's beard; tall too. As he moved, his eyes roved over the spinifex and Lyss ducked her head down, her gaze shifting from his face to his boots as they stopped short of her father's.

"Avi Rhyos," he said. "How many years has it been? Twelve? Thirteen? More?"

Rhyos. Lyss' insides went cold. Never use our family name, *Fa had always said. He'd never said why. Her father paused for a long minute, and Lyss imagined him craning his head up at the soldier and wetting his lips. "You are mistaken, my name is—"*

"Alron Floros, is that it?"

Silence.

"You can grow a beard and change your name, but your reputation follows you. A woman in Tunsby, a child in Port Freda, another in Carradoon, a grandfather in Larouse—all beyond the help of local physicians, yet all healed by an extremely talented mancer whose name the Conclave has no record of."

Her father's feet shifted, a pretense of shuffling back Lyss knew well, but really moving his weight onto the balls of his feet. "What will it be then Capitan Mereor Loric? The noose? Stake?"

"Seize him," Captain Loric commanded. "Search his—"

Fa reached for his sword. No Fa, don't—

One heartbeat. A sliver of steel. Fa's blade drawing, glinting in the noon-light. A shout from the soldiers. Then a crackle of air splitting. A roar. A scream—Fa's scream, Lyss' heart shot into her throat—and a fleshy, crunching sound. The thud of a body hitting the earth. Growling.

Lyss quivered in the grass, breath light and fast in her throat. Fa lay on the road, a six-limbed monster hunched over him, its maw around his neck. Antlered horns curled from the monster's head, a black mane smothered Fa's face, claws sank into his chest opening him up like a knife.

Gnawing. Gurgling. Fa's fists beat the beast's side. No use.

No Fa. Please.

"Noam, cease." The Captain snapped a command, and the monster withdrew, pacing back to its master's side with a purr.

Fa coughed, gagged a breath.

"You got sloppy Rhyos," the Captain said. His feet came within an inch of her father's boots. He drew his saber.

"Stop it!" The words were out and she on her feet before she realized what she was doing. The soldiers spun, weapons snapping out. Idiot, *why had she confronted them like that?*

"Lyss…stay down," Fa wheezed. His throat was a mess of red.

"Please, don't kill him!" She stumbled two steps before gloved hands grabbed her and hauled her to the cart. She twisted in their grip. "Please." Her voice turned high and horse. "He's just a healer. He's helping people, he's—"

Loric's eyes flashed between them. "Who is this?"

"My…apprentice," her father gasped from the dirt.

Captain Loric gripped Lyss' chin between a thumb and forefinger and turned her head. "You're a terrible liar, Rhyos." She blinked back tears, tried to swallow the fear pooling hot in her throat. "Golden-eyed like an Eyos woman," he said. "Desert eyes. You don't see that this side of the Spine." His nails dug into Lyss' jaw, "But that expression is you through and through, Rhyos." He released Lyss with a sneer. "Kill him. Bag the head."

"No!" Lyss threw herself at the man, grabbing for his sleeve. "Please. He has not hurt anyone!" At his side, the monster released a rumble. One clawed paw stepped for her, lips peeling back. Loric stayed the aetherling with a hand. Two soldiers tore her away instead and pitched her to the earth. Her legs folded under her, weak and useless. Pain grazed her knees.

Loric snorted. "A harmless peddler. Is that the story you sold her on, Avi?" His sword slid free of his scabbard.

She should have never pleaded. She should have kicked and stomped; writhed and bit.

"Lyss…" Fa wheezed. His hand reached for her, grabbing at empty air. She couldn't move. Her legs were numb. He found her gaze instead, lips working around the words. "Be brave."

Loric's blade rose into the air. Higher, higher again, then it swung down and into her father's neck.

She screamed. Screamed so loud and so hoarse it sent her head spinning. The musk of the soldier's sweat filled her nose. Then blood. Red, thick, and so much of it.

She should have fought. Should have saved Fa.

The pool grew around her father's body, and still she sat, rooted by fear. Helpless.

"Shut her up." The Captain's voice sounded far away.

If she'd been stronger…

A sword swung at her, dark in the midday sun. She didn't feel its bite. Didn't feel it rip through tunic and skin. All she knew was a blooming red on her chest as the world tilted. She fell to her knees, weakness seeping in, the soldiers' laugher in her ears—

CLAWS BIT INTO HER SHOULDER AND SHOOK. LYSS CAME TO, a scream welling up her throat. Not claws. *Talons.* A pair of red and silver eyes peered over her. *Sepp kratting rarkyn.* She vaulted away, snatched up her sword and swung it like a cudgel. The tip of the sheath cracked against the creature's jaw.

"Stay back!"

The rarkyn yelped and stumbled from the tent's opening, wings flaring, one hand clutching his face. Pain blossomed across Lyss' chin, and she winced, pressing down the urge to cup a hand to her smarting jaw.

Kratting pact.

She bared the sheathed sword at the rarkyn. "Don't make me use this." She flexed her grip. If it came at her, she'd kill it, blow the consequences.

The rarkyn hissed back. "I only wake! Only wake!" The crest between his horns spiked into an indignant tuft. He pointed to the sun rising over the eastern peaks. "Is late."

Late? She squinted through the tent opening at the rose-tinted sky. It was the gods damn crack of dawn. The rarkyn spat something out in his own tongue and stalked off, rubbing his cheek. His shadow danced across the canvas of her tent.

Lyss sank back into her bedroll, wiping sweat from her face with a shaking hand. *Five years, you should be used to it now.* Yet, each time the dream left her shivering. She clutched her nightshirt and focused on her breath. *I'm coming for you Loric.* Her scar pulled under her shirt. Her heart slowed.

Outside, a log popped over the fire. Lyss' eyes snapped open again. A musty meaty smell wafted to her and her stomach growled. She gathered her tunic and coat she'd discarded on the ground sheet. They were cold, but at least they were free of dew. Lyss pulled the gray tunic on over her long woolen nightshirt. The sheepskin coat went over it, held in place by her belt. She left the hood off and pulled on her boots. Wriggling her toes to warm her feet up, she rubbed her hands together, blowing warm breath against her fingers before a twist of her wrist made one hand twinge. She winced, then put them under her armpits and poked her head out from the shelter.

The rarkyn had rekindled the fire. The coals glowed red under the husks of several burnt-through branches, but that was not what caused Lyss to stop dead in her tracks. Something was cooking on a spit over the fire, something chicken-like, only it had scales and a few too many limbs.

She glanced at the crude sliver of rock that had served as a knife at the rarkyn's feet. One edge was stained red with blood. She opened her mouth.

"Cockatrice," the rarkyn said, answering the question before she asked it. Its gaze swung to meet hers, following her as she circled the fire to see the chicken-thing better. It was about the size of a pheasant, only instead of a beak it had tiny sharp teeth and its wings were skin instead of feather. *One of the wilds' creatures?* She frowned. *Here?* She took another step toward the fire.

The rarkyn bristled, snatched the spit from the flames and snarled.

"Mine!"

Lyss stopped, taking in the rarkyn's bared teeth, sweat prickling in her palms. "I had no intention of taking it."

The rarkyn's eyes darted over her, suspicious, snarl slowly fading, but it did not return the cockatrice to the fire. Instead, it tore a leg off the bird and began to bite away large chunks of hot flesh.

Good. Lyss thought, pleased. She had no idea how much a rarkyn needed to eat, but suspected it was more than the rations the Eder had spared her. She turned to her own breakfast: salted venison and some roots she'd unearthed the evening before. She set it to cook over the fire and watched the rarkyn strip all the flesh from the cockatrice before moving onto the gristle and bone. Silence settled over them, long and uncomfortable. *Not much of a talker.* She cleared her throat. A long ear twitched in her direction.

"Sorry, for earlier."

At the mention of it, the rarkyn bristled again. For a heartbeat, something gnawed at the edge of her thoughts. Hot. Angry. *Not forgiven then.*

Darrin's face flashed in her mind, expression consoling. From when she'd first failed one of Iga's tests. *"Give it time. It'll come."* Only it hadn't. She scowled. Screw waiting. If she had to travel across the Empire with this creature, they needed to set some ground rules. She opened her mouth.

"Will not hurt you," the rarkyn said. He tapped his cheek. "Can't." He pointed a talon at the sword on her hip. "You don't need."

Lyss took the aetherling in. Even crouched before the fire, his head was level with her shoulder. Her hand curled around the pommel at her hip. "I'll be keeping it on, all the same." The rarkyn's ears flattened, tail giving an irritable flick at his feet. Lyss sighed. "But keep your claws to yourself and I won't use it on you. Agreed?"

The rarkyn's gaze dropped to the sword. Another quiver at the edge of her thoughts. Anger again, this time milder. Annoyance perhaps. The sensation faded. Lyss' hair prickled and she lifted her sleeve to check the runes on her wrist. They still held, dark and bold on her skin. Across the fire, the rarkyn nodded.

"Agreed."

Well, it's a start. Lyss pulled her breakfast from the fire and began to eat. The rarkyn watched her, miss-matched eyes travelling over her twice. Lyss scowled and put her spoon down. "Sepp's balls, *what?*"

"You have bad dreams often?" the rarkyn asked.

"Most nights."

"Always?"

"Since my father died."

The rarkyn's round eyes—owl-like under that permanent scowl of feathers on its brow—studied Lyss a heartbeat more. As if satisfied, he turned away and combed his talons through the remains of the cockatrice.

Lyss finished her meal and packed up the camp as he completed his second pass. Not a scrap of meat left. A heavy sigh escaped the aetherling when it was done. Its gaze roved the trees.

"You're still hungry?" Lyss asked, incredulous.

The rarkyn started, turning to find her standing with Titch, waiting to leave. It stood up and plodded ahead of her, ruffling its wings open. "Always hungry."

As it took to the air, Lyss was struck by how bony the rarkyn was. While folded, those wings were deceptive. In fact, he looked practically skeletal as he took off. Guilt twinged inside her. She hadn't spared a thought that the rarkyn had almost starved to death on the end of a sigil.

Their uneasy truce lasted through the day—and the next. That evening, Lyss set traps and was rewarded with two rabbits in the morning. When she returned to the camp, the rarkyn was gone. As she searched the brush surrounding the camp, the bond between them gave a faint tug, turning her attention to the north. She took a step for the trees and paused. No need to go looking for it. The rarkyn wasn't in any danger.

Kratting aetherling's probably digging up roots. She sat down to skin the rabbits instead.

Only when she was halfway done with the second rabbit did the thought dawn on her: How did she know the rarkyn was all right? She couldn't feel any pain, but what was to say it wasn't being chased or hunted? Yet even as she pondered, she was certain it was safe. No ifs or buts, simply the knowledge that wherever the rarkyn was, the creature was fine, content even. But how did she *know*?

The pact. Again. *The curse that keeps on giving.*

Fear surged inside her and Lyss checked the runes about her wrist. Still there. Still whole. She pushed her sleeve down again and swallowed. She finished skinning the second rabbit and set them both roasting over the fire, her heart still jumping. The runes were holding. She wasn't mad yet.

A footfall at the edge of camp made her start and she snapped her head around to find the rarkyn had returned. It stopped in its tracks the moment Lyss' attention landed on it, then skirted around the camp, giving her a wide berth. Unease trickled over to her from the other side of the bond. Again.

She clenched her jaw. "Stop that."

The rarkyn looked at her, pausing amidst unslinging its waterskin from one shoulder. The pact gave an indignant tug.

"That," Lyss said. "Whatever it is. Don't." Then on a whim added. "Please."

The rarkyn scowled. "No." It turned its back on her and sat, ire wafting over her like an unpleasant smell. She relaxed her gritted teeth and took a breath. Yelling at the rarkyn would only rile the creature. She turned the rabbits over on the fire and risked glancing at the rarkyn on the side of the camp. It was busy crunching through a small stash of wild turnips it had brought back from its foraging.

"See this rabbit?" Lyss poked the meat and a bit of fat oozed out and dripped over the flames with a hiss. The rarkyn's ears ticked in her direction and it turned. "You can have it."

A flicker of eagerness darted across the link, but the rarkyn's face remained still. It knew it came with a condition.

"If you stop," Lyss said.

The rarkyn's ears flattened and it turned away and spat an indecipherable word out in its own tongue. Then it gave a loud huff. "Can't."

"What do you mean *can't*?"

The rarkyn's mismatched irises fixed on her for a long minute and Lyss felt it hesitate, uncertain again. Slowly, it lifted a hand to its head, "*Hugrokar*," it said and tapped a claw against its temple. "Is not like galdar. Can't stop."

Lyss frowned. "You're talking about the bond?"

"No *hu-gro-kar*." The rarkyn tapped its temple on each syllable. "Mind to mind."

"Our mental link?"

"Yes." The rarkyn watched her carefully. "Hugrokar is always. Doesn't stop."

Lyss paused, not sure if she'd understood. "The mind link between us is rarkyn magic?"

"Yes."

Lyss let out an exasperated sigh. *Great, just great.* Rarkyns were aetherlings and aetherlings couldn't use galdar. Their magic was different. There were no runes she could strike out to make it stop. "The bond means I can…" she floundered. "I don't know…*feel* you? Feel what you're feeling?"

The rarkyn looked up from its turnips and scowled. "You do it too."

Lyss faltered. "What?"

"You have it. Hugrokar. You are using it." It pointed at her. "Right now."

Lyss blinked. She was using rarkyn magic? Without realizing it? Her gut tightened. *Oh Sepp's balls.* She had been doing to the rarkyn exactly what it had been doing to her. "We've been travelling for, what, three—four days, and you're telling me this *now*?" She rose to her feet. "How long have you been snooping around in my head? How do I stop it?"

The rarkyn's top lip curled back into a snarl and Lyss saw—no, *felt*—it tense, but it held its ground and stayed seated. "You not listen. *Can't.* Hugrokar is *always*. It is part of us. Like seeing." It tapped a talon below one long ear. "Like hearing."

Lyss put her palms to her head and rubbed. "Can't you control it?"

The rarkyn's snarl faded. "A little."

Lyss shook her head, repeating the rarkyn's words over in her mind. She glanced over at the rarkyn, watching as it resigned itself back to its turnips and began to crunch through another one. She snatched the rabbit off the fire and marched over. The rarkyn heard her coming and scrambled to its feet, its tail giving a nervous flick as she came close. Lyss thrust the roasted rabbit under its nose.

"Show me how to control my hugrokar and it's yours."

The rarkyn was silent, but it swallowed its latest mouthful of turnip like it was a knot of moldy swampweed. The link, hugrokar, quivered as its eyes followed the bribe she waved before him.

"Deal?" she asked and held out the end of wood skewer for the rarkyn to take.

The rarkyn considered the meat. "Two rabbits."

Greedy bastard. Lyss looked over at the second rabbit on the fire. She'd intended to take it for herself, but she supposed she could make do without it. "Fine. Two rabbits. Two lessons. Deal?"

The rarkyn reached for the skewer. Lyss jerked it away. The aetherling let out an angry screech and glared at her. "Deal?"

"Deal." The rarkyn agreed. Lyss let it take the rabbit and she retreated to the fire, a smile playing across her lips. Maybe, just maybe, she would survive this after all.

If the rarkyn sensed her elation, it said nothing.

CHAPTER TEN

With his free hand he poured a trickle from his waterskin over his fingers. It splashed through his outspread digits and into the dirt. "Holding nothing in. Everything goes out. Like a kit," he said. The girl peered down at him from her horse as it walked down the game trail. She scowled at his description. Skaar ignored the disapproval creeping over hugrokar and curled his hand into a fist. "This is closed off. Nothing gets in, nothing gets out." *Like a human is supposed to be.*

The girl's eyes fixed on his fist. "How do I do that?"

"Can't." Skaar relaxed his hand into a cup and poured another dash of water into it, pooling the liquid in the rough creases of his palm. He held it up, so she could see the water beginning to drip through. "Can't hold everything back. Only some." He released his fingers a little more and the water slipped through.

Lyss' gaze lingered on his hand. "Show me."

Skaar mulled a moment. How to explain something he did without thinking? He held up his closed fist again, hunting for the right words in her tongue. "Picture this. *Here.*" He tapped his head, then opened his hand again, waggling his talons. "Not this."

He sensed the girl's confusion, but she fell silent for several minutes.

"How's that?"

Skaar didn't bother looking at her. "No."

Lyss fell silent again. Her hugrokar gave a flicker—a moment of blissful stillness—before her presence pressed against the edge of his thoughts again. The more she wrestled with the magic, the more her hugrokar buzzed—frustration, hope and anger hummed through her. He tightened his own hugrokar and his sense of her eased.

"Why does galdar hurt you?" Lyss' question broke his momentary peace. She rubbed her wrist, and Skaar felt the prickle of runes there.

He considered her question, unsure how to answer. Once, many years ago, he'd asked Raska the same thing. A mordkyn sighting had forced their pack to flee their territory and seek shelter at Finnafell, the meeting mountain. Fengar had been part of the party that had encountered them. They'd all escaped, but not without injury. Skaar had stared in horror at the roping burn down one side of Fengar's chest and leg, as if he'd been caught in a net of fire.

"It burned cold," Fengar had described. *"Straight into my bones."*

"How was that possible?" Skaar had asked Raska. Human magic was still Aether, and they lived and breathed in the magic. How could it harm them in such a way? The old rarkyn had fixed her gaze on him, eyes pink with age, and put down the block of slate she'd been working a knife out of. She'd held up the beginnings of the slate blade she'd just split from the block.

"Human magic is like this knife," she'd said. *"It might be small, but it's focused; honed to a will."* She held up the block. *"Our magic is like this rock. We have more of it, but it's not shaped for any one purpose."*

"But if our magic is more…" Skaar had started.

Raska had flipped the slate blade in her fingers and scratched it down the side of the block, leaving a long scar in its wake. *"It's the same material, but it's sharp. It can still do damage."* The tip of the blade found a fracture in the rock and with a twist she'd splintered a corner of the block off. Crouched over it, Skaar had stared at the cracked piece of slate, heart sinking. How could they ever fight against that? Human magic was a tool—a weapon. Rarkyn magic was not.

"Our rock is not very useful," he'd concluded, looking down at his talons; dismay turning his wings heavy.

Raska had tutted. *"A rock is plenty useful. You can hunt with it, build with it, use it to grind herbs up for medicine."* She'd propped the slate blade against a log. *"Small and sharp is dangerous if you attack it head on. But attack it from a different angle…"*

With a great swing Raska brought the block down over the slate knife and when she removed the block, the blade was shattered.

"You see?" Raska had said, picking out the shards and stowing them for arrowheads. *"A rock can break a knife, in the right circumstances."*

Skaar had stared at the slate block in her hand, thinking of all the times the hugrokar of one of their number had abruptly severed and fallen silent. *"Then why are we the ones who die?"*

Raska had sighed and patted his shoulder. Her hands had been so big, and he so small, that her talons had flexed about his entire shoulder.

She never did answer my question, Skaar realized, suddenly. And he'd never had a chance to ask again.

Before him, the girl still waited. Skaar ruffled his wings, hunting for the right words. "Galdar focuses Aether. Makes it dense, like ice," he said at last. "For rarkyn, Aether *is* us. Burns inside always."

Lyss nodded, thoughtfully. "Galdar suppresses the fire."

More like smothers it. Skaar shrugged a wing. Close enough.

Satisfied, Lyss fell silent, her hugrokar warping as she wrestled with it. "Now?" she asked after a few heartbeats.

Skaar sighed. "No."

She kept at it all morning with no success and when they crested the ridge of one valley, she took a break to consult her maps instead, muttering something about finding the King's Road. Skaar wandered from the game trail, half-heartedly digging through the leaves on the ground with the talons of one foot to see what he might uncover. To his delight he unearthed a squirrel's nut stash. *Should have made a deal for one of the rabbit skins,* he lamented when he could only stash two handfuls in the pocket of his braies. Pleased nonetheless, he ruffled open his wings to head back to the game trail—and stopped, ears twitching.

Hooves.

Further away, Lyss froze, detecting his alarm through hugrokar. Skaar brushed off the astonishment that echoed back across the link and turned both ears to the noise, listening.

One, two…three horses.

He furled his wings and scrambled up the nearest tree. Through a break in the canopy, he spied the bottom of the sloping valley. A road. Foliage obscured the horses, but the sound came from that direction.

He muttered a string of curses under his breath and clambered down again.

He couldn't fly this close to the road; a well-placed arrow could fell him. Nor was it the time to test his *rasvenger*. If his Aether-flight failed, he'd be easy to spot. *And an even easier mark.* He spotted the rump of the girl's horse plodding down the game trail and loped after it. *If only we could travel at night.*

They descended into the valley, the trail becoming wider, more travelled as it closed in on the road below. Open, exposed road. Skaar kept one ear cocked on the horses. Every step brought them closer, and soon the scent of steel and sweat reached him from the party. His feathers prickled and he turned both ears towards them.

"By Sepp, *enough*." Lyss reined her horse in and turned in the saddle. "You're giving me gooseflesh. What is it?"

Skaar hardly heard her as he listened to the creak of the leather saddles below. *How can she* not *worry?* A draft of wind brought the odor of horse and human closer and the end of his tail curled around his feet.

A crunch of leaves and a twinge of annoyance made him look around to find the girl had slid from her saddle. "We'll wait for them to pass," she said, and took her horse's reins in one hand and sat down on a small moss-covered log on the side of the trail.

Skaar went back to watching the road. He could make out part of it through the trees. When the hooves on the gravel echoed off the walls of the valley, Skaar picked a wide trunk to conceal himself from the road, shooed the shadowlings out from its shade and settled down to wait. Quiet fell over the trail and Skaar closed his eyes to listen.

His eyes shot open again as the intenseness of the girl's hugrokar eased. He turned to find her balanced on the log, gaze distant, forehead wrinkled. Skaar stared. *She's only been at it for one morning.*

Lyss snapped back to herself and cocked an eyebrow. Her control slipped and Skaar sensed her excitement.

"How did I do?"

Skaar turned back to the road. "Better." *Reythr be thanked for that.*

"This sense, hugrokar," Lyss started, "do all Rarkyn have it?"

Skaar nodded. "All."

"So in a pack—"

A voice sounded from the road. Skaar jumped and cursed his carelessness. He peered down the slope. Three horsemen. Their horses were what he'd heard humans call "purebred", well-fed creatures of honed muscle. The riders were armored, each carried a crossbow on their back and a sword at their hips. But it was not the weapons that chilled Skaar's gut before the hot anger roiled in its place. It was the color of their cloaks.

They were red.

Like blood.

CHAPTER ELEVEN

Lyss' breath caught at the first flash of red. She vaulted from the log and scrambled over to the trunk the rarkyn sheltered behind. Gods, ginndir, and Sepp's kratting bollocks. *Order soldiers? Reds cloaks here?* She swore again under her breath and glanced to Titch. The mare's mottled pinto coat would hide her well within the trees at this distance, so long as she didn't make too much noise.

Carefully, Lyss peered down at the group. Reds without a doubt. Their cloaks swayed on their backs, in time with their horses' hooves. Once, she'd admired those capes; lapped up stories of how the Empire's fiercest warriors had driven the Krawan advance back, how the best officers wielded galdar and swords together. A whirlwind of galdar and steel, she'd told Fa during one retelling. *"Folk watch in awe when they come to town."*

Her father had fixed his dark eyes on her over his mug of chara. *"In awe?"* he'd cut in. *"Or in fear?"*

"Of course in awe," she'd argued. *"The Order protected Empire folk."* That was their oath and sacred duty.

Fa's barking laugh had turned heads in the inn; his white teeth baring in his salt and pepper beard. *"Once they did,"* he growled. He downed his drink before continuing. *"Listen Lyss, the Order protects one thing only. Itself."* He leaned in. *"I broke the oath I took, and after what they did, I'd do it again a thousand times over."*

78

In the valley below, one officer said something indiscernible, causing another to laugh. The sound rose up the valley slope and Lyss could have sworn it was mocking. *Bastards.* Her hand found Fa's sword and she twisted her grip on the hilt. Three against one. Not great odds. She shut her eyes and forced herself still.

Eager to draw, eager to die. Fa's old saying crossed her thoughts. Her scar twisted, pain and sadness strafing through her. *Fa.* She squeezed her battered sword again, wishing it was Fa's hand instead.

Then rage bloomed across hugrokar. Hot, fierce, dying to wrap its hands around their throats. Her eyes popped open and she stared at the rarkyn. Its previous caution had evaporated. In its place was an anger that mirrored her own. The rarkyn's top lip quivered, eyes fixed on the road below. His hand gripped the tree trunk before him, talons sinking deep into the wood, squeezing as if to crush the life out of it.

The rarkyn glanced over at her, meeting her gaze with the slight nod of its head, then went back to watching the riders.

Lyss searched the cloaks. What if one of them was *that man?* There was no way to know from up here; their faces were hidden. Chances were, none of them were. *That day* had probably seen the Captain promoted above patrol work. Lyss picked off a piece of bark from the tree and ground it in her palm.

One day. She recited her promise. *One day he will pay.*

Oblivious to their observers, the Reds continued down the road and vanished around a bend. A breath hushed past Lyss' lips. Next to her, the rarkyn muttered something its own tongue, spat on the ground, and stalked away.

<hr>

At dusk Lyss stopped a stone's throw from the road's edge and set up camp. Unlike previous nights, the rarkyn did not wander off. Instead, it sat at the edge of the camp and brooded, not happy about the road being so close and thoughts still lingering on the Reds—if the anger emanating from him was anything to go by.

"What did they do to you?" Lyss asked as she threw the last of her supplies—a few scraps of venison and a couple of tubers—into a small pot for a stew. She was not surprised when the rarkyn did not answer. She would have to go first. "They murdered my father."

The rarkyn looked at her.

Lyss stoked the flames and pushed aside the coals to make room for the pot. "Beheaded him." The pot shook in her hands.

The rarkyn glanced down at the pot, then back to her face. "You saw?"

Lyss placed the pot on the coals and nodded. She pulled the collar of her tunic open, revealing the end of the ridged scar that ran from under her chin, twisted over her collarbone to above her heart. "They nearly sent me to Baer's hall too." The rarkyn's mismatched eyes stared at the scar, hugrokar still, expression unreadable. Lyss let her tunic drop. "You?"

The rarkyn inched closer to the fire and held out his hands. "Reds were cruel. Reds killed…someone kind," he said. Lyss had to lean forward to make out the words. His hugrokar gave nothing away. Someone kind. A friend? A relation? Did rarkyns have families the way humans did? What about a mate, or children? She studied the aetherling warming his hands over the fire. Come to think of it, how old was he? The rarkyn's long, black-padded digits were so close to the flames his talons smoked. There, streaked within the feathers of his forearms, long, white scars. *Knife wounds.* She'd seen wounds like them often enough as her father's assistant.

The rarkyn's hugrokar bristled and he moved his hands away. Discomfort trickled into her stomach. Lyss gave a guilty start. Her control had lapsed again. She refocused, drawing the mind magic tight. *Like a fist.* For a minute she wrestled, before the presence across the link dulled. She sighed. *This will take some getting used to.* She looked into the glowing coals.

"Do you have family?"

The rarkyn eased back and opened a wing to the flames. Light danced across his dark feathers. "Had once. Big pack. All dead now."

"Oh." *Alone, like me.* She couldn't help but wonder how it had happened.

"Mancers."

Lyss stiffened. She tightened her hugrokar again. *Kratting magic.* Across the link, the rarkyn's presence remained still. Whatever he felt, he kept it hidden. In the hush, he toyed with the crystal strung about his neck, one talon tracing a groove over and over in its clear surface.

She sat up. "Is that a rune?"

The rarkyn's hand closed over the stone. "A dead one." He released the crystal and furled his wings tight again; shifted his weight.

"Where did you get it?"

The rarkyn sat in silence for several moments before answering. "Someone kind."

Lyss blinked. Rarkyns didn't use galdar. A human had to have given it to him. *It couldn't have been…*

She goggled at him. "The one who put you in the prison cart?"

The feathers along the rarkyn's arms went on end and he spat out a snarl that echoed off the valley walls. *"No!"* His growl faded to a rumble in his throat. "Not him. *He* was a Red. *Cruel.*" He settled again, but his feathers stayed ruffled.

There had been another? Lyss stared at the rarkyn's back. A new, unsettling thought wormed its way forward. Had they been like her? Had there been others? Her stomach clenched, and she constricted her hugrokar before the rarkyn sensed her fear. *Like a fist.* She eyed the rarkyn over the flames, hoping he might reveal more, but he did not.

Lyss chewed her lip and peered across the valley at the smoke rising from the chimneys of Bardas Post. A dozen fields stood between them and the village. Open fields. Behind her, the rarkyn stood at the edge of the tree line, red and silver eyes narrowed as he took in the settlement. Lyss relaxed her hugrokar and her unease grew, the rarkyn's compounding her own.

"Rark," she said.

Lost in his own thoughts, the rarkyn paid her no mind.

"Rark," she said again. Still no response. Lyss loosened her hugrokar further, letting the magic flex, and stretched out for the rarkyn's mind. Taking the pressure at the edge of her thoughts, she yanked it like a temple bell. The rarkyn jolted, tail flaring as his attention rounded on her, the feathers along his forehead and crest rumpled. Like a frown.

"What's Rark?"

"You are. That's what I'm calling you."

The frown remained.

"It's either that or Grumbles, because that's what your stomach does. All day. So, what will it be?"

The rarkyn's lip twitched. For a heartbeat, amusement flickered through hugrokar. Then it was gone. "Rark will do."

Here I was expecting an argument, Lyss thought. He still refused to give her his name, but she had to call him something. What else was there? No human name seemed to fit. She eyed the creature half hidden in the shade. What would a rarkyn name sound like? Did they even have names?

Lyss shifted on Titch's back, gaze returning to the farm fields. All that open space. It would be a miracle if Rark wasn't spotted. She swallowed, unease doubling again. It would be better to bypass the village, but her supplies were near gone. *Nothing else for it.*

"Stay here until nightfall," she said. "See that ridge?" She pointed down the valley, finger coming to rest on a distant ridge where the forest reclaimed the mountain side. "I'll meet you there tonight. I'll light a fire."

Relief welled across hugrokar and Rark nodded. *He'd been that worried? What would happen when they arrived in Illredus?* Lyss pushed the thought aside. That was future Lyss' problem. Rark turned for the trees, ducking his horns under a low-hanging birch.

"Watch out for galdar," was all he said.

CHAPTER TWELVE

Dearest Elena,

I write to you from Deum, a little hamlet on the edge of the Memnon Spine. The inn here (if you can call this two-dorm shelter an inn) has, against all odds, a messenger service: one eyree, trained only to fly to Fort Chaelus. It's a grumpy old bird, long fluorescent tail feathers dull and wilting, but its beak is still sharp—I have the bruises to prove it! But it's better than naught.

The Council have sent me to investigate rumors of a haunting along the Tros Pass, the same pass that is Illredus's sole trade route through the Memnon Spine to Hannon. Yes, haunting. Turns out country folk are just as superstitious as those in the city. Chances are it's a local summoner up to no good, or perhaps an iele down from Memnon's wilds. In any case, I am to investigate and put it to right.

I'd like to think my Council affairs are proving a handful for you, but I suspect you are thriving. You're a talented mancer, Elena, and a promising politico. Heed me when I ask you to play your hand, our hand, carefully. Most of all, I must warn you of Councillor Keteus. He has had more than a good share of the King's ear of late, and I'm certain he's the reason behind this merry adventure. I've said it before, but I'll say it again, the fellow hungers for power like a starving dog hungers for scraps. He constantly maneuvers and positions, befriends and betrays. Do not trust that smiling face. Where I would have preferred to stay in Illredus and send a battalion to investigate this rumor, Keteus has convinced King Therrin that my presence is paramount. And so, I must obey and leave you at the helm. Little do they know that after years as my daughter and confidant, you are just as capable as I! Perhaps more so. Ha! I wish I could see the Council's faces when they realize you are no pushover.

Isaac is here with me, so whatever these old bones can't handle, he'll be able to. He bade me an early good night this evening, claimed he had some study to do in his room. Study my foot. I saw him sneak out arm in arm with the bar maiden a mere half-wick later. Did he think I hadn't noticed the doe-eyed looks she was giving him earlier? But I digress.

So far, our journey has been uneventful. Sepp willing it will stay that way. I will do my best to keep in touch, but I'm afraid I can't make promises. This is the first town in a fortnight that had an eyree at all.

I know you tire of me saying this but be careful in court.

Love Papa

THE MANCER WOKE WARM, DRY AND WITH THE AFTERTASTE of earth in his mouth. The inside of a tent met his gaze. Thick felt walls of woolen hair and wicker matting spread across the floor. His groggy mind churned into action. *Wildner.* A woven tapestry had been pushed aside from the doorway and he blinked, squinting in the bright as he ran his tongue around his mouth. He tasted blood and spat on the floor. A fire burned low in the hut's pit, its scented smoke tickling the back of his throat. The mancer coughed and grunted as pain ignited down his side. Had someone taken a club to his ribs?

A hand fell on his shoulder. "Be gentle. They're broken."

The mancer started: an old woman knelt beside him. *Kratting Wildner.* He'd not been caught off guard in years.

"What happened?"

The old woman swiveled on her heels and pulled a kettle from the fire. "We found you under the rubble." She swilled the water inside the pot and poured it into a mug. "Half buried," she added, and her eyes turned back to him, dark—an odd color for a Wildner—still and knowing. *Half dead,* they seemed to say. He'd seen eyes like that before; wise, knowing eyes. Eyes that had seen things. His gaze drifted down to her gnarled hands and the roping scars that started above each middle finger. They wrapped around her wrists and vanished up her sleeves. Old oil burns they looked like. *Curious.*

The mancer patted his left breast for the pocket that wasn't there, finding only cotton shift and skin. *The journal.* His heart lurched. He twisted in the bed, ignoring the pain, his one good hand turning over the furs, frantic. *Where is it? Where is it, where is it?*

"I believe you're looking for this." The Wildner placed a stained and travel-worn book on the furs. "We found it on you when we pulled you from the slide."

He snatched it up, unwinding the leather thong. "Did you—"

"Read?" The wrinkles of the old woman's face deepened as she scowled. "No," she said, voice cold enough to crack glass.

Mercies are still with me then. The mancer flipped to the end, checked the last page and released his breath. All there. His sketches and notes just as he'd left them. He snapped the book shut, clasped it tight and listened to the leather creak as he searched for the best way to ask his next question. "What about the rest of my cargo?"

The woman pointed to a small bundle of clothing at the foot of the blankets. A false wooden hand rested on top, runes and circles scored into it, the cloth bindings clean and folded underneath; ready to wear. Next to it, a silver brooch glinted in the low light, the crown and scepter stamp polished clean in the cold metal. "We washed and patched what we could," she said, eyes lingering on the brooch as he picked up the pile.

A small, ceramic bottle dropped from the folds of the fabric, thumping to the matting. The mancer froze, following the grit-stained bottle as it rolled to a stop at the Wildner's fur-lined boots. She turned from the fire, stooped, collected it.

"My thanks," he said as she handed it over and blinked as the weight of it fell into his palm. *Still full.* He uncorked it, sniffed once. A rich coppery smell tingled up his nose. *Mercies indeed.* He placed it on the bed atop his journal, licked his cracked lips, not sure if he wanted the answer to his next question.

"What of my wagon?"

"Crushed under mud and rock," the woman replied.

Of course, the storm. The deep crack of the earth and rumble of rock shivered up from his memory. The mancer forced down a shudder and picked up the false hand, glancing down to the stump of his right wrist. Elbow, forearm, then nothing. Nothing but pale flesh, calloused in places from the bindings, and a twisted lump of skin. He placed the hand against the stump and began winding the cloth. Under, over, round and round.

The Wildner woman watched. A vain thing, she must think. He didn't much care. The runes engraved on it were of far more import—summoning circles, defensive wards, all the tools for controlling belligerent aetherlings. He tied the bindings fast in a deft, practiced motion and turned back to the Wildner. She held out a mug of tea.

"I am Iga. And you are?"

The mancer took the tea and warmed his hand on it. "Archer."

He reached for the Aether within him. It came sluggishly, slinking back into his control like a cowed dog. Drawing a trickle, he unfurled his senses. Galdar had been worked close by, recently, perhaps only a few days ago. A ring of runes still echoed on the earth. A ward. A strong one. "What happened to the rarkyn?"

Iga's attention fixed on Archer and stayed for a long minute. "The rarkyn is gone."

Archer swore and threw the mug's contents onto the fire. The water slopped onto the coals with a hiss. "Blast it woman, which direction did it go?"

"North, toward the Steppes."

What happened to its sigil? Had the runes broken? No impossible. He'd spelled it himself. The rarkyn must have worked the chain free from the wagon's chassis. Archer pushed himself to his feet, fighting back a wince at the pain in his ribs. "There's still time—"

"Sit down," Iga's voice rang sharp over the spluttering fire. "Yes, it was headed north, three days ago."

Archer stopped. "How long was I sleeping?"

"Four days. You were half-fevered for most of it." Iga gathered her skirts and stood, her head stopping short of Archer's chin. She walked past him and opened the door of the tent, sweeping a hand to the world outside. The ground was a dusted white.

"No," Archer scrabbled to the door. "No, no, no, no."

"The first snow arrived last night," Iga said, gaze intent on Archer's face. He opened his mouth, closed it, and ground his teeth together. "I doubt even a mancer as skilled as you is fool enough to follow in your condition."

"Abyss damn it!" Archer spat out the curse and peered out at the snow-covered camp. "Curse it, curse it, *curse it all!*" He retreated into the hut, grating a thumb and forefinger along his bearded chin, feeling the ridge of the puckered scar that ran from cheekbone to jaw. The rarkyn had no pack. It was alone. With Archer's sigil still on its wrist, it would move slowly, trapped on Terresmir and unable to move through the Otherworld. Archer's eyes darted about the tent. He would have to hurry, he had time to make up.

"I need food, water and a horse," he said.

"You intend to go, despite my warning?"

Archer squared his shoulders. "I can't afford not to. I'll see you are compensated."

Iga's eyes narrowed, the edges wrinkling into crow's feet as she glared. "You'd risk your life over a rarkyn?"

"It cannot roam free. It's my—" Archer cut himself off "—the Conclave's property."

Iga's lips pursed. "A curious creature to keep," her eyes darted to the brooch again, "even for a mancer. Difficult to control too. Requires skill beyond the rank of a Mereor. Probably beyond a Praetus too."

Archer stiffened. *She's no ordinary Wildner.* "You're a Conclave woman?"

She delved into the pockets of her skirts, pulling out a battered brooch of her own from the folds. "Many years ago."

That explained the wards he'd sensed. Archer considered the woman. How old was she? Fifty? Sixty? Old enough to remember the days before Kallion's Regime, when Kraw and Illredus had been allies, though she would have been young. He took in her tanned skin, dark eyes—so very un-Wildner like—and the burns on her hands. Burns where runes might once have been tattooed on her skin. Old Kraw magic then? *She's too fair for a full blooded Krawan. A half-cast maybe.*

But that changed nothing. He needed to get the rarkyn back. The rarkyn had a three-day lead. The longer he dallied, the further ahead it got.

"I leave today. With or without your help."

Iga clucked her tongue, then sighed when Archer wasn't dissuaded. "You're lucky to be alive. Remember that. Miracles don't come twice."

CHAPTER THIRTEEN

Lyss pointed to the bundles of rima. "One of those, please." The merchant dropped the white tubers into a hessian sack, then held out the bag and an open palm to her. Lyss caught a whiff of wet soil and something grass-like as she dropped a copper into his palm.

She turned back to Titch and pushed the sack into a saddlebag. Done. *That should last another week.* She took up Titch's bridle and guided the mare down the street. The crowd was thin, Bardas Post was a small mountain town, but the smell was overpowering. It lapped at the back of her throat: sweat, soot, and livestock. When she swallowed, she tasted it, like she'd been chewing on a mud-crusted leather boot.

Gods and ginndir, who knew people stank so bad. She pulled Titch through the crowd and the mare's ears went flat as she tried to bite. Lyss jumped away and scowled. "Keep that up and I'll sell you for horse meat."

Titch stamped the ground and champed at her bit, as if daring her. *Don't tempt me,* Lyss thought at the beast.

Her final stop was in the village square. A town hall stood at one end; a single high-roofed manor that housed the guilds and visiting dignitaries. *Not that this backwater town would ever have any,* Lyss thought, eyeing the peeling paint on the tall, and very shut, double doors.

At the other end of the square stood the Guardhouse, its single tower rising over the town gate and casting a late afternoon shadow over the stocks and across the square. In the tower a watchman stood, gazing out beyond the wall at the sun as it moved low into the sky.

Lyss tethered Titch to a hitching post outside the local inn, pulled out her water skins and went to stand in line for the well in the square's center. Her mind turned to the rarkyn as she waited. He was still roaming north of town. Whatever he was up to had him focused. Lyss concentrated, trying to pinpoint his exact location. *If he's left the woods to pursue livestock…*

A hiss sounded in her ears and the rarkyn shoved her across the link. Lyss started and dropped a waterskin. "Kratting rarkyn," she muttered, rubbing her head with a wince.

"You, girl, stop right there."

Lyss froze. A glance over her shoulder turned her gut inside out. *The Order.* Two of them; eyes trained in her direction.

Oh gods, they know. Lyss' grip tightened around the neck of her water-skin. *How do they know?* One soldier stomped over: the older of the two who sported a thin scar along his forehead. As he came close, the runes on his sigiled armor *pushed* against her, like a faint, but icy, breeze. Miles off, the rarkyn shied away, his hugrokar shrinking small and tight.

Lyss gritted her teeth and kept her face straight. *Hold your ground.* To lean away would reveal herself. *Hold—*

The scar-faced soldier stopped before a young girl standing two places down the queue. In one, swift movement, he snatched the bucket out of the child's hands.

"Sir, my bucket—" the girl, no older than a ten-year, protested.

Scar-face looked the bucket over: a squiggle flashed on the wood inside. "Thought so," he grunted. "A spliced rune." He turned on the girl. "What's it do?"

The girl kneaded the bottom of her tunic. "Makes it lighter, sir. For when it's full. So I can lift it," she murmured.

"Did you make it?"

"No sir."

Scar-face leaned in. "Who did?"

The girl squeezed the hem of her tunic and looked away.

The soldier stepped closer and held the bucket under her nose. His hungry eyes fixed on her small frame like a wolf on the hunt. "*Who. Made. This?*"

The girl swallowed but stayed silent, even when Scar-face's hand clamped down on her arm and pulled her from the line. "Give me a name, child, or it will be your tongue and hands I take."

Panicked, the girl looked around for help, her gaze locking on Lyss. Lyss' heart thudded into her throat. *Stop looking at me. Stop it.*

"Let her go," a voice from further up the queue came to the rescue. A middle-aged woman stepped out of the line amidst a flurry of whispers.

"Miranda, *no!*"

"Fool! Keep yer head down!"

The woman ignored them and approached Scar-face. "Leave her be. Her father's the one you want."

The soldier straightened, and his face quirked, holding back a grin. "His name and where he lives."

"Torben Amsel. Owns the tailoring shop next t' the inn." The woman pointed to a street leading off the square.

Scar-face dropped the bucket to the cobbles. It landed with a thunk and the soldier lifted a sigiled boot onto it to stop it rolling away. His grip tightened around the girl's arm. "You're coming with me."

The soldier's companion, a younger ruddy-cheeked man who had watched the exchange in silence so far, stepped forward and put a hand on Scar-face's shoulder. "Farrus, we have a name. That's all we need."

Scar-face eyed the girl in his grasp. The girl sniffed and he let out a grunt and released his hold. "You're too soft Yannis." He drove his heel through the wood, splintering the bucket to pieces. He turned on the girl. "Beat it, but tell your krat father there is no point in running." His voice rose to a shout as the girl took off.

The soldiers continued down the queue, ruddy-cheeked Yannis falling into step with Scar-face. Lyss forced herself still as the number of runes doubled. Cold pushed against her skin, intensifying to a burn when they passed. She clenched her teeth. Was this what the rarkyn had meant when he'd said to watch out for galdar?

"I'll go fetch the Captain," Yannis said, and Lyss turned an ear to their conversation as they walked off.

Farrus grunted. "No need. You saw how easily that rune broke. The krat's just a dabbler."

Yannis sighed. "Let's get this over and done with then."

A tap at her shoulder made Lyss start, turning to find a man in the queue glaring at her. "How long are you planning on standing there?" he asked. Lyss blinked. She'd reached the front of the line.

"S—sorry," she stammered and with clammy hands, lowered the rope and bucket down the well shaft. It took an age to bring it back up and fill her waterskins from it.

Task done, she hurried back to Titch, stowed the two skins and made for the town gate, eyes down the whole way. *Quickly, quickly...but not too quickly.*

Streets away, her ears picked out a cry: "Papa!"

Lyss' throat turned dry. She closed her eyes. *Don't listen.* But her pact-turned hearing tracked the thud of the soldier's feet, their march steady as a gallows drum. A street away, a shop bell tinkled, its door opening then clattering shut. Lyss tensed, heart quickening.

A beat later the door burst open, the sound of its bell lost as a voice pleaded, pitching upwards, words coming faster and faster, until it began to babble:

"Was but a small charm to help my daughter—please, sirs, I cannot work without my hands. We'll starve—"

Lyss rubbed her ears, trying to block out the begging. No good. The pact amplified it all, even the sob as it broke from the tailor's throat.

"Sirs, please, not my hands, not my hands—"

Curse this hearing. Lyss grabbed Titch's reins and pulled the horse toward the gate. Two pairs of boots thumped toward them, bringing a third lighter step, half dragging, half scrambling.

"Papa!" The girl's voice again, close. Heads turned across the square. Lyss looked up to find the two soldiers hauling a well-dressed gentleman before the guardhouse. His left eye was already puffy and swelling by the second. A smear of dirt ran down one side of his jerkin.

"I'm all my daughter has. I need to provide—"

Scar-face jerked him forward, cutting off the tailor's plea. He stumbled, righted himself and wrestled against the soldiers' hold.

"It was one rune!" he cried. He locked his knees, dug in his heels and threw his weight against their grasp. He brought his hands together, fingers flexing, twisting, as he worked a rune.

Lyss watched, unable to take her eyes off him. She felt...pressure. Not unlike the Order's sigils, but it was fainter, weaker. No cold or pain, just a building press on her skin. It was like watching someone open their mouth and knowing a scream would soon come rushing out.

Yannis grabbed the tailor's hands and wrenched them apart. *Too late.*

Something *twitched* inside the prisoner. The air *pulsed*, its warmth evaporating in a heartbeat. Lyss stopped dead, knuckles white as they clenched Titch's reins. *Galdar.*

Gooseflesh spread over her arms as the power of the fresh rune radiated across the square. *Sepp damn.*

"Farrus!" Yannis managed to garble a warning before the tailor twisted against their hold, landing a strike in Yannis' chest. His fist thudded against the soldier's steel breastplate. The air twinged, engraved runes flashing green. It threw Yannis to the ground, his steel armor screeching against the cobbles as he skidded over the stones and lay still.

Scar-face grabbed the tailor's free arm and wrestled with him.

One, two, three; Lyss counted the sigils as they ignited across the soldier's armor as he brought the krat under control.

"It was one rune! *One!*" the tailor cried.

Behind them on the group, Yannis groaned. Scar-face turned an ear to him. "Yan—"

A flash of blond hair darted from the side of the dazed soldier. *The girl.* In five strides she crossed the stones to Scar-face and sank a dagger between the chinks of his leg plates. He yelled.

"*Kratting bitch!*" His backhand swung for her. She tumbled, the soldier's hand clipped her head, knocking her to the cobblestone.

"Elisa!" The tailor's fingers wriggled. Lyss blinked, recognizing the shape of the rune. *Spellfire.* Pressure built again, then pulsed cold as the rune activated. A small green flame popped to life in the tailor's hand. He rounded on Scar-face, pushing his hand into the soldier's cheek.

The acrid stench of burning flesh reached Lyss' nose as a cry went up from the soldier. He pushed the tailor off him, hands pressing to his face. When he removed them, his skin was blistered and raw. The tailor scrambled over to his daughter.

"You kratting—" Scar-face grabbed at his sword.

"Farrus!" Yannis staggered over, stepping between them. "The law Farrus, the law! He has to have a trial."

Farrus shoved past him. "Remember where you are Private." He sneered. "City laws got no place out here." He eyed the tailor. "Ain't that right, krat?"

The tailor's lip trembled. He pushed his daughter away. She clawed at his sleeve.

"Papa!"

"Elisa no. Stay back!" The tailor detached her, grabbed her frock and pitched her into the gathering crowd. Then he turned back to the soldiers, slowly, a man out of options.

Lyss' heart stopped in her chest. She'd seen this before. Her arms shook and she dug her nails into her palms. *Look away!* Yet her gaze latched onto to Farrus's sword as it rose into the air. *Don't watch.*

Dimly, she heard Yannis's shout ring over the square. "Farrus stop! This is not right! This is not—"

The sword came down.

And Lyss was falling.

CHAPTER FOURTEEN

Skaar sat on the creek bank under the curtain of a
willow. He stared at his hands, listening to the pop of the fire beside
him and the creek trickling through the willow's branches. Nothing.

Tenth time in a row. The voice of doubt whispered. *Give it up, it's not
coming.*

Skaar shoved the thoughts away and came to his feet and paced.
Why wasn't it working? His Aether should be strong enough. Had he
misjudged? He had missed something. He did another lap under the
tree, before abruptly sitting down again. *Remember how we used to work it.*

Of course, you never actually did it on your own back then, his doubt
nagged again.

Shut up.

He remembered soaring on the Otherworld's currents, piggybacking
his brother's rasvenger as a kit, as all kits did with their elders. Something twinged deep inside him and his heart thudded in his chest. Skaar
pulled away, the feathers on his arms bristling. *I don't want to see it. Not
again.*

He sat for several seconds, paralyzed until his heart settled and the
panic eased. He shook himself. *Enough, you're not a kit anymore.* If he had
to go all the way to Illredus, he needed to learn this now.

What about before the elders entered the Otherworld? The Aether
used to do that odd twist, and then they would be…part of it. How had

they done that? Skaar pondered for several minutes. As a kit it had been easy. Natural. All he'd had to do was concentrate on Fengar's hugrokar and follow the draft of the pack.

He paused. Perhaps that was how the elders had done it. Instead of having another rarkyn to guide them, had they simply focused on the Aether itself? The Otherworld was vast and deep, dive in too far and there was no coming back. How did they stop themselves overstepping the mark?

Skaar huffed and rubbed his head, talons brushing against his horns. *You're Aether-turned, maybe it's beyond you.* He jerked his hand away. "No." He had to trust he could still use rasvenger. Without it he was good as dead.

A pang of hunger gurgled over his frustration. He moved back to the creek. The school of fish was still there, sheltering under the willow's branches. Crouching on the bank, he reached out and dipped his talons into the water. Ripples spread across the surface and the school scattered. Skaar paid it no heed and sank his arms in up to his elbows. The fish would return soon enough.

He waited, the creek's current pulling at his feathers as he watched. *If only getting into the Otherworld was as easy,* he thought as he tracked one fish making its return. It darted through the water, stopped, then darted forward again, straight into his talons.

Got you.

Skaar pulled the fish from the water and tossed it onto the bank. It flipped about on the grass, and he grabbed it again before it fell back into the stream. Deprived of water, the fish gulped the air, slowly asphyxiating.

I know the feeling, he thought. All those long years starved of the Aether at Archer's hand. The mancer had given him just enough to survive, but never enough to fill his bones. Skaar dug two talons into the fish's gills, pulled its head back and snapped its spine. It flopped dead in his hands.

He returned to his fire; the coals had burned low again. Skaar broke a few of the dry branches he'd collected for kindling, threw them over the pit and blew a lung full of air over it. The coals gave a pop and the flames rose, licking around the wood. *If only recovering his magic was as simple as rekindling a fire.*

He pulled out his slate knife—a sliver of rock taken from the riverbed that morning—and cut along the fish's belly and dug out its entrails. They went into the fire with a hiss and puff of smoke. Once complete, he picked up the sharpened branch he'd stoked the fire with and poked it down the fish's mouth, lodging it in the meat at the end of the tail before setting it over the coals.

He sat back down, rubbing his palms together. Cold hands again. With a mumbled curse, he pulled the Aether inside him tight, knuckling down as if he were drawing a blanket close against a chill. What he wouldn't give to be immersed in the Otherworld's heat again. Truly immersed. He held his fingers out to the flames before pausing.

What am I doing?

The sigil was gone. There was no need to conserve his energy. He blinked. *Could it be something so simple?*

He fell silent, concentrating. His instinct to cling to his precious little Aether surged through him. Skaar pushed it down. *There was no sigil, nothing stopped him drawing on more.* Bit by bit he coaxed the Aether from his bones. The energy rocked through him, sending a shiver of heat from tail to toe. His muscles warmed and soaked the magic in. Skaar drew in a deep breath and the Aether tingled inside his lungs.

Miles away he sensed Lyss frown, his antics catching her attention. She came close over hugrokar, trying to figure out what he was doing. Skaar flattened his ears and snarled, sending the sentiment across hugrokar as he shoved her off. *Go away.*

She started and pulled back, angry, but did not try to pry again. Skaar growled under his breath and returned to the Aether.

Surely now there was a chance.

Come on, just a little, he urged.

Under his skin, the Aether twitched. *Yes!* He latched onto the sensation and reached his magic out for to the other plane. His talons caught on something not quite air, not quite water. *The divide.* Excitement rose inside him and he pushed on it. The pressure fell away, rippling around his talons. Before his eyes, his fingers blurred, and the heat of the Otherworld slid across his palm.

It was like he'd eased his frozen hands into steaming water. Skaar swallowed hard. *How could I forget this?* The heat sank into his skin, thawing his muscles, seeping up his arms. His muscles and bones drank the Aether in like a rag. A soft current pulled at his downy feathers.

Skaar hesitated, then pushed deeper, up to his elbow. The warmth spread to his shoulders, through his neck, sending a shiver down his spine. *Beautiful heat. Delicious heat. More.* He wanted more. He pressed in further, pulling the Aether into his bones. Hot pain spiked up his arm. Skaar yelped and snatched himself free.

"*Careful*," warned Raska's memory. "*We must always be careful. Balanced. In control.*" Her talons brushed his temple, tapping below his pale eye. "*You more than others. The Aether already touched you when you were born. It claimed your mother, do not let it claim you.*"

Skaar sank back onto the bank, flexing his digits. *I won't,* he promised. The magic was shaky, like a kit's first wobbling steps—it had been years since he'd used it after all—but it was *rasvenger*. He was a long way off from pushing through to the Otherworld and soaring the Aether's currents, but given time…

A toothy grin pulled at his face.

His delight was short-lived. A moment later, the cold burn of galdar trickled through hugrokar. Skaar bristled, head swiveling in the direction of the town.

Reythr damn it, I told her to stay away from it.

He waited; muscles tensed to see if the cold would grow. It did, a little, and Skaar eased away from their link. The cold faded and a sigh eased up his throat.

Safe, for n—

Miles away, Lyss' hugrokar went still.

CHAPTER FIFTEEN

THE FIRST THING SHE REGISTERED WAS THE RARKYN RAGING
at her across hugrokar. Lyss' heart shot into her mouth. He was close.
Very close.

Let. Me. GO!

Lyss rocked on the spot as the rarkyn's snarl boomed in her head. He
tried to pull away, only to find their hugrokar snag tight.

"Witch!" The cry snapped Lyss' gaze up. The town square, the crowd
—why were they backing away? She looked at her feet.

An Order soldier—or what was left of him. His face was crushed,
skull misshapen. Eyes were no more than hollows, each one weeping
bloody tears. She stumbled back, caught sight of her palms and stopped.

Blood slicked her fingers. Wet. Sticky. *Red.*

"With her bare hands," a whisper rose from the crowd. A dollop of
blood ran down the outside of her pinkie. It plopped onto the cobbles,
splattering at her feet like a raindrop.

"Not even the sigiled armor stopped her."

"Only a witch can do that," said another.

"Don't be stupid, there are no more witches. Kallion burned them
all to ashes years ago."

Lyss dragged her gaze from her hands and back to the corpse. The
sigils of the dead man's armor were lifeless, dull little dents in the metal
casing. His shattered face looked up at her, features unrecognizable in

the blood and skull fragments. *What happened? What did I do?* The bile rose in her throat.

"Witch!" The shout rose again from the crowd.

She spun. "No, I—I'm no—"

"Don't move!"

A sword pointed at her from the other side of the corpse. Scar-face, his cheek weeping and welted from the tailor's spellfire, grip tight on his pommel, glared at her over the blade. "Don't move, I said!" The sword-tip quivered.

Lyss stared at him, and the soldier watched her back.

"Arrest her," someone called. Scar-face's eyes darted to the crowd. He swallowed, clenched and re-clenched the hilt.

"Stay where you are," he repeated. He shuffled out, away from his fallen companion and circled towards her.

If he arrests me, I'm dead. Lyss glanced at Titch. Five strides away. Four, if she dashed. If she could get on the mare, she might stand a chance. She shifted her weight. Scar-face's sword snapped up to her throat.

"By the Order's decree I—"

A shrill whistle broke him off. Lyss' breath caught: the local watch. A phalanx of spears pushed through the crowd. *Oh gods, now, I have to go now!* Scar-face sensed her alarm and lunged, stabbing the blade in her direction.

She reacted without thinking, darting around the blade with a quick-step, limbs moving on instinct. Scar-face pitched forward, his sword meeting no resistance and clanking into the cobbles.

Lyss spun around and ran. Four long strides and she reached Titch. She grabbed the reins, hoisted herself into the saddle, and kicked her heels hard into the mare's sides. *Move!* Titch vaulted forward and the crowd scrambled to let her through.

The gate. Get to the gate. A pair from the watch were already at it, shoulders heaving into the wood to push it shut.

No! She kicked Titch again and gave the mare the rein, letting her stretch to a gallop. They vaulted forward. *Make it, make it, make it!*

She passed through with half a girth to spare on each side, kicking at one of the watchmen as he grabbed for her. A mere moment more and she was free.

Open sky and brown farm fields greeted her beyond the gate. Lyss drove Titch down the road, the mare's hooves clattering in her ears. Ahead, the mountain where Rark waited loomed, its peak dark with trees visible between the mare's ears. Lyss dug in her heels and Titch surged forward, just as a shout sounded from inside the walls.

"After her!"

———

SKAAR PUMPED HIS WINGS, WIND RUSHING OVER HIS feathers. His senses buzzed. Scents were sharp, horse and human sweat, and a loose buckle jangled in time with Titch's hooves on the trail.

The girl rode below him, a black ant zigzagging up the slope. Their agreed meeting point, where the road intersected the valley's ridge, was close. A horn-blast swung his attention down the valley. A band of horses, men and dogs followed, red cloaks billowing from the riders' shoulders.

What in Reythr's name is going on?

He swooped low, circling over the canopy, squinting as the orange-gold sun left blots across his vision. *Aether curse it, twilight is no time to fly.* The girl rounded the crest of the ridge and he dropped to the ground and waited on the trail.

"What—" Skaar began before the horse, girth covered in frothing sweat, whisked past, carrying the girl and the scent of blood and galdar with it. "Wait!" he squawked. With a beat of his wings, he flitted down the trail after them. "What happen?"

No response. Just the bellow of Titch's heaving lungs. Lyss' eyes were glazed, miles away. Bloody freckles splattered her cheeks. Her fingers, curled tight around the reins, were a crusty red brown.

Skaar scurried after them. "Lyss!" He grabbed for Titch's reins, but the mare skittered away with a new surge of energy. The girl's knees tensed in the saddle. Her hands whipped out, took control and the mare came, finally, to a standstill. She looked up.

"Rark?" Her hugrokar snapped sharp as she came out of the daze. The smell of blood intensified.

"What happen?" Skaar asked again.

Lyss swallowed. "The Order came. Not for me, for someone else and before I knew it..." she stopped. Bile rose in Skaar's stomach and he jerked his mind away as Lyss doubled over in the saddle and retched.

The Order. That explained the galdar he'd felt earlier. Skaar wrinkled his nose. *And why she smells like runes.*

Lyss wiped her mouth with the back of a trembling hand. "I killed him."

"Who?"

"The soldier." She gripped the saddle horn as if was the only thing real in a midst of a nightmare. "Gods and ginndir, I killed him. I didn't mean to. I mean I don't remember. I just saw the sword and—" She looked at her hands and Skaar sensed as much as saw her shudder. Her thoughts spiraled. "I don't remember," she said again. She stared into her palms and swallowed hard. "I didn't feel a thing."

A hound bayed in the distance and they both jumped.

"Reds come," Skaar said. And from the sound of it they were out for blood. He considered the dimming sky; the moon had not risen yet. "We lose them when dark falls."

Lyss' gaze roved the trees. Her hugrokar quivered as she weighed their options before an uncomfortable twist knuckled into Skaar's gut when she realized there were none. Not when the Reds followed with galdar and hounds.

"Okay."

He felt the effort it took her to force the word out; the swell of will to blot out the events she'd fled from and focus on what was in front of her now. Lyss nudged the mare forward with her calves.

"Hugrokar will help you see," Skaar assured.

Lyss nodded. "Let's keep moving."

At last, something we agree on. Skaar lifted his cold fingers to his mouth and breathed over them, savoring the momentary heat. The Otherworld would have to wait.

He set after Lyss at a steady lope.

LYSS PULLED THE HOOD OF HER CLOAK TIGHTER AND wrapped it around her throat. The last haze of the sun had vanished behind the mountains, taking the warmth with it. They'd descended into a new valley; fir and spruce trees sprung high overhead. Damp earth muffled their pursuers to far off shouts and the occasional dog bark.

In her peripheral, she sensed the rarkyn keeping pace. Every now and again she'd see a figure cut close to the road then vanish back into the trees. *Like a haunting,* Lyss thought and shivered.

With daylight gone, the world had shifted into muted tones of blue, green, and gray. Lyss held her hand out. Rark had been right about their hugrokar. Where once she wouldn't have seen her own hand, she now made out the blood under her nails with unnerving clarity. *Gods, what had that been?* At the image of the soldier's mangled head in her hands, bile rose in her throat again. She forced it down.

"Only those who have never taken life can talk of killing lightly," Fa had once said. She hadn't understood then. She did now, even if the moment between seeing the sword lifting to the air and waking to the soldier dead in her lap was completely blank. A chill crept into her muscles. Was this how the madness started? Moments of time lost? Slips in sanity? Would she kill every time it happened? She shivered and pushed up her sleeve. Iga's runes were still whole, but the knot in her gut didn't ease. She pulled her cloak tighter once more. *Illredus. Get to Illredus, break the pact.* She scowled at herself. *Idiot.* A fool's wish truly, but she clung to it anyway. Maybe, just maybe.

A stumble from Titch pitched Lyss into the mare's neck. Her knees clenched the saddle, holding her balance as Titch righted herself. The mare was at her limit. *Curse it.* She slowed Titch to a walk, stopped and dismounted, and took the reins in one hand.

A ripple across hugrokar made her look up as a rarkyn-shaped shadow stepped out from the trees.

"Why stop?" Rark asked.

Lyss indicated Titch. "She needs to rest."

She thought that might spark a quip from Rark, but he merely nodded and turned to keep pace beside them.

The night deepened and a smattering of clouds rolled in. The road led on. Stillness descended. Twice Lyss strained for the sounds of pursuit; anything to gauge how far off the Order were. She detected nothing.

As Titch's breathing eased, Lyss brought the mare to a stop and dug into the saddlebags, producing a camp pot and a water skin. She removed the mare's bridle, filled the pot to the brim and placed it before the mare then held the skin out to Rark. He took it, talons and padded fingertips brushing Lyss' palm in the exchange. It was like touching ice. Gooseflesh rose down her arm, turning her hairs on end.

"Are you okay? Your hands are freezing."

The rarkyn huffed. "Is normal." He took a swig from the skin and held it out to her. Lyss eyed him in the dark. He was still wretchedly thin. And how well would his feathers insulate from the snow? She might not like the aetherling, but she didn't wish him dead from cold.

Rark sighed, sensing her doubt. "Is normal," he repeated. "Not enough Aether."

Lyss frowned. "What do you mean? Can't you draw in more?"

Rark shuffled his wings and his hugrokar gave a twitch. Irked; almost sheepish. "Takes time to build up, especially in Terresmir." He patted a foot against the ground, indicating the earth under him. His talons left little prick-marks in the dirt.

His explanation set off a dim memory and Lyss recalled a smoke-filled tent and a lecture from Iga. *"Aetherlings need more Aether than us to survive. It is their source of life."* Lyss glanced at Rark, gaze lingering on the chafed band of skin the sigil had left around his wrist. Curiosity got the better of her.

"Rark, how long was that sigil on you?"

The rarkyn's horns tilted in the dark. He was silent for a long minute. "Not sure," he said at last. "Six winters maybe."

Six years starved by a sigil. Six years trapped and alone. Gods and ginndir, how had his mind not broken after all that time? Lyss rummaged through the saddle bags and pulled out a bag of grain and a loaf of bread. She poured the feed into a nose bag for Titch, slipped the nose bag over the mare's ears, then split the loaf in half and offered it to the rarkyn.

"I can't help with the Aether, but at least eat something."

Rark took it with a nod of thanks. He nibbled at it, as if trying to savor each bite to make it last. Lyss checked Titch's nose bag, found it empty and repacked it, then returned the bridle to the mare and took up the reins to walk her again. Rark followed, pacing beside her, just out of reach of Titch's teeth.

"What will you do? When we break pact?" he asked, sounding hesitant, as if worried how she might answer.

Lyss remained quiet. When it was over. More like *if*. A very big if. The foolish wish rose inside her again nonetheless. Say they succeeded. Say they beat the odds, broke the pact, stopped the madness, what then? Fall back on her original plan? Change her name, infiltrate the Order and bring Loric down? She sighed. *No.* She needed mancer skills to get into the Rose Brigade. Her inability to wield galdar hadn't changed. She would have to find another way. If not, well her knife-in-a-dark-alley plan was still on the table. She squeezed her wrist, the faint cool of the runes tingled under her fingers. It all hinged on Illredus and what help they found there—or didn't.

"There is someone I must kill," she said at last. The soldier's imploded head in her hands flashed through her thoughts again. Her stomach flipped. *This is different.* He *deserves it.*

Rark cocked his head, question rising over hugrokar.

"His name is Loric. Captain Mereror Loric. Though he's probably ranked higher now."

"He killed kin?"

In her mind's eye, Loric's sword fell. Blood pooled. Lyss wrenched her thoughts away, gritted her teeth and nodded. Rark's doubt crept over hugrokar and she turned to find him studying her.

"You want to kill? After"—his gaze slid back down the road—"that?"

She stiffened. "That was an accident."

But was it? a part of her mind whispered.

Lyss shook her head. "It was—" her voice trailed off and she gripped Titch's reins, knuckles whitening. *Murder. You're a murderer.* The way the villagers looked at her. *Like a monster,* the thought rose inside her, chilling her skin.

I'm not. I won't be. I won't be like him.

Captain Loric's laugh rang in her head, mocking.

CHAPTER SIXTEEN

ARCHER STARED DOWN AT THE MOUNTAIN HAMLET. SHABBY
was the best word he could muster for it; everything from the rotting
log walls to the open gate and empty guardhouse.

Careless idiots. Practically begging to be raided. He clicked his tongue and
his piebald horse skipped forward. He steadied the animal, wrapped
another loop of the reins around his wooden hand, and took in Bardas
Post again.

"We'll reach it by nightfall." Darrin nudged his horse forward. His
kid brother followed on their packhorse, shaping out runes with his
fingers as the animal plodded along.

Good, Archer thought, vehemently. A few more hours and he'd be
able to pick up supplies, send this wretched horse home with his
Wildner guides, and head North for the Steppes—if that was indeed
where the rarkyn had gone. He watched Hane's hands work the runes,
fingers shaping the ancient letters. *Cen* for heat; *ur* for strength; *ehwar*
for quicken; *nauthis* for bind; the runes of farmhands and merchants. He
cast none but repeated the series over and over. After six iterations the
boy sensed Archer's gaze and his hands stilled.

"How many do you know?" Archer asked.

"Just four."

Just four you'll admit to. Archer had seen the remnants of the invented
runes scratched into the earth next to the wreck that had once been his

wagon. The lad knew at least one other—a bastardized spell that spliced ur's strength with a nauthis binding—and probably a fair few more inventions that would have an Order soldier reaching for a branding iron. A touch from one of those sigiled prods and goodbye galdar.

The boy started up his practice again.

I wonder if his grandmother knows. Archer scowled, the old scar pulling on his cheek. *Of course she does.*

"Have you been to Illredus?" he asked the boy.

Hane shook his head.

"A big city, lots of people; white buildings and flower boxes on every sill. A pretty city, beautiful even," he concluded. "People flock to it from all over the Empire."

Hane gave a half shrug, a gesture that said Archer's words were not news to him. "The King's Court is there," he said. "As is the Order, the Conclave, and the Council of Seven."

"Yes, yes. Home of the Robes and the Reds." Archer hunched forward, saddle creaking. "But did you know it smells something awful?"

Hane blinked, confused. Ahead of him Darrin's head turned, exposing one ear to the conversation.

"But you said—" Hane started.

"I said Illredus is *pretty*. Not that it smells nice. Smells like a tavern's outhouse in truth. No amount of flower boxes can hide it. Sure, there are runes in every house to expunge the smell and some along the streets of the nicer parts, but there's no real way to escape it. Even the sea breeze can't whisk it away. Can you guess why?"

Hane was silent, and when it was clear he couldn't answer, Darrin gave a small huff. "Because of the mancers, Hane."

Hane's brow furrowed.

"Think about it," Darrin went on. "Think about Iga's tent right after she's been casting."

"It smells like bad eggs." He blinked. "Illredus is like that? But to make a whole city smell—"

The youth's eyes darted back and forth as he calculated. All runes burned the Aether when they were cast. The smell from a single rune was undetectable but cast multiple runes in quick succession and a whiff of something akin to burnt hair would hang in the air a moment after. Multiply that by an entire city; whole streets and suburbs... Archer's smile grew as Hane's expression stilled.

"There must be hundreds of mancers there."

Archer leaned back in the saddle, as if he were once again one of the Seven being asked for consult in the King Therrin's Hall. Sniveling Therrin, always so afraid, terrified his subjects might learn how much of a fraud of a mancer he really was.

"Try thousands," he said. "All casting, all the time." He glanced at Darrin. The Wildner's attention was on the trail, perhaps a little too attentively. *Another nudge then.* "That is where your friend is going," he said. *With my rarkyn.*

Darrin twisted in his saddle; his dark irises fixed on Archer.

Hane pursed his lips. "How do you know about Lyss?"

Archer ignored Darrin's stare, feigning mock surprise instead. "Was it a secret? Your fellow Wildners didn't make much of an effort to stay quiet about her."

Hane scowled and looked at his brother. "I bet it was Wellan."

Archer cleared his throat. "If she can handle a bit of stink, she'll be fine, unless…" he faltered.

"Unless what?"

Archer studied the brothers' faces. "It occurs to me your friend left at the same time my rarkyn escaped." He stroked the stumble on his chin. "Awfully coincidental, don't you think?"

Hane's gaze darted to Darrin, but otherwise both brothers kept their faces neutral.

Archer pressed further. "A rarkyn can fetch a fine price in Illredus—if it's dead. If it's alive…well, they'll charge her for breaking the law."

Hane's brow twitched with the start of a frown.

"Kallion's fourth law," Archer recited. *"Thou shall not summon beyond thy station."* He lifted his cloak, fingering the silver brooch on the lapel of his coat. "Has she earned her mancer's brooch?" At the brothers' silence, he smirked. "Thought not. For something like a rarkyn, a creature capable of ripping a hole between this world and the Otherworld, it's the gibbet for sure—if they don't execute her on the spot."

Horror flashed across Hane's face. "You can't know for—"

"Hane!" Darrin interrupted, too late.

Got you. Archer relaxed his features, forcing down his rising triumph. "I was right. Your friend has my rarkyn."

Hane flushed red. He swallowed and looked at his brother. "Sorr—" he started, but Darrin stopped him with a hand.

"Just…stop talking."

Archer clucked his tongue. "You can't blame him for caring. I meant what I said about the fourth law. The Order will execute your friend if she's caught trading a living rarkyn. They won't be lenient, no matter who she is or how powerful."

Even so, getting the beast back from her wouldn't be easy, brooch or not. If she's gifted enough to keep it under control, she's gifted enough to cause trouble. He reached for the Aether inside him, balling it together at his core and taking stock. It had recovered somewhat over the last five-day, despite the Wildners' scant rations. A few more good meals would go a long way to replenishing it, but his reserves were still woefully low.

A direct confrontation was out of the question. At least for now. He felt for the ceramic bottle tucked into the breast of his coat, next to his journal. Still there. Ready. Waiting. *If not for that kratting storm I'd be in the Steppes by now.*

Not to be. Not yet, it seemed. He patted the journal. *A little longer.*

For now, his best option was a trade. But he couldn't compete with what the black market would pay for a rarkyn in Illredus. No, he needed something to force her hand, just in case.

The brothers' silence extended all the way to the town gate. At their approach, a guard detached from the wall and planted himself in their path. A polearm thrust toward them, forcing Darrin to jerk his reins tight, pulling his horse to a stop.

Archer bit back an oath and did the same. The piebald whinnied, its weight shifting to its hind legs, forelegs lifting from the ground as it reared. Archer yanked to the left with his good hand, digging one heel into the horse's side and maneuvering it in a tight circle to regain control. *Blasted creature.*

"State your name and business, Ghost." The guard's knuckles where white around the polearm, teeth bared behind his scruff of a beard.

A scowl flickered across Darrin's face at the Empire's nickname for his people, but when he spoke, his voice was level. "I'm Darrin Eder, of the Wildner. This is my brother," he pointed at Hane, then motioned to Archer. "We're escorting this traveler to Bardas Post."

An interesting welcome, Archer noted wryly as the guard's polearm twitched in his direction.

"Andreas Markides. Seeking supplies," he said, and when the piebald under him pawed the ground he added, "and a new horse."

The guard's polearm roved over them. "You're traveling awfully light. Where's the rest of your supplies?"

"Lost to the road," Archer said.

The weapon dropped slightly. "Bandits?"

"Rockslide. I survived thanks to the Wildners." He indicated Darrin and Hane.

"Our camp is a five-day ride from here," Hane said, nodding, then fell silent as Darrin glared at him.

"How long do you intend to stay?"

"Just the night," Darrin said and Archer nodded in agreement.

The guard eyed the three of them for another long moment before the polearm swept back up and its heel thumped into the dirt. "Go on then," he said, waving them through. He made to turn back for his post, but stopped mid-stride, fixing his attention back on Darrin. "Do not be causing trouble. We've had enough of that of late."

Archer glanced up at the watch tower as they passed. To his surprise, he spotted a tuft of brown hair and bright eyes peering at them over the lip of the rail—a boy, not more than ten. *Not completely unmanned after all,* Archer thought, *but damn well near it.* His eyes skimmed the empty lookouts along the wall. *Where are all the guards?*

After finding the town's only inn and haggling the price down to something reasonable, Archer stowed his few belongings in his room and set out on foot.

The streets were eerily quiet. Locating the traders' quarter, he headed for the livestock pens at the edge of town. The sole horse trader looked apologetic when Archer described the horse he needed. Strong and fit enough to carry a rider through the mountains; nimble enough to traverse game trails; stolid, but alert and responsive.

"Workhorses is all we got 'round here," the horse trader said, swinging an arm out to the pen. Three horses and a pony stood within it. Two were the heavy-set giants, bred and trained to haul heavy loads. Archer circled the pen, eyeing the lighter built steed in the far corner, before spotting the bandage around the hoof of one foreleg.

"A case of hoof-rot," the trader said with a sigh. "If you're willing to wait two days, he'll be good to go again."

Archer shook his head. "I must leave tomorrow."

The trader indicated the pony. "She was ol' Samson's before he passed. Used to pull his cart to town on market day," the trader said. "She's a little old, but a good animal and reliable."

Archer looked the pony over, running a hand over her withers. She was stocky, and her brown coat was thick and ready for winter. A slight dip in her back and a few white hairs around her nose betrayed her age. *She's the best I'll get in this shithole.* He gave a nod. "How much?"

He parted ways with two iron ara for the pony and persuaded the trader to throw in a full set of riding tack and two saddle bags for an extra half-iron demos.

"Can you point me toward a good tailor?" Archer asked when the deal was done.

"'Fraid not. The Order ran our tailor out of town a few days back."

Archer's eyebrows rose. *The Order? Here?* The trader read his surprise.

"Caught him using illegal runes," the trader said and sighed. "Idiot krat fought back when they arrested him. Ugly business."

Archer nodded. "I heard rumors about a fresh inquisition a few months ago, but I didn't think it would extend this far north."

"Aye, it has," the trader said. "Some fancy Regis from the capital is coordinating it out of Nilos I hear."

Nilos, now there's a place I haven't heard of in a while. There had been a time when every report that had crossed his desk had mentioned that cursed little town. Krats swindling in the markets, destroying crops, using spliced runes to break through the mayor's protected manor and graffiti his front door. Things had clearly changed since then. *A new Order outpost will do that.*

"Is there anyone with a few extra winter woolens to trade?" he asked. The trader pointed out a few shops along the street to try his luck in. Archer thanked the man and left.

It was well past sundown when he returned to the inn. Securing his pony—Nela, the trader had called her—in the inn's stables, he ferried his supplies to his room before heading to the tavern next door for a meal. As expected, he found the two Wildner boys seated at a table with a pair of empty plates before them. Archer placed an order with the kitchen then had the barkeep pour three mugs of chara. Carrying two by the handles in his good hand, he thumped them down before the two youths, fetched his own drink, then sank into the chair opposite.

"As thanks for guiding the way here," Archer said when Darrin raised an eyebrow. "It's not much I'm afraid, but it's all I can afford right now."

Hane dragged a mug toward himself. "Thanks." The chara sloshed over the rim, leaving a trail across the table, its sweet honey and spice scent mixing with the wood. His brother studied Archer for a moment before picking up his drink and sipping it.

"You're leaving tomorrow then?" Hane asked, and promptly investigated the inside of his mug when Darrin shot him a look.

"At first light," Archer replied, shifting back in his chair as a barmaid arrived with his meal. Hane opened his mouth to speak again, then shut it and lifted his mug instead. As the silence lengthened, Archer turned his attention to the next table where two guards were hunched over their drinks.

"—patrolling all the road, but I think she's long gone."

"Thank Sepp for that. And the Reds? Are they on their way back?" It was the elder of the two who spoke; the insignia on his shoulders marked him as a Sergeant of the watch.

"No, they opted to push on. They're determined to catch her." Archer caught the incredulous tone of the younger guard. "I only hope the weather holds."

The Sergeant swilled his mug. "She murdered one of their own so it's not surprising."

The younger gave a sigh. "That's true, but I didn't see many supplies between them. They will all freeze if the snows find them."

The Sergeant swilled the last of his drink around his mug, then knocked it back. "They're Reds, they can take care of themselves," he assured. "A krat like that is too dangerous to let roam in the provinces."

Archer sat up and turned to face the guards. "Forgive me for prying, but did you say there's a dangerous krat on the roads?"

The younger of the two gawped at the interruption, his attention flicking from Archer's eyes to the grisly scar on his cheek. Recovering, the guard gave a slow nod. "A young woman, travelling alone."

One of the Wildner brothers choked on his drink. Archer ignored him.

"She killed a Red you say?"

"Aye," the older guard replied. "Crushed his skull. Barehanded."

Archer's eyebrows raised. "Did she now?" He shuffled forward in his chair. "An unusually strong girl then? Perhaps *giftedly* strong?"

The younger of the two guards bobbed his head. "Roll up her sleeves and I bet you ten ara you'd see runes 'graved all down her arms. You know, like what them krats from Kraw do."

"You're sure she was alone?" Archer asked. "No one else—*nothing else*—was with her?"

"Not that we saw."

Archer lifted his glass. "Well, there's good news for a wary traveler. I'm sure it's only a matter of time before the Reds catch up with her." He nodded to the two guards, finished his drink and placed the tankard down on the table with an almost imperceptible thud.

"I leave tonight," he told the brothers, voice low and steady. "And if you care at all about your friend, you'll help me."

CHAPTER SEVENTEEN

Skaar sat, the warmth of the Otherworld soothing his icy fingers in the pre-dawn light. Its power seeped through his skin, sending quivers through his Aether-deprived muscles. He closed his eyes, thinking back to when he used to watch Fengar trying to master the skill.

"*No ripples, Fengar,*" Raska had said. "*Too much disturbance brings the ginndir.*"

Carefully, he drew on the growing pool of power inside him and *reached*. The Aether responded, reaching back, pulling him closer. The Otherworld lapped up to his elbows and swirled around his fingers with an ever-so-slight pull of its current.

No ripples.

Skaar grinned. Fengar had practiced again and again trying to get the knack of it. More than once, the black rings had formed in his irises when he worked the Aether to his limit. Through it all, Skaar had watched and waited for Raska to call the lesson to a close. "*No more for you today,*" she'd always say at the end. "*If you lose yourself to the Aether, I won't be fishing you out.*"

Fengar hadn't dared disobey. Yet for all his grumbling about wasting precious summer days learning rasvenger, his brother's pride had resonated across hugrokar for days after Raska pronounced him skilled enough to fly in the forward pack. From that point, he became an adult capable of navigating the Otherworld's currents on his own. Meanwhile, Skaar, five years younger and half of Fengar's size, had had to stay with the other kits at the back, relying on Raska and the other elders to guide them. How he'd hated that.

"Patience Skaar," Fengar had consoled once. *"Give it time."*

That day they had watched another kit, three years Skaar's younger, go into *ellirsott*—the growing sickness. It had signaled the end of that rarkyn's childhood and the start of their ability to call upon the Aether on their own. How Skaar's feathers had bristled in envy.

"Your turn will come," Fengar had said, and he'd leaned in, his hugrokar going suspiciously still. *"You know, it's said the older the kit is before the Aether touches them, the stronger their skills will be. Raska thinks you'll be the one to replace her."*

Skaar hadn't believed a word. It was just like Fengar to make up stories to comfort him. But he'd not been in the mood. He'd fixed his brother with the coldest, flattest stare he'd been able to muster and uttered one word before taking off in a huff: *"Liar."*

An old, familiar tightness spread across Skaar's chest and throat. Seven years Fengar had been dead. He opened his eyes and eased his hands free. Aether curled off his talons in small, smoky wisps, dissipating into the morning fog. He'd been twelve when ellirsott's call finally came, two years later than the other kits his age. It had come on like a tide, dousing him it its fever. The timing couldn't have been worse. It had been the height of summer—mordkyn season. True to his cursed luck, the mordkyn had found them while he'd been in the throes of ellirsott fever.

He remembered little of that night. Pain searing through hugrokar; fear hammering at his senses, and Fengar scooping him up in his arms and running as the rest of the pack faded into the Otherworld. Alone and burdened with a kit too sick to fly, Fengar had made easy pickings. A shuck had found them first; teeth snapping at Fengar's heels to muster them toward its masters. Skaar remembered the sting of runes on his brother's back and screaming at him to stop, to leave him and run. Instead, Fengar had plonked Skaar at the foot of a pine and rounded on their pursuers.

"Wait here," he had said and vanished into the melee, hugrokar so tight Skaar hadn't felt the galdar burns or the mordkyn's arrows when they finally brought his brother down.

Only when Fengar's mind had come close, hugrokar unravelling like a thread pulling loose from a frayed end of fabric, did Skaar know something was wrong. He had come to his feet, nerves buzzing, and followed his nose to the bloody scene. Three bodies in the soil, gutted from navel to sternum, limbs contorted in blood and piss. Skaar had never laid eyes on a human until then. He'd taken in the strange featherless creatures, far smaller than he'd imagined, with piggish skin, matted hair and strange pointed noses. These were the monsters of rarkyn nightmares? Their mouths gaped, eyes bloated, as if shocked to find themselves dead. Pitiful, weak things they'd seemed.

He had found Fengar beyond, crumpled in a broken galdar circle, pierced through with arrow shafts, lifeblood draining into the earth. The Aether inside him was calm. Controlled. Unnervingly still.

Raska had taught him well.

Skaar had collapsed at his brother's side, talons digging into Fengar's feathers. Grief had cut through his Aether-addled thoughts long enough to draw breath and scream before ellirsott's power engulfed him. Fever wrenched his control away, magic searing his bones, bubbling up inside him like an overheated crock threatening to spill over. Fengar's hugrokar reached out, stabilizing him in the torrent. His brother's talons had wrapped around Skaar's own. *"I'm here,"* he'd murmured. *"Stay with me, Skaar."*

Pig-skin hands had grabbed him and Fengar and ripped them apart like meat off a bone. Fengar had pulled Skaar's mind tight, tighter than he'd ever done before. Skaar had felt the terror drum through his brother, then the press of a knife against Fengar's throat.

Fight it Skaar, his hugrokar had whispered. *Fight. Live. And fight again.*

Then Fengar was gone, mind fading away as the last of his lifeblood soaked the earth.

Skaar shivered. After that it was a blank. He had no memories; just a vivid sense of falling, tumbling in the dark. And so much fear.

He shook himself in the dawn. Seven years. Had it really been that long? He eyed the bald band of skin around his wrist. So much had changed.

A trill of a wren brought him out of his musings. Gold tinged the eastern valley ridge, setting the canopy alight in an orange glow. *Time to go.* Skaar got to his feet and approached the canvas shelter Lyss had strung up and crawled into when he'd taken over the night watch hours earlier. He considered her sleeping form curled, fully clothed, under the blanket. Six days of long hours in the saddle and short nights had taken their toll. Circles shadowed her eyes, the dark tousled braid curling out from the hood of her cloak was matted with dirt. Grime covered her face. Skaar could still smell the dried blood on her too, a pungent odor of iron and earth with a hint of sticky sweetness, mixed with the burnt smell of runes.

Skaar took a step closer and stopped, gaze dropping to the outline of her sword on her hip, then taking in her clenched jaw and fists balled under her armpits. Perhaps it would be better not to startle her.

He loosened his hugrokar from the tight knot he'd pulled it into for practicing rasvenger. His heart thudded in his chest. Terror flooded his senses, sending his feathers on end. He jerked his mind away. Reythr damn. Another nightmare.

Skaar hovered a moment, then gave a huff and pulled himself mind-to-mind with her. He caught a flash of blood oozing out a man's eyes and nose as a pair of hands—her hands—crushed his skull. Skaar heard the bones crunch across hugrokar before he drew close and nudged her mind.

Enough. Wake now. He pushed the thought towards her, then jerked away as Lyss came awake with a gasp, eyes popping open. Her cheeks were flushed, and she gulped down a breath as the last dregs of the dream faded.

"What was—"

"Nightmare," Skaar supplied, then hesitantly, "you alright?"

"I'm fine," she snapped.

Liar, Skaar thought, but kept it to himself.

Lyss ran her hands down her face, her fingers squeezing her eyes into slits as she rubbed the sleep from them. Weariness enveloped Skaar's senses, so thick and heavy he swayed on the spot. His vision blurred and he glimpsed himself standing with the morning fog curling around his feet. Feathers rose down his arms and his heart lurched. *Not again.* He coiled his mind tight and surged away, battering against the pull of her hugrokar. Lyss jumped. For a horrible moment he thought their minds were jumbling together again. He cleared his throat, about to screech at her to let go, when her hold released and his sense of her fell away.

Sweat glistened on Lyss' forehead and cheeks. Hawk-eyes wide, she drew her coat tighter with a quivering hand. "I saw," she started, then stopped. "Did you see—" she took a long slow breath and tried again. "What was that?"

Heart still thumping against his ribs, Skaar shook himself, and the bristling feathers settled along his arms. "Got too close," he said.

At Lyss' frown he knitted his fingers so the talons on each hand interlocked. "Got tangled," he said. Or at least that was what it had felt like.

"Is that normal?"

Skaar ruffled his wings. "No."

Lyss was silent for a moment, her fingers falling to her left wrist and squeezing. "Sepp damn it," she muttered. Her gaze darted to the brightening sky. She cursed again and rolled to her feet, found the mare's nose bag, filled it and strapped it on. As Titch fed, she scurried about the camp, collapsing the shelter and stuffing it into a saddlebag. The blanket followed, then the nosebag once the mare was finished. Lyss practically threw the tack on—saddle first, deflecting a bite from Titch, then the bridle. She circled once, tightened a strap, before she stuck a boot into one stirrup and swung up onto the mare's back.

"Let's move," she said. She gathered the reins, clicked her tongue to the horse, and turned toward the road just visible through the trees. Skaar kept pace on foot as Lyss warmed the mare up with an easy walk.

Twice now her hugrokar had pulled him in and held him mind-to-mind, closer than anything else he'd ever experienced. He stole a quick glance at the girl. It was like her magic was learning, *adapting* itself to him. A shiver ran over him. Was such a thing possible? He had always assumed a human's ability to control the Aether was limited to runes. None of the elders had ever mentioned humans wielding any other form of magic. He'd never seen anything to suggest otherwise. Until now.

The girl yawned in the morning light, her eyes puffy from fatigue. A human capable of learning other magics. There was an unnerving thought. Was it because of their pact? Or were there others like her?

"Rark," Lyss spoke suddenly and Skaar started, realizing he'd been caught staring. "You spoke through hugrokar this morning, didn't you?"

Those hazel-yellow eyes were piercing. Skaar nodded.

Lyss hesitated, and Skaar sensed fear, guilt, and uncertainty warring inside her. She straightened. The leather reins gave a faint creak as she tightened her grip. "Is it difficult to do?"

Skaar blinked, surprised. He'd expected an accusation, not intrigue. "Depend," he said, then added: "We all learn. Useful when flying. And hunting."

And in the Otherworld.

Lyss gave a slow nod. "Yes, I can see how it would be." She ran a hand over her left wrist. She'd been doing that a lot. Something to do with the faint runes that pulled on the Aether whenever she came close.

"Can you teach me?"

"Eh?" The word escaped him without thinking. When the mare carried the girl past him, he realized he'd stopped walking. Two weeks ago, she hadn't wanted to know anything about hugrokar. "You want to learn?" he asked, catching up and falling back into step.

Lyss nodded. "It might be useful." She tapped her saddle bags. "I've got two, perhaps three days of rations left. I'll need to get more soon."

With the Reds on their heels, hunting was out of the question. That meant braving another human settlement. He swallowed. Teaching her to control hugrokar was one thing, but to *use* it? His blood went cold. Rarkyn magic in the hands of a human.

Raska would curse me to the abyss and back.

But Raska was dead, just like Fengar. And Skaar was stranded in the middle of the human's world with nothing but this renegade girl for a pack. They needed every advantage they could get. He ground his teeth. *I'm going to survive this. Consequences be damned.*

"Alright," he said and fell silent, considering how to explain. "Keep mind tight," he began and across hugrokar she reined her mind in. "Now, come close with hugrokar."

Lyss frowned. "How do I do that?"

"You sense me, no?"

She nodded.

"Focus on me," Skaar said. "Reach out. Pull mind toward mine."

Lyss closed her eyes and her hugrokar creeped nearer.

"Closer," he advised, then sighed. "More. Closer."

Her presence grew stronger, then shied away like a hare darting back into its warren. She nudged out again. He waited.

"Now?"

"No. Close—yes, better," he said, when her hugrokar brushed against his, tapping at his mental barrier. This close, he sensed her discomfort and that she desperately wanted to pull away, but to her credit she refocused and stood her ground. *She has grit, I'll give her that.*

"Form words here," he said, tapping a talon to his head. "Like you might talk. Then push them at me."

Lyss' brow wrinkled for a long moment. "I don't think it's working," she said a while later, opening her eyes. "If feels like," she pursed her lips, and Skaar sensed her flounder. "Like my words bounce off you."

Skaar relaxed his mental barriers a little. "Try again. Focus more."

WHAT ABOUT NOW? The words blasted across his mind, as if Lyss had leaned in, cupped a hand to his ear and screamed them. He muffled the yelp in his throat, turning it into an odd, high-pitched gurgle as he staggered. He coiled his mind, slamming his barrier back up, head reeling in blissful silence.

"Too much?" Lyss guessed.

Skaar eyed her on the horse. *Picked it up in mere moments.* A flicker of guilt passed through her. He rubbed a temple. "I said push, not stab. Save that for scrapping," he said, then stopped, surprised to hear one of Raska's early beratings leave his mouth. *Reythr damn, I sounded just like her.* Fengar would have teased him about it for weeks. He snorted.

Lyss tilted her head. "What's so funny?"

Skaar gave a rueful smile. "Someone once said same thing to me," then before she could press, he added, "try again."

They were nearing the ridge of the valley before she began to grasp it without leaving his head ringing. Twice she got too close and they both had to wrench their minds apart before their hugrokars tangled.

"Why does it do that?" Lyss asked, wincing after the second time.

Because your hugrokar is ridiculously strong. Skaar shrugged. "Not sure. Pact makes it stronger, perhaps." The trees had thinned as they'd climbed, and Skaar peered back down the valley they'd come up. The dirt road they'd followed weaved across the land. No sign of the Reds.

"'Byss and blood," Lyss' curse made him turn. Instead of a winding road into the next valley, the trail took a sharp turn to the south-west, cutting into the side of the mountain face to run parallel with a wide gorge that sliced through the valley's bottom like a ragged wound. The vibrant blue water broiled and swirled as the river rushed between the stone cliffs. Skaar followed its journey down the valley and saw the bridge—and the people manning it.

They were dressed in red.

Tents too were pitched on the opposite shore next to the bridge. Most were a dull-brown canvas, not unlike Lyss' lean-to. But one, a large hexagonal thing pitched in the middle, bore a flag fluttering a red and gold shield insignia on it. A hiss curled past his teeth. *The Order. Reythr damn.* He shuffled back under the tree line.

An oath from behind was Lyss consulting her map. "There's

nowhere else to cross, the King's Road is the only point," she announced, folding the worn map back together. Her brows knitted as her eyes scoured the road and the slope above it. Jagged boulders pushed out of the mountain side, like giant knuckles punching through the earth. There was no getting over that on horseback.

"Kratting damn it," Lyss muttered. She ran grimy fingers through her hair, pursed her lips and stared at the road and bridge before them. "We need a distraction. Something to get them away from the bridge." She mulled a moment, and Skaar followed her gaze to the canvas tents of the garrison picketed below, then on the braziers that lit the camp. If those fires went out...or perhaps went up—

The girl's head swiveled, eyes sharpening on him. "If you've got an idea, I'd hear it before the Order's dogs catch up with us."

Skaar hesitated. The last time a human had asked for his help it hadn't ended well. Archer's face loomed out of his memory. Tainted eyes bored into him; hungry, angry. Repulsed, Skaar pushed the memory away. This was different. The pact changed everything. Like it or not, they were stuck together. Until they found a way to undo it, they both needed to survive. Lyss was not like Archer, at least not yet.

Still waiting on the mare, Lyss raised an eyebrow. "Well? Ideas?" she asked.

Skaar flashed sharp incisors. "Just one."

CHAPTER EIGHTEEN

ARCHER STOKED THE FIRE, SENDING A SHOWER OF RED ASH and smoke into the air. He coughed and wiped his watering eyes. The kindling had not only been green but also wet from an afternoon squall. Everything was sodden. The wood, his cloak, his shoes; he wiggled his numb toes and shuffled closer to the fire.

Kratting mountains, it's getting colder by the day.

Archer had resorted to using a rune and precious Aether to get the fire lit. *Better than no fire at all,* he thought, stirring the bubbling gruel in the pot nestled among the coals. The green minty smell of the dried marathos leaves he'd thrown in wafted up from the fire pit.

A loud wooden clank, followed by a thud and a swift curse, made Archer look up. Across the camp, the two Wildner boys were sparring again.

Darrin picked up Hane's practice sword from the dirt and tossed it back to his brother. "Again," he said, taking up his stance.

Hane blew out a lungful of air, wiped the sweat off his face with a sleeve, and repositioned himself. The bout began.

Their stamina is impressive. No matter how long they rode, as soon as Archer called for a rest stop, the swords would come out and they'd be back at it. The only time they weren't practicing was for the few short hours they paused to eat and sleep.

Darrin launched an aggressive attack: stab-swipe, stab-swipe-lunge.

Hane side-stepped left and parried once before falling into a scramble. He dodged, ducked, and dove to the earth, rolled and scurried up to his feet. Darrin drove his brother to the edge of their small camp. Hane stumbled, tripped over the roots of a tree and fell against the trunk.

Another loss then, Archer concluded. He reached to stir the gruel and stopped as Hane's expression turned steely. The boy dropped and rolled, dodging Darrin's sword as it stabbed for his throat. Hane came onto his feet. He ducked under Darrin's swinging blade and found himself inside his brother's defense.

The boy blinked, as if astonished to find himself there. Then he grinned. "Got you!" His sword thrusted for Darrin's belly.

Darrin spun. Hane's practice sword grazed the side of his brother's tunic. The young Wildner had enough time to let out a cry before Darrin stepped in, grabbed his extended arm, planted a boot behind his knee and tumbled him to the ground. Across the camp, Archer heard the huff of air leave Hane's lungs as he landed flat on his back.

"Good." Darrin nodded his approval. He released Hane and stepped away. "Very good."

The boy wheezed in the dirt, chest rising and falling in labored huffs.

Archer went back to the gruel, dipping a spoon into the mush and tasting it while the young Wildner peeled himself off the ground.

"Can we…go again?"

Darrin shook his head. "That's enough for now."

"One more," Hane begged. "Come on Darrin."

"No. You've done enough today."

Hane scowled. "I need to get better." He clutched the practice sword. "I've got to be ready. One more round."

Archer's ears pricked and he peered over the flames at the pair. "Ready for what, boy?"

Hane stared at him, the creases in his brow deepening, clearly thrown by the question. "For the rarkyn, of course."

So that's it. Archer sighed and jabbed a thumb at his own chest. "Let me worry about the rarkyn." He pointed at Darrin, then Hane. "You two focus on finding your friend before the Order does." *And convince her to give up the rarkyn before she learns too much.* He poked a stick through the pot's handle and lifted it off the coals. *If that creature opened its mouth and blabbed*—the stick cracked in his grip. *If word reached the Order…*

Archer fell into a brooding silence and spooned the gruel into three bowls.

"Do you think our message has reached Iga yet?" Hane wondered aloud as he stirred the gruel to cool it. "She will be so angry."

Darrin nodded. "The messenger should arrive at camp tomorrow," he said and flashed Hane a grin. "She will be fuming."

Hane didn't smile. Instead, he stared down at his bowl. Darrin reached over, put a hand on Hane's shoulder and squeezed. "If you want to go back, Hane, I understand."

The boy's gaze snapped up. "I'm not leaving." He set his jaw. "Don't you dare try to make me." He scooped a spoon, put it in his mouth and gulped the contents down, then stirred the gruel again. "I've got to help," he said. "It was my fault."

Darrin rolled his eyes and Archer sensed the topic wasn't a new one between the brothers. Darrin put down his dinner. "Hane, there was nothing you could have done."

"They were *my* runes!"

"It was the sigil. Iga said it released a lot of power when it broke. It wasn't—"

"Wait," Archer interrupted, straightening in his seat. "You broke the sigil?" He eyed Darrin from across the fire. "The rarkyn is free of it?"

The brothers exchanged a look and Darrin gave a short nod.

Archer's skin went cold, then hot. "*Sepp kratting fuck!*" he exploded, coming to his feet. His gruel splattered across the dirt, bowl rolling to one side. *How*? The amount of Aether in that sigil had been—*No, never mind how*. He had to act fast. The longer the rarkyn was free of it, the slimmer his chances of ever catching it again were. His chance was slipping away. He'd never see them again. His chest tightened. No, he was so close. *I'll be damned if I let it get away now.*

He paced about the camp, cursing under his breath. By his count they were still least three days behind, possibly more. His boots thumped to a stop, there was no way else around it, they *had* to move faster.

"Boy," he snapped, causing Hane to jump. "How many runes do you know? How many do you *really* know?" he added when Hane opened his mouth. "Any that grant endurance?"

Hane swallowed. "Just one. Why?"

Archer sank back down by the fire. "You're going to use it on the horses."

Hane's mouth dropped open. "Engrave a rune on living flesh?"

A scowl worked over Darrin's face. "That's against the law."

Archer snatched up his bowl and spoon from the dirt and stabbed the utensil at the brothers. "You'll do it. For the sake of your friend."

Both frowned this time. "Why?" Hane asked.

"There is no other way to catch them now, and we *need* to catch them."

Darrin's dark eyes glinted. "*You* need to catch the rarkyn, you mean."

Archer gave a crooked smile. "Well there's that. But I meant what I said about your friend. She's in danger."

Hane nodded. "From the Order, we know."

Archer snorted. "More than the Order, boy. You better still pray they don't find her. No, I'm talking about the rarkyn, now you've gone and given it unfettered access to the Aether. Once it relearns how to enter the Otherworld—and it will—you better hope it doesn't lose itself to it."

"You mean a Fever," said Darrin.

"Exactly."

"But it's not injured. Not anymore," Hane pointed out.

"Ever heard of a gundhram?" Archer asked. At their blank response, he sighed. "Of course you haven't. It's what mancers call a rarkyn that's lost itself to the Aether, fallen into the Otherworld's abyss *and survived*. Being that deep changes them. *Turns* them. Once the Aether has its hooks in, it doesn't let go. Sooner or later, the rarkyn will lose control of their magic and fall back in, either to be eaten by ginndir or to become one themselves. And they will take anyone nearby with them when they do. *That* is what your friend is travelling with."

The brothers' eyes darted toward each other, a silent look that said everything and nothing. Archer's gaze narrowed. "Is there something I should know?"

Hane looked to Archer, swallowed, then dropped his gaze to his boots. Darrin folded his arms over his chest. "Nothing that matters right now."

"…is that so?" Archer fixed on Hane, who shifted before the fire.

"What are *you* going to do?" Darrin interrupted. "I'll not have Hane risk the Brand without good reason. You're a mancer, why can't you spell the horses yourself?"

Archer rubbed his stubbled cheeks, letting the smirk crack across his face. "Because I'll be spelling *us*."

Hane choked on his gruel and a hacking cough rebounded through the camp. Darrin rocked back as if slapped. "That's—" he started.

"Illegal? Most definitely. The kind of illegal that'd get all of us a one-way ride to the noose if the wrong people find out." The scar along Archer's cheek pulled taut as his face twisted into a smile.

"Insane," Darrin finished.

"You'd break your own rules?" Hane whispered.

"The rules?" Archer snorted. "The Empire doesn't give a shit about rules." He jerked a thumb into his chest. "I should know." He waggled his stump of a hand. "Following them gets you nothing but a knife in the back and twelve pieces of silver for an apology."

Darrin's lips thinned; his shoulders squared. "No."

"You ain't got much choice lads. Your friend will die if she stays near that rarkyn."

"We will too if we're caught. It's too risky." Darrin glared at Archer. "Break the Third Law if you want, but leave us out of it."

"Darrin—" Hane began.

"Lyss would not want us risking our lives," Darrin snapped, then his expression softened. "I promised Iga, Hane. If anything were to happen, I couldn't…" he trailed off and rested a comforting hand on Hane's arm. "We'll find another way, but we can't help her if we become outlaws ourselves."

Hane bowed his head and chewed his lip. Archer watched them across the fire pit. "I take it I'm to travel on alone then?"

Darrin nodded. "We'll continue on our own, *without* galdar."

Blast it. Archer worked his face still. "So be it." He got to his feet. Using galdar on himself and his horse would drain precious energy, energy he'd need to save for capturing the rarkyn again. There were ways around that. Risky ways. The ceramic bottle pressed against his breast pocket and Archer drew on a sliver of Aether, directing his senses towards the container. Power sloshed inside; raw, wholesome. Beckoning.

Just a sip, it whispered. *One sip couldn't hurt,* Archer pulled away, his thread of Aether fizzling out. Not yet. It was all he had left. He had to save it. His stomach rumbled, hungry, even though he'd just eaten. He packed away his bowl and spoon and turned for his bedroll. A few hours kip and he'd be on his way.

Behind closed eyelids, he rehearsed the runes again, practicing the shapes with his good hand, drawing the circle in his mind. His other hand, his stump, prickled with an itch of long-lost fingers. If not for that kratting storm he'd be deep in the Steppes by now casting these very runes. Instead, he was chasing the infernal rarkyn right back to the heart of the Empire. *Mercies damn that creature.*

He outlined the circle on his hand, feeling the bumps and ridges of the runes graved in the wood. He had it right this time, he was sure. This time he would succeed. His hand stilled. All he needed was the Sepp damn rarkyn. And for that, he had to find the girl.

Where to from here? he wondered as he lay there, waiting for sleep to take him. Without the brothers, he would have to find a new way to persuade the girl to hand the rarkyn over. *If not for that damned older brother.* He listened to the two Wildners stomp about the camp, then settle into their own rolls. A few minutes later, heavy breathing issued from their side of the fire.

Archer stared up at the dark sky. Clouds obscured the stars, and a faint ring of diffused light signaled the moon was near full. Perhaps the girl would be heartily sick of the creature by the time he caught up. He nearly laughed. *Don't bet on it.* Greed was a powerful motivator. And the amount of coin she could get for its blood alone...

His thoughts drifted on the edge of sleep. Come to think of it, why take the creature all the way to Illredus? If it was coin she was after, any market would do. Perhaps she had bigger ambitions.

Archer's ears popped as pure, still silence fell over the camp. A hand grasped his shoulder and shook.

"Archer!"

Archer jerked up, grasping for his dagger before he recognized the boy crouched over him. Hane. Over the boy's shoulder Archer glimpsed the soft sheen of a silencing bubble. *Advanced casting that.* Archer studied the Wildner and the second smaller bubble, the spell in miniature, glistening in one of the boy's hands. Not many had that kind of skill. He was more than the backcountry amateur he pretended to be. *I suppose he has his old hag to thank for that.*

"Can you really control the rarkyn?" Hane whispered.

So that's what this is about. Archer shook off the boy's hand. "I have before."

"Can you do it again?" Hane pressed. "Can you do it without the sigil?"

Archer was about to tell the boy to shut up and go back to bed when he paused. Perhaps he could use this. "It'll be difficult," he said, slowly.

"But it's possible?" Hane asked. "You could place another sigil on it?"

"I could, if I have enough Aether left. Trapping it will be tricky."

The boy straightened, his eyes flicking once to his sleeping brother, then back to Archer. His shoulders squared. "Take me with you."

Archer looked him over. "Your brother's not going to like it."

Hane swallowed. "It was me. I shot it," he said, softly. "The rarkyn I mean, back at our camp. Everything that happened after…" He looked down at the bubble in his hands. "It was my fault. I have to help fix it."

"Okay."

Hane looked up. "I can come?"

"Yes," Archer sighed and threw off his blankets. If sleep wouldn't come, he might as well put the time to better use. "Get your things. We leave now."

A second silencing ward saw Darrin slumber on as they stowed their rolls, packed up the leftover utensils from their dinner and tack up the horses. Archer kicked dirt over the fire, smothering the last of its faint glow before upending his canteen into the coals. With the digits of his wooden hand, he stirred the ashes into an inky paste, scooped it up and turned on the horses.

He did his pony first, tracing runes onto each foreleg and then another two on her rump.

Sepp help us if we run into the Order out here. Archer moved onto the boy's mare. The horse flared her nostrils as he approached and pawed the ground when Archer ran the ash mixture over her coat. Hane took her bridle and ran a calming hand down her nose until Archer was done.

Runes in place, Archer took up the reins of his old pony and led her off. At the edge of camp, he stopped, turning on the boy.

"Last chance to change your mind," he said. He nodded at the runes. "You haven't triggered them yet. You're still a law-abiding citizen."

Hane lifted his chin and met Archer's gaze. "I'm coming."

Good.

Archer gave a curt nod. Without another look back, he swung into the saddle and pointed his pony down the overgrown trail toward the road. Behind, he sensed the boy staring at the sleeping form just visible under the trees.

"Sorry," Hane whispered to the silent camp, to his slumbering brother.

CHAPTER NINETEEN

Ha, I was right. It was no haunting. Not at all. But I am getting ahead of myself. Let me start from the beginning.

Isaac and I were sent to investigate a haunting near Tros Pass. It took us three weeks to reach it after our stop in Deum. It's rugged country up here. Once the snows arrive, that's it. The trail is impassable; there's no way of reaching the people here. For half the year, they're on their own. Imagine our surprise to find the town of Tros is a prosperous place, with more than a fair share of its people weaving galdar in ways I've never thought to. Did you know they've created a spell that circulates the heat from their hearths through their homes? Most ingenious. Isaac wasn't so impressed. "Any spell that calls on invented runes is asking for trouble," he said. He forgets invented runes were once the norm before the Conclave established the alphabet we know now. Krats they may be, but their work appears stable—not like the krats Councillor Keteus is intent on eradicating from the streets of Illredus.

But I am side tracking. Where was I?

After a few enquiries with the locals, we discovered the site of the haunting was a week's ride from the Hannon-Illredian border. Traders were reporting heavy fog along the road—even at midday—and whole caravans and livestock were simply vanishing in it.

After reaching the site—a plateau covered in thick pine and larch on the west side of the Spine—it was another three days before we sighted the so called "ghost".

It was mid-morning, and Isaac and I were finishing up a late breakfast. The sun was out and the sky clear, there was no reason at all to suspect what was coming.

With just the fire left to clear, I set Isaac to work mastering a new casting spell and went to douse the coals with a bucket of water. It burbled and hissed, sending wafts of steam into the air. I stood back to let it dissipate, only to find it did not. At a shout from Isaac, I looked down to see fingers of fog curling through the camp. I scrambled over to Isaac and within seconds, we were in the thick of it.

I cast a ward around us. The miasma roiled against its barrier—raw Aether, fresh from the Otherworld. Inside the circle we were safe; the Aether and whatever Aether-born creatures lay within it unable to cross the runes. Should we have stepped out instead, who knows what would have happened.

After a few minutes, a shadow darted through the fog. Its outline shifted, first indistinct, then solid as it moved about, sometimes darker, sometimes no more than the barest gray against the white. I summoned a berigan and sent it off to sniff out whatever it was. It failed! Imagine that. A four-ton aetherling, twice the brawn of any bull and with a grip that can crush boulders—defeated! It lumbered off into the fog and its summoning simply unraveled. One moment my berigan was there, the next it was gone. Poof. Vanished.

Then we saw it.

One moment there was nothing, the next the fog was coalescing, folding in on itself into a humanoid shape. Like I said, it was not a haunting. It was a rarkyn. Tiny too—no taller than my waist—far smaller than I ever imagined, kit or not. Its talons sank into our barrier as if it were water. Only Issacs's quick thinking stopped it tearing the ward open completely; he cast a second circle inside mine, reinforcing the barrier. Its talons raked against the ward; eyes unfocused, silver irises set in pits as black as tar. I wasn't even sure if it knew we were there. Its gaze was only for the ward.

A fresh layer of fog swirled in and with a horrible crackling, the creature's talons tore free. It vanished into the mist, then reappeared four paces to the left. Again, it clawed at the barrier before it was ripped away; a mere plaything in the Aether's grip.

I said to Isaac, "It's stuck."

He said, "It's in a Fever."

We watched the kit dart left, then right, clawing at our runes. You see Elena, it was trying to break free of the Otherworld's hold, and with every attempt it pulled more Aether through to Terresmir.

When Isaac started shaping a casting, I clamped my hand over his fingers to still them. Only fools would spill the blood of an Aether-enthralled creature while the

Otherworld lapped at our feet. If the Aether didn't swallow us, the flesh-eaters of the abyss would.

I told Isaac as much, and he asked, "What would you have us do?"

The answer was quite simple, really. The kit was a conduit. All we had to do was cut its connection to the Aether and wait for the mist to dissipate.

As I said, a simple solution, but far from simple in practice, dear Elena. Together Isaac and I reworked some of our riding tack, burning precious energy to reforge it into a metal cuff and engrave a sigil onto it. I admit I was dubious whether it would work. Rarkyns are not aetherlings in the truest sense. They need no summoning to stay on Terresmir, they come and go unassisted, meaning that part of them is also of Terresmir. What might bind an aetherling, might not hold true for a rarkyn. But our options were slim, so I took up my position at the edge of our wards.

Isaac cast five half-completed circles around our own, their runes glowing faint through the mist in yellow-green arcs, like a whorl of petals around a rose bud. We waited. The kit lunged into view; a ward sparking under its talons to our right. Isaac spun, flinging out a hand. The lines on the half-ward flared and four more runes appeared in the dirt—snapping the circle shut around the kit.

The creature screeched, a high-pitched cry that made my ears throb. It threw itself against its prison. The circle crackled, and Isaac sagged as the kit forced an arm through. He cried for me to hurry.

I flung the metal cuff into the kit's ward. The sigil thumped to the earth, runes inert. Steeling myself, I worked two new sets of runes. The first, another ward to bolster Issacs's trap; the second, a casting to move the metal cuff to my quarry. My casting wrapped around the cuff and it flew into the air, straight for the kit.

It dodged.

Isaac and I cursed as one. The kit tore through Issacs's circle, shredding it like paper, and I gasped as the full brunt of its power slammed into my encasing ward. Sepp, it was strong. I abandoned my casting on the cuff, focusing everything on my ward. With every kick, punch, and raking of talons, my own gift waned, shrinking inside me as I burned through my power to hold it back. A third circle shimmered up around mine, its form patchy, bare of magic in places. I looked over at Isaac to find his face white and veins popping down his neck. He was lucky to have enough Aether reserves left to conjure anything at all.

We counted down from three. At one, I released my circle and Isaac grunted as the kit fell against his runes. I lunged into the kit's circle, scooped up the cuff and sprang. My arms wrapped around the creature, pinning one wing and both arms tight against its sides. Issacs's circle failed, and he slumped to the earth.

The mist rushed in. For a horrible moment I thought the kit would pull me through to the Otherworld.

It squirmed in my grasp. I grabbed one of the kit's arms, fumbled for the cuff, then snapped the metal shut around its wrist. I reached for the runes graved on the metal, fixed them in my mind and activated the sigil.

The shriek half deafened me. It was so loud it rattled my bones. My knees gave way and the kit beat me off, twisting and writhing this way and that, clawing at its sigiled arm. I gathered my remaining strength and summoned my berigan. Its hunched form swirled out of the mist.

I shouted at the berigan to hold it, and in a fluid movement that belied its size, it had the kit pressed to the earth with one giant hand.

The mist began to thin. In mere minutes, our camp reappeared. I reinforced the sigil runes again and went to Isaac. He was unconscious from Aether-drain, but thankfully unharmed. I sank down beside him, the first drops of a summer shower splattering on my forehead. I was too tired to move, so I sat there in the rain, thanking Sepp for our unbelievable luck. Had the kit been full grown, I do not know what I would have done. I'm terrified to think of the power it may have had. Small wonder why only the bravest, the most skillful—the most foolhardy—mancers prey on these creatures, Elena. Their blood might restore life and limb, but no doubt at great cost to those who dare to take it.

A mewling drew my attention back to the kit. It was quite unlike any sound it had produced thus far. The rarkyn had stilled under the hold of my berigan. Cautious, I moved over to it. Its breath was short and labored, and I signaled my aetherling to release its grip. Crumpled is the only way I can think to describe it. Its down was muddy, and more than a few feathers were missing from its half-spread wings. The creature flailed its limbs and continued to rasp as if choking. Its eyes snapped open at my approach, and I was startled to see they were a brilliant red and white—not the all-consuming black and silver I'd first seen. Big, bright eyes, intelligent eyes, not the eyes of the monster we'd just subdued.

"Come back to yourself, then?" I asked it, though I knew the kit wouldn't understand a word. The rarkyn's ears twitched and flattened; a warbling growl worked up its throat and it tried to get up. Its body flopped like a fish washed onto the shore. I crouched down and tried to calm it. Unfortunately, I only scared the poor creature more and it let out an awful keening until I moved away again.

The obvious question was, "What to do with it now?" I couldn't remove the sigil for fear of it falling back into the Otherworld, but the kit was clearly unable to fend for itself as it was. Logic dictated that with the Aether calmed, it was my chance to kill the creature and be done with it. But as I stood there, dagger raised to do the deed, listening to it shudder for air, my skin prickled. A chill washed over me, burrowing deep into my gut and I knew I couldn't—shouldn't.

Yes, your father, a mancer, a Regis, who has fought braggarts and pirates, who has risen through the ranks of Conclave and Order, was cowed by a tingling in his gut. But I've not survived the Krawan war and Therrin's inquisition without learning to trust it.

Which brings me to where I am now. I'm afraid I'll be away a little longer than expected. We're heading north to Talos you see; then on to the Ice Steppes that hem the Empire. I am taking the kit away, out of Illredan, and hopefully to a place where it will find its own kind once more.

Isaac is not pleased, but he'll come around eventually. He always does.

As for the kit, it is still very weak and its breath still rasps, though less so than before. I do believe it's adjusting to the sigil. Though, it's very warm to the touch, and I'm left wondering if rarkyn fall prey to sickness like we do. I guess only time will tell.

That's all my news for now. I'll send you updates on our progress as and when I am able.

Sending you my love as always.

Papa.

P.S. Keep an eye on Keteus for me, lest he get too comfortable in my absence. But do not, I repeat, do not *meddle.*

LYSS PRESSED HER HANDS TO HER MOUTH, BREATHED ON them and then rubbed her freezing fingers together. *This better kratting work.*

She tucked her fingers into her armpits. Under her, Titch pawed the dirt, signaling her impatience. Lyss leaned forward and petted her neck. "I know," she cooed. "Soon."

She squinted down the dark road behind her, its winding path just visible through the valley below. No Reds on it yet, but it would be a close thing.

"Half a day," Rark had said when he had landed from his reconnaissance. "Maybe less."

"How many?" Lyss had asked.

"Six. Two mancers."

Lyss' stomach had curdled. "You're sure?"

Rark had wrinkled his nose, as if recalling a smell he'd rather forget. Lyss had caught the twinge of worry ripple through the rarkyn before it was quashed. "Very sure."

They had given up their precious lead to wait for the sun to set to hatch this hairbrained plan. Now Lyss sat at the top of the ridge, half expecting a cry to go up at her back as an Order dog caught her scent.

Across the gorge, the rarkyn crept in the dark, beelining for the bridge and garrison camp. He was either surprisingly calm or, as was more likely, keeping his hugrokar knotted tight to hide any nerves.

Don't get caught, Lyss wished again. He might be a moody, cantankerous creature, but she had no desire to see him hurt. Especially not when the pact would ensure she'd feel it too. She shivered. *There really is no choice. Try to go our separate ways and the pact would just pull us back.*

Not that the rarkyn's company had been as terrible as she'd expected. Come to think of it, Rark had been quite tolerable at times. Even hugrokar, strange as it was, was oddly comforting as she sat in the dark, waiting for Rark's signal. With their senses overlapped, the night was bright, her hearing sharp, and the shadows less deep. She relaxed her hold on the magic and her senses flowed outward, down to the rarkyn as he snuck along the edge of the camp below. He was tense, slinking around trees, pausing, slinking again. Closer, closer. Talons wrapped around the flint and steel she'd loaned him.

Surprisingly useful magic, Lyss thought, pulling away before their minds tangled.

All rarkyn have hugrokar. That was what Rark had said. What might hugrokar be like in a pack? Would the night appear as day? Their senses would extend for miles, of that she was sure; each mind fortifying the others. Was that how they withstood the Aether's raw power when they crossed into the Otherworld?

Her mind drifted back to her first conversation with Rark: when he had sliced his talon down his palm and she'd felt the pain blossom through her own hand. When a rarkyn died, did the others feel it? The thought made her skin crawl. It was one thing to see death, another thing to experience it over and over as if it were your own.

As if on cue, her hugrokar quivered, an odd sort of nudge that pulled at her senses, a twanging of the invisible string between her and the rarkyn. A moment later, Rark was mind-to-mind with her.

Start moving, was all he said and was gone again.

"Finally," Lyss breathed, squeezing her heels into Titch's side. The mare started forward, ears perked, alert to the muffled *thud-thud* of her hooves. Lyss leaned over the saddle to check the wraps on the mare's feet. The strips of her torn nightshift still held—and worked better than expected. Gravel still crunched under their weight, but there was no clank and clop of metal shoes.

Satisfied, she straightened and stiffened as a new scent reached her. *Smoke.* Below, a telling glow was spreading through the camp. It scattered light across the gorge, sending flickering orange hues across the rocky cliffs.

It had begun.

Seconds later, a tent on the edge of the camp ignited with a *whomp* and flames shot into the night like a bonfire. Shouts erupted. Figures scrambled from their tents. A horse whinnied.

No going back now. Lyss set her jaw. The cries grew louder, and more Reds roused and set to work with buckets and blankets. Another, larger tent was engulfed. The sentries at the bridge dropped their spears and joined the effort.

Now. Lyss kicked Titch's sides and the mare lurched forward, ears flattening as they galloped towards the smoking camp. Over the crackle of flames, Lyss picked out words in the shouting.

"Get more blankets!" someone roared. "Protect the stores!"

Titch's hooves hit the bridge, thudding over the planks like a drum heralding their arrival. Lyss held her breath, expecting a cry to go up at the noise and spears to swivel on her. No alert came. The bridge ended in a haze with no sentries in sight. Lyss sucked in a breath, pulled her cloak over her nose and mouth and plunged into the swirling red miasma.

Her hugrokar hummed again. Rark was close. An image flashed through her mind: the camp seen from above. Smoke billowed up from the tents in great columns, specks ran from shelter to shelter. People. Soldiers. Chaos. *Gods and ginndir, he did all this with a bit of flint?* There, in the vision, a bigger, longer shape galloped through the camp—her and Titch. It was all she needed. She yanked the reins, bringing the mare's head around. *Right, go right,* she snarled at the animal. A red tent loomed up on her left, fabric rippling and snapping as they careened past. A step more and Titch would have charged straight into it. Two more tents flashed by before the smoke thinned. Almost through.

Lyss pulled her cloak from her face and sucked in a fresh breath.

Cool air filled her lungs, but before she could exhale, something twisted across hugrokar and heat seared down her core. She went rigid in the saddle, feeling the warmth blossom and spread *under* her skin.

Light flared from the other side of the camp. Lyss spun, catching the sight of an orange ball erupting from the site of the main fire. Cries of dismay echoed through the night.

As quick as it had come, the warmth dwindled inside her. Lyss shivered. *He's using the Aether to spread the fire.* She imagined him striking the flint, and the flame popping as he blew a lungful of Aether-laden air over it. *Could he do that?* She glanced down at her wrist, fighting the urge to pull back her sleeve and check the runes. *Later.*

She hunched against Titch's neck. From her vantage, she had just enough time to register a tent flap swinging open and a young Order soldier running out, arms loaded with surplus blankets—right into Titch's path. The mare screamed, dug in her hind hooves and reared.

The soldier went down. Lyss grappled, sliding back in the saddle. At last, after what felt like far too long, Titch's forehooves slammed back to the earth. Lyss dragged herself back into place as the mare skittered around the fallen soldier. Blankets were strewn across the road as the man stared up at her.

"Hey, you—" he managed before Lyss took control of Titch again and rammed her heels into the mare's sides. The horse sprang forward.

"Oi! Hold it!" The soldier called after her. Then, *"Stop!"*

Lyss gave Titch the reins, letting the mare stretch her neck to reach her full stride.

"Stop!" The soldier's call fell behind, though Lyss could still hear him hustling after them on foot. Something cold whipped past her shoulder and cracked into the earth beside Titch. A casting! The mare lurched sideways, Lyss clamped down and held on as Titch surged forward.

The blockade marking the edge of the camp swung into view, its thorn-like spikes turned out to the night road. Relief sighed out of her. Somehow, she'd made it. She reached down to Titch's neck, rubbing a shaking hand against the mare's sweat-stained mane.

"Good work girl, good—" her voice suck in her throat as the air—no, the Aether—warped at her back. An icy draft chilled her neck, light flashed in her peripheral. Her muscles locked as the casting hit her. Her scream came out as a croak. Further off, an in-human screech split the night.

Lyss tumbled sideways, thumping to the earth as what felt like a hundred icicles drove into her skin. Titch's hooves thundered down next to her face, wheeled about and a moment later the animal's rump was disappearing into the dark, tail streaming, stirrups bouncing free on each flank.

Lyss blinked back tears. Was this what galdar was like for a rarkyn? *Move!* She commanded her frozen limbs. Nothing. A binding spell. It had to be. Her heart thrashed where her limbs could not. *Helpless.* Again. Fear's cold grip wrapped up her limbs, seeping into the scar on her chest. The road to Caenis flickered in her head, thick with blood, the smell cloying in her throat. Helpless, helpless, helpless—she wrenched her thoughts away. *Get it together Lyss!* Her hugrokar quivered, and Rark's presence arrived in her head.

Get up, he sent. *Mancers are coming.*

Lyss gritted her teeth. *I can't.* She gathered the sensation of her rigid muscles and thrust it at him. He pulled away with a hiss, and the echo of a shudder ran down Lyss' spine. Rark's presence returned. *Break it.*

With what? Lyss snarled. *I'm not a mancer!*

Then don't be one.

Lyss was about to snap a scathing curse at him when she stopped. Could he be on to something? She couldn't use galdar, but nor could Rark. Yet he'd managed to force open Hane's ward once his sigil broke. Could she do the same and break this casting? The pact wasn't a one-way bond after all. They shared thoughts, shared emotions, shared pain —her stomach turned over on itself—*and they shared magic.* Could she tap further into the rarkyn's abilities? Her tongue turned thick and dry in her mouth. She glanced at her wrist. What might that cost her?

A boot crunched down next to Lyss' face. Black and worn—Order boots. She caught a whiff of mud-crusted sock. Nausea rose up her throat. Hands gripped her collar and turned her over. Two soldiers stood above her now, the blanket-carrying youth and an older tawny man covered in ash and dressed only in a set of pantaloons.

"Good work Corporal Hasek," the ashen soldier spoke, wiping perspiration off his forehead with the back of a sooty hand.

"Thank you, sir," huffed the young officer. "But it was lucky you came by when you did."

The ash soldier signed a rune with his fingers and the numbness in Lyss' limbs ebbed a little. She tested her toes. Movement there. No luck with anything above her ankles.

"I suppose I have you to thank for tonight's chaos," the ash soldier said. His eyes, still puffy from being roused too early from sleep, studied the dried blood flecked on Lyss' cloak, her filthy coat and tunic, then dropped to the sword on her hip.

"Corporal Hasek," he said. "Run to my tent and fetch the latest warrant on my desk."

Lyss near choked as her heart vaulted into her mouth. A warrant? *Shit.*

"Yes, Captain." The young corporal saluted and ran off, leaving Lyss alone with the soldier. He leaned over her, smelling of sweat and smoke, grasped her collar and pulled her up to sit against a pillar of the blockade.

Hurry. Rark's mind flitted close again and she sensed him creeping just beyond the tree line. *Fire's almost out.*

Lyss looked past her guard, toward the telltale sound of water hissing against hot coals. A steam plume had joined the throng of smoke at the end of the camp.

She was out of time.

Lyss clenched her jaw and tried to lift her arms from her sides. It was like pulling against tar. For a moment they came free, before the spell snapped them back down against her ribs.

The Captain clucked and shook his head. "You can't break my binding spell with brute force, girl."

Lyss slumped back. It was no use. Impatience flickered across hugrokar. Rark was close. She imagined the glint of his red eye tracking the Captain. Hatred boiled in her gut. It was just one soldier. A mancer he might be, but if she could leap out and snap his neck before—

No! Lyss wrenched her mind away. Across the pact, the rarkyn started and his presence shot away like a rabbit down a burrow. The crunch of running boots made her look up to find Corporal Hasek coming back up the road, a tightly rolled scribers note grasped in one hand. A warrant for her head no doubt, probably sent by a fleet-winged eyree all the way from Bardas Post. She felt ill. Capital punishment at the hands of the Order or madness from rarkyn magic.

"Some choice," she muttered, and the ash soldier glanced at her as she spoke. *I'm damned either way.* She closed her eyes and turned her senses inward as Iga had taught, searching for the Aether's elusive pull within her. She found it easily. *How much that's changed.* Slowly, she unfurled her senses outward, brushing them along the casting to assess its strength.

The binding knotted around her like a rope, its power tightly coiled, shaped it to the caster's will. A flicker of excitement trilled in her chest. She'd never gotten this far before—galdar or not.

Now what? she wondered. Rarkyns didn't use runes, so what did they do at this point? She tried to force her little pool of Aether at the spell. Nothing.

It's not like galdar. Rark's presence was beside her in a heartbeat. *Don't push it. Draw it in.*

Lyss floundered. *Draw it in? How?*

"The warrant, Captain," the young corporal's voice sounded above her. There was a rasp of paper being unfurled.

"Short, medium build, Eyos complexion, especially in the eyes," Lyss tried to blot out the words as the Captain read aloud. "Dressed in Wildner garb and armed with a lightweight sword." A sigh. "The description matches. Instructions are to capture or kill."

Panic cramped Lyss' gut. *Gods and ginndir.* She had to get out. Now.

The Corporal's eyebrows shot up. "What in Sepp's name did she do?"

"She murdered a Red."

Hurry! Rark pressed, and Lyss' muscles crawled as he fretted in the shadows. She refocused. Draw the Aether in. She sucked in a deep breath, imagining she was inhaling the binding with it. Warmth flushed through her core. It roared up her throat and down her spine, easing the cold numbness in her limbs.

Yes, that's it! Again.

Something jangled in her ears: manacles. A glance at the Corporal confirmed it; a pair cuffs joined by a chain dangled from his grasp.

"Good thinking, Hasek."

"Thank you, sir."

Far off, Rark let out a hiss. *Hurry,* he urged once more.

Lyss took another breath, and another. The binding's grip eased. Heat pulsed through her, and her warm winter coat turned sweltering.

"Quickly Corporal, she's doing something," the Captain warned.

Lyss' eyes rolled in her head. Her thoughts fuzzed.

Enough! Do not give in to it! Rark's alarm slapped into her, starting her awake.

The Captain stood, watching his corporal bend and reach for Lyss' wrists.

Worry about that later. Break the binding first. Rark's presence pressed against her mind, panic edging his words.

Lyss reached for the heat inside her, then *sucked* the last of the galdar casting coiled about her. She flexed her arms, straining with all her might. The Aether twitched inside her, spasming like muscle. The binding disintegrated, tearing apart like wet paper.

She was free.

Lyss slammed her forehead into the Corporal's nose. He let out a grunt, reeled backward.

"Hasek!" The Captain yelled before a fist-sized rock whizzed out from the shadows and cracked against his head. The man slumped like a sack of empty clothes.

Ha! Rark's triumphant cry resonated through hugrokar.

Lyss rounded on the Corporal, thrusting the toe of her boot into his chest as he lunged for her, manacles forgotten. His body folded over her foot, lifting off the ground long enough for the breath to whistle out of his lungs before the blow flung him down the road.

Sepp damn. Lyss stared after the soldier, dumbfounded. Beside her, the Captain groaned. His eyes fluttered open.

Don't stand there gawking. Move! Rark near screeched at her.

Lyss turned and ran. For a second time in less than a seven-day, a heart-stopping cry went up behind her.

"Guards! To me!"

CHAPTER TWENTY

LYSS RAN, ARMS PUMPING, DISHEVELED HAIR CLINGING TO her sweat-slicked neck in thick, matted veins. The Aether tingled through her muscles, making her heavy winter boots feel weightless as she fled.

I used rarkyn magic. The thought flashed through her, turning her innards into a writhing knot. *Rarkyn magic.* She shoved her horror down and ran on. Behind her, indistinct cries ran through the camp. Someone roared orders and—Lyss' breath caught—there was a telltale clack-clack of horses crossing the bridge. Many horses.

The hunting party has caught up. Rark sent from somewhere overhead.

The Reds from Bardas Post. Sepp help, they would run her down like a manged dog. Where was Titch? The mare couldn't have gone far. She searched the road. Nothing. Kratting horse could be anywhere. She cursed again. Without a mount, she'd never outrun them.

Lyss slowed, considering her options. She had to get off the road—they'd have a harder time hunting her over rough terrain. Tall pines hemmed in the trail. On her left, the ground was flat for a half-mile before it rose steeply into the rocky side of the valley. On her right, between the trees, she spied the edge of the gorge, a stone's throw away. Left it was then, even if she had to scramble hand over foot up the side of the ravine. Still better than being killed by a Red.

The forest was oddly muted as she ran under the interlocking branches. Pine needles crunched under foot. She slipped on a pinecone, sent another spinning off with the toe of her boot and sprinted on.

Far off, the Aether shuddered. Its power rippled past her, as if a stone had been dropped into a pool. Lyss stopped and turned back, squinting through the trees.

"Rark?" she called and grimaced at the quiver in her voice. That hadn't felt like the rarkyn's magic. She clenched her fists and called again. *"Rark!"*

A shadow swooped over the canopy and with a thumping of wings and a rush of air, it latched onto the top of the pine above. The tree bowed under the rarkyn's weight and a shower of needles fell to the forest floor.

"No stopping. Run!" he shouted at her and she caught a flicker of panic through hugrokar. "Aetherling is coming!"

Lyss sucked in a breath. *An aetherling?* The ripple hadn't been something dropping into the Aether. Something had been pulled *out*. Gooseflesh washed over her arms. Sepp help her, one of them was a summoner! She lurched forward. Trees rushed past and a hot, uncomfortable burn built in her legs. The air felt thin in her lungs. The ground pitched upward as she left the basin and started up the valley slope. Was it her or was there a *pat-pat-pat* of feet behind her?

She dared not look.

The pines gave way to low shrubland and grass, leaving her scrambling up in the open on a rough, rocky slope until she hit a game trail. It cut across the face of the slope and Lyss loped along it, huffing. Minutes passed and the trail leveled off before it pitched back down toward the valley floor. Lyss stopped, doubled over and gasping, and searched for a new route. The slope upward was steep, but manageable, however, a few paces before the ridge it turned to a cliff at least twice as tall as she was. No going over that easily.

She peered at the ridge line, grateful for the crisp vision the pact had granted her. Between it and the full moon, she could see the ridge far off down the valley. *There.* About a mile further down, part of the cliff had crumbled, leaving a rocky, but passable way out of the gorge.

Her hugrokar shivered. Behind, a soft *swish-swish, pat-pat* of feet rushing across the rocks. Lyss froze, hairs prickling. Not knowing why or how, she threw herself sideways. Something snapped against the bottom of her boot but failed to find a purchase. She tucked her knees and rolled. Rocks dug into her back and she sprang up, sliding to a stop down the slope, knife in hand.

A shadow bore down on her. It was dog-like in shape, but shaggy and the size of a pony. Black on black, the only thing she could make out clearly was a bone muzzle and three luminous eyes: a sentient skull levitating in the air.

A *shuck*.

Lyss swallowed. She'd never seen one before, but she'd heard of this type of aetherling. The Otherworld Hound they called it—a favorite among soldiers and watchmen. Fiercely loyal and protective of its summoner, but Sepp help if it was set on you. Holding her breath, Lyss eased away, feeling for her sword at her hip while her off hand bared her knife at the beast.

The shuck sniffed the air, raised its head and howled. The cry began low; a roar that crescendoed to a shriek. It vibrated in Lyss' gut, turning her blood cold. Alarm shot across hugrokar from Rark. He knew that sound, knew it and feared it.

Surprising, Lyss thought, dazed. Surely a rarkyn had nothing to fear from a shuck. Further down the valley, a human cry went up from the road. This time Lyss heard words:

"It's found her! Go!"

Gods and ginndir damn. They're coming.

The hound stared down at her, waiting for her to bolt. Behind it lay the crumbled cliff and the ridge to safety. Freedom might as well have been on the other side of the Empire. Lyss tightened her clammy hand around the knife. Turn her back on it now and its teeth would be in her before she took two steps. She shuffled back, boots scuffing the ground. The shuck stepped forward.

Shit. Lyss' hand closed on her sword, pulled the blade free and she regripped her off-hand knife, balancing her stance. The shuck shifted, black body incorporeal but for its head.

Rark's hugrokar bumped against her own. Urgent. *Use gala.*

What?

Draw Aether in like before, then push it out. Fast. Hard.

Draw it from where? There's no casting.

The Aether is everywhere! He exploded across the link. *Draw it in. Do it now.*

The shuck prowled closer. Out of time, she would have to wing it. Lyss imagined the Aether rising from the earth like steam from a pot.

She sucked in. Warmth tingled in her chest. Another intake. Heat sparked in her belly.

Now throw. Rark urged.

Lyss wavered. *Throw how?*

Too late.

The shuck lunged. Lyss lurched sideways, sword clanging off its bone muzzle. It was solid! *That's it.* Lyss skittered back, flexed her grip around her hunting knife, gathered the heat inside her—and *threw*.

The warmth left in a rush. The blade tumbled end over end. For a heartbeat, she could have sworn the air rippled around it.

Hit! she willed.

The knife struck. Not with the crack of a blade sinking into skull, but the thud of the hilt slamming into bone. *Of all the gods rotten luck—*

The air erupted.

Pressure blasted out from the point of impact, buffeting Lyss. Her ears popped; stomach clenched.

The shuck stopped. No part of it moved. It's nebulous body quivering where it stood.

Lyss gawped. "Sepp's balls, it actually worked."

Rark's rounded on her. *Move! It won't stay stunned for long.*

With one last look at the ridge, so steep she'd have to climb it hand over foot over hand, Lyss cursed and sprinted back down the valley. A low yowl rose behind her. The shuck was already recovering. She crashed over rocks, sending pebbles cascading down the slope, sure that any moment a set of teeth would close on her heels. She hit the tree line and kept running, the burn crept up her legs again.

The land leveled and she burst out onto the road. Flushed out. *Like a damn deer,* the angry thought flashed through her.

Down. Now! Rark's command sliced through her thoughts. Without thinking, Lyss threw herself to the earth. Grazes stung one elbow and both knees as the shuck pounced, maw snapping the air above her head. The beast skidded into the gravel, claws digging into the dirt as it rounded on her.

Lyss rolled and snapped up her sword. She slashed as the beast pounced again. Her blade sank into the creature's neck like it was water —then stuck. A maw of teeth and a lolling blue tongue came at her face.

Terror swallowed her. It locked her limbs, grabbed her guts and twisted. The world slowed, then dropped away—dulling like an old painting. Faded to gray. A hot tingle stabbed down her spine. Needle teeth and a white maw filled her vision.

Her body moved on its own. Her weight shifted, feet sliding out, torso turning. The shuck's jaws missed her throat and buried into her shoulder.

Odd, Lyss thought numbly. No pain. Her free hand raised of its own accord, fingers pressed together, her grit-covered nails honed to a spearhead. Her hand drove into the shuck's chest. For a moment the aetherling's flesh was liquid, then solid, then liquid again. Something firm brushed against her fingertips. Snake-like, her hand struck, grip closing in a vice, nails sinking into something soft and fleshy.

A squeal in her ear. The shuck shuddered.

Heat seared down her arm. From her dim world, Lyss watched as her body braced, then wrenched. For a moment there was resistance, then with a sucking, slurping sound her arm came free, together with the shuck's heart. Hunger pooled in her mouth.

The creature slumped against her, suddenly heavy. Steam rose from its body, its shadow-like form dissolving into the night—everything but its bone white skull still latched onto her. Lyss' sword clattered to the ground.

The world flickered back to full color and pain blossomed across her shoulder. She gasped, fighting down a scream.

Lyss! Panic, then relief smacked into her hugrokar. *Thank Reythr. I thought the Aether had—*

It's fine. I'm fine. She tried to pry the shuck's skull loose from her shoulder, but one touch brought black spots to her vision. Her cry became a grunt.

"What...what are you?"

Lyss' head snapped up to find a crossbow pointed at her and, behind it, a huffing soldier. She gaped. It was the Corporal! On *foot.* How had he—her eyes caught the flicker of a wisp curling about his legs and she understood. He was not puffing from running after her, he was puffing from a summoning.

"Corporal!" A shout came from down the road.

"Here!" the Corporal returned.

Lyss backed up.

The Corporal jerked his crossbow at her. "Don't mo—"

A rarkyn-shaped blur shot from the treetops and slammed into the Corporal's back, sending the Red sprawling. The crossbow twanged. A bolt skittered across the road. Half-dazed, the Corporal pushed himself up from the dirt just as Rark clobbered him with a dead branch. He flopped to the earth and was still.

"River cliffs. Go!" The rarkyn thrust a talon towards the gorge. He spread his wings, sank into a crouch, then launched upwards in a buffet of air and beating of feathers.

Lyss dropped the heart, scooped up her sword and ran, left arm curled to her side. Her shoulder throbbed with every step. The skull's piercing teeth jarred and grated, sending warm blood dribbling down her elbow and forearm.

Behind her, the Aether twisted. A galdar casting splintered into a tree. *More Reds!* She glanced back and made out five horsemen following her. She wove around the tree trunks. The horses' labored breath closed in. Another casting whizzed by her side, cold runes burning her as it passed.

Without warning, the trees ended, as did the ground. Lyss skidded still and looked over the edge of the gorge. It was a long way down. Black water billowed and churned at its bottom. Now what?

Jump.

Lyss stared down at the water. Jump off the gorge? She'd be mincemeat the moment she hit the surface.

Trust me.

Lyss glanced back. The darkness undulated with horses and men; a musty whiff of grime and animal sweat filled her nose. One cloaked figure rose an arm, fingers twitching through a series of runes. Above and behind them, she made out a black dot banking in the sky. Lyss sensed it wheel about and furl its wings tight to begin the dive.

Jump. The rarkyn urged again.

Lyss closed her eyes, sucked in a breath, and leapt.

For half a heartbeat she sailed up and forward. A casting clipped the edge of the gorge with a spray of rock chips. Then the air gave under her. Her stomach dropped. She plummeted.

A set of giant wings unfurled above her and a hand reached out. Lyss grabbed it, her weight sinking into the grip. Talons dug into her skin. Her fall slowed. With a grunt and one almighty downstroke, the rarkyn reversed their momentum and lifted back into the sky. They shot up and away to a cry of *"No!"* and between her dangling feet, Lyss glimpsed the five riders clustered on the edge of the gorge.

A heartbeat later they were lost in the night.

CHAPTER TWENTY-ONE

ARCHER TOOK IN THE CHARRED BARRICADES, THE TATTERED canvases, and the soot clinging to the ragged tents. Ash and dirt caked the bridge. Their horses, cleaned of runes before they descended the valley, left deep crescent-shaped prints in the muck.

"What happened here?" Hane whispered.

Archer didn't answer. Instead, he watched one of a pair of soldiers guarding the threshold step up to them, scroll and quill in hand.

"Name and destination," he said, holding up a hand.

Archer fixed him a pointed look, eyebrow arching.

"Please," the soldier amended, but did not relent. Sweat ringed the neck and arms of his tunic, turning it from red to brown. Ash stained his hair, ageing him twenty years. His eyes were raw from lack of sleep.

"I suppose there's a first for everything. Andreas Markides." Archer jerked a thumb at himself, then over his shoulder. "That is Hane Eder."

The guard made a note in his scroll. "Destination?"

"Illredus," Hane blurted.

The scratching of the guard's quill stopped. "Heading to Illredus? This close to winter?" His eyes narrowed. "On what business?"

Archer shot Hane a look. *Stay silent*, he willed at the boy. The young Wildner gulped and quickly investigated the horn of his saddle.

"Conclave business." Archer opened his cloak, revealing the brooch, its crown and scepter stamp glinting in the morning light. The guard's red-rimmed eyes lingered on the brooch for a long minute, then moved to Archer's face. His expression was steady, non-plussed even.

Unusual.

"Mancers then? Do you have your papers?" the guard asked.

Very unusual. *Why the tight security?* Archer rummaged for the journal inside his coat, careful not to show the scrawled pages to the guard. He pulled free the waxen papers tucked at the back. Only then did he catch Hane's stricken gaze. *Of course he doesn't have papers.* He turned and thrust the folded parchments at the guard. "This should put any doubts aside."

The guard took them but didn't open them. "And your companion?"

"The lad is my new apprentice. He is under my watch."

The guard was still a moment before he uncurled the papers. His eyes flicked over them once, twice, then his face flushed, and he straightened in his boots.

"Apologies, sir," he said, folding the papers up and offering them back in two hands as if presenting a great gift. "My orders are to be thorough, especially after…" The guard gestured at the charred camp. "I'm sure you understand."

Archer took the pile back and tucked them inside the breast of his coat. "What happened?" he asked.

"An outlaw set fire to the camp, sir."

"Just one? When?"

The guard bobbed his head. "One woman, by all reports, sir. Two days ago, it was."

Archer stilled his expression. *Two days.* They'd made good time then. Excellent time in fact. He was closing in. "Where is the outlaw now? Were they caught?"

"No sir, she got away."

Thank Sepp for that. Archer eased back in his saddle. The guard mistook his silence for apprehension.

"Rest assured, we're searching for her now. A proper task force is being prepared to capture her."

Archer's glared. "You'll do no such thing."

The guard blinked. "Sir?"

Archer searched past the guard's head, squinting into the ravaged camp beyond. "Who is in charge here?"

"Captain Mereor Brennus sir."

Archer ground his teeth. "Take me to him, I want a word."

The guard's lips parted, goggling for a moment before his jaw shut and he nodded. He spun on the spot and signaled to his fellow watch-man. "Kovos will take you sir."

The second guard stepped up and gave a short bow. "Right this way if you please, sir." He began to trot off down the road.

Archer kicked his horse forward after the guard, then turned on Hane. The boy's face was white, and he stared at Archer as if he had grown an extra head.

"I know this'll be hard for you," Archer growled in an undertone so only Hane could hear. "Keep your mouth shut."

"But Lyss—" Hane started.

"I'm not about to let the Reds capture her, so *stay quiet*."

Hane's shoulders relaxed. His brow unknitted, and he gave a nod. "Alright."

Kovos led them through the camp and Archer marveled at the amount of damage the fire had done. One end of the compound was nothing more than a few blackened support poles. In other places, men worked in teams refortifying the barricades, re-pitching patched-together tents and sorting through blackened supply crates. They passed a makeshift horse pen, thrown together with an assortment of tent supports and charred barricade planks.

A pair of fingers tugged the sleeve at his elbow. Archer ignored it. The fingers tugged again. Archer spun on the boy.

"What did I just say?"

"That's Lyss' horse!" Hane hissed, jabbing a finger at a pinto moun-tain horse tethered at the far end of the pen. Its forelegs were splattered with dirt and mud, and tattered pieces of fabric were wrapped about its hooves.

"What if they've found her?" Hane whispered.

What indeed. Archer wondered, but before he could answer, the guard stopped them outside a large tent, its canvas walls streaked with smoke stains, but otherwise unmarred. They dismounted and waited as the man ran inside to inform his Captain of the new arrivals.

"Andreas Markides? *The* Colonel Regis Andreas Markides?" came a voice from inside the tent.

A murmur of assent.

"Sepp be. Show him in."

"Brennus, we have urgent plans to prepare," a brusque voice objected.

"This will take but a minute, Captain Draper. Show him in, Corporal."

The guard came out and held open the tent for Archer and Hane to enter. It was sparse inside, but for a few tables drawn together and a map of the region laid out over the top. Four men stood around it. Two were in light armor—graved breastplates, plated faulds covering hip to thigh and sigiled bracers on each forearm. The other two were dressed simply—plain red jerkins over the top of ash-crusted pants. One of them stepped forward; older than the rest but tall and tawny-skinned, some Hannon heritage to be sure, Archer mused. Dark circles ringed both the soldier's eyes but his gaze was bright and sharp.

"Regis Andreas Markides?"

"You must be Captain Mereor Brennus," Archer replied, ignoring the way Hane's jaw dropped at his old title. He took the Captain's offered hand. "You had some trouble a few nights back I hear."

The Captain sighed. "Unfortunately, that is so." He motioned to the first of his armored companions. "This is Captain Draper." Archer caught the flicker of ire before the man inclined his head. "And Corporal Farrus." Brennus motioned to the second man in amour, a soldier whose right cheek was a raw web of peeling skin.

Spellfire burn. Archer noted as the soldier gave a stiff bow.

"Lastly, Corporal Praetus Hasek," Brennus finished, motioning to the fellow Red beside him.

The Corporal started, jerking his gaze away from Archer's face and gave a quick bow. "An honor, sir."

Archer nodded to them in turn and circled the makeshift map table they had cobbled together. "You've not caught the perpetrator yet, I take it?" he queried, eyeing the marks on the map and the King's Road that ran north to south through the ranges.

"Not yet, but it's only a matter of time," Draper replied, cleared his throat, then added: "If you don't mind sir, we've got a lot to plan and a small window—"

"I do."

"Pardon?"

"I do mind." Archer met Draper's gaze and watched as the Captain struggled not to show his astonishment.

"I have just come from Bardas Post," Archer said, running one long finger along the wood grain of the tables. "From what I heard there, I believe we're after the same woman."

In his peripheral, Hane's face paled and his mouth opened. Archer held out a hand to the boy. *Wait.*

Captain Draper's eyebrows rose. "Are you sure?"

"Do you know of any other woman who can crush a man's skull barehanded?" Archer countered and, at his silence, continued, "I thought so."

"Why are you hunting her?" Brennus asked.

Archer hesitated. "She…stole something from me. Something important."

"You wish to aid us," Draper concluded.

"No. I'm here to tell you to desist." Archer gave a thin-lipped smile.

Shocked silence filled the tent, before Draper's young second blurted, "But, sir—"

"I'll be blunt," Archer interrupted. "You have no hope of catching her."

In the quiet that followed, Draper's face morphed through a series of expressions: open mouthed surprise, ruffled confusion, and at last landing on glaring anger. *Not used to being challenged, it seems.*

Brennus laid a calming hand on Draper's elbow. "You saw what happened two nights ago," he warned. "Perhaps he's right, Sergeant."

Archer leaned closer. "Tell me, what did you see?"

Brennus motioned to his Corporal. "Hasek saw more than me, I'll let him tell it. Go on Corporal."

The Corporal cleared his throat. "Brennus knocked her off her horse with a binding casting when she came through camp. We were about to secure her in a ward when she broke free and took off. I summoned a shuck to find and stop her, but when I caught up…" he hesitated, and Archer noted the hairs rising down his forearms. "I arrived just as she pulled its heart from its chest."

"*Pulled* out its heart?" Archer asked.

"Yes. With her hand."

Archer frowned. Soldiers prized shucks for good reason. Their bodies were a mass of shifting shadow, physical attacks didn't work against them. That was the way it was supposed to be. Such a thing should not be possible. Not from an ordinary mancer, krat or otherwise. *Am I missing something?*

"Did you see how she got away?" He asked. "What direction did she go?"

Corporal Hasek rubbed the back of his head with a wince. "Not I. Something knocked me out from behind."

The muscles in Archer's neck and shoulders went taut. He sucked in a soft breath and held it for a heartbeat. "Did you see what...or who?"

The corporal gave a rueful shake of his head. "No. The last thing I remember was being thrown to the ground. It was like getting kicked by a horse."

Archer released his breath. *A bit of luck, finally.*

"Whatever it was, it helped her escape," Brennus concluded. "Draper's riders saw it carry her over the southern ridge. Our theory is she's some sort of summoner."

Corporal Hasek frowned. "Forgive me Captain, but I've found nothing to indicate she cast a summons. No ward, no runes, no residue. Nothing. I checked the valley yesterday."

"She must have summoned it before she came down the north road," Draper said. His eyes ran Archer up and down, lingering for a heartbeat on his silver brooch. "I lost a good soldier to her, Colonel Markides."

"My days in the Order are over, Captain. My rank is Regis, *not* Colonel," Archer corrected.

"Regis Markides," Draper amended and paused to draw himself up. "As I said, she killed one of my men. I would like to see justice done. I'm sure we can be—"

"Justice will be done," Archer cut over him. "Just not by your hand. The woman is now a Conclave matter. It's time for you to return to your post, soldier."

"But si—*Regis*," Draper's second, Farrus, protested, facial burns weeping as first he scowled, then stared in earnest. "Yannis was one of us. That witch—"

"I care not what he was, *boy*. What he is now is dead, and you will go the same way if you persist in following this *witch* as you call her. She's not the ordinary back-country krat you're used to dealing with."

Farrus's mouth opened, then shut again with a clack of teeth. When no one spoke, Archer clapped his hands together. "Good. I've said my bit." He shifted closer to the table and tapped the map. "Now, show me where you last sighted her and I'll be on my way."

.   .   .

They were off again by mid-morning, supplies topped up and leading their horses back to the road. At the final barricade, Archer turned to bid Brennus farewell.

"I appreciate your understanding on this Captain," he said.

"We are a garrison, not a patrol unit. Half my men have no galdar talent whatsoever, the rest are average at best," Brennus replied, then with a quirk of his lip added, "with the odd exception from time to time."

With a glance at Archer's wooden hand, Brennus held out his left and Archer took it. But to Archer's surprise Brennus didn't let go. Instead, he leaned close. "For what it's worth now, I was sorry to hear of your departure from the Council," he murmured. "And of your family."

The words hit Archer like a punch to the gut. His grip clenched about Brennus' fingers. The old soldier seemed unfazed.

"Have you thought about returning?" he asked in an undertone. "A voice of reason in the Seven would be welcome news for many of us out here."

Archer swallowed, tongue thick in his mouth. "I cannot," he rasped. Somewhere inside him the old rage twitched, uncurling from its long sleep. *Some things cannot be forgiven.* His right stump throbbed under the bindings. *Some are not worth saving.* Once he had the rarkyn, he would put these gods-cursed lands behind him. *Rot in your Empire of ashes, Therrin.*

Archer forced his grip open and Brennus let his hand fall. To Archer's surprise, the Captain turned to Hane.

"Take good care of him," he said. The young Wildner blinked, then nodded. "Y—yes. I will."

"Good lad."

Brennus stepped back to let them mount. Archer dug his heels into his pony's flank. They'd lingered too long and there was much ground to cover—even if the girl was on foot. His horse clattered forward, shifting from a trot into a canter. Behind, Hane muttered a curse and raced to catch up. Soon Brennus was nothing more than a distant figure on the road.

***

Brennus turned on his heel once Markides and his apprentice dropped out of sight. He tucked his hands behind his back and waited. A minute later Corporal Hasek came into view, tramping through the camp, freshly washed and dressed in light armor and carrying a heavy rucksack. The only part of his uniform not clean were his black Order-issue boots, which still bore ash and grit from the camp clean up.

"Are you ready?" Brennus asked as Hasek fell in beside him.

"Yes sir," Hasek replied. "Are you sure you want to do this, after what he said?"

Brennus crooked a smile. "We are not doing anything, Corporal. I am simply sending you home for some long over-due respite."

Hasek raised an eyebrow. "Illredus is a long way to go for a respite, sir. Even for a summoner like me. He won't buy it if he sees me in the field."

"You let me worry about Sergeant Draper."

"I was referring to Markides, sir."

"I don't expect him to. But as he said, he's no longer in the Order. He can't interfere with how I run my garrison or where I send my men. I am simply following standard protocol and *you* are simply following my command." Brennus rocked back on his heels and watched the ash swirl in miniature whirlwinds through the camp. "All the same, try to keep out of sight. Markides is up to something," he said. "And I'm not sure he has the good of the realm at heart. Not after what happened to him."

Hasek gave a short nod. "I'll keep an eye on him, sir."

"Thank you, Corporal. Keep me posted."

PART III
ASHES

Across the divide, the rarkyn led,
Asander and men to burrow deep.
Down, down to the Aether's heart,
To the den where the eternals sleep.

Hungry, the ginndir hounded,
Picking off men and kin,
Until last Asander beat the doors, screaming:
Let me in, let me in, let me in!

—Fragment from The Epic of Asander.
c. 500 years before the Illredian Founding.

CHAPTER TWENTY-TWO

A HOOF-STEP ON THE BRIDGE ALERTED THE GUARD TO THE stranger's approach. He straightened in his boots, jerking his spear to attention as he squinted out into the pre-dawn light. A rider approached. They were hunched in the saddle, cloak drawn tight and hood up as they swayed on the back of the steed. The horse plodded forward, head low. As it got closer, the guard spotted dried saliva coating its mouth near the bit and a foam of sweat around the bridle.

"Norri," he hissed, waving down his fellow watchman who was stamping the blood back into his toes on the garrison's threshold. On spotting the rider, his fellow guard hurried over.

"Sepp, another one?" Norri muttered, falling in beside his fellow. "Be careful, Caffery."

"Halt!" Caffery called. "Declare yourself." Silence was their only response. Both rider and horse continued forward, unfazed.

"Halt," Norri echoed, tightening his grip on his weapon. The horse clopped to a stop at the edge of their spears; a hot breath from its nose rolled over their fingers. Norri stepped out, reaching for the reins. "Who—"

The rider folded in the saddle like a hinge, slumping forward, then sideways.

"Catch him, Norri!" Caffery shouted, lunging to take the horse as his fellow grabbed at the rider's cloak, but it was too late. With a ripping sound, the stranger toppled to the ground, leaving Norri standing there with a shredded cloak in his grasp.

"Sepp damn," he muttered, and they leaned over the rider sprawled in the dirt.

It was a young man, fair haired and hollow cheeked, with circles so deep under his eyes it looked like they were painted.

"You all right, boy?" Norri asked.

The stranger blinked twice and with what seemed like a great effort, focused his eyes. "Where?"

"Ira River Garrison," Caffery said as he and Norri bundled the stranger up and back onto his feet. "What happened to you?"

"Been riding for days," the stranger murmured, swaying.

"Non-stop it looks like," Norri said, sliding a shoulder under the stranger to help keep him on his feet. "Idiot boy, do you want to kill your horse?"

"I can't let him take Hane."

The guards exchanged an uncertain glance. "When did you last sleep?" Caffery asked.

The stranger wrinkled his forehead as he thought. "Three days...or four?"

Caffery sighed and pointed to the nearest tent: a supply tent for the night watch. It was full of wet-weather cloaks and woolens, dirt crusted boots and a rack of weaponry, but it was better than the open road. "Let him rest in there," he said to Norri.

"*No!*" The stranger dug in his heels, jerking Norri to a stop. "I must keep going."

"You're damn near dream walking," Norri chided, then softened his tone. "You're going nowhere until you've slept. Just a few hours kip. Then you can leave."

He guided the stranger into the tent and with a brusque word, sent two of the watch scurrying out to replace them on the bridge. Caffery gathered the reins of the stranger's horse and led it to part of the block-ade, tethering it there. He made a mental note to fetch a bucket of grain for it later.

When he returned to the tent, Norri was easing the stranger onto a makeshift bed of guard blankets.

"I can't stop," the stranger grabbed Norri by the forearm. "He's taken Hane and they're going...they're going after..."

"You won't find him if you're dead on your feet," Norri said, prying the stranger's grip free finger by finger. "Rest. What's your name?"

The question seemed to throw the stranger. "My name?" he said. "Darrin…Darrin Eder."

"Ah, a Wildner. A northern name if ever I heard one," Norri said.

The stranger gave a slow nod, eyes fluttering as he fought off sleep. "'S not…important," he mumbled. "He's taken Hane and they're going after the rarkyn. Hane is…I can't let them do it."

Norri turned to Caffery and mouthed *"Rarkyn?"* Caffery shrugged. Fatigue had clearly made the youth delirious. Yet, he paused, only the desperate—or stupid—traveled the road in such a state.

"Who's Hane?" Caffery asked.

Darrin heaved himself out of sleep. "Brother," he managed.

Made sense. "Who's taken him?"

"A mancer…called himself Andreas Markides."

Norri's stiffened, his gaze meeting Caffery's, and Caffery clean forgot his next question. He recalled seeing the pair coming through the camp two days ago—a mancer with a boy of thirteen, fourteen at most. If they had crossed the bridge…

Caffery rose and headed for the writing desk in the tent's far corner to rummage through the ledger sitting atop it. He scanned back through the record. Yes, scrawled there in Perry's barely legible hand: *Andreas Markides, mancer, with Hane Eder, apprentice. Destination: Illredus.*

This could change things.

Caffery cleared his throat. "I'll get the Captain."

CHAPTER TWENTY-THREE

Skaar woke to the far-off rolling of thunder. Rain patted against the leaves of their hap-to shelter, like the sound of tiny feet scurrying across the branches above. He listened, twitched an ear, then listened again. No, not like the sound of tiny feet. It *was* tiny feet. With a huff he sat up and found a flock of smarokk peering down at him. Their shadowy bodies appeared solid, their two-toed feet hooked around twigs, leaves, and branches alike. White pricks marked their eyes in their oval heads. It was like staring up into the stars.

The Aether must be thick here.

Skaar rolled to a crouch, ducking his head under the branches and feeling a horn brush the leaves. "Be off." He shooed a hand at the flock. They vanished like a disturbed reflection in a stream, drawing deeper into the Otherworld and beyond his sight. He yawned and checked on the branches he had propped up against the trunk of the pine they'd taken refuge under. Satisfied they still held, he turned to Lyss.

She lay asleep, face pale and clammy, cloak drawn up under her chin. He lifted the edge with one talon to examine the length of torn-up cloak serving as a bandage around her arm and shoulder. It was red and oozing blood onto the makeshift bed of dry grass and fronds beneath her.

Reythr damn it. He eyed the skull of the shuck pushed up against the base of the tree trunk. Its teeth were needle sharp; he'd cut himself on several just prying the thing out of her flesh two nights before. He undid the bandage and muttered under his breath. It looked even worse in daylight, and despite their bond, it had yet to start healing.

The shuck's teeth had gouged deep wounds into the top of her arm and back of her shoulder. The skin had pulled back, revealing red flesh and, in places, white bone. Lyss was lucky it hadn't taken her arm clean off at the shoulder. He glanced at the shuck's skull again, then at Lyss' sweat-slicked face and ran a talon along his palm, considering. One scratch. Just a prick. A drop or two down her throat and Lyss would be past the worst of it. He curled his fist and shook his head.

Banish the thought. You saw what it did to Archer. No. The situation wasn't that desperate. Not yet.

He undid the blood-soaked bandage, tore another section off the bottom of Lyss' cloak, spat on it, and dabbed the wound clean again.

The edge of his hugrokar twitched, and with a groan, Lyss came to. The pain, a dull ache in her sleep, flared anew in Skaar's shoulder. He yanked his mind free and coiled it tight. The sensation melted away.

Lyss' eyes cracked open. "How long?" she croaked.

"Three days."

She shut her eyes again and her eyebrows knitted together. "Sepp damn," she sighed, and sucked in a breath. Skaar sensed her mentally brace herself, tense her muscles and he pressed two fingers into her forehead to stop her rising to her feet.

"Bad idea," he said. "Just rest."

"The Order. They must be—"

"Quite far away now," Skaar said. "We flew far."

She relaxed a little and winced as Skaar resumed dabbing. Then she frowned, staring up at the branches above them and the pact gave a quiver. Skaar followed her gaze. The smarokk had returned.

"Ignore them," he advised.

"What do they want?"

"Terresmir flesh, like all aetherlings,"

Her face went a new shade of white and her hugrokar gave a distinct flip-flop. "You mean—"

"Not living flesh," Skaar corrected. *At least, not in this case.* "Water, earth, leaves." He snapped a small twig off from the tree and held it out to one of the smarokk. It perked up, making little snatches for it while the others next to it swarmed closer. "Still in the Otherworld. Just very shallow," he said and poked the twig at one of the smarokk. With an odd twist the aetherling's form warped around the object, as if Skaar were suddenly seeing it through thick, uneven glass. "See?"

At Lyss' non-reply, he turned back to find her eyes closed, jaw clenched and a thin film of sweat on her cheeks and neck. She carried no medicine, he knew, he had gone through the pockets of her coat and cloak earlier and found nothing but a coin purse, a coiled and slightly squashed letter, and a small ornate mirror, which had all been buried in the bottom of an interior pocket. *Not good.* He tore another fresh strip off the bottom of her cloak to re-dress the wound.

"Wait." Lyss stopped him with her free hand. "The wounds are too deep." She swallowed. "I have to sew them shut."

"Don't have..." Skaar paused, realizing he didn't know the word in the human tongue.

"There's a needle in my coat," Lyss said, motioning to the garment draped over her legs. "In the cuff."

Skaar picked up the coat and examined the sleeve. Sure enough, when he turned down the cuff of the left sleeve there was a sewing needle embedded in it. She grinned when she saw it there.

"My Fa's trick," she said. Her smile faded when Skaar pulled the needle free and held it out. "Help me sit up."

She tucked her left arm to her chest as Skaar slid a hand under her neck and pushed her up. Then he grabbed the collar of her jerkin and shifted her so her back was against the tree trunk. Her face changed color again and sweat rolled down her jaw and throat.

Skaar relaxed his mental barriers, hoping to gauge just how bad moving had been. He braced himself for a wall of pain, but instead found nothing. The link was silent. The girl had blocked off her hugrokar on her own. Her lip quirked at his surprise.

"I'm a quick study," she said, and despite the pain her shoulder was clearly causing her, Skaar thought she sounded a little smug. She had him pull off a frayed thread from the bottom of her tunic and loop it through the head of the needle. The shaft was long, made for repairing holes in clothes, not skin.

"You sure you want to..." Skaar motioned at her wounds. "Sew?"

Lyss held up the needle, mouth set in a grim line. "They'll get infected, if they're not already." She took a breath and held the needle up to the first wound at the front of her shoulder. Her hand shook, needle tip quivering like a scrawling quill.

Skaar stared at the needle, then sighed. *Reythr, don't let me regret this later.* "Relax hugrokar," he said.

Lyss paused. "But you'll feel it too."

"Just do," Skaar said, and waved her on with a talon.

Slowly, the girl's hugrokar unfurled. Pain rushed across the link to him. He caught the hiss in his throat, feathers bristling.

"Told you," Lyss said, and began to tighten her control again.

"Leave it."

"But—"

He didn't wait for her to finish. Instead, he reached across hugrokar, felt for the throbbing pain that resonated there and drew it in. Relief, shock, and awe clashed into him from the other side of the link.

"You can take away pain?"

"Not take. Share it," Skaar replied through gritted teeth. "Make it less...distracting." He pointed at the needle, now steady in her hand. "Hurry up."

At the first stab, they both winced. Despite only having one hand, Lyss worked deftly, instructing Skaar to tie off the ends of each puncture and break the thread after. Finished with the wounds at the front of her shoulder and arm, she held out the needle to Skaar.

"There are ones I can't reach," she said. "I need you to close them up." She shifted, turning her back to him and revealing two deep wounds in her shoulder blade. Skaar glimpsed a flash of white bone in one. He took the needle and considered the first ragged hole. Unlike the others, the shuck's teeth had sunk in and then raked through her flesh, leaving a jagged gash in its wake. He started at the deepest part of the wound and copied what he had seen her do for the others. Lyss had made it look easy. His work was messy in comparison, but passable. His second attempt was better. He tied it off, coiled the remaining thread around a talon and snapped it.

"Thank you," Lyss said, closing her eyes and leaning her head against the trunk. She let him wind the strip of cloak around her shoulder before sinking down onto her good side to rest. She fell back asleep almost instantly. A deep, exhausted sleep of the sick and injured. There would be no waking her for several hours.

He eased his hold of her pain. It faded into a dull throb, mixing in with the muscular ache in his wings from flying through the night. For a time, he sat there, content to listen to the rain and the thunder roll past in the east.

Hunger eventually drove him out into the weather.

He arrived back at the shelter just as darkness fell, a satchel of river clams scavenged from a nearby stream in one hand and a full waterskin in the other. A biting breeze from the north swept through the trees, swirling pine needles around Skaar's feet. He sniffed the air. A glance up at the overcast sky confirmed it and his gut tightened. Snow was on the way.

He checked the shelter. Lyss still slept, even as he layered extra branches outside; the furry pine needles turning the shelter into a giant green bulb. A flurry of small black limbs greeted him when he ducked inside. The smarokk had remained. They scurried out of the way as he sat down, and Skaar sensed rather than felt them creep closer as he opened the kerchief of clams. He held up one black shell between two talons. It was clamped shut; its edible morsel locked tight inside. He cocked his head. The Otherworld might be warm enough to open it— and it would save him having to build a fire. Then again…his gaze slid to the smarokk. They had encircled his feet like a gaggle of kits at story time, their pointed white eyes gazing up at him unblinking and with rapt attention. He'd be lucky if the little critters only made off with half his haul.

Skaar tapped a talon against his bottom lip and considered. Smarokk weren't known for their intelligence. He just needed to entice them away for a few moments.

Very well, let's see what works. He dug about under the fronds at his feet, scooping up the wet earth underneath and forming it into mud balls the size of his palm. When he had three, he stood.

"Come on you lot," he waved the mud balls near the flock and walked outside, ducking his head as he went. They scurried after him, clambering over one another in their haste. Ten paces away from the shelter he stopped, crouched down and *reached* for the Otherworld. The Aether in him surged to his will, resonated with the essence of the second plane and just like that, his hand slipped through into glorious warmth. He hadn't prepared himself for what came next.

On mass, the smarokk swarmed. In a heartbeat they were all over his hand, toothless mouths sucking beads of water and dirt granules off his feathers like a school of fish. For a moment Skaar was transported back to one spring when he and Fengar had found a school of tadpoles in a stagnant pond and fed them bits of smoked mutton. A pang of sadness rose at the memory. Skaar sighed and brushed the smarokk off.

"Here, this is better anyway," he reached his other hand through and tossed the three mud balls off into the Otherworld. "Go fetch."

The flock split, scrambling after the mud balls. Skaar withdrew, the fresh power of the Aether tingling up his arms. No ripples. Each time he shifted in and out of the Otherworld it grew easier.

Dwell on that later, he thought and hurried back to the shelter for the clams. He rasvengered his hand back through the divide, dripping bundle and all. The mussels smoked as they hit the other plane, as if the bundle had been thrown over a fire. The Aether's smoky tendrils licked the carry-sack, the Otherworld's current pulling on the fabric as the shells popped open one by one. He grinned and leaned forward to put his nose to the other plane. Heat rushed down his airway, warming his throat and lungs, carrying a faint fishy scent with it.

A flicker at the edge of his vision made him swing around. A wave of smarokk was racing toward him. Skaar lurched back, but not before the first of the mass lunged for the bundle.

"Get off!" He shook the kerchief and a few clams slid out, plopping into the Otherworld's shallows. He cursed and plunged his other hand through, flicking the groping smarokk away. Then, with a jerk, he pulled the clams back to Terresmir. The Aether inside him flared and a flicker of heat passed down his core, as if he'd over-stretched a muscle. *Ouch.*

A ragged gasp made him look down. A smarokk lay writhing on the earth, *Terresmir earth.* Its thin, whispery arms scratched at its chest. Mouth open, it sucked at the air as it squirmed.

Reythr damn. He must have pulled it through with the bundle. Skaar scooped it up and reached for the Otherworld again, thrusting the smarokk back through. The aetherling stilled once it hit the second plane, and Skaar watched its chest rise high, then fall, then rise again. Its body twitched, and it suddenly vaulted off his fingers and flittered back toward its flock.

"You're lucky you're so small," Skaar told it. *And that I had enough power to push you back through.* The thought made him stop. If his strength had recovered enough to let him pull a smarokk through with relative ease, was he ready to cross completely into the Otherworld? His stomach fluttered. He'd not been emersed in the Aether since...he swallowed, *since then.* But this time was different.

You have no pack, doubt nagged at him. *If you fall, there's no one to help you.*

He'd stay shallow. Skaar considered the smarokk swarming over the mud ball a mere stone's throw from him. They suddenly seemed impossibly far away, yet he had to learn this—and quickly. Fail to master it and he might as well crow his arrival in Illredus from the top of the city battlements.

How will you get out? Skaar's doubt asked again.

Easy. Use the girl.

She wasn't going anywhere soon, and her hugrokar would serve as a tether. He hesitated. Wouldn't it? He turned his head up to the dark sky and muttered a curse. There were so many unknowns, but he had to try. He forced down the fear and took a breath; the cool night air hit the back of his throat.

Skaar focused on the other plane, reached a taloned finger out and sent his own Aether forward to forge the connection. His index sank through, as if he'd dipped it into a pond. His hand followed, then his arm, shoulder, head. He lifted a foot and the Aether's warmth curled around his toes as he set it down in the Otherworld. Then he shifted his weight and stepped. At the last second, he turned, just in time to see the tip of his tail cross through and his passage close behind him.

For a long moment he stood, holding his breath. The Aether coiled about him, embracing him in its heat, evaporating the water out of his feathers with a soft, faint hiss. Skaar expelled the cold Terresmir air from his lungs and breathed in the Otherworld. Heat and power rushed through him. His head swam, causing him to wince. It burned; right through muscle into bone; reverberating through hugrokar as it went. Lyss stirred in her sleep. Skaar coiled his mind tighter but held on to the link like it was a lifeline and he a drowning kit. He took another breath and the sensation subsided. Then another. His head steadied, and he eased his grip on the link. His sense of Lyss fell away. He waited. The Otherworld was silent; its power a faint hush in the back of his mind and not the roar he'd feared. But spend too long in here and that would soon change.

Skaar looked out to Terresmir. The material plane had dulled as if he were viewing it from underwater. He still heard wind rustling the trees and the hoot of an owl; still smelled the dried blood of Lyss' wounds, but the sounds and smells of Terresmir lacked their usual crispness. It was both a familiar and horribly alien sensation, like recalling a half-forgotten memory in sharp and sudden detail. His feathers bristled and Skaar gave a small shudder. *Time to go.*

He flexed his hugrokar and reached for the girl. Lyss still slept, though his antics had roused her out of her deep slumber. He drew on the Aether, pulling its power into his bones and releasing it again to his will. It came to him easily now, and his body drank in more to replace what he used. Skaar extended his senses to the plane beyond.

He couldn't find it.

His stomach turned over, squirming like a worm in the sun. He reached again. *Nothing.* He could see Terresmir, hear it, but he couldn't *sense* it. There was no weight in the back of his mind that signaled its presence. Of course there wasn't, he realized too late, Terresmir wasn't like the Otherworld. Panic gnawed at the edge of his thoughts. He fought it down.

Think Skaar. All rarkyn learned this. Fengar had done it. He would too. He closed his eyes and focused, hunting for any sense of the material world. *No good.* All he sensed was Aether. Fear did another lap in his belly. *No, there was a way.*

Across hugrokar, Lyss' mind shifted, rising out of her slumber just enough to labor with the mind-magic.

Use the Aether in Terresmir…idiot. The groggy thought came at him with a flicker of annoyance. She lingered long enough to sense the stroke of understanding run through him before her mind fell away again.

Of course. *You drekkag,* Skaar berated himself. Everything in Terresmir had Aether, albeit not much, but some. He seethed it out of the air in on the physical plane. The eyrees flew with it. The humans ate it in their food so they could work their runes. It permeated everything. The earth, the plants, the air.

He fixed his attention on the tree he'd used as the base for their shelter. There was a small glimmer of Aether at its core and a faint power trickling through its wood and roots. Had he not deliberately looked, he'd never have noticed it. Skaar drew power and *reached*. It was like throwing a fishing line. The magic latched onto the tree's Aether. All he had to do was reel himself in.

He leapt. The Otherworld fell away, thinning, then thinning again. With a gasp he hit the frigid air of Terresmir. The cool mixed with the warm Aether in his lungs and sent him into a coughing fit. Compared to the Otherworld, the air was light, almost insubstantial.

"Remember, breathe out first," Raska had always instructed the kits whenever she'd led them from the Otherworld. Ah yes, he'd forgotten that. He didn't care. He'd done it. He sank down to the earth,

scrunching the damp soil between his fingers. He could use rasvenger. He might be Unluck, the stunted kit come Aether-turned rarkyn, but the prized ability of his people was his too. He'd entered the Otherworld, and the Aether hadn't claimed him. Relief clogged his throat, and he bowed his head to the earth.

Reythr thank you, thank you.

CHAPTER TWENTY-FOUR

Dearest Elena,

I'm sorry for not writing, our "charge" has been keeping us up and down worse than a newborn's parents. For its part, the rarkyn is doing well, or well enough. Isaac still worries it will fall back into the Otherworld and take us with it, but I'm confident my sigil will keep it grounded.

We are camped on the outskirts of Tros, far enough away from the townsfolk, should anything untoward happen, but close enough that Isaac can ride into town for supplies (and to post this letter once I'm done). He's been a wonder, Elena, with the rarkyn especially. I dare say he's become quite fond of it, even though he insists he hasn't.

And the rarkyn…

Where do I begin? Much has happened in the weeks since we found it. It spent the first few days in and out of consciousness; quite expected after being trapped in the Otherworld for Sepp knows how long. It was horribly weak, barely able to lift its head. I'll bet it was the first time it ever had to move without the aid of the Aether in its muscles. Not that it stopped the creature hissing and spitting at us like an alley cat.

On the third day after we found it, I awoke to find the rarkyn gone. We caught up with it fifty paces from camp, crawling along the road on its belly. The next night, I set my berigan to watch over it and I settled down in my sleeping roll, unable to shake a growing unease. The kit had developed a high fever over the course of the afternoon and where it once snarled at us, it whimpered. It spoke a little, a soft lilting tongue to the ear, almost like a song, but when it saw we hadn't understood, it fell silent.

Something was wrong, that was all we knew.

Just after midnight, I woke to a rough hand gripping my forearm. I jolted up, scrambling away from the prick of talons on my skin. A faint rasp issued at my feet. I squinted, and by the light of the still-warm coals, I made out the rarkyn. It had dragged itself across the camp—to me. *But why? I searched the shadows. My berigan was still at its post, eyes fixed on the kit, waiting for it to set foot outside the camp.*

Instead, the rarkyn thrust out an arm to me, holding out the metal sigil locked about its wrist.

I sighed and pressed my hands around the cuff. "I can't take it off, not yet," I said, knowing full well the kit wouldn't understand. The metal was warm to touch. So hot I had to pull my hands away before they burned. I turned the cuff over. The runes were faded. Nearly gone!

It was sucking the magic right out of the sigil, Elena.

I'm not one to curse, but I did then. I leapt up, cast a rune to set the fire blazing and crouched over the rarkyn. It was in a bad way. Its temperature was high, even for an aetherling, and it was panting hard, mouth lined with a froth of dry spittle. I examined the rune sigil. Two of the graving spells were completely dead. I made to recast the graving but froze at the sight of the creature's eyes staring up at me from my lap. Black rings darkened its irises. I could practically see them thickening as I watched.

"Sepp almighty." I lurched to my feet, scooping up the rarkyn, releasing my berigan to summon my strongest ward in its place. It flared across the camp like a candle touched to the well of an oil lamp. Bright, comforting light. "Isaac!" I called, stumbling over to him, my clumsy feet kicking him in the shins. He woke with a grunt and a curse. "Get in the circle! Hurry!" I ordered. "It's going into Fever."

For a long bleary second, he stared at me, then comprehension sank in and he scurried into the ward in a tangle of bedclothes. I set the rarkyn down inside with us. It clung to my nightshirt, eyes round, and refused to let go. As I tried to peel its talons away, it pressed the wrist with the dying sigil into my chest.

"Glder," it said, shaking the cuff at me. I frowned and the kit thumped its fist into me again. "Glder." It thrust the cuff under my nose, and as the fading runes caught the light of the fire coals, I understood. Galdar.

I crouched, knowing I should pry the aetherling off me before it Fell, but instead I froze, trying to make sense of its odd request. It wanted more *binding runes? Perhaps it sensed the engraving was all that stood between it and falling back into the Otherworld. I pressed a hand over the sigil, drew on the Aether inside me and fed it power afresh. The runes flared and the rarkyn slumped against me, head lolling. I examined my handiwork, the heat of the kit's fever sending sweat prickling down my back. To my alarm, the spell's power was already fading. In its fevered state, the rarkyn drained the power from the runes, soaking it up like water dropped onto crusted desert sand. My runes, strong enough to summon and bind a berigan to Terresmir, were stripped and wasted in minutes. That's the power of a rarkyn's Fever, Elena.*

Again, the kit rallied, pressing the cuff into my chest. I cast once more, and this time the runes held. I staggered up, cradling the kit in my arms, and stepped back from Isaac and cast a new ward inside my first—around the kit and myself. A stern look silenced Issac's objection.

"If this fails, I'll not have you dragged in too." I told him. "Focus your energy on those." I nodded to the circle's lines arcing around him. He wanted to argue, to curse at me I suspect, but instead he nodded and sat, closing his eyes to concentrate.

That was the beginning of a long, sleep-scarce night. Several times the kit drained both the sigil and my circle. I don't think it was intentional. In fact, I think it would have stopped had it known how. The kit was as much a victim of its own magic as we were. You see, Elena, I do not believe it was a Fever, at least not a true one. It was something else—perhaps something just as dangerous. Either way, I'm convinced we saw a kit become a rarkyn that night. I've never seen anything like it. It grew by two feet at least, I swear! The best way I can describe it is like a caterpillar emerging from a cocoon—transformed. Gone is the tiny kit no higher than my waist. The banding on its shoulders has darkened, and it now stands close to my own height, with more growing still to come I suspect. The Aether has left its mark too, the kit's horns are now as long as my hand—and still growing. One eye remains red, but the other has turned as silver as the moon. Silver like the aetherlings of the Deep. But for all that, it seems in remarkably good health, if somewhat ungainly.

It has become more tolerant of us since that night too. I've strengthened the sigil with more 'gravings than I care to count and modified it to allow the rarkyn to draw in just enough Aether so his magic doesn't turn on the sigil itself. It must be the most spelled piece of metal in all the Empire, surely! The sigil irritates the rarkyn of course, but I've no doubt it would have fallen back into the Otherworld without it, and I think it realizes that. I only hope it doesn't have to be a permanent solution. It's quite the lucky critter really. Across the North Sea, the people of the Kalana Isles have a word for that kind of Gods-touched luck: Tykee. So, that is what we're calling it.

As for Isaac and me, we're faring, although roughing it eventually got the better of Isaac. He spent our remaining coin on a wagon in Tros yesterday.

Nothing too flash, it'll allow for a comfortable sleep off the earth and a shelter from the worst of the elements. Given where we're headed, it might turn out to be one of his wiser purchases (don't let him know I said that, or I won't hear the end of it!).

We're planning to set out the day after next now the rarkyn has recovered from its sickness. I'll send you another update on our progress when we reach Klymene.

Sending my love as always.

Papa

P.S. Word has reached Tros that Councillor Gyras was found guilty of treason and his family forced to flee across the straights to Kraw. Gyras was a dear friend of mine and was as loyal as they come. The wheels of politics churn. Please be careful.

ARCHER STARED AT THE PONY IN GRIM SILENCE. THE animal's eyes rolled in its head, the normally thin, oblong pupils were round and dilated in the morning light. She threw her head back, rising on her tether, neck arching.

"What's wrong with her?" Hane asked.

"It's the runes," Archer said, grunting as he strained to keep hold of the pony. On the animal's legs, the galdar runes had burned gangrene-black into its flesh. He reached one hand down and smeared the markings out. "No rune-riding today," he said. *Blast it.*

Hane winced and checked his own mount. The Eder's horse fared better; the runes Hane had graved on it hadn't marred its flesh yet. Hane saddled the creature, stowed his bedroll in its bags and waited for Archer to do the same with his pony. The stocky little beast was having none of it. She skittered about, launching a savage bite at Archer when he tried to lift the saddle over her back. In the end, he gave up. With a sigh, he slung the tack over one shoulder, saddlebags over the other and began to walk, pony in tow.

"Why yours and not mine?" Hane asked as he hurried after.

"Could be any number of reasons, age, breeding..." Archer said. "It's like asking why certain people can control the Aether and others can't. Some are sensitive to it, some aren't."

They travelled in silence, which suited Archer fine. At noon he stopped to summon a nizer, calling the leathery, foot-tall, creature out of the Otherworld with a circle graved into the thumb of his wooden hand, and ignoring Hane as the boy ogled.

"I never thought of that," he muttered, staring at the galdar wards scored into the grain.

There was a lot, it seemed, the boy did not think about.

"What's the big one in the middle do?" he asked.

Archer glanced down at the fine lines and arcs marked in the palm of his false hand. Unlike the other wards graved into the wood, this one bore no runes. Just inert lines; a reference for the day when he would trace those lines on the earth for the last time. Hane's mouth moved as he counted its points. *Twenty-three, twenty-four.* He stopped and gaped at Archer.

"Never you mind." Archer shifted his hand under his cloak and turned on the nizer. The aetherling's six eyes shifted to him, waiting, expectant. It knew the drill; Archer had trained it well. From his coat he produced an old scuffed rarkyn feather and held it out to the creature. The aetherling sniffed, nostrils flaring, its long-spindly fingers twitching at its sides.

"Where is it?" Archer asked.

The nizer quivered, round eyes blinking owl-like in the noon light. Its hands lifted, curling and tapping the air as if it were a spider testing the lines of its web. Hane shifted closer to Archer.

"What's it doing?" he whispered.

Archer made to tell the boy to shut his trap and wait, but at his earnest, curiosity-filled expression, he faltered.

"It's searching for the rarkyn's imprint in the Aether," he said instead, folding his arms as he waited for the nizer to finish.

"Imprint?" The boy echoed curiously, not understanding.

Archer sighed. For a child so talented in galdar, there were surprising gaps in his knowledge. *What has that old crone been teaching him?* "All things that use Aether leave an imprint of their workings behind."

The boy's face lit up. "Oh, a bit like the smell galdar causes when it's cast?"

"Yes, but in the Otherworld most workings are too small to trace— even by aetherlings—but nizers are particularly apt at sensing it." He gestured at the creature crouched before them.

They looked down at the creature and its quivering hands. Its blinking had slowed and four of its eyes were glazed over, staring off down the valley, while two on the side of its head remained alert and fixed on Archer. One skinny finger twitched, then the creature chirruped and shook itself.

Archer leaned forward, prompting the creature. "Well?" The nizer lifted an arm and pointed over the ridge. Archer grunted. "Thought as much." He put a hand on its bald head, ignoring the aetherling's flinch. "Show me."

An image flashed through his mind. The ridge, but not from his perspective. A faint line of smoke weaved over it and over the ridge beyond too, heading south and east.

Archer removed his hand from the nizer, and the vision receded. That the trail was there at all meant it was still fresh. But its direction led off the King's Road, toward Memnon's Spine. *Where in the Mercies are they going?* Too east for Nilos. Perhaps she intended to bypass the city altogether what with the Order outpost there. If the girl's destination was Illredus, she and the rarkyn would ultimately turn westward again and strike back to the coast. But when?

Either way, they still have to cross the Gesham plains. Miles of grassland full of bones—not all of them human—from a war forgotten to time. There were giant things lodged in the soil there; femurs as tall as he was, teeth the size of forearms. Few dared to brave the plains without the protection of a caravan and a Conclave mancer. The beasts of the Deep still haunted the place, or so the drovers claimed.

If she's fool enough to take a rarkyn to the capital, she's fool enough to try her luck on the plains.

Archer dismissed the nizer and considered the valley's ridgeline. Gone were the crumbling ridges of rock from days before. Rolling pine forest had taken over the land like the waves on a green sea. Thick, yet passable. *But slow going.* Archer rubbed the thickening beard on his jaw, considering the road and the winding Ira River they'd been following for the last three-day. The path was clear, well-kept thanks to Brennus' men coming and going between Nilos and the garrison.

With the nizer, he could head the girl and rarkyn off over the mountains, before they reached the plains—if they traveled fast. He glanced over at his Aether-scored pony. The marks from the runes had faded, along with its wild look and temperament, but riding it was still risky.

Then there was the boy.

Hane stood quiet, holding his horse's bridle, stroking its nose as he waited. As the mancer glanced at him he perked up, coming alert like a pup graced with attention.

If he had a tail it would wag, Archer thought, wryly. If he were to avoid a clash with the girl, he needed the boy. Yet the Wildner's fond description of her didn't match up to the facts. An honest, and by all accounts loyal, girl turned murderer and arsonist? It didn't make sense. A familiar gnawing feeling grew in his gut; the uncomfortable pressure snaked under his ribs, beginning its slow squeeze. Something wasn't right.

"What is it?" Hane asked as Archer stared at him.

Either she was a con-artist or something else was at play here. But what? Archer pondered another moment, then gave up. He knew too little. He pointed at the trees lining the valley rim. "How're your tracking skills?"

The youth's nose wrinkled, and he scratched his head. "Not terrible." He scuffed the toe of one boot in the dirt and averted his gaze, then added softer, "Darrin was always better."

Archer waved off the boy's guilt. "We'll make it work." He stepped off the road, pulling the pony along with him. Hane followed. *No questions asked,* Archer noted. He had to give the boy credit. The youngster had done everything he'd asked without fault.

"How are your reserves?" he asked over his shoulder as they walked.

"I've still got two canteens of water left and—"

"I meant your *Aether* reserves."

"Oh, I'm fine," Hane replied, hurrying to close the gap between himself and Archer.

"Good." Archer snapped a twig off a low-slung branch and cleared the pine needles away from the forest floor, exposing the dirt underneath. He drew four runes on it with the twig. Then he handed it to Hane.

"Copy them."

Hane studied the runes for a moment before carving his own set of four below Archer's in swift, confident strokes of the branch.

"Again," Archer said.

Hane copied the runes out once more.

"Good." Archer pointed at the first rune. "*Tyth* is the anchor. Always cast this one first." He indicated the following two runes. "These two are the binds. And this"—he tapped the last rune with his foot: a line with two spines coming off it—"this is the tail."

Hane looked up at Archer. "The tail to what?" he asked.

"To a casting that can down a rarkyn."

Hane gaped at him. "I can't control a rarkyn."

Archer snorted. "We're a ways off controlling it yet, boy. This is just to catch it." He gathered the Aether inside himself and lifted a hand, fingers mimicking the shapes in the air. The runes crackled to life, waking before him in a gleaming white cross, the anchor at north, binds at east and west and the tail at the south. "It's a striking cast designed specifically for aetherlings."

Archer flicked his wrist and the casting shot off, plunging straight through the closest tree trunk as if it were not there at all. "It takes time to learn to control its movement," he said, and with a motion, the spell arced in the air and streaked towards them, stopping a yard short of them at Archer's signal. With a snap of a finger, he released the spell, and it fizzled into the afternoon breeze. "You have two days to master it."

Hane was still a moment, attention lingering on the air where the spell had been. "Will it..." he hesitated. "Will it hurt the rarkyn?"

Archer pursed his lips. "Of course it will, it's a galdar casting," he snapped. *After all that begging to come along and* this *is what he worries about?* The boy's brow wrinkled like a prune, but his right hand tapped against his thigh as if he were eager to start casting.

"It's not going to go into Aether Fever from a few runes," Archer reassured.

Hane's frown didn't ease. If anything, it grew. He stood under the trees, the sinews in his jaw straining as he clenched and unclenched his mouth, gaze fixed on some far-off place.

Archer scowled. *What isn't he telling me?* He retraced his last few steps to the boy, who came back to himself with a start as Archer stamped up to him.

"Start talking."

Hane shied away. "It's not—"

"You either tell me now or you start walking back to Ira Garrison."

The Wildner's gaze skimmed the forest, searching for a haven that was anywhere but Archer's face. His fingers scrunched around his woolen leggings.

Just one more push. Archer waved an arm back down the valley. "Start walking then. Go back and apologize to your brother for leaving him on the side of the road for no reason at all."

Hane stiffened. The knuckles around his bunched leggings turned white. "We can't harm the rarkyn," he said. His voice was soft, head bowed, yet his words cut through the air like a crisp wind through woolen fleece. The hairs rose on Archer's arms.

"Why in Sepp's name not, boy?"

Hane swallowed, and his lips, when they did open again, trembled. "They're bonded." A gulp. "Like familiars."

Archer stood still, jumbled thoughts falling together, understanding sinking in. *Bonded like familiars.* A few weeks ago, he might have scoffed at the notion, even now he wanted to. It was absurd. Yet, it explained much: how the girl controlled the beast and why she was headed to Illredus.

Who would willingly bond themselves to a rarkyn?

Their mind-magic had driven more than a few foolish mancers mad across the pages of history—unless...his mind clawed the pieces together. *Unless it hadn't been intentional.* He thought back to Hane's words to Darrin by the campfire: *It was my fault.* A working gone wrong. Horribly wrong.

"Of course," he muttered. He almost felt sorry for her. Almost. "Her control is being eaten away." *Her hopes are pinned on that stinking city.*

Hane's head snapped up, eyes bright, hopeful. Relieved. "Yes."

Archer clenched his teeth to stop the curses from spilling out. "You only thought to tell me this *now*?" He managed to keep his voice calm, but Hane seemed to sense the danger and shuffled back a step.

"No one else can know. If the Order find out—"

True rage flared inside Archer. In two strides he crossed the space between them and grabbed Hane by the jerkin. "Do I look like an Order lackey, boy?" he growled, nose to nose with the youth.

Hane froze, quivering like a hare caught in the open. His gaze darted to the silver brooch pinned on the inside of Archer's coat, then back to Archer's face before he managed to squeak, "No sir."

Easy does it, you still need him.

"Good answer." Archer shoved the boy back. "Don't compare me to those two-faced snakes in the capital."

To his surprise, Hane seemed relieved. "You won't report it?"

Archer scowled. "No, I won't. I've better things to do than police the five provinces." *I have more important things to think about.* The girl and rarkyn were bonded. That changed things, but not the fact he needed to stop the rarkyn from hightailing it into the Otherworld once they caught up. In fact, Archer's lip quirked upward as he considered, if he could restrain the girl, the rarkyn wouldn't be able to flee at all—at least not far. Yes, the bond changed things, but in a way, it made his job easier. He patted the journal in his pocket, glanced at the twenty-four-point tracing on his wooden hand. He'd have to adapt his plans, move them forward before the bond grew too strong. No matter. His spell was ready. All he needed was the rarkyn.

"I need to think this over," he told the boy. "Master the casting." With that, he gathered his pony's reins and stomped ahead. "Two days," he reminded, pointing at the runes in the dirt before moving out of earshot.

CHAPTER TWENTY-FIVE

She watched the sword rise into the air.

No, not again.

Its tip glinted in the dry sun. Horror locked her limbs. Why? Why didn't you run, Fa? *The sword swung down with a meaty, wet—*

Lyss jerked awake, cry catching in her throat. For a moment her mind floated, still enthralled by the dream. Then the pain came roaring back. Little needles of fire stabbed in her shoulder. She clenched her jaw, pushed herself up and shifted the too-warm coat off her. Cool air caressed her skin, and she let out a sigh of relief as the pain eased to a dull throb.

Thank Sepp for that.

She peered about the shelter. The rarkyn lay asleep on the other side, crammed under the lean-to roof. Smarokk surrounded him. They were perched on his shoulders, head, horns; every available place was taken. Their shadowy forms were transfixed, like birds staring down at a fresh pile of seed. The rarkyn himself was curled in an odd fetal pose, long limbs tucked tight against his body to fit into the space. Like a dead bug, Lyss thought, blinking as she took in the scene.

The pressure in her bladder eventually made her move. Gingerly, she found her boots and pulled them on one-handed and stuffed the laces down the sides. She wasn't going far. She wrapped her torn cloak tighter around herself—its frayed hem above her knees now rather than her feet—collected her sword, and crawled for the entrance, wincing at the movement. A faint flicker across hugrokar signaled the rarkyn rousing at the noise. She glanced over to find an ear cocked in her direction. Without thinking, she reached her mind out, brushing Rark's with a reassuring touch—*yes, just me, pay it no thought*—and the rarkyn's hugrokar slipped away as he sank back into sleep. Her lip quirked; she was getting better at this.

Outside, her boots crunched into fresh snow and she sank up to her ankles in it as she straightened. She stared out into the forest, barely recognizing it. In one night, it had transformed into a pristine, unsullied white. She hurried for a tree, cursing the cold as she squatted. Relieved, she straightened, kicked snow over it and turned back on her tracks.

Around her, the air hung still; silence pressing in. Not even a breath of wind. She stopped, listening in the chill quiet with a gnawing unease in her stomach.

Winter.

And she was not even halfway to Illredus.

She glanced down at her bare wrist. The dark runes leered up at her. Crisp, clean runes. The teeth in her belly eased. Still intact. *One, two, three, four*—she turned her wrist to count the remaining two—and her gut turned over. *They're gone!*

Her knees wobbled and her sword dropped to the snow. She slumped, cupping her clenched fist to her breast. She bit her lip to stop the rising sob. *I am not helpless.* Her scar twisted down her chest. She clenched her fists. *Not helpless.*

Iga's runes were failing, fading away to nothing. She was going to lose herself—every thought, every memory wiped from her mind.

How would it happen? she wondered, numbly. Would they fail all at once? Or would it be a long, drawn-out horror as she lost herself piece by piece until she shattered?

Either way, you deserve it, murderer, the thought rose inside her like a sneer. Lyss shifted, drew her knees into her chest, ignoring a stab of pain from her shoulder. Cold seeped through her trousers. Perhaps she did deserve it. She'd killed that soldier, killed the shuck—all without thinking, without *knowing* what she was doing. But unlike the soldier, this time she remembered. She remembered the shuck's teeth grinding in her shoulder. Her hand plunging into its chest. The hunger that wet her mouth at the sight of all that blood; joy coursing through her muscles. Horror rose inside her, setting her hands shaking. It *was* real.

Something slept within her. Something that drove her into the mind's recesses as it took over. *Something monstrous.*

In its thrall, she'd torn through sigiled armor, crushed a man's skull like a grape, and ripped out an aetherling's heart.

Lyss stared at her hands. Red stained in the lines of her palms, clung under her nails. A killer's hands. She knew what those looked like. An image of a bloody body lying, headless, on the road to Caenis flashed through her thoughts. Soldiers laughing. Her heart thudded in her throat and her stomach lurched. She scrunched her eyes shut and sucked in a breath, trying not to scream. *Gods and ginndir, what am I becoming?*

A rough hand fell on her good shoulder and gently squeezed. The faint pressure of talons pricked through her coat. Lyss started and the rarkyn's presence suddenly winked into her thoughts. *Kratting damn,* she'd forgotten about hugrokar again. She wound her mind in, but even as she did, his hugrokar flickered across, grim yet determined.

"Not over yet," he said. His talons released and he stepped past her, leaving deep tracks in the snow and a flock of smarokk trailing after him. Anger flared in her for a heartbeat. Easy for him to say, it was his magic causing the problem in the first place. Then she reined her head in. *No, that was unfair,* the rational part of her pointed out. Rark was just as much a victim as she was—and who knew what would happen to him when her mind finally unraveled.

She sniffed and got to her feet. Rark did have a point. For now, she still had her sanity. She could still run. Her fingers ran along the blood-splattered sheath of her sword. She could still fight. She picked the weapon up, looped the belt and sheath back into place and drew the blade. It came out clean with a soft, yet audible ring to her keen ears. Further off, the rarkyn rustled about, digging something up in the snow.

They were utterly alone. The knowledge was comforting.

I suppose the pact isn't all bad, she thought, listening. If not for the monstrous madness creeping closer day by day, it would have been convenient. She sliced her sword through the air one-handed, holding her breath, anticipating an angry flare in her opposite shoulder. It never came. A steady throb to be sure, but no deep stab that caught at her lungs. She swung again, then again, feeling the tension fall away as she focused on the task and the steps. She kept the movements slow, working on precision and form. At the end of the pattern she stopped, frowned and held the hilt under her nose. Was it her, or had the weapon become lighter? She launched into another series. *Yes, it was lighter,* she decided as she thrust, feinted, then sidestepped. She examined the blade again. No damage, nothing to suggest why it practically floated in her grip.

A flicker of curiosity across hugrokar and she turned. The rarkyn crouched in the snow watching; smarokk perched on his horns and shoulders. He tilted his head as she sheathed her sword, and she sensed him puzzling.

"Who taught?" he asked after a long moment.

"My father," Lyss said, and her answer confused him more. "Why do you ask?"

"You move different to others."

Lyss nodded, she'd heard that before. *"Not bad, just different,"* Darrin had once said. She weighed the sword and sheath in her palms. Unlike most Illredian swords, it was a single-edged weapon—its leading blade facing out at her opponent—and light enough to wield one handed. Its curved tip and canted hilt allowed her to slash and thrust with uncanny control and precision. To the Eder it had been something of an oddity. To her it was old and familiar, its battered ebony sheath a remnant of the days spent traveling with her father and learning the art. At the time, it had been an entertaining hobby, a bit of sport to break up the long days of walking. She never thought she'd ever need to use it. Her chest squeezed.

"Fa claimed he learned it from an exile of the southern continent," she said, turning the weapon over in her hands. It was exactly as she'd always known it—a worn grip in need of replacing, scuffed pommel and a long scratch down one side of the sheath. If the sword had not changed, then it had to be her. Her gaze returned to the runes on her wrist. If the pact enhanced her senses, did it enhance her strength too? Why the change now? Was it because she'd lost two of Iga's runes?

"What will you do, once you kill your kin-killer?" Rark's question bumped her out of her musings. She stared down at the sword. It had never occurred to her to think about what she'd do after she dealt with Captain Loric.

A smirk cracked her features. Drink a whole keg of chara. Maybe two. She stilled. But what about after? What *would* she do? It'd been a long time since she'd thought of her future beyond ending Loric. The soldier had consumed all her dreams. She paused, considering. She'd leave Illredus for a start. Put the whole kratting Empire at her back, buy passage to Kraw and...what? Journey to one of the ports across the Galcus Sea? The thought set off a thrill inside her. She could see the minstrels of Calahe! Explore Hannon's bazars. Learn a trade—she wasn't sure what, but something that would let her earn an honest living. She'd never have to set eyes on a Red again. Then her stomach gave an unexpected twist.

The Empire was her home.

Darrin's face flashed through her head, grinning, dark eyes glinting with pride and glee—a memory from one of their sparring sessions. A pang caught in her ribs and Darrin's words echoed in her head, *"You have brothers here, if you wanted."*

Friends.

Family.

She stopped the thought there before it wormed deeper.

"I...I don't know," she answered, honestly. She turned on the rarkyn crouched in the snow. "What about you? What will you do once the bond is gone?"

He blinked, evidently not expecting the question to come back at him. "Go far from Illredus," he said. "Away from mancers. Find a pack."

Thoughts still partly on the Eder, Lyss almost missed the flicker of anxiety that twinged as he spoke. She looked at him over her sword, surprised. "You're worried you won't find another pack?"

"No..." Rark hesitated, gaze sliding from her. His wings ruffled. "Worried other packs might turn me away." He said at last.

Lyss frowned. "Why would they do that?"

Rark stayed still, but his hugrokar squirmed and the crest on his head rumpled. "I am Sigra. Aether-turned."

"I don't understand."

Rark huffed and pointed at his silver eye. "Fever has claimed me before."

Lyss' blood chilled. "You've fallen into the abyss?"

"Close to. Yes." He tapped one horn, scattering the smarokk on it. "I am Sigra. Turned by the Aether. Other rarkyn don't always like. We fall to Fever easily."

Lyss sucked in a breath, her hugrokar clenching with her stomach as Rark's words sunk in. A rarkyn prone to falling into Fever. A laugh welled up her throat. She couldn't help it. "What a pair we make." He with too much magic and she with absolutely none. Yes, Sepp, Baer, and all the rest must be having a right old hoot at them. Kratting gods.

Rark stared at her. Confused, until she said as much. He smirked, flashing canines. "A curious pair, agreed." He stood. "Think you can travel?"

Lyss returned the sword to her belt with a nod and wiped her sweaty palms on her tunic, then stopped. Her gaze flickered over the trees, taking them in anew. Overhead, the sloping side of a valley loomed. A sliver of panic stabbed through her. Her heart quickened. *Where are we?*

She snapped around, searching for the road. Nothing but the thick roping trunks of pine trees.

Rark lifted a finger, pointing down the valley. "That way."

Lyss released her breath. Not totally lost then. *Thank Sepp for that.* She turned back to the shelter, thinking to check her maps to get a better idea of how far Rark had brought them.

Her stomach dropped, hope crashing with it. Her maps had been in Titch's saddlebags. No Titch; no maps. Inconvenient, true, but she could replace them. What set her scrambling back into the shelter to rifle through the pockets of her coat was the thought of Iga's letter to the mancer of Illredus. When had she last had it? Had she stowed it in her saddlebags, or in her coat? She turned out the pouches along her coat front, no letter. A sinking feeling plucked at her stomach. Lyss scurried about, fumbling for the interior breast pouch. She found it, plunged a hand in and pulled the crumpled parchment from it. She undid the string, opened it, and read the first line:

Dear Eris,
The girl who gives you this letter is my apprentice.

Lyss coiled the letter again and returned it to the interior pocket. *Thank Sepp.* Without it she was just another girl from the provincial backwaters begging assistance from the Empire's best mancers.

"We go?" Rark asked, turning in the direction he'd indicated the road.

Lyss eased her coat over her wounded shoulder, then slid her other arm in. Cool air seeped through the holes the shuck's teeth had torn in the garment's shoulder. The chill didn't bother her. Strange that. She shrugged it off. Perhaps some of the Aether was still in her. She left her coat unbuttoned and slung her torn cloak over her shoulders, then reached into the shelter to retrieve the shuck skull. Maybe she could sell it for coin. She tore a fresh strip off the bottom of her cloak, wrapped it around the skull and slung it over her back.

"Show me the way," she told Rark.

FOR A WHILE THEY WALKED IN SILENCE, RARK WINDING through the trees with a trail of smarokk following him. The little creatures were infatuated. Every time he stopped, they alighted back on him. Like chicks imprinted to a hen. Despite everything—the pact, being on the run, her lost runes, and her stomach folding itself over in hunger—a smile quirked Lyss' lips.

"What did you do to them?" she asked, holding back a laugh as the rarkyn stopped to shoo them off.

Rark sighed. "I fed them." He hissed, swiping at several as they returned. Their forms warped around his talons, distorting like reflections in a pond. "Big mistake." He swatted again.

Lyss lingered a moment, then kept walking. He'd catch up once he'd managed to lose the critters. She crunched up a low rise, feeling the snow seeping through her boots and chilling her toes. Her fingers were getting cold too. She reached the top of the small hill and paused, listening to gauge how far Rark was behind. No sound of him. She relaxed her barriers and hunted for him across hugrokar. His link felt oddly muffled, like trying to listen to someone from behind a closed door.

"Rark?" she called. No response. She waited another moment and reached out again, pulling her mind close to his. He didn't seem to notice her presence. Odd.

Rark?

Her sense of him seemed muted, blurred even. *Obscured*, Lyss thought and wondered if she'd need to shout down hugrokar to be heard.

Rark? she tried again, with more force.

She sensed him grunt, then, "What?"

Lyss jumped and spun on the spot, just in time to see the rarkyn shift from a sylph-like shadow to his usual solid eight-foot frame. Steam curled off his feathers, eddying in circles before vanishing from sight. His hugrokar snapped sharp and Lyss caught a flash of annoyance at her interruption. She gaped. What in the five provinces had that been? A tendril of steam curl off one of his wing tips. *No, not steam,* she realized. *Aether.* By Sepp, he'd just stepped out of the Otherworld!

"Rasvenger," Rark said.

Lyss blinked.

"Is what we call it," Rark amended. "Means Aether flight."

"Have you always been able to do that?"

"No. Had to learn," Rark said. "Now have to practice before Illredus." He flashed her a toothy grin. "And good to stay warm. Works well, no?"

Lyss touched her hands together, nodding. He was right. Her toes were blissfully warm again. *Guess that's why I didn't need my coat earlier.* She paused as a new thought occurred to her. If she was sharing in the Otherworld's warmth, surely that meant some of the Aether's power trickled from Rark to her. Was that how she'd been able to use his magic to free herself from the galdar binding at the Order camp? How she'd used his gala ability? It had to be. She thought of the soldier she'd sent flying with her kick in the scuffle. Was this, and not the loss of Iga's rune, the cause behind her sudden strength? She cocked her head, curious.

"Why do you need to practice?"

"To go deeper," he said, simply, as if the answer had been obvious. He pointed a talon at her face. "To where you can't see. Even with second sight."

Lyss' eyebrows rose. She hadn't given any thought to how she'd get him into the city of mancers. It was too far off a problem to solve. But evidently Rark had. "Isn't that dangerous?" she asked.

Rark scratched the base of one horn. "Otherworld is always dangerous," he said.

"How dangerous?" Lyss pressed. Rark's hugrokar shied away from hers, like a child clasping a secret thing behind their back. Lyss scowled. She didn't know much about what lay in the Otherworld, but she knew there were things in it even mancers dared not summon. *"They lie deep,"* Iga had said once. Was that what she meant? She put her hands on her hips and waited, and the rarkyn shifted under her gaze. When he offered nothing, she gave a sigh. "Never mind." She waved the question off. *Whatever the risk, it can't be worse than walking into Illredus in broad daylight.* "Do what you like," she said and continued walking.

A crunch of snow at her back signaled him following.

"Might fall," Rark suddenly blurted.

Lyss stopped, heart thudding, legs turning heavy. "Into the Otherworld? Like a Fever?"

Rarkyn nodded. "Deep in, and no coming back." He ruffled his wings and lifted a hand to his head. "Aether eats at mind if I stay in for too long. Mistakes can happen. Is why we have hugrokar, helps keep us alert."

"I see," Lyss said, slowly. It must be why they shared pain too. Distracted was a dangerous thing to be in the Otherworld. She started walking again, turning the news over in her mind. If he fell into the Otherworld's depths, what would become of her? Rark caught her up with a few loping strides; anxiety radiated off him in waves.

Is he waiting for me to weigh-in? Lyss wondered. *For my nod of approval?* She lifted her head and watched her breath rise into the cloud-mottled sky.

"This...this could work," she said, thinking aloud. Time was short, winter in full swing, and the Order was after her head. If they were to survive this, playing it safe wasn't an option. "You said you needed to practice?"

Rark nodded.

A smile pulled at her mouth, and she swept a hand out at the forest. "Then practice."

CHAPTER TWENTY-SIX

Hasek,

I hope my eyree reaches you in time. Markides is hunting a rarkyn that has found its way into the Empire from the north. I believe the woman who assaulted our garrison is also after it. To what end I have not discovered.

I'm sending a young man to meet you at Nilos. His name is Darrin Eder, and he is brother to the boy Markides had with him. From what Darrin has told me, the boy has quite the talent for galdar and Markides has tricked him into his service. Darrin believes—as do I—that Markides has some plan to use him to trap the rarkyn. I worry what might happen should he succeed.

Do what you can for the pair, but do not get between Markides and the rarkyn.

Lastly, see if you can uncover more details from Darrin, I suspect I have only heard half the story.

Brennus

"Ho, young man."

Something hard prodded Darrin in the shoulder. Bleary-eyed, he woke to the bargeman standing over him.

"This is you."

Darrin unwrapped himself from his oil-skin cloak and peered over the lip of the barge. The boat bumped against a jetty, sending hollow thuds shivering through the craft. A connecting rope was looped over one pylon, twine creaking and straining as the water tried to pull the barge downstream. Beyond the jetty all Darrin could make out was mist. Mist and a dim gray sky.

"Go to the end and follow the road up," the bargeman said, jutting a finger out to the invisible shoreline.

"How do I get to the King's Road?"

The bargeman waved a hand at the mist. "Jus' follow the trail and you'll find it."

Blinking off the remainders of sleep, Darrin gathered his two saddlebags and threw them onto the jetty before stepping out himself. The wooden planks squeaked underfoot, and Darrin grabbed for a pylon as his boots slid on the dew-slicked timbers.

He turned to watch the bargeman unsling the rope and push the barge back into deeper water.

"Good luck lad," the man called and waved. The glow of runes along the barge's bow was the last thing Darrin saw before the fog folded over. He stood, listening to the quiet gurgle of water underneath the jetty, then threw his saddlebags over one shoulder and trod toward the embankment. It loomed out at him, the trees gradually taking shape within the shadow as he drew close and ascended the log staircase cut into the bank. At the top he found the track the bargeman had described snaking through the undergrowth, well-trodden and clear of debris. Darrin followed it, noting the deep ruts on each side of the trail.

A laden cart passed here not long ago. He pulled the red cloak tighter about him and lengthened his stride, recalling Captain Brennus' words.

"Don't dally. If you hurry, you'll make it."

The trail soon turned into a path, and the path into a churned and muddy road. Ahead, Darrin glimpsed the thatched rooftops of Koth hamlet peaking between black branches of pine.

"Go to the inn there," Brennus had instructed. *"They'll give you a horse. I've sent an eyree ahead of you."*

He reached the hamlet and counted down the row of cottages. Fourth one up from the river road, on the left. It was larger than the others, with a barn sharing one outer wall. Darrin pushed open the metal-work gate, and as its piercing squeak rang across the yard, a thin red-haired and bearded man poked his head out from the barn.

"You from Ira Garrison?"

Darrin nodded.

The man ducked back inside. Darrin heard the snort of a horse before the door swung open, and the man came out leading out a roan pony tacked up and ready to ride.

"Best I got at short notice," he said.

Darrin walked around the animal. The pony was a pale comparison to the mount he'd left behind at Ira Garrison. A small pang of regret twisted in his chest at that, but Darrin ignored it and gave the man a nod. "He'll do fine." He pulled out his coin pouch and handed over two iron aras.

The man turned the reins over and watched Darrin drape his two bags over the saddle, tie them down and then swing into the saddle himself. "How far to the King's Road?" Darrin asked, gathering the reins.

"'Bout a mile down road," the inn keeper said, pointing.

"And Nilos?"

"Half a day's ride."

Darrin nodded. "Good. Thank you." *I may just make it.*

"Take care on the pass into Nilos," the inn keeper said as Darrin drew level with the gate. "There have been reports of banditry."

"I will."

Darrin kicked his pony into a canter and in few heartbeats the hamlet of Koth dissolved into the mist like a dream. True to the inn keeper's word, the lane met the King's Road at a marked junction. Here Koth's travelers turned onto the wider, more traveled road. In summer months Darrin imagined the steady stream of merchants and journeymen feeding into the road like a tributary, bearing their loads of wares and produce south to Illredus. Out of the backwaters toward civilization he'd overheard a merchant say once.

Now, at winter's edge, the road was deserted. Darrin squinted at the weathered letters carved into the junction's stone waymarker. *Nilos. Fifteen miles.*

The arrival of the supply barge into the Ira Garrison couldn't have been better timed. No more than an hour after Brennus had got the story out of him, Darrin and his belongings were bundled up, packed on the barge and floated off down the Ira River. A day and a night on the water had covered what would have taken three on horseback. Luck had been on his side, Darrin knew, and he hoped it held just a little longer for him to find Brennus' scout.

The Captain had said his man would likely spend the night in Nilos.

"There's an Order outpost there," he'd said. *"He's burning galdar with a summoning, so he'll stop to rest, send news and collect supplies before heading off again."*

"What if I miss him?"

The graying Captain had sighed and squeezed Darrin's shoulder. *"Then you're on your own lad. I feel for you, I do, but my job is to protect the peace. I can't waste more men and resources chasing after lost children."*

Darrin had bit his lip. His lost child of a brother was in collusion with a mancer who was hunting his best friend and a kratting rarkyn for Sepp knew what purpose. Surely finding them before they did something reckless classified as keeping the peace. He had wanted to argue the point but knew better. He liked the Captain, but he doubted disputing the subject would sway the soldier's mind—or do himself any favors. The best thing for Hane now was to find him and get him away from Archer.

Use your head, Hane. Darrin thought as he spurred the pony on. *Don't do something you can't undo.* Fresh rage bloomed inside him at the thought. Curse that mancer. Curse him for bringing a rarkyn into Eder territory, curse his sly words and vain promises, and a double curse on himself for not seeing through it sooner.

Iga should have let him die in that rock-slip, he brooded. *If not for him…*

The thought spiraled into dark places, devouring time as he slipped into visions of what he might do to the mancer once he caught up.

His pony's gate dropping into a trot roused him. *"Don't dally,"* Brennus had warned, and the words stayed with him. Darrin put all thoughts of Archer aside, pulled the animal back into line and pushed him back into a canter.

Hours later, he rounded the top of the Nilos pass and spied the town sprawled across the distant rolling hills. He rode on, one hand resting on the pommel of his sword as he went, half expecting highway men to spring out of the bushes. No bandits came.

Perhaps his borrowed Order cloak had put them off, he mused. Many mancers were recruited into the Order to bolster the Illredian military. The result was that one could never be sure whether a red cloak was an ordinary soldier or one of the Empire's trained battle mancers—at least not at first glance.

The first sign of the Order's presence in Nilos came as a smell; a stomach-turning stench of sour decay that caught in his nose and wouldn't leave. Next, a caw of a carrion eater on the wind. Darrin steeled himself and pressed on. A quarter mile down the road, he passed under four towering gibbets, their hardwood beams bearing fruits of wrought iron cages. Three had occupants, all dead and slumped against the bars. Hanged first, then put on display; examples made. Darrin wanted to look away, but the grisly scene drew him in like an insect to a flame.

Livid bruising marked the neck of one as he rode past. Another corpse was missing a hand. An old injury Darrin guessed, the skin had long since healed over into a twisted, knotting scar. On the stump that remained, just below the elbow, was a faded red brand. The krat's brand. Darrin's stomach clenched, and a chill crawled up his spine. He stared at the circle of burned flesh. Two parallel lines cut through it; a krat of the second degree. He'd used illegal runes to deceive and swindle.

The third in the row bore six runes tattooed on his arms, three to each side. Darrin stopped. *A Krawan? Here?* He took in the olive skin and the mass of black hair that masked the man's face in tangled clumps.

What in Sepp's name were you doing so far from home? He wondered.

What had once been fine clothes were torn and spotted with ruddy stains, and a whiff of rotting fruit drifted down to Darrin as he passed below the cage.

This one hasn't been dead long.

"...Mercy."

Darrin started and glanced up. The corpse shifted. Its tangled hair parted revealing a withered face, sunken eyed and cracked lipped, and with a shock, Darrin realized he was staring up at a girl not much older than himself.

"Mercy," she croaked again. Her fingers reached between the bars; the fresh brand on her bony arm showed a circle with three strikes. Darrin stared at it. *A killer.* He swallowed. "I can't."

Her eyelids fluttered wider, and a pair of brilliant purple irises looked down on him. A prickle ran up Darrin's neck. A halfling: part human, part something else. A krat in the truest sense, damned from the moment she was born. He glanced back at the other two gibbets and their corpses. Had she been mixed up with them?

Darrin cleared his throat. "I cannot give you anything." To give her anything would only prolong the torture.

She rested her forehead on the bars, her broad face pressing into the metal. Definitely Krawan in there, but her slim jaw and pointed chin hinted at Illredian blood too.

Those strange purple eyes bored into him. "Please...kill me," she said, her voice as thick as her swollen tongue. "Make it end."

Darrin rocked back. "I can't," he blurted, snatching a glance down the road to the rooftops of Nilos. "I'm sorry." He gripped the pony's reins and squeezed his heels against its sides. The animal started walking again.

"Please..." the voice echoed after him. Darrin steeled himself, nudged his mount again and it sprang into a trot. Only when he reached the gate of Nilos did he unclench his fists from the reins. Even then, his hands still shook. *She won't end up like that.* The thought alone made the breath catch in his throat. *Gods, don't let Lyss end up like that.* He wiped his sweaty palms on the bottom of his tunic, dismounted and led the pony into town.

NILOS WAS A BUSTLING TOWN; A JUNCTION BETWEEN THE King's Road and Ira River to the west. History told that the Ira River had once run through the heart of the settlement, but a great earth tremor centuries ago had diverted the stream west—or so claimed a beggar-woman when she saw Darrin puzzling over the town's ambling and twisting main road.

White snow dusted the rooftops, but on the streets, it had turned to a boggy, cold slush that clumped on the soles of Darrin's boots. He rounded one corner and found himself in a wide town square. The dry riverbed ran through it and, within, a warren of stalls had sprung up, their canvas tops poking up in line with the cobblestone square. A bridge arched over this basin of commerce, and across the other side of the square, a flag bearing the shield insignia of the Order fluttered atop one archway.

"Steady up," a guard said, stepping out from the arch as Darrin's approached. "Papers please."

Darrin fumbled for his pocket, pulling out the scrawled note

Brennus had handed him before he'd left the garrison. The guard took it, glanced over it once, then nodded.

"We've been expecting you." He pointed down the road. "Follow this to the end and leave your pony with the stable hand." He indicated a long three-story log building on the left. "You'll find lodgings in the barracks there."

"Is Captain Brennus' scout here?" Darrin asked.

The guard raised one eyebrow. "We see a lot of scouts through 'ere. You got a name?"

Darrin furrowed his brow as he tried to recall the name Brennus had mentioned. "Havel? Harric?"

The guard shook his head and scratched his belly. "Ain't seen anyone like that today. Check at the barracks."

Darrin thanked the man and headed for the stables. Once his pony was seen to, he wandered back through the quarter, spying a busy kitchen and laundry room through the windows of the first-floor barracks. He found the entrance the guard had pointed out and went in.

"Name and unit," said a man at the desk just inside the door. He tapped a bound volume lying open on the counter. Darrin picked up the quill and hesitated.

"Can't write?" The man beckoned for the quill. "Pass it over."

"It's not that," Darrin said, and handed over Brennus' note instead. "I'm not part of the Order."

The man's eyes darted over the note. "Ah, you're the one from Brennus." He rummaged under the desk, clicked a key in a lock and thumped another smaller volume open on the desk. He flipped through several pages before finding a blank one.

"Name?" he asked, quill poised over the paper.

"I can write it myself," Darrin offered.

"No can do. These pages contain sensitive information about some of our guests," the officer said.

Sensitive information on your informants you mean, Darrin thought as he gave his name, where he'd traveled from and who'd sent him. His gut twisted, did that mean he was one too? An Order spy who reported any dubious behavior and magics to the realm?

No, it was just a once off. Brennus had made that clear. The Order's help and resources to catch up to Hane in return for carrying the intel about Archer and his pursuit of the rarkyn to Brennus' scout.

"You're in room twenty-four," the man at the desk said. "Up the stairs and on the left. If you're quick, you'll make the lunch hour in the mess."

"Is Brennus' scout here?" Darrin asked.

The man shook his head. "Not yet, I expect he'll arrive just before sundown." He held up a hand as Darrin opened his mouth. "I'll let him know you're here."

Darrin thanked the man and left.

The room was plain: a bed, closet, writing table, and a single window overlooking the barracks' interior courtyard. Rows of wooden training mannequins lined one wall, several sporting crossbow bolts embedded in their barrel chests. Darrin turned away and slumped onto the bed, his thoughts returning to the halfling girl trapped in the gibbet. No one, no matter how bad the crime, deserved that kind of slow death. Yet here he was in the belly of the beast that had sanctioned it. A beast that would do the same to Hane and Lyss if it found out what they were. His skin crawled.

A KNOCK SOUNDING AT THE DOOR OF HIS ROOM JOLTED Darrin out of a doze. He opened his eyes to find his room awash in the red-orange light of late afternoon. He'd been asleep for hours. The knock sounded again, and he levered himself off the bed, massaging out a crick in his neck as he went to answer it.

A sandy-haired soldier stood outside. His chin bore a week-old beard of red stubble and his cloak was flaking dry mud.

"Good, you're dressed," he said and held up a scroll with a broken wax seal and a smudged claw print of an eyree on its surface. "Brennus says you're joining me."

"You're—" Darrin began.

"Corporal Praetus Galen Hasek," the soldier said, offering a hand. He looked Darrin up and down as they shook hands. "How soon can you leave?"

Darrin glanced back at his unopened saddlebags hanging on the back of the writing desk chair. "Depends on where we're going."

"North-east, back into the ranges."

A glimmer of hope rose in Darrin's chest. "You mean Archer and Hane haven't come through Nilos yet?"

"They left the King's Road some days ago to take a more direct line over the ranges. It's rugged country up there, they won't be through for some time yet. I suspect they'll bypass Nilos entirely and emerge somewhere near Torin."

That meant Lyss and the rarkyn were probably somewhere in the ranges too. If that were true, it also meant long days and cold nights for him with no food and shelter waiting at an inn on the road. "I'll need to restock my supplies," Darrin said, collecting his bags from the chair.

Hasek gave a nod. "Talk to the kitchens downstairs. Take only what you can carry. Meet me at the north-east gate at dusk—the one flying the flag of an eagle. Don't be late," he said, and turned to leave. Halfway down the corridor he stopped. "Oh, and don't worry about bringing your horse."

He left Darrin frowning in his wake, but his confusion soon vanished when he caught sight of the sun out the window. Its golden disc hovered over the tip of the western range. He had barely an hour before the Corporal's deadline. He darted about the room, checking nothing was left behind before he scooped up his saddle bags and headed downstairs.

At the kitchen he managed to beg two loaves of hard, crusty bread, cheese and a sack of gruel from a belligerent cook. He left the kitchens with the man loudly swearing to any who'd listen that his stores wouldn't last another ten-day at this rate.

"First Lady Leandre with her fifteen, then Corporal Hasek, and now *this*," he cussed.

"Careful sir," came the voice of his young kitchen hand as Darrin rounded the hall. "Don't let the Lieutenant Regis hear you call her that, she'll burn holes into you with her eyes."

"Ha! I'd like to see her try."

Darrin lost the end of the conversation as he hurried on, stuffing the supplies into his saddlebags as he went. After signing out of the guest registry by the non-plussed attendant, he made his way back through the street. The crowds were out, and they strode the street with bent purpose as they made use of the last daylight to run their errands. Darrin bumped past several townsfolk, earning glares as he went, and broke into a run when he saw the eagle flag atop a parapet in the distance.

He arrived at the gate just as the sun dipped below the peaks and the long shadow of the mountains eclipsed the town. Panting, he scoured the people milling about the great wooden walls and its threshold. No Hasek. He checked at the guard station and with the two city guards watching the crowd. Nothing. A bell sounded from the parapet above the gate. Two more guards appeared and together with the two on duty, they heaved the doors free from their resting place. The hinges groaned like an elder forced out of bed too early in the winter.

Where is he? Darrin ground his teeth, casting his gaze back through the street and then to the dry, grassy meadow beyond the wall. *After all that talk of not being late.*

"Which is it lad, in or out?" Darrin jumped and turned find the doors half shut and a guard's head poking out from behind one.

"Out." Darrin scuttled through, then watched the streets of Nilos disappear behind the thick timbers. Abruptly the groaning stopped, and from behind the doors, a great beam was dropped into place with a wooden thud.

For a moment Darrin stood, looking up at the gate some twenty paces high. If Hasek didn't come he was in for a long, cold night outside. He shifted his saddlebags on to his other shoulder. Best get on with it then. Hasek had said Hane and Archer were still in the western ranges. That was where he'd go. He eyed the mountains rimming the valley—they were a long way off, on foot or not.

"Ho! There you are," a familiar voice made Darrin look round. Hasek jogged into view along the eastern perimeter, two saddle bags slung over one shoulder. Jogged Darrin noted, but not out of breath. Where had he come from? And where was his mount?

"You're late," he said as Hasek met him.

"Some business up by the east gate to see to," Hasek said. "Are you ready?"

When it was clear that was the only explanation Hasek would offer, Darin nodded.

"Good." From around his neck Hasek produced a whistle and Darrin caught the telltale green glow of a summoning circle engraved into its surface before the soldier put it to his lips and blew. No sound came from it, but the hairs on the back of Darrin's neck prickled. *Just like when Hane casts. The man's a mancer. A strong one.* A little stab of envy pricked inside him and he quashed it. Wishing wouldn't change anything.

When it came to runes, he was even more inept than Lyss. Only he accepted it, where she did not. Had not. Now, he wasn't so sure. The rarkyn had changed something in her—that much he knew.

"Stand back," Hasek warned, jerking Darrin back to the present. "Let him smell you."

The air shifted before them, shimmering and roiling like a heat haze. At its epicenter a great shadowy paw emerged, then another. A long white muzzle of bone followed as the creature stepped out.

A burning in his lungs made Darrin release the breath he'd been holding. A shuck. Its three silver eyes swung to fix on him.

"He is bound to my will, he will not harm you," Hasek said, just as Darrin caught himself taking an involuntary step backwards. He planted his foot back on the ground, forcing himself still. *Bound to his will,* he repeated Hasek's words. *That means he knows its name.* Aetherlings did not give up their names willingly. To prize it out of the creature he would have had to best it first. Or consult the Book of Names. Darrin couldn't imagine the Conclave permitting a mere Corporal the right to the creature's name, not when so many other higher ranked soldiers could make use of it.

Darrin stared as Hasek placed a hand on the beast's shoulder and it lowered its belly to the ground. *He's no ordinary mancer.* To best a shuck meant his galdar abilities were at least at the rank of Praetus. Such skill was highly sought after, even Darrin knew that. What was he doing out in the far reaches of the Empire?

"We will make good time with Naqamal," Hasek said, then grimaced, "even if it's not entirely comfortable."

Comfortable? Before Darrin could ask what he meant, Hasek kicked a leg over the beast's back.

"We're *riding* it?" Darrin choked out, composure forgotten.

"Of course, how else are we going to head them off? Nothing can outrun a shuck." Hasek motioned to the space behind him. "Naqamal can easily carry the two of us," he patted the crown of the bone skull. "Normally I'd summon my second shuck but—" he cast an accusing eye at Darrin "—your friend killed it."

Still battling to get his head around the thought of riding a shuck, Darrin almost missed what he said. *My friend?* He couldn't be talking about Hane or Archer. That meant—his heart gave a lurch. "You've seen Lyss?"

Hasek's eyebrows rose, a wiry smile crossing his face. "Ah, so that's her name."

Kratting loud-mouthed idiot. Darrin cursed himself, grappling to keep his face impassive. He must have given something away because Hasek gave a chuckle.

"It's fine," he said. "I won't tell." He waved the issue aside with a gloved hand. "Now get on, we're wasting time."

THEY RODE WELL INTO THE NIGHT. IN THE DARK, DARRIN felt like he was riding the night itself. Despite the shuck's translucent body, it was firm under him. It was impossible to gauge how fast they moved. The shuck's body stretched and bunched in a rolling, loping gate, its feet no more than a whisper over the earth. The wind tossed Darrin's hair, dragged at his cloak, and burned his cheeks. Cold began to bite through his clothes. Grimly, he clung to his saddle bags, fastened tight around the shuck's middle. *Hold on.*

The chill worsened, and Darrin thought longingly of the oilskin bundled in his saddlebags. He closed his eyes, trying to ignore the ache building in his legs as he gripped the shuck's sides with his knees. *I'm coming Hane.* But it wasn't Hane's face that flashed through his mind. It was Lyss', with the wry grin she wore when she thought she had the upper hand in one of their sparring matches. If not for the rarkyn. *If not for Hane and I.*

Stop it.

Darrin opened his eyes, and with a start realized the shuck was standing still.

"Why'd we stop?"

"Camp ahead," Hasek said over his shoulder. Darrin peered past him and wondered how the soldier could see anything in the dark. "Another squadron."

Hasek shifted on the shuck's back and a far-off fire winked into view. He squinted.

No good, all he could make out were the dancing lights of the flames and shadow upon shadow.

"It must be the Leandre," Hasek muttered.

Darrin didn't recognize the name.

"A Lieutenant Regis up from Illredus," Hasek continued, and Darrin heard the sneer in his voice without having to see it. "Here to lend assistance to the north." He sniffed. "A show of force more like. A reminder to us up here that Illredus is watching."

Darrin raised an eyebrow, even though he knew Hasek wouldn't see it. "Aren't you part of the Order?"

Hasek turned on him. "You think we all get along like pigs in a trough?"

Well, yes, Darrin thought, but knew that was not the answer the Corporal was looking for. At his silence Hasek gave a sigh.

"We're not all monsters. Not all of us. Some of us are trying to do good."

Darrin stared at Hasek's back, not sure how to respond, or even if he should. Hasek straightened. "We'll go round," he announced. "I have no wish to cross paths with Leandre. She's as fanatic as they come."

He tapped the crown of the shuck's skull and the beast took up its lope again.

As they moved past the light, Darrin could have sworn he saw two red orbs track their progress from beside the fire. *Sighted eyes.* The thought left his skin crawling.

Under him, the shuck shuddered. Its shadow-coat thinning, and Darrin glimpsed rock and grass through the aetherling's back. Hasek spat out a curse, brought the shuck to a standstill with a tap to its shoulders.

"I am Corporal Praetus Hasek of Orthus Brigade. Let me pass."

Footsteps sounded in the dark, heavy and shuffling. A light flared—a fire rune set in a lantern—held up by the biggest man Darrin had ever seen. He hunched as much as stood, neck corded muscle, red jerkin glowing under the rune light. A night watchman. A sword hung on his hip; his free hand relaxed against it.

Hasek slid off the shuck, Darrin followed. Behind, the shuck shifted, and in the dim, Darrin spotted a rune point and the arcing circle of a ward before the aetherling's feet, activated at their approach. He squinted back at the guard. A second ward encircled the giant's feet.

"Orthus you say?" the man rumbled. "One of Brennus'? You're a long way from your garrison." His eyes narrowed. "You a deserter?"

"Not a deserter. On assignment."

The rune-light swung to Darrin and he blinked as it flared brighter. "And this one?"

"My aide."

"And your assignment?"

The shuck released a low growl, circling around its master. Hasek pressed a hand to its white skull. "That's between me and my Captain."

The giant's fingers squeezed around his sword hilt.

"Let them pass, Hecaelon." A voice drawled from the black. Hasek stiffened as a tarsie-like creature stepped out. It was shorter of fur and lither than the antlered tarsie the Wildners mustered in the mountains. Cloven hooves picked soundlessly toward them, the gray and black bands on its flanks shifting under the rune light. A single horn rose out of its head, shaved down to a half-stump. *Kardunn,* Darrin recognized. *Windrunners,* Iga called them. Very rare.

On top of it rode a woman, hair the same color as her gold-plated armor, red eyes flashing from him to Darrin to the shuck between them. "I know him, he's one of Brennus' scouts. Isn't that right, Corporal?"

Hasek's jaw clenched. "Yes, Lieutenant."

The woman surveyed them, searching the dark at their backs. "You seem to be missing an aetherling, Corporal. Last we met, you commanded two." She cocked an ear, listening to the night.

"Just the one now."

"Ah, unfortunate. A krat then?" Her expression hardened and she leaned forward in the kardunn's saddle, her stare unblinking. A chill rippled through Darrin. Hairs prickling as a faint pressure washed over him.

Hasek remained steadfast. "It was."

"You delt with the heathen?"

"Brennus is seeing to it."

Leandre studied them a moment longer. "Well then, Corporal. I shall not keep you." She nodded to her second. "Release the circle. Let the men be on their way."

Hasek gave the woman a short salute. "Thank you, Lieutenant." He led the shuck toward the runes and guided it over. The aetherling shivered as it crossed.

"And Hasek," Leandre called as Darrin settled back onto the creature. "We received an eyree from Nilos this evening. A young krat escaped the gibbets. You wouldn't happen to know anything about that, would you?"

Hasek paused. Only Darrin saw the slight quiver in the hand around the shuck's neck. "No, sir."

CHAPTER TWENTY-SEVEN

S KAAR'S HUGROKAR TWINGED, PULLING LIKE AN overstretched muscle as he dove deeper into the Otherworld. The trees of Terresmir lost their color, fading to muted tones of gray and brown, their shapes appearing ever-so-slightly out of focus.

The Aether thrummed in his bones, pulsing through every fiber. It hummed through his skull and into his ears, coating everything in a faint echo that fuzzed his thoughts.

You're at your limit, Raska's voice lectured out of his memory. A twitch of his tail leveled out his dive and he coasted on a misty current that wove through Terresmir's shadows. Just a little longer. He closed his eyes and drew the heat into him.

Stop. Lyss' warning flashed through hugrokar and with unnerving power the bond snapped tight, gagging him like a dog on a chain. His lungs emptied, chest constricted, and he flared his wings. For a moment he flailed, unable to sense Terresmir at all. The bond twinged once more. He wheeled upwards, following the link, reaching for the dregs of the Aether he sensed in the air of Terresmir.

He ripped out of the Otherworld and straight into a frigid gale sweeping off the mountains—and dropped like a stone.

Reythr curse this thin air. He beat his wings to regain altitude, wind buffeting him as he circled down toward the ridges. The peaks rose into the sky like jagged teeth, and he dipped over into one valley, spying the rooftops of a human settlement nestled in the trees of its western slope. The girl was some distance up the road, trudging through ankle deep snow, her cloak loose and coat tied about her waist. A ring of sweat stained the collar of her tunic and she'd pushed the sleeves up past her elbows. Her face turned skyward as he passed overhead. Skaar caught the white-orange glint of the shuck skull on her back in the long afternoon light.

"That was unpleasant," she said, pursing her lips as he dropped the last few feet to the snow. Displeasure radiated from her, almost as much as the pinching emptiness in her belly that doubled Skaar's own. "Felt like someone sitting on my chest." She rubbed her breastbone and frowned. "I thought you'd be able to go further than that before it pulled taut."

"Otherworld is not like Terresmir," Skaar said, furling his wings. "Distances are different." *Especially the deeper you go.* He stepped off the open road, sheltering under the trees. The forest had turned into a sparse woodland along this section of valley, but it was better than nothing. "Village ahead," he explained at Lyss' quizzical look. She brightened.

"How big?"

"A few homes."

Lyss fell silent a moment, pondering. Her hands dug through her pockets and loose coins rattled as she drew out a pouch and opened it. The lines on her forehead grew and she chewed her lip.

"One ara; three quinus," she muttered. "That won't go far."

"Enough to eat?" Skaar asked, hopefully. He'd long grown tired of their diet of wild mushrooms foraged from the side of the road.

"Yes, enough to eat." Lyss rolled her eyes. "For now."

Skaar shrugged. "Is good then."

Lyss sighed. "I was hoping for a horse."

"You're making good time on your feet," Skaar pointed out. Even he'd been surprised. With the Aether in her muscles, she'd struck out at a mile-eating pace and stuck to it for the last three days without trouble. It was unnerving. Nothing a normal human was capable of.

Lyss returned the pouch to her pocket, cupped a hand to her brow and squinted into the distance. "At this point, I'll take anything that's more than the clothes on my back."

THE NIGHT HAD WELL AND TRULY TAKEN HOLD BY THE TIME they saw rooftops from the road. Skaar took to the sky without a word, leaving Lyss to continue to the settlement alone on foot. The gale battered him as he climbed, whistling in his ears as he circled east over the opposite side of the valley and alighted on a narrow plateau to wait. It began to snow and Skaar watched entranced as the wind spiraled the flakes through the air.

It's empty. He started as Lyss spoke across hugrokar. His ears pricked, gaze turning to the village across the valley, not sure he'd understood.

No one is here, Lyss said. Her heartbeat quickened across the link. Something wasn't right. *Do you see any lights?*

Skaar examined the town from his perch. It was dark and silent.

No lights, he confirmed, and imagined Lyss' curse in reply. If the town was abandoned, chances were they'd find little of use there. He stood up, ruffling his wings open.

Lyss' hugrokar gave a sudden wrenching twist. Fear crashed into him so intense a half-strangled cry escaped him before he could stop it. *Too close again.* Across the valley, a shout rose on the wind. Panic plumed in his chest, sending chilling fingers of ice rippling through his veins.

Skaar pushed his mind close. *What is it?*

An image flashed into his head: a cobblestone street littered with— the gorge rose in Lyss' throat and Skaar wrenched their hugrokars apart.

I'm coming.

Skaar shook out the ruff of feathers turning on end around his throat and spread his wings. The wind pulled at his feathers, catching under him as he sprang. His wings beat down and he lifted into the night. At the center of the valley, he stopped climbing and glided towards the village.

He passed low over the thatched roofs. *I hope she's right about it being empty.* With a twist of his magic, he crossed into the Otherworld, just in case. In rasvenger, the soothing heat of the Aether washed through him, gloriously warm. At the back of his skull, the pressure built, grinding away at his mind like a whetstone. *Too much Aether.*

He passed over the village. Lyss had been right. No people. No lights. He circled back to the center: a small square of intersecting roads. At its heart lay a raised flowerbed of trampled shrubs with a stump of a giant tree trunk in its middle. Lyss stood before it, head bowed, waiting. At his approach she turned, eyes tracking him through the Otherworld as he glided down and slipped out of rasvenger to land on the cobblestones.

Not deep enough. Skaar noted and stopped as the smell of blood hit him.

What he'd thought of as a tree trunk was not.

It was a mound of corpses.

Human corpses.

They were piled on top of one another, gruesome building blocks of hacked limbs, gutted bellies and slit throats. A hand, fingers twisted and broken, poked out from the mass. A blistered burn graced its palm: a circle with three lines. Skaar stared at it. He knew that symbol. He searched the pile, found one burned onto a forearm, another on a neck. These were not the first humans he'd seen branded this way. What had Archer called them? *"Krat,"* he said. "They all are."

Next to him Lyss' hugrokar wavered. "These are, but it's worse up the road." She swallowed hard and pointed down the lane she'd come in on. "Back there they were cut down in the street. Even children. They didn't have the Brand."

Skaar crouched before the pyre and sniffed. No stink of rot. They'd not been dead long. Half a day, maybe less. Browning blood still oozed down the garden bed and into the cobbles, spreading a red web across the square. The sight was eerie, yet familiar. He felt it pick at the old ache in his chest. He shuddered and coiled his hugrokar tight. *So much cruelty.* Baffling.

Lyss moved to a large wooden wall erected on the opposite side of the square. A noticeboard. He'd seen others like it along human roads before. Just like the others, this one had paper of varying degrees of yellow nailed to it. Some bore pictures, yet most were covered in the human's illegible scrawl, their ink fading and corners peeling. However, unlike the rest, this one board displayed two sheets of fresh parchment nailed at its center. Each sheet bore an insignia at its top: a red and gold shield.

A growl rumbled up Skaar's throat. *The Order.* Next to him Lyss stood, fists clenched eyes darting along one fine-script line to the next.

"What does it say?"

For a moment she didn't answer, and when Skaar relaxed his hold on his hugrokar her anger roiled through to him. She cleared her throat.

"Notice is hereby given to the occupiers of Bern hamlet that they are guilty of the following charges: insubordination, harassment of public officials, sympathizing with criminals, tax evasion, and the aiding and abetting illegal magics.

"By breaking the First Law, your lands are to be seized and turned over to the Crown immediately. Lieutenant Regis Eugenia Leandre of the Rose Brigade." Lyss' gaze lingered on the last words. Something flickered in her hugrokar; a yawning rage that echoed in the pit of his belly. It was gone as quick as it had come as she pulled her hugrokar tight. "They must have fought back," she said.

And were slaughtered for it, Skaar thought. He pointed at the second paper. "What this?"

Lyss' glanced over it. "It's a warrant. For Asen Marin, Petya Manus and Nina and Brinhild Reiner. Wanted by the Crown for wielding illegal magics and inciting violence."

The first three names on the list had sharp, precise strikes through them. *Probably caught during the raid,* Skaar guessed, turning to take in the rest of the square. The houses were not big by any measure. Most were simple one-story cottages, many with their front doors ajar, one even half-cocked on a single hinge. True to Lyss' assessment, they were empty; their windows dark, hearths silent. All this he knew, yet his insides crawled, and he couldn't shake the feeling that no matter which way he turned, a crossbow bolt was being wound up and trained on his back.

Across the square, Lyss shuddered. "Let's check the storehouse and then get out of here," she said and made toward a long, high-roofed structure at the square's southern end. The giant double doors were shut, secured with a simple drop latch. Lyss lifted the timber and pushed a door open.

A clamor of scents reached Skaar's nose: wood, grains, herbs, and livestock.

"Sepp damn," Lyss' muffled voice sounded and Skaar stepped inside, squinting as his eyes adjusted to the dim light. Rows of crates, barrels, and bales were stacked high to the roof. Several lay open, their contents spilled across the floor, mingling with a series of dry, muddy footprints, as if the village folk had grabbed all they could carry and fled.

Skaar went over to an open clay crock and sniffed, a faint gamey smell wafted up his nostrils. *This is—*

"Salted meat," Lyss finished his thought. She tapped a barrel. "This one's grain. And those," she pointed at the bales at the end of the store-house, "un-spun wool."

Skaar eyed a long drag mark on the floor. Someone had hauled further supplies away from here.

Lyss drew her cloak around her, suddenly cold. "All their winter stores. Just left behind."

"No time to take it," Skaar said, simply. *Especially if they were running for their lives.* The thought welled inside him, stirring an old edge of panic and a flash of that heart-in-mouth flight with Fengar. He shivered and pushed the memories away. The girl's hugrokar gave a guilty, almost embarrassed, quiver as he did, like a kit caught nosing where they shouldn't. Skaar ignored it. The memory had lost much of its sting anyway. But best not to dwell on it too long; others from that time still cut to the bone.

He lifted the lid of the crock and the game smell hit the back of this throat. Mutton he guessed. Saliva pooled in his mouth.

"I wonder if any escaped?" Lyss pondered as Skaar helped himself to the contents of the crock. She walked down the row, stopping to pry off the top of a crate and rummage inside. She came away with a handful of red bulbous roots, which she rolled between her fingers. "These fends are still fresh. They can't have been gone long."

She bit into one, grimaced at the taste, but kept chewing. At another crate she was rewarded with dried linca fruits. These released a sickly-sweet smell as she dug into them, pocketing several as she went. She continued down the length of the store house, pausing only to try the knob of a single door built into the wall. "Locked," she announced with a sigh, turning away.

Skaar finished the rest of the crock as they explored the storehouse and began on another until the salt made him so desperately thirsty he had to stop.

"Here," Lyss emptied a bale of wool and presented him with its empty sack. "Fill it with as much as you can carry." She made another one for herself and set about the storeroom with it.

Lyss broke the silence again much later as she tied off the end of her sack with a bit of twine she'd undone from a dangling bundle of gammun leaves, "That should last a while." Skaar twisted the end of his own bulging bundle into a knot.

Outside the wind had begun to howl, rattling the storehouse's single window. Skaar turned toward the entrance, mood evaporating at the wet slap of sleet hitting the roof. Lyss stood next to him, staring at the doors in grim silence.

"There will be no sleeping in that tonight," Her gaze slid to the wool bales. "We could make do here."

The thought of the dead right outside their door sent Skaar's feathers bristling. All that blood…

If it were in the Otherworld the place would be crawling with ginndir. He thought of the stories Fengar had told him of the Eaters of the Deep. Monstrosities of flesh, he'd called them. Some the size of trees, others no bigger than a rodent, each a jumble of limbs and body parts morphed and grew with every new thing they ate—including each other. He shivered.

"I don't like it either," Lyss continued, "but it's just one night. Until the storm blows over."

Skaar mulled a moment longer, listening to the sleet clattering on the timbers, and nodded. Lyss let her bundle slump back to the floor. Skaar stowed his own beside it and returned to the clay crocks, opening another: fish this time. Further off, Lyss had returned to the single door. She pulled at the door's iron handle. It still didn't budge. She examined the keyhole, furrowed her brow, then turned on Skaar.

"Can you use rasven-whats-it to get past this?"

"Rasvenger," Skaar said, ducking his head as his horns scraped a rafter. He considered the door. There was a gap underneath, and no sign of runes. "Yes, probably."

"Probably? You're not sure?"

Skaar shrugged. "Is more difficult."

"You can't just pass through it like the snow?"

"Wood is solid, snow is not. The Otherworld flows around it, not through."

Lyss cocked her head, "How do you fly through the forest while in rasvenger?"

"Like this." Skaar stepped forward, shifting into the Otherworld. The door became indistinct, and he concentrated on the flow of Aether around the object. He stepped closer and slipped his fingers underneath the gap. *Reythr, it's small.* Not like slipping between a couple of tree trunks at all. Skaar followed the pull of the Aether's current, drawing deeper, then deeper again until the pressure of the door against his hand eased. He took a breath and pushed through, feeling the magic contort around him. A heartbeat later the pressure let up and he was able to straighten back to his feet.

The dim room beyond was just visible through the Otherworld. Its features sharpened as he tried to make out its shape: a low ceiling and wood floor. *A hallway*. He reached for Terresmir. For a moment he grappled to sense the material plane, then with a flash of relief he had it. He shifted out of rasvenger.

A hot burn stabbed through his horns and down his skull, all the way to the tip of his tail, sending his head spinning as it went. He grunted, staggered and sucked in a sharp breath of cool Terresmiran air.

What was that? Lyss' mind snapped close, alarmed.

Too much Aether in one day, Skaar sent back. Clutching his head, he groped for the door, found a latch, lifted it and let Lyss in.

"Are you sure you're alright?"

Skaar nodded. "Just need rest." He padded down the hall, leaving Lyss to untie her sodden boots, tuck them under an arm and continue in her socks. They emerged into a room with a stone hearth at one end and a variety of pots, pans and ladles hanging on hooks above. A set of knives gleamed on a workbench next to it.

Skaar stepped forward, thinking to inspect the knives, when a cold prickle spread up his arms. He vaulted back into the hall, hissing, feathers flaring. *Galdar!* He braced himself for the icy stab of a casting. None came. He shuffled closer and peered in.

"It's a kitchen."

Skaar started at the sound of Lyss' voice behind make him. "They probably used runes to cook." She wrinkled her nose and gave a small shudder. "Does all galdar feel like this?"

"Some kinds are worse than others."

Lyss studied him, hazel eyes glinting in the low light. "What kinds?"

"Castings hurt more," Skaar said, and tapped his forearm. "Since they touch."

"Double punishment," Lyss mused. "First the touch of the casting, then the intended effect of the spell." She rubbed her gritty nails over one wrist, right above the runes Skaar sensed there—as had become her habit. She sighed as if the news were lead on her shoulders. "Wonderful."

Skaar edged along one wall toward the door at the room's end. It opened into a wide chamber filled with tables and chairs, several upended.

"Must be an inn," Lyss remarked, running a hand over the head of a chair. "Fa and I used to stay in these all the time." Something tremored across hugrokar and she closed her eyes. "What I wouldn't give for a mug of chara and a warm bath."

"Not good idea to light a fire here."

Lyss weaved between the furniture, leaving damp footprints in her wake. "I know."

Skaar followed and a loud creak sang out from the wood floor under him. He started, scurrying back a step. *Reythr damn it, jumping at crickets again.*

A laugh sprang from the girl. It echoed around the room; loud and brazen against the still of the house. Skaar shot her a look and her smile faded, understanding taking over.

"You've never been inside a human dwelling, have you?"

Skaar's ears flattened, crest bristling into a scowl. *I was locked in a prison cart for six summers, what do you think?* He didn't let the thought reach her, but something of its intent must have trickled through because Lyss' smile vanished and guilt rose through her hugrokar.

"Sorry," she said. "I forgot."

Skaar huffed. "No matter." He moved past her into the hall, stopping outside the first door and tentatively testing the handle. It shifted, and the door opened. They peered in. Some sort of sleeping quarters.

"What was it like, with him? That mancer."

"Archer?" Skaar paused, mulling it over. He hadn't started out hating the man. After all, Archer had saved him from the Aether. At one point, Skaar might have considered him a friend, as much as a strange, featherless, flat-toothed creature—as he'd thought of them then—could be. Archer's company hadn't been anything like being part of a pack, but it'd been the next best thing. All that changed at Myron Keep.

"He was kind once, until he lost his heart," Skaar said, finally. "Lost family. It changed him. Made him angry."

Lyss nodded. "I can understand that."

Skaar fixed his gaze on her. "Made him cruel."

Her hugrokar flickered, uneasy.

"We made deal. He promised to take me back to the wilds if I helped him. Lent him power. Then he got greedy. Refused to take off the sigil." One more month, Archer had kept promising. Lies every time. Skaar shifted, half expecting Lyss to ask what he meant by "lent power". But she stayed quiet, listening. "He wanted more. Took more and more. I tried to escape, but he caught up, put me in the cart," he finished. "The rest you know."

He recalled his brief window of freedom. The rush; the elation; the joy of the air in his feathers again. He'd run until his legs could carry him no more and then taken to the sky. Archer's berigan had found him a day later. With the sigil clamped on his wrist, he'd not been able to stop it. The aetherling had knocked him senseless, and when he'd next woken it had been from inside the prison cart. The despair that had followed had been crushing, a giant pit of black worse than the abyss.

"I won't do that to you," Lyss said.

Skaar turned, surprised, and studied the girl. Her hawk eyes met his, a fierce ball of muscle and willpower—albeit quite a grubby one now— whose head barely reached his elbow. "I swear it," she said. "We'll break this pact. You will be free to return to your people. And I will be free to go after Loric."

Skaar took in her set jaw. She was determined, he'd give her that. But her conviction niggled at him, and all he could think was: *If only promises were enough.*

CHAPTER TWENTY-EIGHT

Dearest Elena,

Apologies for the long months with no news. We are in Klymene. It boggles the mind how the province of Phaia stretches so far into the Spine. Up here, they call our Illredian tongue Trader speak—yet the locals know it, even if their way of intoning is odd on the ears. They are a friendly folk, yet when we tell them we're from the capital there is always a near imperceptible shift. Their backs stiffen, their smiles turn forced, and the warmth vanishes from their eyes.

There is little love for the Empire here.

These folk were the worst done by when Kallion came into power. His and Therrin's iron-clad stance on galdar and other magics has all but branded these people as krats. The rest of Phaia, indeed the Empire, shuns them, so I guess it's no surprise they are wary. There are signs of what these people once were: beautiful stone works through the mountain side, balanced at impossible angles, turning slowly in the breeze for no other reason than to awe. Many are no more than piles of rubble. I do not know what drives our Crown's fear, but I worry it's eroding everything our lands once were.

Enough depressing talk, what of Isaac you ask? And our charge? Isaac is well, although a bit grumpy since I told him we would only remain in Klymene for a few hours; long enough to pick up provisions and for me to scribe this letter. I told him he should send word to his father—despite all the man's faults—but he turned down that idea before I had even finished airing it. You know what he said to me?

"You are more of a father than he ever was."

Word for word. Turns out my old rambunctious apprentice has a soft spot. It was quite touching.

Tykee fares well too. He has not stopped growing. As he stands, he is a head taller than Isaac. If he grows any more, he will not be able to fit in our wagon! The kit, if you can still call him that, has picked up our "Trader speak" too. Far quicker than I would ever have thought. Rarkyn are no dumb beasts or half-men, Elena. There is a shock of intelligence there, but it is more than that. They are cunning. Or, at least, this one is. He's already worked out how to pick the lock to our food chest. I had to put a sigil on the lock to put a stop to it. He found a way around that too—Sepp only knows how, the sigil on his wrist is still on. Not long after my last letter, he got hold of a cooking knife and tried to pry the manacle off. Near slit his wrists. Blood everywhere. And he wouldn't let either of us near him to heal it. Not that it mattered. A day later it was little more than a scab.

I've since engraved another rune on the sigil to stop him tampering with it. He did not appreciate that at all. For three days he hissed at me every time I got close. It's taken some weeks for him to understand the sigil is a temporary thing. He was trapped in the Otherworld for a long time, months at least, and it's left its mark—that silver eye and ginndir horns. If I release the sigil now, he'll fall straight back in. Once I'm sure the Aether has released its hold, I'll begin reducing the power of the runes. It's slow progress, but I hope to have the sigil off before we get too far into the Steppes. Isaac has begun teaching it Ludus in the hopes the game will take its mind off the sigil.

I know I was the one who set this mission for us, but I'll be glad once it's done. Six months is a long time to be away. I miss my home and my family, as small as we are. While I'm sure you've done a superb job in my absence, I worry what Councillor Keteus is up to. There are rumblings of discontent wherever we go these days. People out here praise the rebellious few who stand against the Crown—though never openly. I feel it in their gaze, in every interaction with us. I feel it, and I am certain Isaac does too. It concerns me. These people here are a gentle folk, but push them too far, and they are sure to push back.

Love,

Papa.

IT WAS CLOSE TO DAWN WHEN SHE HEARD THEM. THE STORM outside had masked their approach; the rain and sleet had stopped, but still the wind gusted. At first, she'd thought them creaking timbers from a neighboring building, or a loose fence plank toppling in the squall. Slowly, the sounds resolved in the noise, a grating, grinding of wheels on stone, a creaking of axles, and a persistent knocking of a trace and pole. *A cart.*

Lyss rose from her watch at the window, wincing at the pull of new skin at her shoulder as she reached for her boots. They were icy as she slid her feet inside, the leather gone stiff in the cold. Mud flaked into her hands as she tied the laces, and she stopped short of wiping them on her new-found tunic, taken from the inn's washroom the night before.

She crept across the storeroom to Rark, asleep on the bales of wool. Neither of them had been able to stomach the idea of sleeping in dead men's beds. Her more than Rark, she suspected. Rark's issue had been with the house itself. His hugrokar had been wound taut like a wire as he'd taken in the sights and smells of the inn. His relief had been palpable when they eventually returned to the storehouse to rest.

His sleep was deep. *Unusually so,* Lyss thought. His ears stayed still, making no sign of detecting her approach as he normally did. *Seems the Aether does take a toll.* She rested a hand on one shoulder and nudged him. Rark's eyes snapped open, hugrokar unfurling along with his wings in a flash of panic. He blinked again, confusion ebbing, recognition taking its place.

"Someone is here."

The rarkyn rolled to his feet, coming to his full height in one fluid motion.

"Who?" he asked. "Where?"

"I'm not sure, but listen." Lyss nodded to the window.

Rark's ears swiveled, long ends twitching in the dark. "A cart," he said, cocking his head as he listened. "Seven, maybe eight horses."

Lyss moved back before the glass and peered out into the dim morning light, her breath leaving a spot of fog on the dirt-streaked pane. A light winked into sight as it rounded a corner of the road.

Sepp damn. She ducked away.

"Safer to stay here and wait for them to pass," Rark said, watching from over her shoulder.

Could they be other travelers? Returning townsfolk perhaps? Brigands? The Order? Lyss wondered. The last thought sunk like a rock in her belly.

She scooped up the small pile of clothes and the tinderbox she'd gathered from the inn and began stuffing them all into her supply sack next to the shuck skull. Her fingers closed around an old cloak, its hem frayed from a lifetime of dragging in the dirt, and she paused.

"Put that over you," she said, tossing it to Rark. He caught it in one hand and opened it out to see what it was. "Just in case we have to run."

To her surprise, the rarkyn stared at the garment a moment longer, then gave a nod and put it on. It came up above his knees, but at least it hid what he was. *Mostly,* she thought, eyeing the tail at his feet and the two horns curling out from under the hood. She only hoped it was enough to stop a stranger shooting him on sight.

"Take this too," she added, holding out a leather belt. Two sheathed knives were buckled to it. She would have preferred to give him a proper dagger, or a sword if he could manage it, but all the inn had turned up was an abundance of cooking and hunting knives, one of which rested on her hip, replacing the blade she'd lost in the shuck attack.

Rark weighed the belt in his hands, his hugrokar turning oddly still, almost...wary, like he expected her to snatch the knives away.

"They're for you," Lyss said.

There was a flicker of something she couldn't quite place, but it was warm and gentle-like. The rarkyn's talons closed around the leather. "Thank you."

They crouched around the window, watching the light—a lantern Lyss guessed—sway closer. Figures came into sight. Eight people on horseback, just as Rark had said, their shoulders hunched into the breeze, cloaks hugging their figures. Lyss swore and ducked down again, and Rark pulled away from the glass.

Reds!

She tightened her hugrokar, sucking in a breath to calm her thumping heart.

It can't be a troop from Ira River. Rark's flight over the ranges had lost them, she was sure. She stole another look into the street. They'd come from the south-east, up through the valley's mouth she guessed.

The group marched on, attention ahead, ignoring the silent village. Too much to hope they were just passing through. Even if they were, once they saw the grisly sight in the square they would undoubtedly stop.

Lyss squinted. Perhaps it was the low light, but their cloaks didn't seem like the same vibrant red she remembered. These were darker. *Dirtier.* Even their mounts were flecked with mud.

Next to her, Rark stiffened, a flash of something—disgust, fear perhaps—snapped across hugrokar and he wrinkled his nose. "Fresh blood," he said.

Gooseflesh rushed up Lyss' arms. She checked the group again. Her eyes followed a long streak up the back of one soldier's cloak; splattering across an emblem of the rose and crown on the rider's sleeve. *The Rose Brigade.* A chill cramped Lyss' gut. She saw the sword rise, the rose emblem riding atop Loric's sleeve. *That* brigade. What were they doing here? *Gods and kratting ginndir.* Had they just routed the fleeing villagers?

A cart piled high with kegs rolled behind the squad, a drunnel in the harness. Its hooked beak swiveling from body to bloody body as it prowled past. With each step of its scaly, long-toed feet, its rear haunches flexed as it pulled the cart along. One swipe from those claws could gut a man.

Lyss held her breath as the squadron trod past the storehouse. Next to her, Rark shifted back from the glass, the reflection of his silver eye tracking the squad crossing the square. The horses stopped before the human pyre and Lyss' heart sank as the riders dismounted.

Now what? Could they afford to wait for the squad to move on? Her fingers found the runes on her wrist and squeezed. The cool prickle of Iga's galdar seal spread up her arm. Across the square, the soldiers began unloading the cart, each one taking a keg.

"Abel, Backus, deal with that mess on the north road," a lanky, black-bearded man ordered, pointing a gloved finger at the road Lyss had come in on. "Nash, take the west side."

A lithe, spider-looking soldier straightened his sword-belt, hoisted his keg onto a shoulder and slouched off.

"Millas, Cottis, go to the farm down the hill. Take the salt with you," the leader continued.

One soldier hawked and spat on the cobbles. "Get the cart, Cottis," he said, turning on the pale, sweaty youth next to him. The young man reached for the drunnel, only to snatch his hand away as the beast snapped at him. On his second attempt he caught the drunnel's lead rope and jerked the creature forward. The cart rolled off out of sight, along with the two men, leaving the leader and a brawny, red-headed soldier behind.

"And me?" he asked.

"You're with me, Platt," the leader said. "Torch everything. Do it quickly. The less time in these kratting mountains the better." He wrinkled his nose. "Start with this." He nudged the corpse pyre with the toe of a boot. "Before it starts to stink."

With a curt nod, the red-headed soldier picked up his barrel, uncorked it and sloshed its contents over the nest of woven limbs. A strong fishy scent wafted over to the storehouse: *oil*.

"We must go," Rark whispered from behind her. Lyss nodded, but didn't move, her gaze locked on the scene in the square. She sensed the pressure building around—no, *inside*—the leader. His hand snapped out, signed a rune. *Spellfire*. Lyss quivered, almost able to *see* the Aether within his body surge forward, concentrating at a point just beyond his fingers. With a sharp, decisive flick, he cast the spell into the bloody mass. It ignited with a *whoosh-whump*; flames roaring for the sky.

A taloned hand grabbed Lyss' shoulder, and her healing skin smarted. "Now," Rark hissed. "They coming."

Lyss glanced out; the red-haired soldier was crossing the square, keg in tow. Straight for the storehouse.

"Shit." She scrambled backwards, scooping up her supply sack and spinning for the doors. The sound of feet scuffing over cobbles came from beyond it. *No good*. She wheeled around. "The inn, quick!"

They piled through the interior door, Lyss catching it just before it slammed and easing it shut. Outside, liquid splattered the storehouse's exterior. One of the double doors creaked open.

Footsteps inside. More sloshing. A pause. "Sergeant," a voice called.

Further off, another twinge of Aether and Lyss heard a spell crack against one of the cottages lining the square. Boots tramped over to the storehouse. "What is it?"

"Someone's been here."

The leader spat out a curse. "Like kratting rats."

"Should I search the houses?"

"No, get on with it. The flames will flush them out."

"An' if they don't?"

The leader snorted. "Good riddance. We'll have done the King a favor. Make sure all those supplies burn. I don't want any more of them coming back."

They listened to the leader stride away, his cloak snapping behind him. The floorboards creaked as the second soldier made his way about the storehouse. Gently, Lyss eased the door latch into place and stepped back—something crunched under her boot. Rark's hugrokar twanged, and jaw-clenching pain bloomed in Lyss' foot. She gasped once before Rark's hugrokar snapped tight. The pain vanished.

Too late.

Footsteps crossed the storeroom, stopping short of the door.

"Come out."

Lyss turned to find Rark already hurrying down the hall, a slight limp in his gait. Behind, the door shook as the soldier tried the latch, failed, then kicked it. He growled a curse and the Aether twitched on the other side of the threshold. The door exploded open, green spellfire caressing the frame.

Lyss sprinted down the hall. Ahead, Rark's form rippled, shifting into a sylph-like shadow as he dove into the Otherworld. Heat rushed through Lyss' limbs and they plunged through the kitchen and out into the hall. Chairs scattered under her feet, clattering to the floor as she crashed into them. Overhead, flames ripped across the thatch roof. Smoke and fragments of straw filtered down through the rafters. Spinning about, she searched for a point of escape, catching herself before she bolted for the porch and front door beyond it. *No. Calm down. Think!* That route ran straight into the square; straight into the arms of the Order. A window overlooking a scraggly yard caught her eye, ashen sunshine glinting through its panes. Wisps of smoke ran along the outside of the glass. The inn was going up like kindling. Beyond the yard and to the west, black plumes clogged the air. The town too. Soon the smoke and flames would consume everything, and them too if they couldn't get out. Perhaps it was the gods getting even after their stunt at Ira River.

A grimace pulled at her lips. *Not yet.* She ran over to the window, pushed it up as far as it could go.

Rark's mind pressed against hers. *Hurry.*

She kicked a leg over the sill, then the other, wriggling through with space to spare. She dropped to the yard outside, landing cat-like in the long grass. She turned to wave Rark through. Had he not been in the Otherworld it would have been a tight, almost impossible fit. Instead, his shadow twisted, limbs distorting as if she was still looking through the warped glass of the window. She watched, fascinated as he touched down onto the grass, form becoming more distinct and rarkyn-like. Suddenly, his hugrokar gave a sharp pull, and his shape vanished back into the Otherworld's depths.

Behind!

Something sharp pricked against Lyss' neck. "That's far enough miss."

Lyss froze, glancing down to see the silver gleam of a blade just under her chin. *No!* she cried at Rark as she sensed him readying to pounce. He lurched still. *No,* she repeated. *He's a trained soldier, he'll cut me open before you bring him down.*

The sword pressed into Lyss' neck. "Turn around."

She did so, shuffling on pinpoint. It was the spider soldier. Hook nosed and thin lipped, his face was expressionless, almost bored. He was keg-less now, no doubt having thrown the barrel onto the blaze in the west. He looked Lyss over once, then glanced at the hollow of the window.

"You're trespassing."

Lyss forced a look of surprise across her face. "I—I'm sorry, I didn't know. I—I'm not from here."

The man gave a pointed look at the supply sack at Lyss' feet. "Stealing from the Crown is a serious crime."

Lyss' temper flared. "It's not *your*—" the blade bit into her neck and she stopped.

"You were saying?"

Lyss forced down her anger. "Nothing important."

"Good. Come with me. Alrend likes to deal with thieves personally." He motioned at the sword on her belt. "Hand it over."

Lyss glared as she undid her belt and dropped it into the soldier's outstretched hand. With his weapon still at her throat, he forced her through the yard and out onto the street.

"Ah, Nash, you found the rat," the leader exclaimed, turning from his red-headed compatriot as Lyss and Nash rounded a burning potter's shop to come out into the square. The pyre roared at its center, filling the air with the scent of burning flesh that mingled with the smell of baked clay and oily fish.

Nash's boot planted into Lyss' back, shoving her forward. "An opportunistic thief," he said, flinging her sword onto the ground before the leader. "Do with her as you wish, Alrend."

Lyss' stomach curdled as the leader's gaze fell on her, black eyes beady and hungry. *As you wish.* The words repeated in her thoughts, snuffing out the slow, red rage that had begun to bubble inside her again. A cold husk took its place and sweat broke down her back.

To her right, at the edge of her vision, Rark's shadowy form shifted, coiling to spring.

Wait, she bade, snapping her mind close. She glanced at the leader, and the red-haired soldier beside him. *Not yet. They're mancers.*

Rark stilled. None of the soldiers showed any sign of seeing him. *Not sighted then. A bit of luck at last.*

Alrend's gaze caressed her figure, lingering on her breasts, then her hips. Clenched jawed, Lyss met his look. *I am not your plaything.* She shifted onto the balls of her feet.

Nash's sword tip pressed into her back. "Steady, don't go doing something you'll regret, girl."

Alrend chuckled, a wide, leering grin cracking over his features. "I'm not sure Nash. I like them wild, but this one might eat me alive." He nudged the hilt of her sword with his boot, flipping it on the cobbles and leaving a fresh red smear on its sheath. "A fine weapon," he observed, stooping to pick it up. He popped the top of the sheath, inspecting the shoulder of the blade. "A Kalana make." He snapped it shut again. "You steal it from a noble house in Nilos?"

"It was my father's," Lyss ground out, staying the urge to ball her fists.

Alrend slid her sword into his belt, next to his own. "Too good for a thief."

Lyss glared at him and gave into the urge. Her fingers curled tight at her sides, nails cutting into her palms. Alrend laughed and sidled closer, pressing a thumb and finger to her chin. "Yes, I am going to—"

A scream rented the air, cutting through the hiss and crack of the burning village like an axe; terrible and bloody. *And close.* The soldiers started, the red-haired man twisting around to the south.

"What—" he began, before his words were lost to a deep, gut-shaking roar. Its low hum reverberated in Lyss' ears, building into an odd pressure in her temples. At the sound of scrambling boots the soldiers turned, just as the young, pale youth came careening into the square, sliding on the blood-slicked cobbles. His face was no longer pale, but bone white and flecked with blood. His red cloak was torn in half, the tattered fabric fluttering behind him as he ran.

"Alrend!" he gasped, spotting the group. "Alrend! It got Millas. It's—"

A shadow moved in the smoke behind him. Hunched over, its indistinct form lumbered forward in slow deliberate steps, like a wolf that knew its prey was cornered. *Or a bear.*

It lunged. Its hazy shape turning solid in the fire-lit morning. A giant paw lashed out, battering the fleeing youth down like a fly. He tumbled to the cobbles, managed one scream before he vanished under the mass of fur, tooth and claw with a crunch of bone and ligament.

Silence.

The beast released its hold of the youth's neck and turned on them. A nose twitched, blood dripping off the shaggy fur at its neck. Lyss stared, rooted to the spot, not quite able to believe it. It *was* a bear, but it was unlike any bear she'd ever seen. This one was huge. Its shoulder half a head taller than her.

More boots sounded, and the remaining two soldiers of the squad ran in from the north road, almost colliding with the creature as they sprinted into the square.

"Alrend, Nash, what—" one managed before horror overtook his features and he leapt back. The bear rounded on the newcomers.

"Kill it!" Alrend shouted.

One of the men scrabbled for his sword; it looked pitiful next to the beast. Behind him, his companion shaped out a casting, sending it lancing into the beast's side. The creature stiffened as it struck. The first soldier lunged in, sword swinging like an axe at the bear's neck. With a roar, the beast lurched away, pivoting. The blade clanked to the cobbles, and a paw lashed up and out, slamming into the soldier's gut. Across the square, Lyss heard an audible pop and crunch as the blow crushed the soldier's lungs and ribs.

She swallowed back bile and sought out Rark's mind. *Be ready.*

"No! Stay away!" The second soldier shrieked and flung another casting at the bear. A spinning knot of spellfire smacked into its shoulder. Flames seared across its side. The beast ignored it, and charged, paws thumping across the stones. The man turned and ran, screaming as the bear's claws whipped out and tripped his legs, as it would to a fleeing deer.

Now.

Lyss slammed a shoulder into Alrend's chest, grabbing for her sword tucked in his belt. He went down with a yell and her hands closed around the hilt, pulling it free.

"Stupid girl," Nash spat. His weapon raised behind her. Lyss' skin prickled, and she dove, rolling across the cobbles to spring back up in a fighting stance. With a piercing, grinding sound, Rark was there beside her, Nash's sword pressing into a cross of two kitchen knives. The utensils screeched under the weight of the soldier's blow. One knife-edge caught the soldier's blade and the utensil let out a crack. The rarkyn flashed his teeth and pushed forward, rising to his full height, dwarfing the soldier before him. A curtain of panic dropped over Nash's face, his skin turning sallow in the ashen light.

"Aether's mercy," he croaked before Rark kicked out, thumping a giant taloned foot into the soldier's chest and sending him crashing to the cobbles.

Leave this one to me, he sent.

Movement in her peripheral made Lyss spin, intercepting Alrend's wild swing aimed at Rark's back. Their blades met, their clang echoing across the square. A mental nudge and a brush of feathers against one shoulder signaled Rark shifting behind her back.

"Kratting bitch!" Alrend spat, sweat lathering along his brow and neck. He lunged again, feinting right, then diving forward with a stabbing blow at her hip. Lyss darted sideways, twisting around the blade. *A dance,* her father's voice sounded in her head, in time with her pounding heart. *Just-like-a-dance.* Only in this dance, her partner was trying to kill her.

A cry sounded behind her. Nash stumbled back, one of Rark's knives buried deep in his shoulder. The rarkyn muttered a soft, "Tch, missed," and pressed forward again. Lyss did the same, sidestepping Alrend's swinging strike.

Too late she realized Alrend had taken one hand off his sword.

The galdar casting hit her head on, releasing from the soldier's free hand a bare two feet from her. Its power wrapped around her. Cold seared to the bone, seized her limbs. A binding. She bit down a shriek and fell to one knee.

Behind, Rark staggered, hugrokar cinching tight, and managed to dodge a half-hearted swing from a flagging Nash. With preternatural speed, he ducked through the soldier's outstretched arm, form hazing as he shifted in and out of the Otherworld. His knife sank through the man's breastplate like it was butter.

One down. Lyss probed the binding spell, ignoring its galdar sting. She reached for the Aether inside the casting and pulled its power into her. It rushed to meet her and she drew it in, gathered it and pushed back against the binding. The casting shed free of her like water. Far easier than last time. She turned on the grinning Alrend.

Already, his fingers were weaving again. She gritted her teeth, tightened her grip on her sword hilt. Aether surged through her limbs. She sprang, lunging across the distance between them, sweeping her sword in an arc for his side. He shifted, moving into position to parry the blow. At the last second, Lyss switched her sword from two hands to one, her reach extending an extra foot. A flick of her wrist darted her sword tip around Alrend's weapon, then back up at his open hand.

The blade sliced across his fingers mid-cast. Alrend yelled, his body folding around his hand, one digit dropping to the ground in a splatter of blood. Lyss swept in, her vision darkening as she sank a knee into his gut, then drove an elbow into his neck. The soldier sagged, took two breaths and rallied, spitting out a glob of blood.

"Who—*what* are you?"

Lyss didn't answer. Instead, her hand rose of its own accord, Aether thrumming through her limbs. Horror surged inside her.

"No!" She lurched away, leaving Rark's back wide open. Seeing his chance, Alrend swept in.

Lyss flung out her hugrokar, wrenched herself close to Rark's mind. *Move!*

Rark twisted. Lyss' vision shifted, lurching free, and suddenly, the blade was swinging *at her*. No time to move. She reached for the Aether, into the place beyond and dove.

The tip of the steel blade followed, lancing down her back.

She shrieked. The sound echoed from across the divide, from Terresmir, from...*her*. Rark's mind rounded on hers, coiling tight, the fire down her back fading to a throb.

Go back, he said.

Back? she echoed, staring at the square. Thick swirling mist layered the cobbles. *This is the Otherworld,* she thought, numbly.

You're here. A rough finger pressed into her temple. No, into Rark's temple. A talon rose before her eyes, pointing to a figure crumpled on the ground. *That's you.*

Together, they watched Alrend turn and nudge her form with his boot, then wave a hand before her vacant eyes. His face contorted from a look of surprise to one of triumph. His sword lifted over her neck.

Gods and ginndir, he was going to—

Lyss tried to pull her mind free, but the bond felt tacky, as if the

Aether had glued them together. She strained; a twinge lanced behind her temples, jolting whatever slept inside her awake. A dark joy rolled through her. In Terresmir, her body jerked, hands clenching and unclenching, as if something gave it an experimental flex. Her fingers honed together. *Something* peeled her lips into a glee-ridden grin.

Like a hand to a shoulder, Rark's mind came up behind and gave her an almighty shove. Her vision snapped sharp, world flooding into vibrant color—and the face of Alrend bearing down on her.

Her sword stabbed up, straight into the soldier's neck—just as a pair of enormous shaggy paws closed about Alrend's head and lifted him off his feet. Alrend managed a single gurgling scream before the bear's teeth crunched into his skull.

With a final shake of the soldier's body, the bear flung it to one side. Reared on its hind legs, the beast towered over her, twice the height of a man and three times as wide. Blood clotted its muzzle, dripped down its chest, each hooked claw the length of her wrist to fingertip. Lyss swallowed, the sword in her hands feeling like a pocketknife next to the creature's sheer size.

Don't move. Rark's voice sounded. He shifted in the Otherworld, becoming fainter still. *It's not what it seems.*

The bear dropped to all fours with a thump, sending loose pebbles bouncing over the cobbles. It prowled forward, and despite Rark's warning, Lyss scrambled back on her hands and bottom, sword scraping stone, until the heat of the burning pyre singed her back. The bear came on, heedless. Its blood-slicked nose twitched, nostrils flaring as it snuffed. Aether hung thick around the creature, like an odor. She licked the tingle away from her lips and held her breath. When she found her heart still beating and limbs still attached, she dared to look beyond the nose. Two gray eyes watched her. *Intelligent eyes,* Lyss thought, gazing back.

A paw lifted, slowly, reaching for her face. She sucked in a breath, closed her eyes and waited for the inevitable blow. Instead, something soft and smooth pressed against her cheek. Like a hand. Her eyes snapped open. A woman crouched before her, naked, but for an enormous bear skin draped around her. The head and maw of the beast rested on the woman's brow; a helmet of teeth, matted fur and two storm gray eyes. Raw, red blood slicked down the woman's jaw, mingling with strands of long golden-blond hair.

"Those eyes," she said, and Lyss became acutely aware of the pyre at her back. "Red and silver." The woman gave a sad half-smile. "You are a krat too."

Suddenly, Lyss was back in the tent as Iga moved the lantern away and uttered those life-changing words: *"You've been bonded"*. "No, I—" she stopped. To continue that train of thought was a lie. *She's right, I am.*

"You chose a bad time to visit Bern."

The woman pushed away, coming to her feet to stare at the burning pyre. She was tall, very tall, Lyss realized, a head higher than her at least. Lyss got to her feet, feeling the sting of half a dozen cuts made fresh with her fading adrenaline.

"Who are you?"

"I am Brin," the woman replied, voice distant as she stared at the flames. "Monsters," she whispered. Her eyes ran over the charred bodies, filling with tears. Then her head snapped up, pupils dilating. *"Nina!"*

Paying no mind to her nakedness, or the cold, Brin sprinted off across the square and into the west street. With growing foreboding, Lyss followed, Rark trailing behind her in the Otherworld.

Do you know what she is? Lyss asked.

No. But she's no mancer.

They found Brin outside a small, thatched cottage at the far end of the west street. Flames were eating up one wall from the houses beside it. The fire had not yet reached the roof, but once it did, it would burn with fury until there was nothing left but charred beams.

"Nina!" Brin called. She jumped the stone fence and ran to the open door. "Nina!" Her cry echoed inside the silent cottage. Dread rooted Lyss next to the gate, one hand resting on the wooden post. Was Nina a mother? A daughter? Sister? Lover?

A half-scream, half-cry rose into the air, building into a wail. The sound gripped Lyss' heart and squeezed. She knew that sound. She'd made it that day on the road to Caenis as her father's body slumped to the ground.

A faint step at her back signaled Rark shifting out of the Otherworld.

"Go," he said, and with an odd, unreadable flicker through hugrokar. "She should not be alone." He leapt onto the stone wall. "I will keep watch. More may come."

Lyss doubted it, but she nodded and pushed open the gate and entered the cottage. It was dark inside. Smoke hazed the rafters, clogging the air with the smell of burning thatch. Brin knelt on the floor next to a cold hearth, fresh logs still in its grate, waiting to be lit. In her arms she cradled a still and silent figure: a woman, hair long and blond like Brin's, features almost identical, but for the shroud of death's white mask. Brin pressed the body to her, rocking back and forth, shoulders shuddering in great huffing sobs.

"Oh Nina, oh Nina," she croaked over and over, clutching at the woman's hair.

Lyss moved closer, edging around the pool of dried blood on the floor to lay a hand on Brin's shoulder. Her fingers sank deep into the shaggy gray fur of the bear skin. It was warm to the touch, hot even. A tingle spread up her palm, and Lyss could have sworn the skin shivered under her hand. Brin paid no notice. A pop and crack above them signaled the fire had reached the beams holding up the roof.

"Bring her outside," Lyss said. She eyed the deep wound in the dead woman's chest, the blood stains purple on her blue frock. *Run through with a sword.* A pang, so sharp it hurt, lanced across her chest and she bit her lip. *Gods damn them.*

A questioning probe rose from Rark outside. *I'm fine,* she assured, and he pulled away again.

Cuts laced the woman's arms, and her fingernails were torn. *She'd gone down fighting.* Lyss reached under Brin's elbow, giving it a little push. "Come, I will help you see to her."

Brin rose, lifting her twin with ease. Without so much as a glance at Rark, she walked out beyond the gate and onto the street. There she stopped, blood-streaked face turning to take in the burning village; she scrunched her eyes shut and screamed.

CHAPTER TWENTY-NINE

T HEY BURIED THE WOMAN IN A SHALLOW GRAVE BEYOND THE village. Brin, in fresh pantaloons and a too-short tunic scrounged from the ruined homes, stood silent over the small, rocky mound. The bear skin hugged her shoulders, fur rippling in the breeze. Lyss stood off to one side, head bowed, staring at the snow-patched earth.

Skaar hung back, feeling like he was intruding on something intensely personal as Brin stooped to place the last stone on the mound.

"Why?" her whisper carried on the wind. Skaar pricked his ears. "We never hurt anyone."

The bear-kin might not have hugrokar, but he sensed her crushing, bone-aching grief as clear as a summer sky. It was how she moved. Her limbs dragged as if draped in chains, her shoulders hunched, arms dead at her sides. Even the bear skin looked dull.

You should not be here. The nagging thought picked at his mind. He pushed it away, turning his attention to the grave. Burial was an odd way to say goodbye, but it was not his kin lying there. The thought sparked an image of a rarkyn crushed in a rune circle; blood soaking the earth, throat slit from where the mordkyn had drained him. *Fengar.* The memory hit him like a hungry ginndir, its teeth sinking into his chest. It drew a glance from Lyss and Skaar coiled his hugrokar tight.

"I promised I'd be there for her," Brin said. "I left to catch a pig for feast day." Her voice trembled. "I should have made her come with me."

Lyss stepped forward and placed a hand on Brin's arm. "You couldn't have known."

Brin's shoulders gave a quiver, then she crumbled to her knees. "We should have stayed in the mountains," she said. "Nina…she wanted to be with other people like her. With normal folk." Brin pressed her hands to her mouth, stifling a sob. "They were so kind to us."

Lyss reached out, hesitated, then patted Brin's back. "They're in Baer's hall now," she said, and Brin sank down even lower.

"It's all my fault."

Anger surged hot and fast through hugrokar. "No, it's not," Lyss growled. "It's the Order's fault."

Brin made no show of hearing. Slowly, her sobs eased, and she fell into a stony silence. Skaar cleared his throat.

"We cannot stay here," he said. "When squad doesn't return, others will come looking."

Lyss shot him a glare from across the grave, her hugrokar flaring. "Not now Rark, she's just lost—"

"No, he is right," Brin wiped her nose with the back of her hand. "We can't stay here." She touched two fingers to her lips and pressed them against the last stone she'd placed on the grave. Fresh tears rolled down each cheek. The bear-kin drew a long breath and rose to her feet and strode toward the road. The scent of blood and earth trailed after her, along with something not quite human, but not quite bear either. It turned Skaar's feathers on end.

He nudged Lyss' hugrokar, jolting her out of a deep reverie that had her brow knitted together. He gave Brin a pointed look. Lyss chewed her lip.

"Just until the next village."

Skaar scowled, adjusted his new belt of knives pilfered from the dead soldiers, and turned for the road.

They traveled in silence. Lyss leading, Skaar behind, Brin trudging along between them. It was slow going. Lyss kept the pace steady, checking every half mile that Brin was keeping up. They heard no complaint from her. She walked head down, gaze unfocused, mouth set in a grim line.

When they stopped to make camp, Brin sat and stared into the fire, stroking a white rabbit's foot strung long about her neck.

"Your sister's?" Lyss asked.

Brin said nothing, just peered into the flames, eyes glassy.

"Here," Lyss handed her a piece of salted venison and some dried linca fruit. "You've got to eat."

With what seemed like a great effort, Brin came back to herself and let the rabbit foot drop. "Thank you." She took the food and held it without taking a bite. "I'm sorry. You've helped me, and I don't even know your names."

Lyss sank down opposite and reached out her hands to the fire. "I'm Lyss." She prodded Skaar over hugrokar.

He gave a soft hiss and coiled his mind tight and ruffled his wings. "Rark," he said.

Brin leaned forward. "What are you?" Her eyes flicked between them, nostrils flaring as she sniffed. "You smell of the Otherworld. Both of you."

Lyss stiffened, her tension echoing down Skaar's spine. "Rark is a rarkyn," she said. Skaar sensed her choosing her words. "I'm human." Something fluttered in her as she spoke. He blinked, recognizing it. Doubt, no *fear*, gnawed at her.

Brin nodded, attention lingering on Lyss. On her shoulders, the bear fur rippled in the firelight. "Where are you headed?"

Skaar and Lyss exchanged a glance. *Tell her?* Skaar queried over hugrokar.

I doubt she's going to report us to the Order, Lyss agreed, then to Brin. "South," she said, then after a moment's hesitation, added, "to Illredus."

Brin's eyebrows shot up and she looked at Lyss, to Skaar, then back to Lyss again. She let out a sharp bark of laughter. It cut through the glade like the sound of splitting stone: cold, dead and without mirth. "Illredus? You must be mad. We just killed eight Order soldiers."

Skaar bristled as her gray eyes turned on him. "You too?" she asked. Her gaze wandered over him, and he sensed the bear behind sizing him up, calculating if he was predator or prey. He bared his teeth and flared his tail feathers. *Don't you even try.*

Lyss stepped between them, flashing a warning look at him before turning on Brin. "Yes."

Brin shook her head. "Madness," she said. She tugged the bear skin tighter around her shoulders. "How do you plan on getting there?"

"King's Road," Lyss replied simply, then as Brin's eyebrows rose again, asked, "What?"

"You're some way from the King's Road." She pointed a long, yellow-nailed finger to the west. "It's a good ten leagues that way."

Shock swept through hugrokar, roiling into Skaar's belly. He reached across the link and held it firm. *Steady*. He kept the thought to himself, but let its intention carry in the look he gave Lyss. She swallowed, not quite buying his calm.

"Where are we? I thought we'd reach Nilos in a day or two."

Brin palmed the dried fruit Lyss had given her. "We're closer to Torin. Bern is—" she faltered, her rough hands curling tight around the fruit, crushing it, "*was* three days from Torin."

Lyss' brow furrowed, and she closed her eyes. "Torin, that's one of the towns that skirts the Memnon Spine, right on the edge of the Geshem plains." Her eyes roved behind their lids, visualizing some internal map Skaar could only begin to guess at. A flicker of dismay pulled her eyebrows together and she bit her lip. "We're miles off course."

"That you are," Brin agreed.

Lyss shot a look at Skaar, anger simmering through hugrokar. "I thought you knew where you were going. How did you lose track of the King's Road?"

Skaar bristled, ears flattening. "We were fleeing! You said we travel south." He gestured at the woods. "Is south, no?"

They glared at each other over the fire before Lyss sighed and rubbed her face. Her hands fell to her wrist and squeezed. "We'll have to backtrack," her voice sounded flat, resigned.

"No, you don't. You just need to get to Torin," Brin countered. At Lyss' confusion, she continued, "There's a ferry there, it'll take you all the way to Illredus' doorstep."

Hope and dread clashed through hugrokar so fast Skaar swayed at the fireside. Hope, dread, delight, horror, the emotions flashed through him so fast he struggled to distinguish which was his and which was Lyss'. He wound his thoughts in, extracting himself from the tumult as Lyss clawed her own mind free. He knew a heartbeat of stillness before a sick unease settled into his stomach, like he'd eaten bad meat. Illredus. Surely not yet.

Lyss shifted, her face of forced calm, attention entirely on Brin. "How long would it take?"

"I'm not sure," Brin admitted. "A week, perhaps a little more. It's a damn sight quicker than walking though—at least from here to Nilos and then down the King's Road." She uncoiled her fist, revealing the sticky mess in her hand. "Of course, you need to get to Torin first." She dug a finger under the squashed fruit, flicked it off into the fire, and wiped her hands on her leggings. "You need a guide."

Skaar snapped his gaze up and onto the bear-kin, not sure he liked where the conversation was headed. "We just follow road," he said as Lyss held up a hand to say, "That's really not necessary."

Brin folded her arms. "Do you know the way to Torin? These mountains are easy to get lost in. You've already done so once already. If you miss Torin, it's two hundred leagues across the Geshem plains until you reach anything remotely like a village. And let me tell you, there's not much between."

Sounds ideal. Skaar thought, wryly. No humans, no Order, and open skies to soar. Judging from Lyss' expression, she didn't share the feeling.

"How far is it to Torin?" she asked.

"Three days, maybe two," Brin cast Skaar a long look, lingering on his wings. "Depending on how fast you can travel."

"I can keep up well enough," Lyss blurted before Skaar could object.

"Good, it's settled," Brin said, easing back before the fire. "I'll guide you to Torin. In return you'll take me with you to Illredus."

Skaar choked on his piece of dried venison. He hacked it out. "No," he managed to get out as Lyss intoned the same response in time with him.

Brin's gray eyes glittered across the fire. "No?"

"It's not a good idea," Lyss began. "We're not exactly...traveling with us is..."

Skaar huffed and jabbed a talon at his chest, then at Lyss. "The Order hunts us."

Brin dug into her tunic, pulling out a crumpled piece of parchment. She slapped it down by the fire. Skaar recognized the Order's insignia stamped on it. The Crown's warrant. *When had she taken that?*

"You think I'm not the same?" Brin asked. She pointed to the scrawled letters. "My name. Brinhild Reiner. Right there." She glowered at them, daring them to argue otherwise. "The Order razed my village. Slaughtered them like vermin. They were good people. Hard working people. And"—she swallowed—"I wasn't there for them." Her eyes turned bright, glinting with rage and grief. "They—Nina deserved better."

"Brin you can't bl—" Lyss began, but the bear-kin held up her hand.

"If they did it to Bern, they've done it to others. And they'll do it again." She met Lyss' and Skaar's gazes in turn. "I am going to stop them." Her hands curled into fists. "For Bern. For Nina."

"Why Illredus?" Lyss asked.

"Because," Brin met Lyss' gaze, then Skaar's, her chin lifted and jaw set, "the quickest way to kill a monster is to go straight for the heart."

PART IV
MORDKYN

The door swung shut, the eternals boomed
*   "Why seek us, son of flesh and bone?"*
*   Upon the hearth, Asander wept*
*   For the heart lost so far from home.*

"Ancient aetherlings, I beg of you
*   My queen is dead, claimed too soon.*
*   Free her from Baer's hold*
*   And to you I'll pledge my boon."*

—Fragment from The Epic of Asander
*   c. 500 years before the Illredian Founding.*

CHAPTER THIRTY

Elena,

I'm not sure how long I have to pen this, so I must be brief. We have been arrested. Two days from the boarder of Talos province we encountered an Illredus-bound troop. From what I've been able to tell, they'd been fighting insurgents in the Spine —for what little good it will do, those peaks are vast, a warren for the iele and other beings us city folk have neither seen nor heard of. The news boded well for Tykee and his chances of finding others of his kind in the wilds, but alas, I doubt we'll get there now.

Perhaps it was the sight of two mancers travelling alone into Talos, or perhaps it was simply part of their routine patrol. Whatever the reason, we were stopped, our belongings searched and brooches seized. Worst yet, they found Tykee. He put up a fight, even with his sigil, knocking one of the soldiers out cold before the rest of the squad subdued him. Last I saw, he and Isaac were in irons at Myron Tower. I only hope the soldiers do not try to kill him in his current condition—I shudder to think what might happen if they try. In preparation for the Ice Steppes, I've been removing runes from his sigil. It's weak now, just four runes bind it.

They think us criminals, Elena. For what I am not sure. They claim I've broken the fourth law. Apparently sheltering a rarkyn is beyond my station as Regis. Apparently not even a mancer of the highest rank is qualified to handle these crea-tures. If that is the case, pray tell who can then? I asked. Other than the Arcas, King Therrin, himself? They couldn't answer to that. Nonetheless, they are adamant I am a liar and a krat. Somewhere along the line they learned we'd passed through Klymene and eastern Phaia—and now traitors and insurgent sympathizers are added to our list of crimes.

I am worried, Elena. This stinks of Councillor Keteus. If we are found guilty, it will be the Brand at minimum. The maximum does not bear thinking about, not now. I may be spared the worst of it; my name is known, even here. But Isaac? He is a drunkard's son with no family titles. He will be a calf in a court of wolves.

I do not like to get you involved, Elena, but Keteus has left me no choice and I fear this is the only way. Petition the King, remind him of our history, remind him who helped him keep his throne if you must. Make him see reason.

Please Elena,
  Bring us home.

Papa.

ARCHER WATCHED THE TWO BINDING SPELLS FLASH OFF through the trees, their white arrows hazing into the fading twilight. *He's got quite the talent,* he thought as Hane turned to him, the corners of his mouth twitching as he fought to control his grin. Had they been in the capital, he'd have the Order commanders squabbling over who got to groom him for an officer. But they weren't in the capital, and Archer not in the mood to sing praises.

"Good," he told the boy. "Show me your half-ward."

Hane spun on the earth, the toe of one boot tracing an arc in the dirt as his fingers worked. The single point ward flared under him. *Interesting use of his feet.* Most mancers visualized simple wards such as this and cast them in one go, lines and runes both. Not all mancers could manage it, and the feat grew more difficult if the circle-to-be was complex. Many lower ranked mancers had to trace their circle out first, losing precious time in the process. To get around that, Hane let his toes do half the work, freeing his mind to focus on the runes alone. *A Krawan approach if ever I saw one.*

Archer shifted from the fire and prodded the ward with his wooden fingers. The ward flexed and wobbled like an undercooked pudding. Archer pushed harder and the crescent-shaped barrier popped, the mid-air sheen fizzling into nothing.

"Needs work," he said. "No cheating with your feet. It's a half-ward for Sepp sake, not a sixteen-point circle." He tapped a fleshy digit to his temple. "Memorize the spell properly. Rarkyns are quick; you can't afford to waste time scratching in the dirt. Now come and eat."

Hane sat, and Archer spooned him a plate of roasted tubers and the remnants of a rabbit. When the creature had burst out before them on the trail the day before, Hane's hand had flown to the blowpipe at his waist, only to have Archer stay him.

"Use the spell," he'd instructed.

And he had.

Archer had offered no congratulations, but for hours afterwards, the triumphant gleam in Hane's eye had been impossible to miss. He wore the same look again tonight, despite his failure with the half-ward. Archer scraped a rock out of the dirt, thumbed off the wet earth and tossed it at Hane's feet.

"Engrave it," he said.

Dismay crashed over the boy's smug look as if he'd been struck over the head with one of Archer's cooking pots. His jaw clenched into a grimace and he gazed down at the stone as if it might bite.

"You're not a 'graver," Archer guessed.

Hane opened his mouth, licking his lips. "I don't know. Gran tried testing me once." He winced. "It didn't go well."

Archer smirked, imagining the hundred different ways it could have gone wrong. Perhaps the rune hadn't set properly, turning Hane's power back on him, or maybe it had scored itself onto something, or someone, else. Perhaps it had appeared successful at first, only to channel uncontrolled magic once he activated it. Archer jabbed his fork at the stone at Hane's feet.

"Try. A simple fire rune. You should know that."

After a long look, Hane put down his bowl and reached for the stone. He cupped it against his chest in one hand, head bowed over it, eyes closed as if in prayer.

Trust me, boy, the gods aren't listening.

With a crude finger—having not the finer tools for graving on hand —Hane traced a rune over the stone, but there was no power in it.

"Try harder, boy."

Hane flushed pink, then traced again. Power trickled into the stone.

"More," Archer insisted. "Unless you want to collect wood every other hour through the night."

Hane glowered at the rock as if it had spoken instead of Archer. The power increased and from under his fingertip, faint green lines emblazoned over the rough surface, forming into the shape of the galdar rune. Hane's shoulders relaxed, and he straightened, holding out the sigiled rock.

"You're not done yet. Finish it properly."

Hane frowned. "But it's—" Flames sprung from the stone. He yelped and snatched his hand away. The sigil struck the dirt and sparks flew off it, landing on Hane's trousers and burning holes through them. The boy leapt up, thumping the heel of his boot at the rock over and over.

In two strides Archer was around the fire. "Stamping won't work!" he snapped, grabbing the collar of the youth's tunic with his good hand and hauling him back. The popping of threads accompanied him. "It's feeding off your Aether. Sever it properly."

Hane swiveled under Archer's grip, hanging there like a pup gripped at the scruff. Archer resisted the urge to shake him. "Sever it."

"How?" Hane managed after a moment.

"It's not a spell or a ward, it's a sigil. You don't need to hold the runes in your mind. Release it."

With a shaking hand, Hane made a sharp, cutting gesture with his fingers, as if slicing an invisible blade through the air. The physical representation that focused the mental act was big and over-the-top. *A novice's approach,* Archer thought, but it worked nonetheless. The sigil snuffed out like a cap over a candle. He released the boy. "Better."

Hane stumbled over to the stone and picked it up between a thumb and forefinger, holding it out as if he expected it to ignite again. He blinked. "It's cool."

Archer grunted. "Of course it is, you're not channeling Aether into it anymore." He stomped back to his side of the fire and sank against a tree trunk, pulling at the bristles of his beard. *All three aspects of galdar,* he mused as the boy pocketed the stone and went back to his dinner. *He'd make a fine mancer. One of the best—if he trained properly.*

With a scowl he roped in his wandering thoughts. *Don't be a fool. You are not fit to tutor any more apprentices.* He rested his head on the trunk and gazed into the fire as it burned down to its coals. Opposite, Hane practiced shaping the runes Archer had taught him, before a gasp slipped out as a cramp wound through his hand. He shook it out with a grimace. *Naïve idiot.*

Archer got up and spooned the last of the tubers and meat into his bowl and crossed to the boy. Hane looked at the bowl, then up at Archer, brow wrinkling.

"I've already eaten."

"Eat it." Archer thrust the bowl onto the boy's lap. "Tomorrow will be a long day. You need to restore the Aether you've burned through."

"What about you?"

"Unlike you, I am good at conserving my Aether. I will be fine." As he spoke, the dry well inside him twisted. *Liar,* it seemed to say.

Before him, Hane gave a slow nod. "Alright." He grinned at Archer, smugness glinting again. "I'll catch two rabbits to make it up to you tomorrow."

With a huff Archer sat back down, doing his best to ignore his groaning Aether-sapped muscles. His legs quivered and throbbed, as if he'd run across the mountains instead of ridden. Stiff shoulders wormed tendrils of pain into his neck, his left stump ached under the cloth bindings. *Damn runes.* He patted the bottle in his coat pocket, tempted once more. One sip and his sores would fade, reserves brim and douse him in power. *Not yet.* He sighed and rummaged for his journal, flipping through the scrawled pages until he found the one he wanted.

A diagram stared up at him, nearly lost in a haze of etchings; some faded, others fresh. He traced the markings, taking comfort in their familiar shapes, the same way a huntsman might follow a worn track through the woods. Twenty-four points. A ghastly size. There was no casting all those runes and lines in one go, no matter how well he memorized it. He closed his eyes, bringing first one rune then another to mind. He continued until he held all twenty-four points. Inside him, his Aether stretched its small mass, unfolding through his limbs, waiting for him to throw his will into the spell. The runes hung there in his mind, clear and sharp, as if he'd cast them yesterday. *Good.* The next question was how to draw the layer of lines to ward the rarkyn in before it took off into the Otherworld. *Curse that girl. If I still had my sigil I wouldn't have to—*

Leaves crunched beside him. "Looks difficult."

Archer's eyes snapped open. Hane peered over his shoulder, empty bowl in one hand, forehead knitted as he squinted at the journal on Archer's lap. "You're going to use it on the rarkyn?"

"Yes." No sense in denying it.

Hane hesitated, seeming to ponder, before abruptly asking, "Why?"

"Why what, boy?"

"Why go after the rarkyn?" Hane said. "Why is it so important that you're willing to…"

His voice petered out, leaving the end of his question unspoken. *Why are you willing to risk so much for one aetherling?* Archer wondered how many times the lad had tried to summon the courage to ask before now. He gazed into the flames. Why indeed? His desire had gone from an all-consuming fire at the heart of his soul to a grim, icy determination. Unlike a fire, ice didn't splutter and die at the slightest breath of wind. It was solid. Heavy. It ground on, like the glaciers of the Steppes. Every season its tracks grew deeper, more resolute.

"For answers," he said. "A chance to do one right in a world of wrong."

"What answers?"

Sepp, where are all these questions coming from? He turned on the boy, glaring. "None of your kratting business."

Hane flinched, hurt flickering over his face.

Was that really necessary? A soft voice wormed into Archer's thoughts. He tried squashing it, but as the silence lengthened and the boy showed no sign of breaking it, it began to nag. *Abyss curse it. I'm growing soft.* With a glance at his still open journal, he sighed.

"You know of the Eternals, boy?"

Hane perked up, bobbing his head. "Everyone's heard of the Eternals."

"Heard yes, but what do you *know*?"

Hane stood, quiet for a moment. "They're old aetherlings. No one knows their names, so no one can summon them."

"They're more than old, boy. They're ancient, as old as the Other-world itself. And *powerful*."

Hane's shifted, sinking down next to him at the fireside, listening. "You're not saying you're going to try to summon—" his voice quavered.

Archer smirked. "I am. I will."

"But, *why*?"

Archer hesitated. "They know certain…things." The words felt awkward and heavy in his mouth, like they came from someone else. But Hane's brow was already wrinkled, staring at the runes sketched in Archer's journal, eyes semi-glazed as he tried to make sense of it.

"What do you need the rarkyn for?"

Bait. He didn't say it aloud; that might alarm the boy. "To open the door," Archer said instead. "I'll use its magic with mine to forge a path to the Eternals." *Not strictly true, but close enough.*

Hane stared at him. "That's—"

Illegal? Law breaking? Blasphemy? Archer waited for the accusations to fly.

"Brilliant!" Hane breathed, face lighting up. He leaned in, suddenly eager. "Is it possible? Can you really mesh two magics?"

Archer blinked. Not the response he'd expected. He smoothed the yellowing pages of his journal. "That's the plan," he muttered.

"*Gods and ginndir,* the possibilities could be..." Hane trailed off, lost in his own imaginings. He gestured at Archer's sketches. "That's the ward that will help you reach the Eternals?"

Archer flipped the journal shut and stowed it back in his coat. "Something like that."

Hane held out a hand and beckoned for the utensils at Archer's feet. "Pass them here, I'll wash up."

Archer grunted and handed them over, but not before Hane's brow creased again and he chewed the inside of one cheek, mulling. "That ward will take time to cast. Even Iga would need to trace it first."

Compared to a Wildner half-blood. That stings a little.

"How are you going to get the rarkyn to cooperate?"

There it was again. That question. Archer stroked the back of his wooden hand, his nails finding the twenty-four-point tracing there as he considered. How to indeed. His fingers brushed the graved circle inside his palm that brought forth his berigan. *If only Isaac were here.* He needed another mancer to stop the rarkyn slipping away while he traced the ward. He sighed, opened his mouth—just as the idea struck him in the face. He blinked, astonished he hadn't thought of it sooner. He didn't need to contain the rarkyn. Just keep it distracted. Glee curled his lips.

"Boy, how'd you like to learn how to summon a berigan?"

ON THE DAWN, THEY PACKED DOWN THEIR CAMP WITH A practiced efficiency. Hane saw to the horses while Archer put out the fire. He kicked away the coals and retrieved his own fire sigil, a small pebble not unlike the one he'd given the boy the previous night.

His mountain pony was not faring well. The runes had burned into her legs, turning the blood vessels black. Dark veins snaked over her fetlocks and knees, crawling upwards to her chest. The moment those tendrils reached the pony's heart, it was over. She would become the Aether's creature for one heartbeat and then die the next. Even now, her once placid eyes had a wild, hungry look, and Archer cursed as she rounded to bite when he put a foot in the stirrup.

Hane grabbed the pony's bridle and with soft cooing noises, stroked the beast's nose until it was calm again. Black tendrils laced the legs and hooves of his own mount too, but not to the same extent as Archer's pony.

"How much more can they take?" Hane asked, petting his own horse on the neck.

Archer grunted. "Not much more. The runes are pumping Aether into their bodies. Sooner or later it takes over."

"Is that why you can't cast runes on people?" Hane asked, a look of understanding crossing his face as they left camp.

"It's why it's against the law," Archer corrected. "At least in the Empire. Krawan mancers specialize in it."

Hane started. "Gran is Krawan. Well, half Krawan. On her mother's side."

Archer shrugged, thinking back to the old woman and those dark knowing eyes. *Guess I was right.* No surprise the old mancer disliked the Order. It was difficult to recall a time in the records when tensions between Kraw and the Empire weren't high. There had been a peace, an alliance even, until Therrin's father, King Kallion, had broken it and cast the Krawans out forty years ago. The full-blooded ones anyway. He'd been but a boy then. A stupid, naïve, foolish boy with too much talent to know what to do with.

Archer glanced at the Wildner. A familiar story. A twinge pulled at his side, like an elbow to the ribs. *Don't start now. Spare your guilt until the task is done, Markides.*

"What happens when the Aether takes over?" Hane asked as they turned onto the narrow winding road they'd been following for the last two-day.

"We put them down," Archer said, gruffer than intended. "Before the Aether burns them from the inside out."

Hane's face paled, and he reached out, rubbing his horse's mane. The animal twitched its neck, shying away from his touch. Hane's jaw clenched, and he swallowed. "There are runes to calm the Aether. Gran told me there was."

"They work to an extent," Archer said, he stretched his senses towards the sigils on his pony, preparing to activate them. "Go too far and they crumble under its power."

Hane stared down at his saddle. Archer pushed his pony past, reached for the little well of Aether inside him and funneled it into the runes. His pony snorted and lurched forward, stamping her hooves until Archer gave her the rein. A prickle at his back signaled Hane's power flaring through the runes of the Wildner horse. The beast whinnied and soon it thundered after Archer.

IT WAS NOON WHEN THEY FOUND THE VILLAGE. OR WHAT was left of it. They spotted the wisps of smoke still weaving through the air from miles off. Only once they descended the valley did Archer make out the skeletal rafters of the tumbled homes.

"What happened here?" Hane wondered aloud, slowing his horse to a trot.

Good question. Archer tightened his grip on the reins, half expecting bandits to spring out from the charred buildings.

They remained mounted, the ash-churned tracks of their horses the only sign of their passing. In the square, they found the smoldering mound. And the fresh, red-cloaked bodies.

Looks like they were interrupted.

Hane gasped. "Mister!" he hissed and pointed at the ground. Archer followed his finger to three black feathers lying in the ash. Large feathers. Each severed down the middle as if from a knife—or a blade. A small thrill ran up Archer's spine. *We're close.*

A thump signaled Hane half tumbling, half scrambling from his saddle. He scurried over to the feathers, scooped them up and turned to take in the scene. His eyes darted over the dead soldiers, face tinged green as he took in the blood, exposed bones and spilled intestines strewn across the square.

He wet his lips. "It was quite a fight," he said, moving through the bodies. His keen eyes tracked the movements of the soldiers before they died. He stopped before a long-toed footprint in the dirt. There was no heel to it and prick marks above the toes indicated a set of talons.

"Lyss was here." He moved over to the two fallen soldiers at the edge of the town square, paling at the long gashes in their torsos. Archer nudged his pony past and the boy's head snapped up, staring at him in panic. "You think…"

"Those wounds aren't from rarkyn talons." Archer eyed the smudged series of bear prints before his pony. He was no huntsman, but they seemed far too big. He wandered the scene, counting the Order boot prints. Eight soldiers in all. No easy feat. And those giant lacerations… "They had help," he concluded.

Hane swallowed, attention lingering on two soldiers at the edge of the square. Their faces were crushed, chests ripped open from throat to navel. "What kind of creature can do that?"

More than you know. Archer shrugged. "Who knows." He steered his pony toward the last buildings of the hamlet, waiting for the boy to mount again. "Ride on boy, they're all dead. There's nothing to do for them now."

Hane stared at the earth, brows furrowed as he examined the clutter of footprints, handprints and scuffed cobbles in the ash. "You're wrong," he blurted. "One of them survived."

Archer leaned from his saddle and squinted at the patch of ash Hane pointed to. A long drag mark jutted out of the fray as if someone had heaved themselves off on their elbows. A dry red-brown smear blossomed in its wake.

"Probably wolves," he said, tracking the smear down the road. *Probably.* He hoped so. He did not have time to tend a lost cause.

They left the town and the trail led on. Straight down the middle of the road the smear went. Thin in some places, thick in others where the man had stopped to rest, blood seeping into the dirt. On it went.

Damn fellow. Just die. They rounded a bend at the end of the valley and the bloody mess continued down it, caking the road in its thick, musky smell. Was it him or had the flow of blood lessened? *Yes,* he decided a mile later, *it had.* Not long after, they came across a silver breastplate cast away on the roadside. Archer dismounted, investigated the dead runes on the blood-slicked thing and found the hole where a knife had punctured through the sigiled metal. *The force that would have required,* Archer mulled. *Either the rarkyn or the girl did this.*

Even so, the breastplate had put up enough resistance to stop the blade driving through the soldier's heart. The man had been lucky.

Archer's eyes roved the frosty ground, then the snow-laden cloud swilling above the eastern peaks. Or unlucky.

Hane leaned over his shoulder, breath heavy on Archer's neck.

"Move off," he snapped, shooing a hand at him.

Hane stepped back, but he'd seen enough. Archer saw the question forming even before the boy opened his mouth.

"Doesn't it take a sigil to break another sigil?" he asked, pointing at the puncture.

Archer tossed the breastplate aside and dug a toe under the torn cloak lying in the muck, examining it. "Stronger magic eats weaker magic," he said. "That's the rule of the Aether." He searched for more drag marks on the way ahead. Nothing.

Either patched himself up and walked off, or someone found him.

That meant someone else might hear of a girl and a rarkyn traveling together. Such an oddity would spread through the north's taverns faster than a wench through an Order barracks. He kicked the ruined cloak off his boot, turned for his horse, but stopped as the fabric flipped in the dirt. A half-stained emblem stared up at them from the back of the cloak. A white rose and a crown. The blood drained out of Archer's legs.

Leandre's emblem. *One of the Rose is here?*

With a curse, he turned and swung back into the saddle, ignoring the pony's chomping teeth as it aimed a bite at him and missed. "No more dallying," he said, kicking his heels into the pony's flanks. She arched her neck, whinnied and jerked into a galdar-fueled trot. "Quickly boy!" he snapped when Hane didn't follow. Hane wheeled his horse about and cantered up beside Archer.

"What is it?" he asked.

"Lieutenant Leandre is here." At Hane's expectant silence, he added, "From the Rose Brigade."

Hane's eyes bulged, mouth popping ajar. "The Crown's Rose Brigade?" His jaw see-sawed like a hinge: open, shut, open again. "I thought—why are they so far from Illredus?"

A good question. One tiny rebellious village didn't warrant the King's brigade getting involved. He pondered a moment more, then gave it up. No point in trying to guess. Whatever the reason, he hoped it was enough to keep them too busy to chase down rumors of a rarkyn. Otherwise, Lieutenant Regis Eugenia Leandre would hunt the creature down and kill it without thought. *And present its eyes to Therrin as a gift.*

Not that Therrin would ever eat those cursed things, no matter how much he might want the gift of second sight. *But Keteus might.* The Regis coveted power in all its forms. As far as the Crown was concerned, it never hurt to have another mancer able to see into the Otherworld, consequences be damned.

"Sir?" Hane asked, and with a start Archer realized the boy was still waiting for an answer.

"I don't know," he said. He dug his heels into the pony's side, spurring the mount on. "But she's not taking my rarkyn."

Not yet.

CHAPTER THIRTY-ONE

Darrin eased off the shuck's back feeling like he'd been trampled under a horse. Everything ached; his legs, his back, even his feet, which were swollen from dangling unsupported at the shuck's side for the last three days. With a groan, he stretched, twisting his spine in the long afternoon shadows. Hasek slid from the shuck, landing light on the ground with a distinct spring in his knees.

Seeing Darrin watching, Hasek flashed him a grin. "You get used to it," he said.

I'm not sure I want to, Darrin thought as Hasek strode off to find a tree, leaving Darrin alone with the massive Aether-hound. He eyed the creature, pausing on the haunting skull and needle-sharp teeth. *Lyss killed one of these? How?*

He dug out a small hollow in the earth and begun to hunt through the undergrowth for fire kindling, never turning his back on the creature. The three eyes watched him work, and Darrin was relieved when Hasek returned and dismissed the creature. It melted away, form dissolving into threads of shadow, like smoke in a breeze.

"We made good time today," Hasek said, slumping down at the fire. Perspiration lined his forehead, despite the cold. "The trail is becoming fresh."

Darrin tossed him a slice of bread, then a bit of dried sausage, and frowned. He hadn't seen anything remotely like a trail, and he considered himself a decent tracker. "Why do you say that?"

"The shuck," Hasek waved a finger at where the creature had been. "They get eager when they start to close in. They run a bit quicker; become more fixated. I dare say we'll reach them in the next two days." The corporal reached for his saddlebags, drawing a large waterskin from one. Darrin caught the sweet scent of chara as the soldier unstopped it and took a swig. "Ah, nothing like a good Nilos brew." Hasek smacked his lips and held the skin out. Darrin shook his head.

"Suit yourself," he said, taking another mouthful before corking the skin again. He returned it to his bags and set on the bread and sausage. It was finished in seconds.

"There's more," Darrin said when Hasek gave a small sigh at the sight of his empty fingers.

"Save it," the Corporal said. "I've plenty of Aether left, I just need rest."

Darrin paused in his chewing, seeing an opening to ask the question he'd been wondering, but hadn't dared to ask. He swallowed his mouthful, then made up his mind. "I've never met anyone who could maintain a summoning for so long."

Hasek grinned. "Aye, I'm not a particularly powerful mancer, but I'll outlast just about anyone."

"You were trained in Illredus?"

"Gods no," Hasek snorted. "Won't catch me going there. Not likely. No, it was Brennus."

Darrin blinked. "I didn't realize the Order trained mancers, I thought recruits started at the Conclave's academies."

"Most do," Hasek agreed with a nod, "but there are not many in the north, and they're not like the ones in Illredus. You have to pay, and I was just a brat from the streets of Nilos." He chuckled. "I actually tried to steal from Brennus once, if you can believe it."

Darrin looked across at the rangy soldier and decided he could.

"Of course, I got caught," Hasek went on. "Instead of sending me off to have my Aether sealed with the Brand, he made me an offer."

Darrin waited to hear more, but Hasek pulled out his skin again, sipped, and offered no more of the story, even after he'd swallowed. For a minute they sat in silence, both staring into the flames, before Hasek cursed and pulled his cloak up from the earth. A tear a hand long ran down one side. With a sigh, he reached for his bags again, pulling a small kit with needle and thread from it.

"They give us sigiled armor that lasts an age," he said. "These cloaks on the other hand...I swear they're more trouble than they're worth." He motioned to the hood and the galdar lining the rim. "You think they'd weave runes to make it hard wearing, but no. Just warmth and weak protection wardings. 'Course you can get other weavings added if you're prepared to pay." He snorted. "But who can afford *that* on a corporal's wage?"

Darrin watched him mend the rip, clamping his jaw to stop a laugh when Hasek stabbed himself with the needle and cursed. From his own bags, he produced an oil rag and, unbuckling his sword from his belt, began to wipe down the blade. It had been nearly two weeks since he'd last taken it out. He hadn't practiced since the night Hane had left. The thought sent an anxious twist through his stomach. *It's fine, Hane will be fine.* He dabbed oil onto the rag and ran it along the edge. The metal gleamed back at him, orange in the firelight.

Had Hane and Archer caught up to Lyss and the rarkyn? The thought of Archer riding her down like an auroch in the Ice Steppes made his belly give another uncomfortable flutter—until a more disturbing idea surfaced. Lyss would fight back. There was no way she wouldn't. What then?

"You're thinking about her, aren't you?" Hasek's voice made him start and jerk his head up.

"Who?"

"The girl, *Lyss*," Hasek said, a smile curling onto his face. "There aren't many men who stare so deeply into the steel of their swords—or for so long."

Darrin pressed the rag into the blade with renewed interest. "I don't know what you mean."

The soldier laughed and stretched out before the fire, his lanky limbs blending into growing shadows. "Let's speak plainly then," he said. "You love her."

Darrin's head snapped up. "No, I—we," at Hasek's knowing look his words petered out and the heat flushed into his cheeks. His gaze slid to the sword. "It's that obvious?"

Opposite, Hasek grinned like a jackal, white teeth catching the firelight. "Let's see," he held up a hand, "you disobeyed your elders, ran away from home, journeyed halfway across the north *in winter*," he listed on his fingers, "all for a girl?"

He pieced all that together from a few conversations? Darrin pushed out a lip and huffed. "Well, when you put it like that..." he muttered. *He must be guessing, surely.* If he was, it was unnervingly accurate.

Hasek chuckled. "There's no shame in it." He offered Darrin his chara flask. Darrin sighed, took it, sipped then handed it back.

"What I don't understand is where Markides fits into it all. How in Sepp's name did you get tangled up with him?"

Tread carefully. Darrin wet his lips. "Brennus told you about the rarkyn Markides is hunting?"

Hasek tapped a gloved hand to his breastplate, as if it contained the missive in question. "Aye, he did." The Corporal's smile vanished, and he met Darrin's gaze over the fire. "It's traveling with your friend, to Illredus of all places. I believe I met it. Briefly." He rubbed the back of his head.

Darrin gave a slow nod, not sure what to make of Hasek's words. He pressed on. "Hane and I were the ones who accidentally set it loose."

Hasek sat up. "*You* did?"

Darrin told Hasek the story about how they found the rarkyn, how he'd shot it with a dart and how Hane had bound it in a warding circle. He even mentioned the part where Hane had run to get Iga but returned with Lyss. He skipped over the fight and the sigil breaking. Anything that might allow Hasek to guess what the link between the rarkyn and Lyss was, he omitted. Hasek asked anyway.

"Why south?" he queried when Darrin finished. "And why her?"

"That's *not* my business to tell," Darrin said, emphasizing his words so Hasek knew he'd say no more on the matter.

The Corporal's eyebrows rose instead. "Then there is something to tell?"

Damn the gods, the abyss, and the Eternals all. Darrin shot the soldier a look over the fire. "No." He squeezed the hilt of his sword as it rested across his knees.

"Easy, easy." Hasek held up his hands, placating for peace. "No need for that. I just want to know what we're dealing with."

Hasek's words jumped out at Darrin. What *we're* dealing with. "You're going to help?"

It was Hasek's turn to look shifty. He mulled a moment, tongue running over his teeth. "Do you know why rarkyns are hunted?"

Darrin shrugged. "Their eyes. It's said they give whoever eats them second sight." He stopped, unable to keep the disgust from working over his face. "You're not—"

Hasek dismissed Darrin's suspicion with a flippant hand. "Gods no. I'm not that stupid. As they say in Illredus: look too deep into the abyss and the abyss looks back into you." He shuddered. "No thanks." He leaned forward, and despite himself, Darrin mirrored the move. "Do you know the *other* reason why the Conclave sends mancers out to kill rarkyn?"

So the stories are true. "Their blood."

"Yes."

"It really does heal?"

"Yes, but not only wounds. Magic too. Think about it, they draw on the Aether itself, they travel in and out of it all the time, their blood is teeming with its power."

A knot of unease grew in Darrin's stomach. "And mancers restore their Aether reserves with the food they eat," he said, thinking of how hungry Hane got when he worked galdar. He glanced up at the soldier to see if he was on track. Hasek gave a nod and Darrin wrinkled his nose. "They drink rarkyn blood."

Hasek clicked his fingers. "That they do. When they can get it. It's rare stuff, and expensive. Beyond expensive, from what I hear."

"Let me guess, that's what you want too."

Hasek tutted. "Suspicious, aren't you?" He heaved a sigh when Darrin didn't let up his stare. "No, I don't need it—" he flexed one arm "—endurance, remember? I'm not the one to worry about. It's Markides." He stoked the coals of their fire. "If Brennus is right, he's planning something. If the rarkyn features in those plans, I'm betting it's something to do with its blood."

His words washed over Darrin, lukewarm. Did Hasek expect surprise? Horror? Darrin didn't feel any of those. Just sullen resignation. Of course, Markides had something planned. Why else go to the trouble of keeping a rarkyn bound to Terresmir? As far as he was concerned, Markides could do what he liked, so long as he didn't drag Hane and Lyss into it.

Wishful thinking. If that kratting rarkyn is involved, then so is Lyss.

Across the fire, Hasek steepled the tips of his long fingers together and propped them under his chin. "Back to my original question," he said. "Why her? And where is she taking it?"

Darrin hesitated. Should he tell the Corporal about Illredus? *No,* he decided. That would only invite more questions. No matter how friendly Hasek was, he was still part of the Order. A vision of the violet-eyed halfling trapped in the gibbet outside Nilos flashed through his head. And the Order still executed krats.

Especially krats who kill the Order's own.

A shiver ran across Darrin's arms. He pulled his cloak tighter and hugged his elbows underneath. *Why did she kill one of the Order?* The question stomped around the well-worn track in his thoughts. *Why?* Had it been self-defense? An accident? A lapse in sanity? The chill spread down his spine. *Was the pact's madness already beginning to take root?*

"You cannot help her." Iga's voice lectured in his ears, and he was back in his grandmother's tent, Hane beside him, watching their grandmother pacing between them. Her Reading runes were scattered over the floor, but she did not appear to notice. *"Do not go after her,"* she had said. *"Let her go."*

Darrin clenched his fists. "Not yet."

Hasek rocked forward, chin lifting. "What's that?"

Darrin straightened. "Not yet," he said again. "Ask again once we rescue Lyss and Hane."

Hasek was silent a moment, then he gave a nod. "Very well, agreed." He cocked his head, grin returning. "I'll get you to her and your brother, but I don't think your love is the one who'll need rescuing."

Darrin's blush got a chortle out of the soldier.

"Get some rest," he said, settling back before the flames.

Darrin unrolled his sleeping kit, propped his saddlebags under his head and shifted about until he was comfortable. He lay there, suddenly wide awake, thoughts spiraling round and round. Blood. Magic. Madness. Fresh fear bloomed in his chest.

What if I'm already too late?

It took a long time for sleep to come that night.

CHAPTER THIRTY-TWO

Skaar sat on the back of the wagon, staring up at the cloudless sky, watching the faint streams of Aether flow through the Otherworld beyond it. Beneath him, the cart juddered and bounced along the winding road, iron axles emitting a periodic squeak as the wheels turned.

He cupped his hands to his mouth, blowing hot air over his freezing fingers. He had thought he'd known what cold was. That had been before he met the mancers and come to know what cold truly was. Its icy tendrils burrowed deep, turning his limbs sluggish and heavy. Down it sank, right into his bones, and stayed there. He glanced at the manacle and its faint runes about his wrist and inched a tentative talon under the metal. The Aether inside the manacle buzzed as if he were prodding a wasp hive. He jerked his hand away, bristling all over. Reythr curse the thing. His fist thudded into the wagon's floor. Every part of him loathed it. Its cool weight as it burned through feather to flesh, the agonizing jolts when he tinkered with it, the utterly enraging power it held over him. It was everything the elders had warned him about. Yet, it was all that stood between him and the Deep.

That thought alone made his heart gallop. Blood surged to his limbs. It's fine, I'm out, I am safe. *Even as he thought it, the pressure of the manacle hung heavy around his wrist. No. He tried to shove the worry aside, but it returned like a gnawing hunger.*

Fengar would know what to do, but then Skaar remembered Fengar was dead; body broken on the earth. He curled himself into a ball on the back of the wagon, biting his lip to stop the tears. Think about something else. Anything else.

What had happened after? *All he remembered was his grief, rage and heat rolling into one, then…nothing. It was all blank.*

He knuckled his temple. *Why don't I remember?*

"Here."

Skaar started as the voice sounded behind him. He turned just in time to catch a rock as it was tossed to him. The young mancer, Isaac, flopped down beside him.

"For you," *he said, pointing at the stone Skaar held.*

Skaar looked down at the glittering rock. It was oddly clear. He ran his tongue over his teeth, then forced it around the word he wanted. "What?"

"A sigil."

Skaar dropped the stone as if it had burned him.

Isaac laughed. "It's alright. I haven't activated it yet." *He scooped the rock up from the floor.* "I want you to try it." *He held out the rock again.* "If it hurts you, let it go." *He held the rock out in his palm.*

Skaar hesitated, then slowly unfurled his talons to let Isaac place the sigil in his hand.

"I'm going to cast," *Isaac warned, and the Aether in the human rippled, like water pushed by a breeze. Such a small pool he had inside him, yet with it, so much power. The mancer pressed a finger to the rock and a faint glow welled up from the rune, along with the familiar pressure of galdar. Skaar bared his teeth but made no sound. With a flourish, Isaac removed his hand and stood back, hands on his hips as he admired his handiwork.*

Skaar was about to ask what next, but at a sudden trickle of heat through his fingers he started, gaze drawn back down again.

"Is warm."

"It's a heating rune," *Isaac said, and gave him one of those strange flat-toothed grins.* "It's not strong, and I figured it might emit enough heat to mask the galdar."

Skaar only knew half the words Isaac said, but he thought he understood.

"Should help with the shivering," *Isaac went on. When Skaar cocked his head, the mancer made a motion of chaffing his hands over his arms and blowing on his fingers. Skaar nodded, but Isaac wasn't done.*

"Draw on it," *he said.*

Skaar looked down at the rune, confused. "What's draw?" *The word felt odd in his mouth; he wasn't sure he'd said it right.*

"Pull the Aether out of it."

Skaar jerked his head up. The glimmer of panic that rattled through his hugrokar got no response, but his expression must have given something away. Isaac thumbed his nose and grinned again.

"Yes, I know about that."

The mancer seemed…pleased? Skaar reached out with hugrokar to gauge what the human was feeling, but there was nothing there. Just a well of empty. A pang burned his lungs, then snaked into his heart and he sucked in a breath and bit his tongue. He counted in his head. One, two…four, five, six. The ache faded.

Oblivious, Isaac tapped the stone and Skaar forced himself to concentrate on what the human was saying. "We need our locks, so drain this instead. Go on."

Isaac gave his hand a nudge and Skaar folded his talons around the stone and reached for the Aether within it. A small, quick stab of cold lanced through his palm before wonderful, glorious heat spread through his bones. A heartbeat later it fizzled to nothing. Skaar uncurled his fingers. The rune lay dead in his hand.

"Sepp damn," Isaac said, peering over it. "I hoped it'd last longer than that."

"Too weak," Skaar told him.

"Can I?" Isaac asked and Skaar handed the rock over. The mancer held it up before his nose, squinting at the rune while clucking his tongue and muttering to himself. He pressed a finger back over it and the rune shone bright green under it. Skaar eased away as the Aether surged into the rune, yet when Isaac held it out, he found it still pleasantly warm to the touch.

"Should last a bit longer this time," Isaac said. "Come find me when it dies. I'll rework it again for you."

Skaar opened his mouth to thank the man, then realized he had no idea how to in the human tongue. He hunted for any words that might do, and the best he could come up with was, "Is good."

Isaac gave a knowing smile. "You're wel—"

A cry sliced the air, a high, piercing call that rang in his ears and reverberated down to his bones. Skaar came to his feet. A flight-cry! The wagon was gone, and a red sky pressed down upon him. The cry came again, high and urgent. He knew that call. Flee. Mordkyn were coming. Skaar staggered forward, feet turning heavy under him. He spread his wings and tried to leap for the sky. The air slipped away from him, tumbling him back to the earth. He slammed face-first into some-thing wet and sticky. Mud, water, and—he sniffed, stiffening at the metallic scent —blood.

He scrambled up, tripped over something long and solid, and splattered onto his knees. Blinking away the muck, he made out the headless corpse at his feet. He lurched back. A groan issued from Isaac's disembodied head in his grip.

"Help me," it whispered. "Help—"

The skin on Isaac's head shifted, features twisting and writhing until a new face stared up at him. A gentle face. Curious and earnest, until the eyes turned cold, and a livid scar twisted its way down its cheek. Archer.

"You owe me," the mancer growled.

Skaar threw the head away. It bounced twice in the muck and was still.

Stop.

Skaar turned on the spot, eyes roving the churned meadow. Bodies hung in the trees. Stop. His feet carried him forward.

They were strung upside down; ankles bound, throats slit, eyes gouged out. Skaar slowed as he got close, dreading what he'd find. He tried not to look at their faces, but still he recognized them. Ruk, Kata, elder Talla. Vlak, Lopor, even little Sorr. He wanted to look away, wanted to—his gaze landed on a familiar figure. He choked back a sob and ran to it.

"No, Raska, not you too." He dug his talons into the rope, pulling at the binding that dangled the elder. Suddenly he was small again, back in his cursed kit's body, flailing at the bonds.

Unluck once more. Unluck the tainted, Unluck the Ever-child.

He strained anyway, but the binding was too strong for his tiny talons. He slipped, fell and landed on his back in the muck with a splash. It soaked into his feathers, coating them in a cloying mess. Overhead, the pack's blood rained to the forest floor. Drip, drip, drip. He scrunched his eyes shut, knowing what would come next. I don't want to see, I don't want to see.

But he did.

The rarkyn was apart from the others, splayed in the mud, rune-burns snaked its body. The magic had seared through feathers to leave blackened, scaly skin in the spell's passing. His limbs were a twisted mess, broken in a hundred places, eyes missing like the rest.

Fengar.

Skaar sank to his knees.

Fengar had fought with everything he had. Everything to save his kit of a brother. Yet Skaar had fallen into the Otherworld anyway. He reached out and put a hand to Fengar's cheek. Why turn and fight? You knew you had no chance. *At his touch, his brother's body shifted. Feathers gave way under his fingers and, like a dandelion in the wind, they dissolved into dust.*

"Fengar!" Skaar screamed, grabbing after the wisps. He pitched forward, sinking up to his elbows in blood, then up to his neck. Heart thumping, he struggled to get free. The earth held him, refusing to let go.

"Fen—"

The world twisted and Lyss watched the sword fall. The scream burned in her lungs, roaring up her throat, out her mouth to pierce the air in a long screech that didn't pause for breath. Before her, Fa's body hung for an impossibly long moment, silhouetted in the red sky. Then it folded, crumpling into a pool of blood.

The shadow behind it laughed, then spat. "A quick death is more than you deserve, traitor."

Lyss' jaw clenched. Her insides boiled. You. She grabbed for her sword. Her fingers closed around air instead. She lunged anyway, fists swinging. The shadow danced away, form sliding around her knuckles.

Her boots splattered into something wet. Blood lapped against her toes. A pool of it. Her eyes traveled further, breath catching in her throat. A lake. It extended as far as she could see, its color blurring with the sky. Nothing but red. So much red.

And her father's body was gone.

"Fa!"

Silence. She couldn't see him. Couldn't see his body. Couldn't lay it to rest.

"Fa!"

With a cry she splashed up to her knees. A head bobbed above the water, turning this way and that. Fa, he was alive? Joy surged through her. "Fa!" She pushed in up to her waist, then her chest, and with a kick, began to swim—frog-stroking just like he'd taught her.

"Fa!"

The joy crashed into her heart like a cudgel.

It was a head.

Fa's head.

It bobbed and buoyed before her: a piece of driftwood on a bloody sea. Mouth open, eyes sightless. Lyss swam to it, clasped the swirling hair in her fist and pulled it close, hugging it to her chest.

"I miss you Fa." Heat built in her throat, threatening to release as a sob.

A groan burbled up from her breast. "Why?"

Lyss looked down. The face had changed, a young man in a mangled sigiled helmet stared up at her, his brain a soggy yolk underneath the ripped steel.

"Why?" It gurgled again through broken teeth.

With a cry, Lyss pushed it away. The head dipped and rolled. Then it sank, vanishing below in a hiss of bubbles. She blinked back tears and turned for the shore. Be brave, Lyss. Her mouth turned dry. The shore was gone. She floundered, kicking her feet down, searching for a purchase. Nothing. She stroked in a widening circle, coat and boots turning heavy as she swam. Her head slipped under. She kicked hard and surfaced again, spluttering, clawing at the sky.

Winged shadows flew overhead. They wheeled about, their shrill cries in her bones. Mordkyn. Mordkyn come. She opened her mouth to cry for help. The red waters rushed in, coppery tang hitting the back of her throat. She coughed and spattered and reached upwards. "Wait!"

The lake sucked her down, deeper into the dark. The air burned in her lungs. She drew in a breath—a breath of blood. Her head spun. So much blood.
In her mouth.
In his ears.
In her lungs.
In his eyes.
Rivers of red pouring. Drowning.
Falling—

W ITH A STRANGLED SHOUT, S KAAR LEAPT AWAKE, COMING TO his feet, heart pounding. Paces away, Lyss started up, a ragged cry ripping through the camp. For a jarring moment he saw double. Human hands flew to his mouth, gagging, while rarkyn talons dug into his chest. With a wrench that burned like tearing muscle, he pulled his and Lyss' minds apart. Pain lanced through him and his knees hit the earth. Gulping down air, he pressed a shaking hand to his temples, listening to the blood surging through his ears.

What in Reythr's name—

He glanced over at Lyss. She was huffing hard, a ring of sweat soaked into the neck of her coat. When she looked up, her face was gaunt and eyes sunken. The thumping fear reverberated between them, and behind it, a weariness settled its weight over her limbs. She opened her mouth and a breath rasped out. Her tongue licked over her cracked lips and she tried again.

"You saw it too?"

Skaar nodded.

"What was it?" she whispered over the smoldering coals.

Skaar slumped against a tree and ran a hand down a forearm, flattening the ruffled feathers. "That was not hugrokar." The thought of the red meadow, dripping corpses and the red lake flashed through his head. Bile rose in his throat. He clenched his jaw and swallowed it down. "Hugrokar doesn't do that."

Lyss' gray face took on a distinct green tinge, even in the firelight, and Skaar didn't need the mind magic to know exactly what went through her thoughts. *The pact.* Her gaze dropped to her left wrist. With a trembling hand she pushed the sleeve up, exposing the flesh and runes underneath. Only there were no runes. Lyss gave an odd, muffled squeak, and turned her hand over, frantically searching.

A single rune marked the inside of her wrist.

"Sepp," Lyss breathed. Her hugrokar twisted, relief and worry warring inside her.

One rune left. They were one rune away from the full brunt of the pact.

Then what? Skaar wondered.

"Ursa was right, you *are* bonded." Brin's voice made them both start. The bear-kin leaned against a tree at the edge of the firelight. Her back was to them, but her head was cocked, one gray eye watching. On her head, the bear's teeth glinted, as if daring one of them to disagree. Brin turned from her watch and sidled over to the fire; she crouched over it, hands out to the flames.

"It's the little things," she said into the silence. "The way you move, the way you cock an ear to the same sound, the way you share a look—just now."

Skaar jerked his eyes from Lyss and Brin laughed. "See?"

Lyss cleared her throat. "You could tell that easily?"

Brin shrugged. "You can't fool Ursa. But me," she rubbed her chin and shrugged, "had I not seen you together, I would never have known."

Ursa? Skaar sent to Lyss, but she pushed his hugrokar away, the lines on her forehead deepening. "'Byss curse it," she muttered. She tugged down her sleeve and rubbed her face.

Brin tilted her chin. "It's not a curse," she said, her gaze shifted from her to Skaar, and his feathers prickled down to the end of his tail as those storm eyes landed on him. "It's many things, but not that." She shrugged and the spell of her stare broke. "Or so Ursa tells me." She slapped her thighs, stood, and stretched, spine popping like the snapping of twigs. "There's scarcely an hour 'til dawn, might as well make the most of it." She strode over to the singed blanket that had served as her bed and began rolling it up.

Skaar watched her work, not quite sure what to make of her. Sometimes she seemed so very human, other times he was sure he was talking to a bear masquerading in a woman's skin.

Just like a mancer, the Aether's power burned inside her as sure as a flame in the night. *A very bright flame,* he thought as he looped his supply satchel over his shoulder, wincing as it bumped the scabbed wound from Alrend on his back.

Despite that, Brin did not carry the telltale scent of galdar, he thought as they set off. There was no cold pressure of runes about her body. Stranger still, the Otherworld seemed drawn to her, though she appeared not to notice. To his eyes, its power hung about her on the other plane, coalescing around her body like a cloak.

Not so different from a rarkyn, he mused, as he and Lyss trudged after Brin, following her lead. *Only she doesn't draw on it.*

The way was still dark, and a thick fog clung to the earth. Above, a half-moon shone down from a clear, star-pricked sky to guide the way. No lanterns needed. *Just as well.*

Skaar glanced at the bear skin again, its gray fur rippling on Brin's back as she strode. Perched on her head, the bear's eyes shone. Shone, and as Skaar stared, *shifted.* He stopped dead in his tracks, drawing a look from Lyss. He paid it no attention. Behind the bear's head the thing shifted again, making its presence felt. Fear prickled down his arms. Whatever it was, it was fierce and strong. Skaar swallowed. And old. Very old. He was not sure how he knew that, but he sensed it down to his bones. Beside him, Lyss pulled up short, a breath whittling from between her teeth.

Brin stopped and turned, a wolfish grin on her face.

"You don't need to fear Ursa, she will not harm you."

Under their watch, the presence stretched, its pressure arching out like a cat after a long nap, then it settled once more and vanished from his senses. Brin gave a sigh and shrugged. "She sleeps a lot this time of year." She pointed to a distant rise and a ridge of trees running along it. "Torin is on the other side," she said. "If we hurry, we'll make it by noon."

A flicker of curiosity ran through hugrokar and Lyss began walking again, coming up beside the bear-kin. "What—who is Ursa?" she asked.

Skaar's ears perked and in two bounds he caught up to the women, and with a final wary stare at the bear-skin, fell into step with them.

"She's my guardian," Brin said. "She was my mother's guardian too, and her mother's before that."

I was right, she's no mancer. But that didn't answer what the Ursa *was.*

"Hereditary magic," Lyss said with a nod. "Iga mentioned it once. Your mother taught you?"

Brin shook her head. "It's part of our coming of age. We enter the wilds to seek out Ursa's gift," she patted one of the giant paws on her shoulder. "If we find it, we become one of Ursa's kin—and she becomes a part of us. If not," her voice petered out and she was silent for several paces, one hand wrapped around the rabbit's foot at her neck. "If not," she continued. "We remain human, never to hear Ursa's voice." She gave a sniff.

"Nina," Lyss guessed, with a guilty stab through hugrokar.

Brin nodded. "We took our trial together. I found Ursa's skin, she did not." She lifted her head to the stars. "She was an ordinary girl who dreamed of an ordinary life. A life with ordinary folk." Her lips pressed together, and her chin gave a wobble. "I should never have gone with her. If not for me, the Order would never have come." Her next breath, when she took it, was ragged and Skaar heard the pain there. She wiped her nose with the back of a hand. "What of you?" she asked, glancing between them. "How did you come to be bonded?"

Lyss cast Skaar an uncertain glance. He shrugged. Lyss seemed to wrestle with some internal debate before relenting. She told Brin about the Eder Wildner, about the fight over the warding circle and the sigil breaking. How she'd killed the soldier in Bardas Post and their crazed flight from the soldiers at Ira River. Twice she glanced at Skaar to see if he wanted to add anything. He stayed silent, letting her tell the story as they walked.

They kept a fast pace. Brin matched Lyss' stride with ease, long legs taking one pace for two of Lyss'. Skaar loped behind, half listening, half watching the forest wake as the sky lightened in the east. A pair of aetherlings idled through the sky above, the scales on their serpent-like bodies catching in the Terresmir light. Skaar watched them a moment, then realized Lyss had stopped her conversation with Brin to stare wide-eyed up at them.

"What is it?" Brin asked, following Lyss' line of sight.

"Noomos," Skaar said. At Brin's blank look, he added, "Aetherlings." The bear-kin searched the sky again, furrowed her brow and gave up with a shrug. Skaar turned to Lyss. "You see them?"

Lyss tore her gaze away from the creatures. "Shouldn't I?"

"You haven't before. They dwell deeper than smarokk," he said. "Much deeper."

The look of wonder melted from her face. Her right hand made an involuntary jerk for the seal on her left wrist. This was more than weakening runes. The pact was growing stronger as well. He pointed to a kwark, its spiny body moving in and out of a tree as if it were nothing more substantial than the morning's fog.

Lyss followed his finger and blinked as she spotted it. "It looks like a lizard, with two heads." She chewed her lip. "Will I keep seeing them?"

"Yes, probably," Skaar admitted.

"Are they dangerous?"

"Not these ones."

She nodded and gave a sigh. "Better get used to it then."

At the ridge their pace slowed, the road forcing them into a single file as it zig-zagged up the slope. Lyss followed behind him, head down, watching her footing.

"Fengar was your brother, wasn't he?" her voice sounded just above a whisper. Skaar quirked an ear at her, heart sinking. *So, she'd seen that after all*. Hardly surprising, his memory of the red lake was just as vivid as the blood meadow.

"Yes."

"What happened? Was it like the dream?"

Skaar huffed. "Close enough. Mordkyn raided our pack."

"Mancer hunters," Lyss confirmed and Skaar gave a nod.

"They scattered us. Most took off into the Otherworld."

"Except you."

"Yes, and Fengar."

Her hugrokar reached out, probing, and he sensed her confusion. It was as though she'd expected to find something there, only it wasn't.

"You're not angry?"

"No."

"Why not?"

Skaar paused. "My people have a saying," he said, slowly. "*Bregda vigr, standa taka vidh*. Fight what you can change, accept what you cannot." He cast an eye over his shoulder to find her listening, face rapt in attention. "Was angry once. But can't change it. Besides," he let out a rueful sigh, "the mordkyn who killed Fengar is already dead."

She blinked and Skaar gave a crooked smile. "Fengar took the mordkyn with him. He saved me." *For all the good it did.*

Lyss sensed the bitter thought. She cocked her head. "Then you fell into the Aether."

"I was in ellirsott. Couldn't fly with growing sickness in the Otherworld. Lots of magic, but no control yet." He sighed. "No pack to help control new magic, I fell. Very deep."

"I'm sorry."

Skaar peered down at her, surprised. "Why? Not your fault."

Lyss shrugged. "I'm sorry all the same."

Skaar snorted, shaking his head. "Strange human."

Ire flickered in her hugrokar, then amusement. "Strange rarkyn," came the retort at his back.

They kept climbing. Ahead, the road curved away through the thinning trees and up over the apex of the hill. Brin waited at the top, knuckles on hips, a knowing smile playing across her face. She swept out a hand. Below, a foamy sea of rolling, snow-spotted pasture stretched as far as Skaar could see. Herds of livestock dotted the fields like dark colonies of ants. A winding river ambled in from the north, twisting and turning with the land, the last of the morning's fog hanging over its dark waters.

Then he saw the settlement.

In the glare of the sunrise he almost missed it, until he saw the long, towering shadows stretched across the fields. Built atop a rise, stone walls—not wood—stood like man-made mountains. Beyond them, five fingers of stone jutted upwards. *Like teeth,* Skaar thought.

Flags flew from each of the towers, their blue deep against the azure sky.

Brin's grin widened. "As promised, the city of Torin."

CHAPTER THIRTY-THREE

THE RARKYN'S HUGROKAR NUDGED HER LIKE A PROD ON THE shoulder. Lyss turned.

"What is—" Rark floundered for words. In the end, he pointed up at the towers.

"It's a castle," Lyss said, and turned her attention back to the road. It was a steep descent, and the path was overgrown with grass and lichen. One slip, and she'd tumble, and likely break bone as she went. With her luck it would be her kratting neck.

"Torin Keep," Brin supplied from further down the path. "Story goes the Erdesin sang it up out of the earth eons ago, long before humans came to these lands."

Lyss peered over the treetops at the towers. "The Earth Singers?" she said. It was difficult to tell from this distance, but the walls looked smooth. As if they'd been cast from clay. "I thought they were a myth."

"That's what the city folk say," Brin said, picking her way along the trail.

"You've been to Torin before?" Lyss asked.

"Many times. We go every spring. Nina likes to—" her words cut short, and she sucked in a breath. Lyss imagined the burn in Brin's throat as the bear-kin fought down grief. She knew that feeling well. *Idiot,* she berated herself and hunted for another topic.

"Do rarkyn have any stories of the Erdesin?" she asked Rark.

Trailing behind, Rark lifted his head, ears perking forward. "Only that they were once many. Now not so. Songs say they built Finnafell."

Lyss turned, curious. "What's Finnafell?"

"Rarkyn meeting place. Deep in the wilds."

"What, in Memnon's Spine?"

Rark shrugged. "Not sure. Only pack leader knows where." As he spoke, his hugrokar twitched, walling off his emotions, and Lyss realized the lie. *Can't blame him.* If her people were hunted by mancers, she'd guard that knowledge too.

They continued down and soon their view of the fields and valley was lost behind trees. The trail ended at a crossroads at the bottom of the ridge. Here, two more roads from along the ridge's baseline joined theirs to become a wide, graveled highway. With a sigh Brin stopped, pulled her bag from her shoulders and eased the bear skin from her back. It was the first time Lyss had seen her without it. The sight of the woman's bare head and shoulders made her look oddly naked, despite her woolen tunic and pantaloons. With gentle hands, Brin rolled the skin into a bundle and stowed it away.

"Folk are wary around here," she said, straightening. "Keep your talk to a minimum or people really will think you're mad." She searched the air around Lyss. "You hear that rarkyn?"

Lyss started. Rark stood next to her, clear as day. A faint tendril of smoke coiled around one horn, then vanished into it as if inhaled. "You're in the Otherworld," she realized. *Sepp's balls, how did I miss that?* No wonder she'd been getting so warm, she'd thought it was from coming down the ridge.

Rark shrugged. "Quite shallow," he said. As he spoke, Brin cocked her head as if straining to listen.

"You can hear him?" Lyss asked.

Brin nodded, blond braids swinging. "Aye. It's like listening through a wall, but I hear." She shouldered her bag. "I have good hearing, but so might the next man."

Be careful, her back seemed to say as she set off down the road.

A prickle tickled the hairs on Lyss' neck. She stiffened and looked back up the trail they'd come. No one followed. She glanced at Rark. The rarkyn stood with a languid ease, one wing half open, basking in the Aether's warmth. Hugrokar calm. Catching her watching, he frowned, cocking his head.

What is it?

Lyss shook her head. "Nothing." She shifted her make-do sack on her back, the shuck skull bumping through the hessian as she set after Brin. *Best go deep until we're past Torin.*

She only hoped his ability held in a throng of people. *Only one way to find out.* Better to test it here in Torin than in the mancer's nest that was Illredus. With a slight wave of pressure, Rark pitched deeper into the Otherworld, and when she glanced behind, he'd vanished.

They passed fields of sheep, thick-wooled and fat from a summer spent out on pasture. Soon barns and the odd homestead began to appear, their chimneys puffing smoke into the cool air. In some of them, Lyss made out people moving behind the closed windows. It brought back vivid memories of her and Fa warming their hands before roaring inn hearths. She smiled at that, and as her eyes landed on a horse and cart on the road ahead, her stomach tightened.

A driver sat hunched on the seat, a crooked hat atop his head as his horse plodded. As they neared, her insides began an uncomfortable flutter. Was he a farmer? Townsfolk? Again, Lyss' senses prickled, gooseflesh spreading down her arms. She checked the fields, half expecting to catch a flicker of a red cloak. But the fields were clear, the road behind empty. Still her stomach clenched, and her palms sweated. Was the man a Red in disguise? Was that it? She'd heard they sometimes dressed as ordinary folk in the backcountry to unmask krats wielding illegal magics.

Wheeling high above, Rark's attention turned on her and a query rose through hugrokar.

She clamped her mind tight with a scowl. *It's fine,* she sent. She was overthinking it.

They caught the cart up with ease, and the driver, a wiry old man with sun-spotted cheeks, hailed them. "Need a ride travelers? We don't go fast, Rhyla and I, but it'll save your legs for the dancing later." He indicated the back of the cart.

Lyss blinked. *Dancing?* Then before she could object, Brin jumped up and settled herself between the crates stacked in the back. "Thank you, err…"

"Timo, Arvus Timo."

Brin caught Lyss' eye and jerked her head at the cart. "Get on," she mouthed. Grudgingly, Lyss clambered up beside her.

"Less conspicuous," Brin murmured as Lyss sat down between two crates that smelt of fresh turned earth and tubers. "Especially if any of the Order are about."

The moment she said it, Lyss' stomach balled itself into a cold, hard knot. A city meant people, and where there were people, there was galdar, and were there was galdar…

She rubbed a fist into her gut, trying to ease the tension. *There's no guarantee they're here.*

There's no guarantee they're not, doubt whispered back.

"Looks like we're in for a fine feast-day this year," Timo said over his shoulder.

Feast day? Lyss' mouth went dry. Surely not. Perhaps Torin folk celebrated winter feast-day at a different time, it must be. She tried to count back the days, but her memories blurred together. She pressed her palms into her temples and massaged. *Sepp help me.*

"I'm a bit past my dancing days, but I always enjoy the music," Timo went on. "Where you lasses traveling from?"

A look of indecision came over Brin's face. She hadn't thought about that. "Nilos," Lyss said, quickly. Conscious of her travel-gritted hair, grubby tunic and distinct lack of belongings she added, "We had a few setbacks."

"Ah," Timo said, "We've had quite a few of you coming in from Nilos. Bad business over there I hear."

Lyss hesitated, not sure how to respond. With his attention on the road, Timo saved her from answering.

"Yes, bad business," he said. "All over one krat girl."

Lyss' heart, which had begun to settle back into a steady rhythm, jolted once more. *Relax, there's more than one krat girl in the north.*

"Hear she escaped the gibbets and the Order's upturned the town to find her," Timo continued. He heaved a sigh, "With the Order's new decree turning neighbor on neighbor there…yes, a bad place to be."

"Decree?" Brin asked. "What decree?"

Timo's thick, bushy brows rose, and he lifted the edge of his hat to look at them. "You've not heard?"

They shook their heads.

"They're turfing out all the krats from Nilos. Calling it a *cleansing*. Anyone found to harbor a krat shall hang in a gibbet beside them. Got some folk here scared." Timo cast a worried look over them. "If you lasses don't mind some advice from an old farmer, perhaps keep you're from Nilos to yourselves."

Lyss felt for the sword under her cloak and gave the hilt a reassuring squeeze. Had they not gone off course at Ira River... She rubbed her palm over the smooth pommel. *We would have walked right into the maw of the beast.* Her senses prickled afresh, this time down her spine. *Gods curse it.* Perhaps she was coming down with something. She shivered and peered up the road to the white walls of the city.

It was late afternoon when they reached the gates of Torin. The walls, which had seemed big, even at a distance, had taken an age to reach. Now, Lyss craned her neck, taking in the smooth white stone that stretched fifty paces above her head. At the top, a pair of guards strode past, silver chain mail glinting in the sun. Ahead, the iron gate stood open like a giant mouth, swallowing a steady queue of travelers and spitting none out. Timo's cart rolled to a stop at the end of the line.

Brin leaned over the lip and peered up at the gate. Lyss copied her, and from the vantage of the cart, made out four guards, two a side, watching walkers, riders, carts, and wagons roll through the threshold. A faint pressure rippled through her and Lyss knew Rark had alighted in the cart beside them. She checked he was still too deep to see. He was.

Sepp, I hope he's right about this.

With a jerk and a clomp of hooves, Timo's cart trundled forward, and as they neared the guards, Lyss held her breath. She forced herself to sit and rest her back against a crate on the end of the cart. Brin dangled her legs over the side, kicking first one then the other out in time with the cart's clanking axel.

"Afternoon gentleman," she called out to the guards when they passed. "We haven't missed the dancing, have we?"

That drew a chuckle from one. "No miss, there's still plenty of dancing to be had." He nudged his younger compatriot with an elbow, drawing a furious glare from the fellow.

They rolled past, and Lyss relaxed her breath. Double story homes lined the street beyond. Each side of the paved thoroughfare they stood, white-washed walls gleaming with frost and icicles. Buntings of red, yellow and blue ran between the second stories, dressing the street in cheer. Below, a throng of people moved, their clothes almost as bright as the flags above. From within the hubbub, doorbells jingled as shop patrons came and went.

"Wait!"

The cry snapped Lyss' head around and a stamp of boots drew her gaze back to the guards at the gate. One of them was running after them, hand raised. Her eyes darted to the space where Rark was. Not a feather, tail or talon to be seen.

"Hold up!" The guard called. Lyss shared a glance with Brin and didn't need hugrokar to get her intent across. *Run?*

The ursa gave a slight shake of her head.

The guard caught them up, huffing. It was the young compatriot. Breath recovered, he straightened and turned to Brin. "What's your name?"

Brin was silent a moment before answering, "Matrie."

"Would you—" the guard paused, and a flush burned up his neck, not quite to his cheeks. "Would you care to dance later?"

Brin drew herself up, storm irises wandering over the man, as if she were a trader sizing up a lamb for sale in the markets.

Is she planning to eat him? Came Rark's question through hugrokar.

Don't be stupid.

Brin's face was still as she considered, and the guard shifted on his feet and wiped his palms on the fabric of his jerkin. A whiff of musty sweat reached Lyss' nose as he did, and she wished Brin would hurry up and put the poor fellow out of his misery. Brin tapped her chin, a smile playing across her face. "Alright," she said at last. She pointed down the road. "Meet me at the fountain at sundown."

The guard perked up, surprised. "Yes, milady!" he said with a boyish grin. "Sundown at the fountain." He gave Brin a short bow, and suddenly remembering Lyss next to her, gave another, shorter bow in her direction.

"Ladies," he said by way of farewell and hurried off. Lyss waited until he'd returned to his post before turning to Brin.

"Is that a good idea?" she asked.

Brin shrugged. "What harm is one dance?" She jumped off the cart and leaned close. "Besides, it's winter festival. Even if they know to look for us, no one's going to be in the mood to arrest anyone."

The city guard maybe, but not the Order. Lyss peered down the street. Aside from the guards at the gate, there were no sign of any other armed forces. Perhaps Brin was right. She stepped down and adjusted her satchel.

"Where to?"

Brin put a hand on her hip and her other to her brow, shading her face against the sun as she considered. "How much coin do you have?"

Lyss grimaced. "Not much." She unslung her supply sack and

opened it to show Brin the shuck skull stowed inside. "I'm hoping I'll have enough with this."

Brin glanced up at the sun, then nodded. "Go sell the skull," she said. "I'll find us a boat."

With a farewell to Timo and his cart, they set off into the street. Crowds thickened the further in they went until Lyss found herself brushing shoulders as she passed. They flowed down the main road, heading toward the city center and the marble smooth spires of the keep. At every side street more people joined them, and Lyss winced as a heel trod on her toes. Above, Rark glided past. No screams, no cries of horror.

So far so good.

There, in the press of bodies, her hairs prickled again. All of them. Adrenalin surged through Lyss' core, clawed around her limbs, and froze her still. Her breath went shallow. Suddenly she was five years old again, rigid with fear at the thought of the darkness waiting outside her and Fa's tent.

An elbow in her ribs jolted her back to herself. "Move girl," someone growled and Lyss staggered on.

Rark's mind butted next to hers, suspicion flowing free across his hugrokar. *You've been jumpy all morning. What is it?*

Lyss clutched the rune around her wrist. How did she explain something she didn't understand? She felt hunted. Haunted. *It's nothing,* she sent back. *The last time I was around townsfolk it didn't go so well.* She shied her mind away from thoughts of Bardas Post.

It was a half-truth, but if the rarkyn detected it, he said nothing.

Lyss took breath and re-joined the pressing crowd. *No one is following.* Yet, the feeling persisted, setting her teeth on edge.

Just when she thought they couldn't possibly cram more people between the town houses, the street ended, crowd thinning as they dispersed into a wide marketplace. It was hexagonal in shape, stalls lined over the broad cobblestones. A large fountain dominated the center. Beside it, a fiddler played to a menagerie of children. A dog ran around the mob, tail wagging, its short legs scurrying as it nipped the children's heels.

As they neared the fountain, a familiar pressure grew on Lyss' skin. *Galdar.* The white-stone basin was smooth stone, green runes glowing beneath the burbling water. She'd heard of these kinds of monuments before, with runes that lasted an age. *Odd,* she thought. *They're not cold either.* She dipped her index into the water, and feeling none of the usual icy burn, pressed it to one of the marks.

Warmth rushed through her, up her hand and into her arm. The glow under her finger snuffed out. One moment it was there, the next not. The water in the fountain slopped still. There was a chorus of surprised cries from the other side of the basin, and the fiddler cut short mid-tune, turning to see what had captured the children's attention.

Gods and ginndir, I destroyed it. Lyss pulled her hand from the water. Under her, the Aether gave a flicker as if twitching a muscle. A faint glow welled up from the runes once more. Then with an agonizing slowness, the water began to swirl again.

Lyss' mouth dropped open. Self-perpetuating runes. Such a thing seemed impossible. It defied everything she thought she knew. Once a rune ran out of Aether, it was dead. Someone had to pour power into them to make them work. Yet these—they'd managed to do that all on their own.

On the other side of the fountain, the children gave a collective sigh as the water burbled again. The fiddler struck up another tune. Lyss turned to find Brin watching her, and the woman cocked an eyebrow. Lyss pulled her hands back under her coat, stuffing them into her pockets.

"How long will it take you to find a boat?" she asked.

"To find? Not long at all," Brin indicated the streets sloping away from the south end of the markets. Another white wall rose up behind them, and beyond it, the tip of several masts prodded the sky. "But bartering the price of our passage," Brin went on, "that'll take a good hour." She flashed Lyss a grin, and Lyss felt sorry for whichever captain she cornered.

"I'll meet you back here," she said, and at Brin's nod, she turned and began searching the shop fronts. It took her nearly half an hour of asking directions and going door to door until she found the right place: a dingey little store in the west corner of the square. Its windows were lined with pickling jars, only it wasn't fruits or vegetables sealed behind the glass. There were gelatinous frogs, coiled serpents, and a collection of internal organs: hearts, livers, tongues. A giant yellow femur the size of Lyss' entire leg rested in the window's top shelf. The fascia above the door read *Matter's Emporium* in red and gold letters.

The Order's colors.

With one hand gripped about her sword hilt, Lyss pushed open the door. A bell sounded above her head, along with a barely audible creak as she shut the door behind her. The small shop was crowded with more shelves, but immaculate. Boxes and jars were stacked in neat columns with labels on every row. *Newt's tongue* read one. *Ground shendu horn*, stated another. Lyss made her way to the counter just as a short, bald man appeared from the back of the shop. His eyes cast over her, lingering longer on her scuffed boots, filthy trousers and ragged cloak and coat.

"Can I help you?" he asked, voice light, yet precise.

Lyss unhitched the carry sack from her shoulder, pulled the shuck skull from it and set it down on the counter. It gave a weighty clunk as she did, and it dwarfed the wooden ledge. The man wiped his hands on the greasy apron about his middle and came forward. A slight rise in his eyebrows betrayed his interest.

"Where did you get this?" he asked. He ran a finger along the bone, as if checking it was real.

"Does it matter?"

"No." The shopkeeper tapped a hollow eye socket. "I suppose at this point it does not." He was silent a moment, and his gaze returned to her, assessing her along with the skull. "I'll give you two geis for it."

Lyss' heart jumped in her chest. Two geis? By Sepp, she could buy a passage to Illredus and then some. She pushed the excitement down, forcing her face still. "It's worth twice that."

The shopkeeper returned her look. "I'm not a back-alley haggler, girl. That's two geis, and *no questions asked.*" His eyes narrowed on those last three words.

Lyss tensed but kept her expression impassive. She reached for the skull. "I'll take it somewhere else then," she said. "I saw another emporium on the east side, much bigger." She made to lift the skull, but the shopkeeper grabbed it and held on.

"Brenton's?" he asked, nostril's flaring as he leaned over the counter. He looked down at the skull. "I'll be damned if I'm going to let *him* have it," he muttered, then to Lyss, "Alright, *three*. That's the highest you'll get, here or anywhere else."

Lyss pretended to consider. "We have a deal."

With a huff the shopkeeper released the skull and began rummaging under the counter. Lyss leaned back, a brief grin spreading across her face before she forced it down, lest the shopkeeper see it. Her gaze wandered the shelves, nose wrinkling as she passed over a long gray intestine pickling in one jar. Behind the counter, coins clinked as the shopkeeper counted out her pay.

Bundles of rare roots and dried leaves were stocked in a locked glass cabinet at his back. *Probably wears the key around his neck,* Lyss thought as she recognized several Iga had used once to heal a fractured leg. She spotted a small jar on the top shelf and stopped.

Rark's eyes stared back at her. In the jar, a pair of fleshy eyeballs floated, stringy optic nerves coiled like a fleshy wire at the bottom of the glass. They faced out to the store, irises the splitting image of Rark's —or at least one of them. Fierce blood red. The image of rarkyns hanging from the trees flashed through her thoughts, throats slit, blood drained, eyes gouged,. Cold prickled down her arms and she pulled her hugrokar tight.

He does not need to know about this.

"Rarkyn eyes," the shopkeeper said, reappearing and turning to see what had caught Lyss' attention. "From the far south, beyond the Empire. Specially preserved." He stepped in front of them and slid three silver geis across the counter at her. "Too expensive for you."

Lyss took the coins and stowed them inside her coat's inner pocket, next to Iga's letter and Darrin's mirror. When she left the shop, it was with a slow, unwinding relief, like a knot being released. The door clanked shut behind her and Lyss shook herself, found her fingers wrapped around Iga's seal again and pulled them away.

Across the market, she heard fiddles and clapping. Pressing a hand to the coins in her pocket, she set off toward it, winding through stalls and the jostling crowd. Four more fiddlers had joined the first at the fountain and they'd had struck up a fast, lively tune that had the city folk dancing in pairs, stomping their feet in time with the music. A twist of the Aether made her spin, only to find a performer manipulating bubbles of water before a small crowd. A moment later, it pulled the other way and she glanced up in time to see a fire-breather spout flames from his mouth at the end of a row of stalls. Delighted cries from several children and a scattered applause celebrated his effort. Lyss stared transfixed as the mancer's fingers worked and changed the shape of the fire.

To see galdar used so freely for entertainment seemed, she hesitated, unlawful? As far as she could tell, the runes were harmless, probably even part of the legal series, yet somehow, she suspected if the Order were to see it, the performers would each walk away with the Brand.

At the thought of the Order, Lyss cast her eyes across the square. Not a red cloak in sight. She let out a breath and rolled her shoulders. *Relax, it's fine.* She sat and leaned against the lip of the fountain to wait for Brin, then leapt up as if burned by a hot poker, stomach crashing around her ankles.

Atop the roof of an adjacent stall and tapping the talons of one foot in time with the music, sat Rark. Or rather, *lounged* Rark. He was spread across the roof, taking up its entirety, wings, tail and all. Her first instinct was to shout at him, to tell him to get the krat out of sight, but she bit her tongue. Below, people bustled to and fro in the market, paying him no notice. Their gaze, if they did look up at all, slid straight over him as if he weren't there.

Still in the Otherworld. Lyss sat down again, wiping her sweaty hands on her tunic. *Could have fooled me.* Beside Rark's shoulder, a plated centipede-like creature, nearly as long as Lyss was tall, scuttled into view. Only a slight twitch of an ear gave any indication Rark knew it was there, his attention was fixed on the fiddlers and the dancing folk below, captivated. Lyss released her hugrokar a little and a rush of pleasure flowed across from the creature. She sensed him humming along with the tune, even if she couldn't hear it. A smile played across his lips.

Lyss pulled away, relaxing a little. If Rark noticed, he gave no sign. What harm was there in letting him enjoy the spectacle? She closed her eyes and leaned back on the fountain. *Relax,* she bade her jangling nerves. *There are no Reds.* Illredus was a week's voyage away. They would make it. She squeezed her wrist. She'd make it. *You're safe—*

The world dropped away.

Darkness filled her senses. Sight and sound vanished. In the dark, somewhere, *something* rose. Something monstrous. A shadow. And it was hungry. Lyss felt, no sensed, it turn on her. Darkness made real. Suddenly, she was back on the road to Caenis, frozen under the Red's sword, too frightened to move.

Helpless.

The monster lunged. A cavernous mouth opened wide, then wider again. Bigger than her. It loomed over her head, neck arched, mouth ready to swallow her whole. She tried to scream, but terror stole her voice. And the shadow swallowed her. A joyful glee filling her head.

Hungry.

Lyss jerked awake with a gasp, sweat clinging her tunic to her skin, heart in her throat. *Gods and ginndir.* She hadn't been imagining it. It wasn't the Red. No, her senses had been trying to warn her. *It was coming. Coming for her. The madness.* She felt it there, fraying the edge of her thoughts, trying to pick her apart. Heedless of who might see, she pushed up her sleeve, exposing her wrist. Iga's last rune was faint, an echo on her skin, like a healing bruise. And fading.

A croak welled up her throat. *No. No, no, no. Not now. Not here.*

Lyss? Rark stood over her, his form shadowless in the high afternoon. Worry flashed through his hugrokar. *What is it?*

Lyss swallowed. *"When the runes vanish, you will have a few hours. Days at most."* That's what Iga had said; but she could already feel it coming. The madness was gaining on her. Stalking her scent like a wolf. She imagined how it might howl as it closed in for the kill. Gooseflesh shivered over her arms.

Lyss pulled herself up and searched the crowd. Where was Brin? They had to get on that boat *now*.

A face at the back of the crowd, beyond the fiddlers caught her eye. It had turned toward them—and stayed turned. A man's face, rough and bearded, with a shabby hat pressed down over his head. A scar ran from under one eye to his jaw, cutting his beard in two. Lyss' heart lurched afresh. He was looking at Rark; eyes boring into the rarkyn.

As if sensing her watching, the man's gaze shifted, locking onto hers. Cold drenched through her core, as if she'd been doused in a bucket of frigid water. His eyes were no more than dark pin-pricks at that distance, but for a heartbeat Lyss thought she'd seen a flash of red —rarkyn red. Horror coiled its hand around her gut and yanked. *Mordkyn.* She was not sure how she knew. She just did.

Get deeper, she shot at Rark.

He vanished, form melting away from the street. Lyss searched the crowd again. The mancer was gone.

What was it? Came Rark's question. He felt close, like he was still standing beside her.

Lyss searched the faces. *A man. He could see you.*

Doubt welled across the link. *Are you sure? I was already deep.*

Yes, I'm sure. Lyss clutched her wrist. The pact was getting stronger; the madness creeping in. She took a breath and quashed the fear down. She gave up looking for the man and searched for Brin again. The bearkin couldn't be far away. Beside her, Rark shifted, the faint pressure of the Aether buffeting her as it rippled through him.

I cannot stay this deep for long. It's—

"There you are," Brin's voice made her start. Lyss spun, hands falling on her sword before she could think. The ursa held up open palms. "Easy." As she took in Lyss' face, Brin lowered her arms. "What is it?"

"We need to leave," Lyss said.

Brin frowned. "I just got us two places onboard the *Nishant*. Can't it wait?"

Lyss chewed the inside of her cheek. "When does it set sail?"

"Tomorrow morning, first thing."

Lyss swore an oath and turned back to the markets, scanning the faces there. No sign of the mordkyn. Dare she risk staying? She recalled her first conversation with Rark and the pain that had fired down her palm when he'd sliced his talons into his hand. *If I die, you die.* If the mancer caught Rark, what then? No, they had to leave. She gripped her wrist. *But the boat. Illredus.* She imagined the last of Iga's rune fizzling out, blot by inky blot. She was running out of time. They had to be on that boat when it sailed.

"We'll come back in the morning," she promised. "Stay if you want, but Rark and I need to leave now."

Brin cast a long look at the fountain, brow wrinkling, hair turning orange as the first touches of sunset hit it. "Okay," she said at last. She pursed her lips, then puffed her cheeks and exhaled. "Let's go." She indicated the south gate. "That way is quickest from here."

Lyss nodded and shouldered her sack. As they set off, Brin turned back to look at the fountain again. She gave a sigh. "I was looking forward to that dance."

CHAPTER THIRTY-FOUR

Dearest Elena,

Isaac is dead. I saw it all. Early this morning the guards marched us out before the Tower. Us and the rarkyn both. Isaac limped, face puffy from a beating. The Krat's Brand glowed on his wrist, just as my own throbbing welt did, each one blocking our sense of the Aether. Nulling our magic. Forever.

The rarkyn followed in a circle of spears, men jabbing him into an inactive nine-point circle on the paving stones. With a twitch of a hand, one of the spear carriers activated the runes and the soldiers stood to attention.

I don't remember much of what was said. Traitor, spy, unlawful magics. Isaac was hauled up the steps and onto the platform, forced to his knees. His face was white. So white and scared.

And then he was gone.

As quickly as I write these words. Gone. *My apprentice, my second son, stolen from this world. All that hope, all that talent, gone. Axed to death like a common criminal.*

I stood numb, staring at Isaac's body, until hands grabbed me and pushed me up steps and onto the blocks.

A flash of green and a soul-raising screech drew my gaze down to the rarkyn. A soldier's spear pierced its belly. A pace away, one of the Order men lay, head twisted askew. Fool had crossed over the ward's runes—perhaps to jab the rarkyn still with his weapon, only to have his neck snapped for his trouble.

Shouts erupted from around the ward and the spearheads stabbed in.

One of the soldiers yelled a warning, something about not crossing the lines. He was the only one with any sense among them.

The rarkyn struck, snatching two spears loose and thrusting them into the soldiers before a third spear caught its thigh and the rest drove home.

The same soldier yelled again. He shouted, "Don't kill it. Not yet!" But his warning came too late.

The rarkyn collapsed, blood spilling onto the stones. For a heartbeat I waited, wondering if the sigil had been enough. At the circle's edge, the soldier shouted at the men to get out and get back, jabbing the butt of his spear at those who had crossed the runes. Fools all of them.

It was slow at first. The rarkyn's blood blossomed where it lay, a well of red collecting on the cobbles. Then the red began to move. Thin tendrils trickled of their own accord, spiraling outwards as if a greater hand were painting a web around the aetherling.

I felt it in my gut first, then the roar in my ears took over. The air split. A wall of heat crashed over me, sending a hot numbing tingle into my chest, burning the Brand on my arm. The rent tore wider. A rumble echoed through the courtyard. The glow of the nine-point circle flickered once like a candle in the wind, then went out.

Fog rolled over the men in a wave, shadows dancing within it.

And the screaming started.

I laughed. I am not proud of it.

I'd expected a Fever. I thought the Aether would spill out and suck them through to the Otherworld—as had almost happened to Isaac and I all those weeks ago. But it was more than that, Elena. It summoned the ginndir. From my vantage, the human-shaped figures crumpled under shadows the size of houses, wails subsiding into a crunching of bone.

I spied a figure. It was unlike the others; smaller, slighter; human, yet every part of me screamed it was not. It watched it all with a power that terrified me, dredging up a mania I've never felt before.

The fog spread, reaching the base of the blocks. Flashes of sinewy muscle, scale, feather, and fur, glinted in the cloud. Fear crept in, paralyzing me in its embrace. Fog curled over the wood planks and I stumbled away, beginning the casting of a ward only to feel my Aether rise then slump inside me, slipping from my control— the Brand. A thump of wings snapped my head up.

It was the rarkyn. Or at least, it had been. Gone was its mismatched gaze, instead the silver orbs of a ginndir stared back at me, lips peeled back in a feral grin.

Mancers tell tales about this kind of rarkyn. Gundhrams they call them. A rarkyn that has survived the Aether's abyss, but not before the abyss has started to turn it into one of its own. I thought the Aether's hold on Tykee was superficial. Physical things: those horns, his silver eye. I was wrong. The Aether's teeth have sunk in, and it hasn't let go. Now, I know the truth. Tykee is more ginndir than rarkyn.

I backed away, calling his name in a dim hope my words would reach him. The rarkyn cocked his head, a flicker of something, recognition perhaps, crossed its face. Around his wrist, the sigil gave a weak pulse. Against all odds, the runes held; probably all that stood between the rarkyn succumbing to its ginndir instincts. I knew a heartbeat of hope.

Then he lunged.

I shouted at Tykee again, useless though it was, and my fingers flailed, working runes they could not cast. The rarkyn closed in. Silver raged in those eyes. Gone was the kit I'd known. All that was left was ginndir.

Galdar-less, weaponless, I did the only thing I could think of. I ran at the monster. Yes, ran. To my surprise, it worked. I slammed into him, arms wrapping around his middle and together we tumbled from the platform. His talons struck deep as we fell, lacerating my face. I lashed back, fist clobbering the wound in his side. He yelped and swooped away.

I thudded into the stone courtyard below. My wrist snapped; lungs emptied. I wheezed, sucked in air. Heat cloyed down my throat, burning. Aether. I was in the thick of it. I clapped a hand to my mouth, scrambled up and ran. A ginndir was upon me in a heartbeat. Claws sank into my calves, pulled me down to the cobbles. I yelled and beat at it with my fists until a serrated beak caught my hand. Dimly, as if watching from far off, I saw the teeth go deep, hewing through bone and muscle.

I don't remember screaming. As for the pain, that came later.

The ginndir thrashed its beak, teeth grinding through flesh, until with a snap and pop—tendons probably—it came free. The beast threw its head back and gulped. My hand, fingers, thumb, wrist and all, slid down its gullet. I have never felt so powerless.

I was certain I was dead, Elena. Off to join the rest of the Tower's guard.

But not to be.

Above, the mist shifted, folded back on itself like a curtain parting. My feasting ginndir froze, quivering as if under the gaze of a predator. Its claws eased around my legs, beak clapped twice, before it darted away into the fog. It was then that I felt it. A presence. It pricked at my senses, huge and weighty. Through bleary eyes, I made out a human shape in the mist—made of mist—with a face of white clay. A shadow in a mask.

It said to me, "Work your magic now or the ginndir will claim you."

I groped for words, almost too addled to think. I wish I had. What I could have asked it. Instead, all I thought to choke out was, "I can't, the Brand—"

An ethereal finger pointed at my injured arm.

Confused, I looked down at my limb, the first flecks of pain pulling my thoughts this way and that. My arm ended in a ragged stump of flesh and bone. Hand gone. Wrist gone. The Brand gone with them. Eaten. I nearly laughed.

The mask spoke to me once more. It said, "Best hurry, human. Before the Aether poisons you." Before I could blink, it melted into the mist as if it had never been.

What happened next is a blur. I recall summoning a ward, which one I don't know. I remember the sweet taste of Terresmir air as it rolled in, causing me to gape and gasp lungful after lungful. The shadows retreated until only one remained.

Tykee. He staggered to my circle. Drawn to it just like the first time we'd met.

In a moment of clarity, I gathered the last of my strength, knowing what I had to do.

Sepp pray it was the right decision.

I reached my senses to his sigil, flooding power into the runes. The markings flared, a brilliant green that lit up the walls of the tower. Tykee screeched and dropped, forgetting me entirely as he clawed at the metal. I cast again, strengthening the sigil twice over. The Aether retreated, and he flagged. Bit by bit, the ginndir rage ebbed; the silver gleam in his eyes faded, until with a final sway, he slumped to the ground unconscious.

I waited. Wounds throbbing, weeping blood all over my castings—I never was good at healing. Beyond the glow of my circle, the mist ebbed; roiling back to the spiderweb of blood that had summoned it.

I was alone.

Above, the tower was quiet. No movement. No tramp of feet or cry of men, nothing but a faint breeze snapping the Illredian flags on their turrets. I waited until the sun was high overhead before I dissolved my wards.

The walls of the tower still stand, not much remains within. The stores are ravaged, furniture and equipment strewn across the halls. It will take some time for me to take stock of what is left.

As for the rarkyn. I know not what to do with him. I dare not kill him. But I dare not release him either. I should not blame Tykee. Yet, deep down, a part of me does. My rational side knows it was my decision to help him. That the men of Myron Keep brought their fate upon themselves. Yet, when I close my eyes and see Isaac die all over again, listen to the ginndir crunch through those soldiers' bones, I wonder that in saving him, have I unleashed something horrible on the world? It nags at me. Even as I write on this piece of salvaged scrap.

But monsters aside, I do know one thing.

It's time to leave this cursed country, Elena.

You must be ready.

THE NIZER'S SPINDLY FINGERS TAPPED THE AIR, TESTING ITS invisible web. Its six owlish eyes blinked once, twice, paused for an agonizing wait then blinked again. Archer shifted on his horse, biting back the urge to jump from the saddle and shake the creature. Nizers performed tasks in their own time. They were slow, but they always worked.

"What's it waiting for?" Hane asked, his disembodied voice coming out of the black. Archer turned and managed to make out the silhouette of the boy and his horse against the night.

"Who knows," he growled, and at the noise his pony jerked its head and snorted. Its rune-spelled hooves stamped, and it released a high-pitched whinny like a knife screeching over stone. Gooseflesh prickled down Archer's spine. The pony was on its last tether, those creeping black, Aether-laden veins were nearing its heart. When they reached it, he'd have to leave the beast behind.

If it doesn't give our position away first.

The girl's face swam through his thoughts again. After Hane's reverence, he'd expected a lithe, fair-haired slip of an Eder Wildner. Instead, the girl had been the splitting image of an Eyos woman: dark-haired, olive skin, eyes more gold than brown. The end of a white scar snarled up under her pointed chin. Young too, no more than twenty. While not broad shouldered like her blond-haired companion, she had the look of someone who knew their way around a sword.

Moved like it too. She'd weaved through the crowd and vanished down a side street with ease, leaving her companion wrestling in the throng behind.

Back at their inn, Hane's face had lit up when Archer described her to the boy.

"That's Lyss! She's here?" He'd almost overturned his mug of chara as he'd jumped to his feet. "Where?"

"Easy boy, she's already left." Archer had put his good hand to the boy's shoulder and pushed him down. "They won't get far."

"But—"

Hand still on the boy's shoulder, Archer had tightened his grip and leaned over Hane to whisper. "We'll ride out tonight. Don't worry, we'll get them."

Hane's face had turned up to him, hope brimming in his eyes. "You're sure?"

"I'm sure, boy."

Hane had slumped against the back of his chair and released a long breath from between his cheeks. A smile had crept over him and he'd gazed up at the ceiling. "This time tomorrow we'll be on our way home," he'd said. "You'll catch the—*it*," he corrected, "you'll seal its magic and Lyss will be free. Everything can go back to the way it was."

Archer had just enough heart not to laugh in his face. *Naïve fool.* She might look of sound mind, but by now the rarkyn's magic would have sunk its claws into the girl's mind and begun to shred it like wool. Yes, the boy would return home. But it would be with his tail between his legs once he learned there was no saving her.

A bang at their backs made Archer start and twist in the saddle. A quarter mile behind them Torin stood, its festive lights setting its walls aglow. A line of fire arced up over its spires, fish-tailing through the air, then exploding in a shower of color. Archer thought he heard the cries and claps of the city's inhabitants on the wind; the joyous tumults as they wished away the winter's evils. He hunkered down. *Wishing won't make it so.* Another line of fire, another bang and the road ahead lit up in hues of red, blue and yellow. Next to him Hane shifted, coming to his feet in the stirrups as he peered into the night.

"Relax, they're a while off yet," Archer said.

Before them, the nizer gave a shiver, its face turning to Archer. His saddle creaked as he leaned forward to see the creature better. The nizer raised one long finger and pointed. *South.*

"That will be all for now, Bruck." Archer dismissed the aetherling with a curt nod, and the night folded in around it as it vanished. Another pop and spark from the city lit the way as Archer wheeled his pony about. The pony gave another whinny and stumbled.

"Is she alright?" Hane asked, the clatter of his own mount's hooves close behind.

"No," Archer said. *She'll be lucky to last the night.* He'd deal with the pony later. First the rarkyn. He kicked his mount into a gallop.

They rode for an hour, circumnavigating the city in a wide arc, their rune-spelled steeds foaming at the bits as the land fell to their hooves.

Between the fireworks and the half-crescent moon, there was just enough light to see by. Only when Torin's glow was a small halo on the horizon behind did Archer stop and summon the nizer again. The summoning circle on his false hand glowed as he poured his remaining Aether into it, grimacing as his reserves thinned. With a swish and rustle, the nizer appeared. It blinked twice, before its form shuddered and shrank into shadow, retreating for the Otherworld as its power pulled at Archer's dry core.

Drat it. He fumbled with his cloak, drawing out the bottle from beside his journal and unstopping it. A sweet, coppery smell wafted up to him. It was the last he had. He'd hoped to save it for later, for the real summons. *You won't be summoning anything if you don't catch him first.* Resigned, Archer lifted it to his mouth and tipped the bottle. The liquid coated his tongue and throat and burned all the way down.

Hane sniffed and stiffened. "Is that…?"

Archer ignored him, relishing instead the heat blossoming in his chest, down his arms and up his neck. Aether pooled back into his core, tingled into his muscles, snapped his mind sharp. *Yes, how he'd missed this.* He pushed power into the summons. The nizer's form solidified, straightened, and stepped closer. Archer held out the crumpled rarkyn feather to it. The aetherling drew in a long breath and fell still, face glazing as it set to work.

"What happened?" Hane's voice broke the silence as they waited. There was an edge to it Archer hadn't heard before.

"What happened where, boy?"

"I meant to you," Hane said. "What happened to you."

Archer turned in the saddle and glared at the Wildner, knowing full well the lad would not see it. "What makes you say something did?"

He sensed Hane shrug in the dark. "You were an Order mancer once. Now you're not."

Archer gazed back across the plains. When he squinted, he made out a line of trees that marked the edge of the Torin River winding through the fields. Now there was an ugly story. His pony pawed at the ground and with a glance at the nizer—its fingers still plucking the air—he sighed. *You're getting softer by the day, Markides.*

"I had a family once, a daughter." He cleared his throat. "Beautiful girl, like her mother was. Heart of a goddess. Charmed the cottons off any who met her. Had a wit and tongue sharper than a Kalana blade too, mind. Got her into trouble more than once." He felt his expression grow wistful and was suddenly glad of the night.

"And?" Hane prompted.

"Therrin and the Seven had her executed."

Silence from the boy. His mount stamped, then, "What for?"

Archer squeezed his reins. "To punish me." The ruins of Myron Keep rose in his mind; the crumpled letter shaking in his single working hand. He'd read and re-read the letter under the candlelight, the ruins of his severed stump throbbing in its tourniquet.

I'm sorry, Papa. I failed. Those words would haunt him forever. He had read on, horror rising like a tide with every line. *I tried, but King Therrin dances under Keteus' strings…I snapped. I am so sorry. I lashed out without think-ing. The casting didn't hurt anyone, except, perhaps, Therrin's pride…*

…They burned our house to the ground three nights ago…I sleep in the dungeons now.

He'd read the charges in disbelief. Near identical to his own. *Treason. Traitor. Enemy of the Empire.* The liars. Keteus had saw an opportunity and he'd taken it. Or perhaps it'd been his plan all along. Get Archer out of the capital where he could not defend himself or his family. A scheme to finally be rid of their voice, their vote—their veto.

How had they known? The thought still bothered him. Had they found his letters? He should have told Elena to destroy them. Better yet, he should never have written. But he'd been too caught up in wanderlust and purpose to care.

By the time this reaches you, I will be in Baer's keeping…

No parent should outlive a child. He'd imagined her face pale as she was led to the gallows, hair straggly in her braid. So young, barely eigh-teen. Pale, but defiant. No tears. Brave until the end. Or so he hoped. And then the heart crushing words.

…I will wait for you in His hall. I love you, Papa.

He remembered crushing the letter in his grip and thinking, *it should have been me,* over and over. He might have screamed. Might have wept. Might not have done anything. The hours after were a fog, right up until something in his brain sparked. *It's not right,* he'd thought. *I'll make it right.* He couldn't summon the gods, but he knew the next best thing. He'd seen it.

A sound from Hane jerked Archer back to himself. He blinked in the dark, throat tight. What had the boy said? I'm sorry?

"Not your fault," he said, gruffer than he'd intended.

A chirrup from the nizer saved him from having to say more. The creature's eyes swung to him, its top two reflecting the star-spotted sky as they fixed on Archer's face. He knew that look. With a huff he dismounted, grabbed the reins as his pony tried to rear, and placed his hand on the aetherling's scalp.

A vision of a fire with three indistinct figures hunched around it appeared in his mind's eye. Archer stared. Where he'd expected one trail, there were now three. The nizer's vision rendered the night sky a deep purple and in it a smoky line of Aether ran, a wake left from the rarkyn's passage. It was darker than the other two, and denser, the rarkyn shedding the Otherworld's power like excess water. He examined the trail, smooth and steady to the nizer's sight. *Still in control.* Archer shook his head. *Tykee's luck still rides with him.*

The other two trails were fainter, each one leading to a figure at the fire. Archer studied them, squinting as he traced them to the blaze. The nizer's vision quivered, as if it were scared to go closer.

"Do it," Archer growled.

The picture in his mind crept forward, the figures started taking on distinct shapes. One tall, winged and horned, the Aether's fog hanging over it as if it'd been puffing on a pipe. The rarkyn. Archer turned on the figure beside it, while it appeared human the shadow of a hulking bear curled around it, its head turned to him, gray eyes watching. *An ursa.* Archer cursed under his breath. *Inconvenient, but manageable.* He turned on the last figure—and froze. There was no figure at all. Where he'd expected to see the outline of the Eyos girl, a gaping black hole of nothing stood. He peered into it, waiting for the nizer's gaze to penetrate. Emptiness stared back. A chill crept up his spine. It was like peering into the void, the abyss itself.

Under his hand the nizer squeaked, and he clamped his fingers about its skull to stop it pulling away. He tried to will the creature closer, but it refused to budge. Instead, he had it circle the camp. The girl's black veil remained.

What power can defy a nizer's senses? As if in answer, a new thought entered his head: *the Aether itself.* An unpleasant, melting sensation wormed in his gut.

"The madness has taken root," the words slipped out of him.

"Madness?" Hane's voice pitched upwards. Archer's focus broke and the nizer pulled free of his grip. The aetherling scuttled away, wary he would make it return to the campfire. Archer touched the ward on his hand, reached inside himself for the Aether that channeled the creature's summons and severed it. The nizer didn't melt, it simply vanished, turning into the Otherworld and fleeing.

"Are we too late?" Hane's whisper cracked, as if on the edge of tears.

Archer opened his mouth to answer; to utter the single word that would crush the naivete out of him like a truncheon to the ribs. He wet his lips.

You still need him.

"Not yet. There's hope still."

The Wildner's breath released in a whistle and Archer's chest twinged. *The truth would destroy him,* the voice inside him cooed. *You can't risk it.*

The boy gave an audible swallow. "How far?" he asked.

Archer mulled a moment more, then pushed his guilt aside. Let the boy enjoy his last few hours of childhood. "A few miles," he said. He drew his pony to the side of the road and dismissed the runes from its hooves.

"What are you doing? You just said they're close."

As the Aether's glow faded from the pony, the animal gave a shrill wicker and tried to bite. Archer kept a firm hold on its bridle. *Not long now.* "They're not going anywhere," he said. He rummaged through his saddle bags, fingers brushing over the contents until they landed on a waterskin and a wrapped loaf of bread from the inn in Torin. He dug into a pocket, flipped out a small stone and pressed a finger to it. The rock heated up, its surface turning red, emitting a soft glow to the night. Archer tossed it onto the dirt and channeled more Aether to the rune. Its glow brightened enough for him to make out the boy staring at him from his horse.

"Come, sit, get your strength back."

"But—"

"This is not something to rush into without a plan," Archer said, he indicated the ground beside him. "Now *sit*."

The boy obeyed, slithering off his saddle to rest in the dirt beside Archer.

"Sever the runes," Archer reminded as he handed Hane half the loaf. With a huff, the boy made a sharp gesture and the runes on his horse dulled.

"No more channeling those tonight," Archer said. "Save your

strength for the rarkyn." He pointed at the bread. "When you're done, try to get some sleep."

Hane's face turned on him, blinking at him in the rune light. "We're not going after them tonight?"

Archer broke off a piece of bread and chewed it, not paying attention to the taste. "Rarkyn don't see as well in the twilight hours," he said. "We'll strike then, when they're least alert. You remember the runes for the binding spell?"

Staring at his bread, Hane nodded.

"Good," Archer said. He rolled onto his side, cupping his head on his elbow. Cold earth seeped through his cloak. He shuffled closer to the fire-sigil. "I will wake you in four hours. Rest while you can."

CHAPTER THIRTY-FIVE

SKAAR SHIFTED IN THE GRASS, UNABLE TO SLEEP. HIS BONES ached, his head pounded, and his mind felt frayed, numb, as if he hadn't slept in days.

Reythr damn, and we're not even in Illredus yet.

He tried to remember the last time he'd spent a full day in the Otherworld. A full day *willingly* in the Otherworld, he corrected as he cast his thoughts back. Probably before the last mordkyn raid. He skirted around those memories, turning his mind to the times he'd spent gliding on the Aether's currents to Finnafell and the last great gathering. That flight had been days in the Otherworld, and he didn't remember it ever being this much of a strain.

You had a pack to share the burden, he reminded himself. *And a mara to read the currents.* Yet even as she'd guided the pack, Raska had never shown signs of exhaustion. An exemplar of balance and control. Meanwhile, here he was, lungs burning, sweat clinging to his palms and bones resonating so hard he thought they might sing. To think weeks ago he'd struggled to draw on the Aether at all. Now he drew on it too much. He didn't remember Fengar struggling this much to master his magic.

I really am Aether-turned. He hugged his elbows, talons pricking flesh under feather. If only he'd paid more attention to Raska's lessons with Fengar. If he could see his own eyes, he knew he'd find rings of Fever in them. He gave a shiver. *Think about something else.*

Across the fire, lit for Brin's benefit, Lyss slept in nothing but a tunic. Perspiration prickled her forehead and her eyes roved under her eyelids, dreaming. Indistinct dreams, Skaar knew, hugrokar too calm for a nightmare. Though that hadn't stopped her fear twisting his gut when she'd made him promise to wake her if he sensed anything approaching a nightmare during his watch. That responsibility had ended when the moon had reached the zenith and Brin had taken over. Now, the thought of shutting his own eyes and surrendering to whatever horrors his mind —or Lyss'—conjured set his feathers on end. He ruffled his wings. *Think about something else.*

Off to the north, a roll of thunder sounded. Before the fire, Brin lifted her head and sucked in a deep breath as if tasting the air. She muttered an oath, drew the edges of her bear skin tighter and went back to staring into the fire. A moment later, she glazed over once more, and stroked an absent finger over the rabbit's foot around her neck.

Thinking of her sister again, Skaar guessed, running a talon over the old rune-stone on his neck as he waited for sleep to come. Isaac had shown him humans could be kind. Then the Order had proven once again they could be monsters. If he ever got free, he'd go far into the mountains, far away from anywhere the Order or mordkyn could ever reach. *If I ever get free.* What if the mancer city couldn't find a way to undo the pact? He would be trapped in the human world and all the dangers that went with it. The thought sent his stomach writhing. *Think about—*

Archer's face swam up through his memories like a ghoulish fish, red-tinted gaze latching onto him.

Skaar sighed and sat up.

Brin looked up from the fire. "Given up sleeping, cousin?"

Skaar nodded, then cocked his head, puzzling over her choice of word. "Cousin?"

Brin picked up a long stick and poked the coals. "You are of the Aether too. Like Ursa," she said and sent a spray of embers into the air as she turned over a log. Flames sprang along the wood and the shadowlings danced around it, like rarkyns around the fires at Finnafell. The day's celebrations in Torin had reminded him how long it had been since he'd last heard music and any of the great songs.

"Do you know the man she speaks of?"

Brin's question pulled him out of the daydream. She was looking at

Lyss, still sleeping at the edge of the fire. Skaar nodded. He'd recognized the description the moment she'd given it, and it had set his nerves racing. If they hadn't needed to return to Torin, he would have urged them to travel through the night.

"Who is he?"

"A mancer," Skaar said. "A strong one. He—" Skaar hesitated. "He trapped me on Terresmir."

"Why?"

To save me. Skaar thought, but the idea of trying to explain all that had happened was too much for his buzzing head. Instead, he said, "To use me." For what he'd never been sure. Archer had kept that secret close to his chest, bound in the leather notebook he carried. But the way the mancer had stared at him as he poured over the journal had made Skaar's hackles rise every time. He shuddered and opened a wing and began preening dirt from his feathers with a talon. Anything to get his mind off that wretched mancer. If not for him…

If not for him you'd be bones at the bottom of the Deep.

He pulled one secondary feather hard; pain stabbed down his wing. *Stop thinking about it.* He glanced over at Brin; she had gone back to stroking the rabbit's foot. *Cousin.* She had more in common with Lyss than he. Yet, despite their magics being worlds apart, the thought was oddly warming.

"You've seen the human world?" he asked.

Brin paused. "Some of it," she said. "Nina and I traveled. Well," she shrugged. "Nina traveled, I followed. Us ursas usually lead solitary lives, but Nina…she wanted more." She gazed into the fire. "We came over the Spine into the Empire. Had I known about the Order, I would never have stayed in Bern."

Skaar nodded and stopped as her words truly sank in. *She'd come from somewhere the Order was not. Somewhere far away from their ridiculous laws and hungry obsessions. A free place.* He straightened, excitement shivering over him. "Where—"

Off in the darkness, the Aether gave a sudden twist. His heart lurched. He sprang to his feet. "Mordk—"

Blinding light crashed into him. Cold lanced across his side as something coiled around his body. A casting! He shrieked, and across the camp Lyss yelped and came to her feet. Then he was falling, pitching into the ground, limbs locked stiff. The acrid smell of galdar filled his nose, along with something else. Burning feather. *No. No, no, no.*

Blinking furiously, he tried to clear his head. Another flash. A bright binding spell slammed into Brin, sending her to the dirt with a grunt.

Reythr, this can't be happening. Not now.

"Rark!"

Hands fell on his back and pulled at the spell coiled about his wings. Cold pain welled in his arms. Lyss. Skaar strained. He might as well be trapped under a horse. He managed to turn his head enough to make her out. She was tearing at the casting, making no headway at all. *You spent six years fighting a sigil,* he growled at himself. *This is nothing.* In the distance, the Aether gave another twist. Another flare of light.

He grabbed Lyss' hugrokar. She winced as the binding's cold rocked from him to her, and he pulled his mind close. *Move!*

Without thinking, she threw herself sideways and the spell cracked into the ground behind him, right in the space she'd been. She scurried back.

"It's okay, I have it," Skaar huffed. He forced his head in the direction he sensed the Aether building. "You stop the casting. I get Brin out."

A roar sounded from beside the fire. Brin heaved against the white binding. Across her shoulders the bear-skin rippled, like grass in the wind. And kept rippling, skin stretching and shifting. The fur moved along her arms, down her legs and across her belly. She hit the ground on all fours, clothes tearing, buttons popping. Muscles bunched along her neck and the head of the skin dropped forward over the ursa's face. The storm eyes flashed. Alive and angry.

Full bear, she twisted, a giant claw ripping into one of the casting's white arms coiled about her leg. It bowed, then snapped under the sheer force of the blow.

Lyss smirked. "I don't think we need to worry about Brin."

The Aether flexed again, and Lyss ducked as another flash shot over them. Brin roared as the second binding hit her.

"Go," Skaar told Lyss, and with a nod she was up and running, one hand on the hilt of her sword.

Skaar ground his teeth and probed the galdar binding. It was strong, even for Archer. *Just you watch. Castings won't hold me, not now.* He released the power from his bones and reached for the heart of the spell—and yanked. The binding fizzled out, its pulsing cold tearing to fragments and he seethed the dregs into himself. An icy burn washed through his limbs, then was swept up into the Aether inside him.

Skaar rolled to his feet and scampered to Brin. Another twitch of Aether and he dove, tumbling—almost into the fire—as another casting smashed into the earth. He vaulted up again and pulled at Brin's bindings. Her gnashing teeth had done most of the work and she came free with a roar.

"Don't stay," Skaar warned. Brin didn't listen. She reared up onto her hind quarters, dwarfing Skaar as she fixed her gaze in the direction Lyss had run. Skaar half expected a binding spell to batter her head on, but nothing came. Beside him, the bear snuffed the air, gave a bellow, thumped down onto all fours and began to run. Skaar made to follow until a pulse through the Aether lurched him to a stop mid-step. He snapped around to the south. Blood drained from his legs. He knew that feeling.

"Stop," he shouted after Brin. "There are two mancer—"

The Aether bucked, power rushing to fill the gap of whatever had just been drawn out of it. Ahead of him, Brin stopped and lifted her shaggy head to the air. Skaar peered into the night, ears twitching as he tried to still his breathing enough to listen. Then he heard it. A thump of heavy feet moving across the earth. He spun and made out the shadow moving through the night.

It was big, twice as tall as he and three times as wide. It lumbered forward, ape-like on its knuckles. Its head was all bison snout and two ram-like horns curling out of its tiny skull. *Berigan.*

Brin's head whipped around, taking in the berigan then turned in the direction of Lyss.

Skaar flitted into the Otherworld to Brin, feeling the Aether chafe at his mind as he skimmed the shallows.

"Two mancers," he huffed as he dropped out of the Otherworld. She had time to nod her muzzle before the aetherling bowled into them. He darted one way, Brin the other as fists the size of boulders slammed into the ground. Skaar came up onto his feet, pulling a knife free from his belt.

Go for the tendons. Stop it moving. Fengar's old advice echoed through his head.

I know, brother, I know. Skaar flexed his talons and unfurled his wings to a half-span, just as he and Fengar used to practice. Beside him, Brin reared up and roared. The ursa's gray gaze met his and gave a knowing glint. *Cousin.*

Skaar sprang forward, ducking a swinging fist, flitting through the

Otherworld to aim a strike at the berigan's heels. He darted in, sliced, and darted out again. *Reythr be damned.* The creature's hide was tougher than leather. A giant hand grabbed for him and Skaar leapt away, berigan following. For several paces he and the aetherling danced. It grabbing and swinging, he ducking and weaving—sometimes in the Otherworld, sometimes out. It made no difference. The berigan followed his every move.

Rough nails nicked one wing, sending him sprawling into the grass. He rolled away, dodging the fist that hammered into the ground after him. A flash of gray fur bowled into the berigan's side and Brin was upon it, claws ripping and tearing. She struck at the creature's chin, just missing its throat. With a bray, the aetherling pulled back. Four red welts scored its jaw and snout. Then its knuckles ripped round and buried into Brin's side. Skaar heard the distinct crack of ribs breaking before the ursa was flung to the earth.

The berigan swung back on him. A host of scratches marked its chest, but aside from the deep wounds on its jaw, they'd done little to it. *Reythr damn, this isn't working.*

The aetherling lumbered forward, and Skaar set off into the Otherworld, leading it in a circle to buy time to think. By the fire, Brin rose and shook herself with a booming growl. She reared up again.

"Wait," Skaar darted out before her, the Aether running off him in misty spirals. Brin's claws were half-way to his face before recognition flashed in her. The paw paused and the ursa's attention fixed on him. "I have idea."

The berigan ploughed into them and they split again. Skaar flitted up around an extended arm and sank his knife into one of the aetherling's eyes. It howled. The sound rattled inside Skaar's skull worse than the Aether. Fingers snatched after him and he dodged one hand and kicked away the other. Pain smarted through his foot and he choked back a yelp. He might as well have tried to kick a rock.

What is going on? Lyss' voice sounded in his head. Anger simmered in her hugrokar, but not at him. The berigan tried to grab him again and he ducked away.

Aetherling. Busy. He sent, then added. *Hold on.* He landed next to Brin.

"Distract, but do not touch when I do," he told her, pointing at the berigan. "Keep distance or you end up in Otherworld."

The bear cast him a quizzical look, all pointed gaze and wrinkled snout, as if to ask, "How?"

"Trust me. Keep distance or you die."

Brin nodded, rabbit charm swinging at her neck. She dug in her claws, bunched her shoulders and roared at the aetherling. The berigan responded in kind, lowered its head and charged.

Skaar dove into the Otherworld, circling with his Aether-flight. Brin leapt away from the berigan's horns, then reared again as the aetherling skidded to a stop and rounded on her.

Reythr, it was big. *And no pack to help you.* Skaar pushed the thought aside and jumped. He released rasvenger, coming out of the Otherworld just above the creature's back, landing on its shoulders and sinking his talons into its thick mane. The beast started; tried to shake him off. Skaar hung grimly on and wrapped his legs around its neck. A flash of gray fur retreating to one side. Brin. Good, she was clear. No chance of her getting caught up in his rasvenger. He wound his hugrokar tight, reached for the Otherworld—*Reythr give me strength*—and *pulled.*

Heat seared through his skull, down his arms, through his chest and into his bones. His muscles screamed, sockets and joints throbbing. His head spun. He shrieked.

Then quiet. Stillness.

The berigan shuddered under him. Skaar opened his eyes to the Aether's swirling fog. He'd done it. He'd pulled the berigan back to the Otherworld. Back where it belonged. He relaxed his grip and slid from the aetherling's back. The berigan blinked its single good eye at him. The compulsion driving it was gone, along with the mancer's power over it. So long as the mancer didn't summon it again—with any luck Lyss would put a stop to that.

As Skaar watched, the wounds on the berigan's snout began to heal over. With a huff, the beast turned and ambled away, sinking deeper into the mists until it was nothing but a shadow.

Skaar let it go, heat building under his feathers. He fanned his wings and panted. *Too much Aether.* The thought felt sluggish as the raw power gnawed at his concentration. He could stay here, give in…drift. With an effort, Skaar shook himself. *Get out now. Before it consumes you.*

He reached, feeling for a pocket of power that had seeped through to Terresmir. It felt far away, so far away. *Curse it.* He sought out Lyss' hugrokar, found the lifeline, and hauled on it. On Terresmir, he sensed her start and wince. *That way.* He banked, wings pumping as he gathered speed. The mists thinned. He made out grass. And above, stars. With a final twitch, he tumbled out, hitting the earth in a heap. His head rang—blood and Aether in his ears. For a moment he lay there, every fiber buzzing, panting to rid the Aether from his lungs.

Footsteps behind. A bear's muzzle swam into view. Its fur shivered and writhed as he stared at it. At first, he thought it was his spinning vision, but then the long jaw and black nose morphed into a human face. Brin flashed him a grin.

"Not bad, rarkyn," she said.

Skaar sat up, clutching the base of one horn, his head swimming. He pulled his hand away, opened his mouth—

His voice died as the Aether's current stilled. His feathers turned on end. *That feeling.* He staggered to his feet. "Get—"

Runes flared across the grass, illuminating the lines scratched into the earth in long, sweeping arcs. Skaar spun, horror blooming in his chest as the circle spread around the camp, joining with other runes in the distance.

With a lurch, the ward activated, sealing them in. Its twenty-four-points glowed around them.

And it was huge.

CHAPTER THIRTY-SIX

Dearest Elena,

I know this letter will never reach you. How could it? We are worlds apart now. But somehow, it feels right. Like maybe these words will reach across the void to you.

You did not fail me. It is the other way around: I failed you.

I left you.

You have paid the price of my mistakes, and that's not right. No child should bear a punishment meant for their father.

I have come to a decision. I will summon the Eternals and make a proposition. A trade to restore the way of things. My life in exchange for yours.

Before you curse me for an idiot, know that I go willingly. To die first is a parent's right; and I'm claiming it. I will pay anything, do anything, to see the world has you back in it.

The answers lie in the Otherworld, in those ancient creatures that dwell in the abyss. The Aether's keepers. The Eternals. I will summon them and make the trade. I have just the rarkyn to reach them.

Do not get comfortable, Elena. I am bringing you home.

Lyss raced through the grass, dry blades cutting at her leggings. Ahead the figure ran, arms pumping, cloak billowing behind. The moment the mancer had spotted her—a jerk of his cowled head and a distinct intake of breath—he'd stopped casting, wheeled about and fled.

Lyss lengthened her stride, closing the distance and ignoring the heat building in her chest. The rarkyn's binding ached down her arms. She pulled her hugrokar tighter, blocked out the pain. The figure glanced over his shoulder, flashing a face of fair skin, and sprinted on.

Not so fast.

She pounced. Her hands snared the mancer's shoulders. A foot to the back of his knees and she slammed him to the ground. He landed with a huff, lungs emptying. Lyss pressed her sword against the collar of the cloak. Just hard enough for the blade to bite through the fabric.

"Why are you attacking us?" the words came out as a snarl, surprising even herself. She pushed away the rarkyn's hugrokar again and cleared her throat. "What do you—"

Face down in the grass, the mancer coughed and wheezed out: "Lyss, it's me. It's me!"

That voice. She stopped. A hand wriggled out from the huddle of limbs, found the knee in his back and tapped it, conceding to the tussle. Lyss stared down at the white fingers. She grabbed the mancer's cloak and heaved him over.

"Sepp be, *Hane?*"

The Eder Wildner blinked up at her, a crooked smile growing across his face. Lyss released him, dropping her sword onto the grass. *Sepp, I was ready to gut him.* She ogled. "Hane, what the 'byss are you doing here?"

The Wildner boy sat up, rubbing the back of his neck, eyes darting to the sword then to Lyss' face. "We've been following you ever since we heard what happened at Bardas Post."

The memory of a bloody head in her hands flashed through her mind's eye. *Oh gods, had they seen—*she sucked in a breath, forced her mind away from the picture. His words sank in.

"We? Darrin's here too?"

Expressions washed over Hane's face: guilt, sadness, and for a moment a spark of anger, then he shook his head.

"Just Archer and me," he said. His eyes brightened, as if suddenly remembering something. "Lyss, he's a mancer from Illredus! He says he knows how to break the rarkyn's bond." He sprang to his feet. "I'll take you to him."

Lyss stiffened. "You're with the mordkyn—the mancer?" She tried to keep her voice light, but it came out harsh, edged in anger. She imagined how it might have unfolded. A few smooth words and Hane would have bought whatever story the mancer told. She could only guess what the man wanted him for, but after those binding castings he'd used, she was sure it wasn't benign.

"You idiot, Hane."

Hane frowned and made to take her sleeve, but she pulled away. A stab of pain in her foot made her forget the thought. Wincing, she spun on Rark, easing her hugrokar closer so it lapped against the rarkyn's mind. Borderline panic rocked through her, jumping her heart into her ribs.

What is going on?

For a moment nothing, but she sensed him moving, drawing Aether into himself, even as it burned inside him. Then, *Aetherling. Busy.* The words were frayed, fuzzy in her head, before: *Hold on.*

Hold on to what? she managed, before heat burst inside her. Pleasant to warm, warm to burning, burning to searing. It rushed down her spine, across her skull and behind her eyes. Pain fired down her limbs, and for a heartbeat she felt a pop of ghostly joints in a pair of wings on her back. She jerked her mind away but before she was clear, the pain subsided into a dull throb. She sagged where she stood.

"Lyss?" Hane's voice whispered. He sounded far away; out of breath, as if she'd winded him again. A sweaty hand clasped her elbow and shook.

Across hugrokar, the rarkyn drifted, thoughts growing murky as the Aether thrummed through his head. His hugrokar stretched for her, reaching out like a hand. She reached back. Their hugrokars caught and Rark latched on and hauled. Lyss swayed, imaging her hugrokar bending like a rod with a fish on its line. The rarkyn swept up and out, tumbling free of the Otherworld's grip and her hugrokar snapped straight again. She came back to herself with a gasp.

"Lyss?" Hane's voice sounded again. Fingers nudged her shoulder. "Are you still there?"

Lyss shook herself and swallowed. "Yes, I'm still here."

Hane stared at her. Stared at her eyes, transfixed, then edged away. "Are you still Lyss?" he whispered. "You look different."

He flinched as she faced him but didn't step away. She took in his travel-stained tunic, smudged face, and gritty hair and put a hand on her hip. "As do you." He looked older too, and he was sweating profusely; more than earlier. She picked up her sword and sheathed it. "Why did you come, Hane?"

"Archer said he could help you."

Lyss tried to ignore the twinge of hope that sprung up inside her. *It's probably a trick.*

"And the Order," Hane blurted. "The Order are after you…but I suppose you already know that."

"I meant, why did *you* come, Hane? You don't owe me anything."

The youth studied the ground. "Yes, I do," he mumbled to his feet, but her pact-enhanced hearing picked out the words easily. He looked up again, eyes bright. "Archer has taught me a lot," he said.

Lyss rubbed the place where his binding spell had hit Rark. The echo of it still simmered down her arms. *He certainly has.*

"I really think he can help you."

Lyss scowled, temper fraying. "Help me? By having you cast binding spells on us?" she asked. "That wasn't helping Hane, that was Sepp damn hurting!"

Hane faltered. "I didn't hit…that was," he began. "Archer said he needed a distraction while he…" he tapered off and bit his lip.

Lyss' gaze snapped to his. "While he *what,* Hane?"

"Don't be angry," Hane said. "He needs the rarkyn for something. A summoning. Something to do with the Eternals. When he's done—"

Cold doused Lyss, turning her hairs on end. At her back, the Aether fell still. She staggered, the pressure in her head fading. It was like the ability to breathe had been ripped away, not missed until it was gone. Heat fled from her muscles. Her teeth chattered. Before her, Hane gasped and green-tinted light illuminated his face. Lyss turned, already knowing what she'd find.

A ward. She goggled at it. It was massive. Some fifty paces across, green lines arcing across the grass, joining the rune points together. Lyss counted, breath catching when she came to the twenty-fourth rune. *Sepp be, the amount of magic that would require…*

Two figures stood within, one winged and horned, the other a mass of shaggy fur. Trapped. At the ward's edge, the air rippled as if something, someone, were curtained behind it. She squinted and made out a moving shadow. A spell of some kind. It came to the edge of the ward and stopped. The Aether twitched around the shadow, and across hugrokar the rarkyn stiffened. He too sensed it.

Blood rushed to her legs, surging her into a sprint. "Rark! Rark look out."

"Lyss, wait!" Hane shouted, stumbling after her.

The casting cracked through the warding, its bolt shredding the air. Inside, Rark lunged away, but the casting followed, forking out to hit his leg. Searing cold struck just above Lyss' knee and she cut back a yelp.

"Kratting pact," she growled, pulling her mind close. *Like a fist.* She forced her feet over the grass; first in a stagger, then a loping stride. The burn eased, but through the pact its icy tendrils were latching on, wrapping up her back, around her arms, tightening the web around her.

In the circle, Rark flailed, wings beating as he tried to pull the spell off. Brin arrived at his side, teeth closing about one arm of the binding. She tore at it, head shaking as if trying to rip flesh from the bones of a kill. She came away empty.

Lyss drew her sword and made for the mancer and their cloak of shadow. The ground closed between them, and behind, Hane let out an inaudible cry. A warning? The mancer looked up, and within the shadow Lyss glimpsed a long pallid scar and black eyes simmering with the light of the rune-circle.

Gritting her teeth, Lyss forced her muscles on. She lifted her sword, leveling it like a lance, and charged for the shadow. The Aether twisted.

Lyss threw herself sideward—too late. Light flared and twelve runes and the encircling lines of a ward seared the grass around her. Cold surged up her legs. Her head collided with something hard and invisible. A wall. No, a barrier; the edge of the ward. Her vision went dark, and she slumped. The air crackled.

Slowly her sight ebbed back and Lyss made out runes pulsing under her fingers. With a shaking hand, she felt along the earth, reaching for the edge of the ward. Pressure met her fingers. Her gut shriveled. The circle was warding her. Warding her *like an aetherling*. Panic stabbed into her chest. *Calm down.* She bit her lip and tried to force the blind terror away, but it danced around her head. *Aetherling, aetherling, aetherling,* it crowed.

Despair rose in her throat, clogged her nose, blurred her eyes. Lyss blinked hard, clearing the tears and she ground her teeth together. *No tears. Get free. Fight.* She counted the points of her own circle again. Twelve. Gods and ginndir, the mancer wasn't messing about. Beyond her twelve-point prison, Rark still squirmed against the binding inside the giant twenty-four-point ward.

"The boy was right. You do share the rarkyn's magic. It has its talons in you, well and truly."

Lyss jerked her head up. The air outside her ward shifted, parting as a shadowy figure stepped out, galdar fading from the sigiled hood of his cloak. An itch built in Lyss' nose as the whiff of dismissed runes reached her.

"You must be Lyss." He knelt at the edge of the circle, inspecting the runes, then her. His eyes were black in the rune-light, but as they studied her, a red glint flickered through them. Slowly, he reached down, fingers passing through the ward and took up Lyss' hand. Mesmerized, she let him. He turned over her palm to take in the last rune of Iga's seal on the inside of her wrist. He tutted.

"Krawan magic won't save you, girl," he said, then added softer. "You don't have long." Lyss snatched her hand away.

Don't believe anything he says. He twists the truth. Rark's voice sounded in her head, far off and strained, as if a great weight were crushing the air out of him.

As if he'd heard, Archer's lips pressed together. He rounded on the rarkyn trapped in his casting.

"Enough interference from you, Tykee." He flicked a finger and the binding spell tightened. Rark grunted and Lyss sucked in a wheezy breath. *Tight, like a fist.* Her breathing eased a little, giving her enough time to wonder: *Tykee?*

"Archer, the ursa!" Hane staggered over to them, pointing. Pink flesh and loose bear skin flashed in the corner of Lyss' vision as the ursa leapt *across* the glowing lines of the twenty-four-point ward, swinging a smoldering campfire log at the mancer's head.

The mancer spun. The log missed, snagging his cowl instead. With a ripping of fabric, the bark tore through it. Lyss stared, watching the mancer's single hand blur through a series of runes—too quick to register—and snap out a casting. Brin was blown off her feet, an arrow-shaped spell striking into her gut. The spell slammed her into the grass with a sickening thud and wrapped around her with a pulse of cold galdar. Brin groaned but didn't move.

"Clever for an ursa, slipping my ward like that." Archer straightened. His gaze landed on Hane. "Get her skin."

The Wildner started. "But—"

Archer glared at the youth. "The skin, *Hane*. The ward won't work on her while she's human, she'll cross straight over the runes. If she shifts, she'll break free of that binding all over again."

Hane swallowed and shuffled over to the ursa. At the tilt of the mancer's head, the binding moved, its bright tendrils readjusting its hold on the woman.

"Don't you kratting—" Brin snarled, only to have her jaw clamped shut as one tendril wrapped around her head. With shaking hands, Hane leaned over and lifted the bear skin from her back. It came away slowly, as if the skin itself resisted Hane's pull. With a final heave it came free. Brin's naked shoulders glistened with sweat underneath.

Hane held the skin out to Archer.

"Burn it."

Brin gave a muffled cry and thrashed.

"No!" Lyss pushed herself up, pressing the barrier above one of the runes of her twelve-point ward. "You can't." She sought Hane's face. "Hane, you mustn't." The youth's eyes slid away from hers, but he hesitated, one hand paused over his pocket.

"For Sepp sake," Archer snapped. He thrust a hand into his cloak, pulled out something small and round and sparked the rune on it. He snatched the skin from Hane, threw it to the earth and tossed the pebble on it. The shaggy gray fur singed under it, smoke curling up around the stone.

Brin screamed, writhing as if it were her the fire stone burned. Hane stared dumbly down at it, hands dangling at his sides, useless.

Lyss pounded the ward, the blows turning her fists numb. *Helpless.* Her scar twinged. *Not again. Please.* "Stop!" she shouted. "Do what you came to do but leave her out of it!"

Archer ignored her. A small pop from the skin and a flame licked up around the rock. Brin gave a stifled sob, eyes tracking the fire as it crept across the fur, leaving a black trail in its wake.

Lyss threw her shoulder into the ward. It crackled against her skin. Crackled and *bowed.* She sucked in a breath, hope welling inside her— not all of it hers. At the back of her mind the rarkyn hovered. A glance over her shoulder found him, bound and silent on the earth, watching.

How do you break wards? she asked. *How did you break Hane's when we first met?*

Overwhelm the runes.

Lyss turned back to her twelve-point ward. *How?*

Find a weak point. Work it open.

Lyss reached her senses out to the ward. What if there were no weak points? She pushed the thought aside and hunted, forcing her mind calm even as the spell radiated cold through her head. A weakness, there had to be one. No circle was perfect.

Twelve-points. The kind of ward used on high-ranked aetherlings. She probed the runes with her fingers, waiting for one to give under her. The first three were solid, but the fourth gave ground and she was able to push half a finger through the ward above it.

There. She jumped as Rark's hugrokar snapped close. Had he been sensing it through her? Lyss burrowed her fingers to the ward and clawed for an invisible purchase. Her nails snagged on the barrier and she gritted her teeth as a pulse of cold stabbed down her hands.

Her muscles strained. The barrier quivered against her. "Come on you bastard," she growled and pressed harder. The barrier gave another shudder and stilled. *No. Just a little more.* She planted her feet, locked her knees and reached for the heat that had once filled her, for the power that had driven her across the Iros Mountains. *I am not helpless. Not today.*

She seethed the Aether in.

Heat flushed through her. Though her skin, through muscles into bone—warming the air in her lungs. The Aether trapped in the circle with her vanished; power soaking into her. Lyss wrenched as hard as she could. The ward fizzled and cracked, then began to give. One inch, then two.

Archer's head jerked up from the flaming bear skin, mouth agog. For a moment he stared, then as Lyss placed a foot over the edge of the runes, he shook off his shock and faced her. He thrust a hand at the ward, eyes flashing red again. The runes of the circle flared; the strength of the weakened rune rebuilding. Lyss grappled with it, gathering up her Aether and pushing back. Cold pricked inside her—she was running out of magic!

Push through it. Rark's voice was beside her in her head. And as surely as if he were standing next to her, a taloned hand fell on her shoulder and pushed her forward. *Go. Tear it down.* Fresh Aether rocked through her. Her vision hazed; a cord of power stretched away from her, through her ward, through the giant twenty-four-point circle beyond, joining with Rark on the other side.

The pact.

Power channeled down it, flowing from the rarkyn to her. *Don't think.*

Don't question. Lyss rounded on her ward and pressed. The barrier trembled under her hand, its flimsy film warping as their magic buffeted it.

It crumpled. Shattered like glass, falling away under her fingers and stinging as it went. *Free.* Lyss rocketed out of the circle, lunging for Brin's burning bear skin. She snatched it up and beat out the flames, smoking rune-stone tumbling to the grass. Brin gave a shout from behind her binding, her body turning limp in relief.

"I've got you." Lyss threw the skin over Brin. It clung to her, worming around the tendrils of the binding spell. Where it touched skin, fur sprouted. Brin struggled against the binding. *Stronger than Hane's,* Lyss guessed, leaning down to help.

The Aether twitched. Lyss leapt back, just as two binding spells split the ground where she'd stood. Brin grunted as pebbles sprayed her face. Mere paces away, Archer glowered.

"Just go quietly," he hissed.

Lyss' sword came to her hands without conscious thought. "I will not."

She lunged, stabbing for the mancer's chest, then scythed the blade up under his throat. He twirled away as if he were her dance partner at a ball, left hand knocking her blade away with a wooden *clunk.*

Not just any mancer, he moves too well. Even with a false hand. A glimmer of fury rose in her. *He's Order trained.*

She darted in, swinging wide, gaining ground as the mancer stepped back. Lyss stabbed again. Her blade caught the fabric of his coat and with a popping of threads, she drove it into the ground, tethering the mancer still. She swept in and delivered a boot into his gut. Archer grunted, and Lyss had enough time to register the Aether's pulse before a casting cracked across her brow. Her vision swam.

She clenched her teeth, pulled her sword free and sliced at the mancer's head. Her blade met earth instead as Archer rolled and came to his feet—the remnants of his last galdar-strike dissipating in the air. Lyss reset her stance and fixed her eyes on him. She rocked onto her toes, readying to spring.

"No, Lyss!" Hane rushed in, grabbing at her tunic. "He's your only chance—"

Lyss shook him off and waded forward, sword ready.

Hane spun on the mancer. "Archer *please!*"

The mordkyn spat on the ground. "Nothing can be done for her, boy.

You saw how the circle held her. She's more aetherling than human now."

His words sawed through Lyss' chest like a surgeon's knife. Her breath caught in her throat. "I'm human," she whispered. Sweat prickled down her neck. She was, wasn't she? She palmed her sword hilt. "I'm still human."

A sneer worked over Archer's face. "Saying it doesn't make it so. Look at you. You look like something that crawled out of the abyss."

Hane's outstretched arms fell to his sides and he stared between them. "But you said—"

Archer's fingers stilled mid-cast, and Lyss thought she saw a flicker of guilt. "I'd hoped," he said. "Until I saw that." He jabbed a finger at the broken twelve-point ward behind Lyss. The lines on the ground were scuffed, runes already dead. "The Aether's in her veins, boy. There's nothing you can do."

Lyss' stomach turned over. *Aether in her veins.* Her fingers twitched, recalling the soldier's skull crushed in her grip; her hand speared through the shuck's chest, an aetherling heart in her fist. Recalled the hunger pooling in her mouth. How Archer's ward trapped her like an aetherling. Time slowed. A slow chill seeped over her, blooming into terror.

Monster. I'm a monster.

Hane reached for Archer, almost pleading. "You have to try. There must be something."

"There is nothing," Archer snapped, eyes blazing. "Get it into your thick head."

Hane recoiled as if he'd been struck, and he sank to his knees. "But I —" his voice wavered.

Lyss rested a hand on his head. Hoped he couldn't feel it tremble. *Monster,* her mind whispered again. She sensed the darkness twitch inside her; gathering its strength to consume her. Soon. She wanted to scream, to run, to hide. *Monster. Shut up!* She took a breath, ignored her heart in her ears, and forced the words out. "It's alright. Let it go, Hane. You can't help me."

His face turned up to her, eyes shining. A fresh tear rolled down his cheek. "It's not alright. It's my fault."

"Hane, I told you before. It's not your fault."

The youth's face scrunched tight, and he pulled away. A silent sob shook his shoulders. "But they were my runes," he choked.

Archer sneered. "If it were those half-baked scribbles I've seen, I doubt it."

Lyss stiffened as he circled, ready to strike if he showed signs he was about to cast.

"Galdar doesn't bond you to an aetherling. That's old magic, from the days before the Empire."

Lyss kept her face still but reached for Rark's mind. *Can you move?*

The rarkyn shifted and she caught the fierce burn of the binding as he relaxed his hugrokar to reply. *No.* Weariness settled into her muscles, ached in her bones. It blurred her thoughts and pulled her eyes shut. She wrenched her mind clear, tightened her hold on her sword, and stepped away from Hane.

She tilted her head to Rark in the giant twenty-four-point ward. "Release him."

"No." Archer's hand rose and Lyss braced. The casting never came. Instead, Archer darted over the runes, *into* the giant circle. Where she could no longer follow. *Gods damn him.*

Rark? She reached for the rarkyn. His mind slid away. She pincered it still. *Are you alright?*

He stirred and Lyss' vision doubled, turning fuzzy at the edges as he opened his eyes. The rarkyn's blood thundered in her head, and she fought the urge to pull away. Through his eyes, the mancer's scarred face loomed close. Panic flickered across the pact.

Rark? Lyss pressed.

Get away. A half-hearted push across hugrokar. *Fever's coming.*

"Tykee, Tykee, Tykee," Archer's voice rang in their ears and the mancer knelt beside him. He ran a hand over Rark's crest, smoothing the feathers. Lyss felt as much as heard the rumble from Rark's throat.

"This is the last time, I promise."

A blade glinted in the mancer's hand. A dagger. Fear bloomed, crashing through Rark's chest. She lurched away, forcing the threads of their hugrokars apart.

Hands shook her shoulders and Lyss flinched before recognized Hane standing before her. "Lyss, I—"

Lyss pushed him aside. "Free Brin," she told him. The ursa chimed in with a muffled grunt from her binding.

Hane tried again. "Lyss I'm—"

"I know."

She felt the prick of a dagger against one forearm. Heard Rark snarl as it sliced. Across the circle, Archer pressed a bottle to the wound.

What is he doing?

He's going to drink. Rark's voice was stronger, but still fuzzy. The burns seared anew as he shifted in the binding. Archer grinned and came away, white teeth flashing. Then he lifted up the bottle and upended it over his outstretched tongue. Blood lapped over the rim. Thick, red. Coppery scent filling the air.

Bile rose in Lyss' throat.

A growl at her back signaled Brin breaking through the glowing bindings. Hane joined the ursa, pulling at the tendrils until one paw slipped free. With a swipe of those black claws, the bear-kin severed the remaining bindings. Hane scrambled up and away as if wary those claws might turn on him.

Brin lumbered over to Lyss. Burns singed her fur and she limped on her left forepaw, but her eyes glittered with rage and Lyss grinned. *Monster it's to be then? I'll fucking show him monster.*

"Sepp be," Hane whispered, coming up on Lyss' other side to stare at the Archer through the ward, expression caught somewhere between horror and disgust. "What are you going to do?"

"I'm going to end it."

A huff of approval from Brin. The young Wildner stared at her, dumbfounded. "He's mad, Lyss."

Lyss grinned again, wider this time, and with too many teeth. "So am I."

PART V
MONSTER

At night the raiders come,
screams cry 'til day dawns.
By light the raiders sleep,
the broken wails of rarkyns morn.

—Old Illredian Proverb

CHAPTER THIRTY-SEVEN

Brennus,

I hope my shuck finds you in time. We have found Markides and the boy. They are in the fields of Torin. They are preparing something—something that requires a twenty-four-point ward. From its shape, it looks like a summons, but it is beyond anything I've ever seen. Whatever Markides has planned, it has been a long time coming and I fear Torin and its people will be the victims of it.

Whatever comes out of that circle will be powerful and, I fear, dangerous beyond control. The city needs reinforcements, Nilos is the closest, but they'll not rally to a call from a Corporal. Do what you can. Send whomever you can.

Hasek.

P.S. Leandre and the Rose are camped near Nilos. As much as it pains me to say it, she may be the best option—if you can convince her. I fear any effort I make will be torn to shreds.

Hasek rolled up the parchment, cast a galdar seal around it and slipped it into the bag tied about the shuck's neck. He patted the beast's back.

"Go Naqamal, as fast as you can," he said, stepping back from the creature. The shuck's bone head lowered, as if in a nod, then it whirled about and streaked into the night, north-west.

Hasek winced and Darrin wondered whether even his unparalleled Aether reserves would last until the shuck reached Brennus. From their hillock, he looked out across the valley, taking in the glowing circles in the distance. If he squinted, he could make out the twenty-four rune points and a smaller twelve pointer beside it. The sight of them on the horizon had made Hasek release a string of profanities—something about traders and their horses—that Darrin had never expected to come from the mouth of one of the Order's men.

"How long will it take for your aetherling to reach them?" Darrin asked.

The Corporal sank to the grass beside their saddlebags, unstopped a waterskin and took a long draw. "A few hours at least, even without us on his back," he said, and smacked his lips. Darrin caught the whiff of chara on the mancer's breath.

"Why not send an eyree in Torin?"

Hasek made a noise in his throat. "And have the message change hands twice—first in Torin, then Nilos—before it reaches him?" He shook his head. "It's too important for that." He flipped up the cover of one saddlebag, delved through it and pulled out a portion of tough, dried bread and a lump of cheese.

Darrin stared at the soldier. "What are you doing? There's at least a mile still to cover."

Hasek balanced the bread and cheese between a thumb and fore-finger and looked at Darrin from over the top of his bony hand. "I'm waiting," he said.

"Waiting?" Darrin almost exploded at the soldier, but he clenched his fists and held his tongue. He stabbed a finger down the hill. "That's my brother down there! And my friend!"

Hasek followed Darrin's finger, then looked to Darrin again. "Go, but my orders are not to get involved."

Darrin gaped at him. "You said you would help."

"I said I would get you here." Hasek nibbled the bread and cheese, and Darrin fought the urge not to sweep in and clock the two-faced soldier on the chin. "My duty is to protect the people," Hasek said, nodding his head toward the walls of Torin a quarter mile to his back. "From the look of those circles, they might need it soon."

As he spoke, a flicker of light pulled Darrin's gaze back to the circles. One pulsed, green light flaring before it deadened and the night fell in around it. Anxiety gnawed into his stomach. *Hane. Lyss.*

Behind, the soldier sighed. "Give your sword here." He beckoned with a hand.

"What for?"

"You're clearly going to go," Hasek said. "I'll 'grave a sigil on it. Give you a fighting chance."

Darrin unbuckled the blade and handed it over, hilt first. Hasek sat, legs folded, sword resting on his knees. His long fingers twitched over the cold steel, tracing a rune on the metal. It flared green for a heartbeat, then faded. Hasek traced another.

Darrin paced the road, waiting for Hasek to finish. Back and forth, clenching and re-clenching his fists.

"How long—"

A scream rose up on the wind. *Lyss.*

Without thinking he snatched the sword from Hasek and ran, heart banging against his ribs. *Sepp, let them be all right.*

"Be careful! Markides' a powerful mancer," Hasek called after him.

And you are not. The unspoken words hung in the air at Darrin's back, but he was already gone.

CHAPTER THIRTY-EIGHT

Sweat dripped down Archer's neck. The rarkyn's blood burned inside him—far more than it ever had. He wiped his brow and sucked in a breath. The crisp winter air hit his lungs, giving him a moment of relief. His fingers tingled; black veins pulsated under his skin, burning him from the inside out.

Fool. Should have known it'd be more potent with the sigil gone. He's been popping in and out of the Otherworld like a Sepp damn mole.

At his feet, the rarkyn glared from the glowing bindings, his silver eye blazing in the moonlight.

"Don't give me that look," Archer muttered. "You promised."

The rarkyn barred its teeth and hissed and jerked its bindings. "Not this."

Archer ignored it and ran his gaze over the aetherling. Returning to the Otherworld had wrought noticeable changes to it. The skeletal thinness was gone; the sheen of his feathers restored, fresh as the day Archer had first pulled him free of the Aether's grip. And his eyes—they were bright and full of fight. Determined to live.

Something plucked inside Archer's chest, like a thumb testing the tautness of a bowstring. He scowled and pushed the guilt aside. *Curse that Wildner boy.* He steeled his will, feeling the press of the journal against his breast. *Remember Elena. Remember what they stole from her. This time, it would work.*

"Why?" The rarkyn's question made him pause. For a moment, he was back with Hane, the young Wildner staring at him in the dark, face earnest as he asked the same question.

"Because you owe me."

The rarkyn twisted in the bonds. "Owe you no more," it spat.

Archer's temper flared. "I *saved* you. You owe me everything," he thundered. "They *all* do." Years of service, months of devotion and duty. Inside him, his well of Aether bubbled, hot as a forge, the rarkyn's blood stoking the heat. He reached for the runes of the binding and funneled more power to them. The spell crackled and constricted around the rarkyn. His snarl spluttered into a wheeze.

"I gave them everything," Archer hissed. In return, his everything had been ordered to death with the casual wave of a jeweled hand. *I will bring her back.*

A shift of the rarkyn's eyes alerted him: a flicker away from Archer's face then back again. He spun, throwing up a half-ward as a strike casting smacked into it. Ten paces away Hane stood, the runes of Archer's twenty-four-point circle at his feet. A pile of scuffed dirt lay at his heel.

Tried to rub out the runes, eh? Archer sneered. *Try as much as you like. It won't work.* He glanced along the rim of the circle and spotted the girl and the ursa clawing at the barrier above one of the rune points. Hane pressed in, one foot inside the ward, one out, runes glowing under him.

Archer lifted his good hand and worked a lazy rune. "Don't test me, boy." He snapped the end of the casting out.

Fingers dancing, one foot digging an arc across the ground, Hane managed to get a half-ward up before Archer's casting hit. The spell smattered against the barrier, and the runes of the boy's defense glowed like molten steel. Archer spooled more power from his core and cast again. This time, Hane's ward shattered. His runes flickered, then dissolved to nothing but scored marks in the trampled grass.

Behind, the rarkyn's binding quivered. Archer spun. The creature hadn't moved, but he sensed it drawing on the magic in the binding, trying to weaken it enough to break free. He spat out a curse, reached for the runes and surged power into them again. The rarkyn grunted, face contorting. At the edge of the ward, the girl hunched over with a groan.

Another casting dashed against Archer's half-ward. *Like a bug fizzling out in a fire.*

"Archer, stop," Hane shouted. "Please." He fired off a strike, then another as if he were hurling a spear. They were large, easy movements to read. *Amateur.* Archer dodged one, blocked two and sent a volley in return. Hane threw himself to the ground and rolled—not quick enough. A strike lanced his side and he yelped.

"Hane?" the girl's call sounded from her rune point. "Go Brin, help him!" The bear gave a rumble and abandoned their effort, muzzle swinging towards the Wildner.

"I'm okay." The boy dragged himself to his feet, clutching his side. His hands worked again, and Archer batted his following strike away with one of his own. With the flick of a finger, he sent Hane sprawling.

Stay down boy. He raised a hand, readying to strike a final time if he saw so much as a twitch.

Silver flashed in his peripheral vision. Archer jerked his head back just as a hunting knife sliced through the air next to his cheek. It embedded itself in the earth behind him with a soft thud.

"Don't you dare," the girl growled from beyond runes. Her hard eyes fixed on him. The hairs prickled on Archer's arms as something shifted behind her gaze.

Curse her meddling. If it weren't for her, he'd be in the Steppes by now. But he knew how to deal with her. He spun and delivered a kick into the rarkyn's gut. She buckled, issuing the same grunt as the rarkyn beside him. "You've interfered enough."

Archer reached for one of the circles graved into the thumb of his false hand. *To think I'd need this.* His finger pressed against the ward-graving, driving Aether into it. The sigil responded, the circle and runes forming whole and clear in his mind. He snapped the sixteen points up around the girl, severing her from the edge of the twenty-four-point circle. A thrill pulsed through him at how easy it was to conjure.

"No!" The girl rammed her shoulder into the ward. It *shuddered.* Archer stared. Blinked, stared again. One galdar-less girl against a sixteen-point ward. A non-contest. *Yet she was harming it.* A chill seeped through his limbs; panic surging in a cold wave. The black void the nizer had sensed filled his head. He pushed more power into the runes. The ward steadied, and the girl slumped against the barrier.

A cough sounded from Hane. *Curse it boy, don't get up.* Archer ground his teeth as the Wildner's leg twitched and bit by bit, the youth levered himself onto his elbows.

"Hane, stay down," the girl shouted, but her voice was lost to the ursa's roar. The bear thudded onto all fours and charged, abandoning the girl to the sixteen-point ward. It tore across the grass to the boy's aid, fur shifting and shimmering in the rune light.

"I have to—" Hane lifted a finger and began tracing a rune.

Gods, curse it. Archer focused his power, shaping another sliver of the furnace inside to his will. He'd make it quick. Painless.

Movement caught the edge of Archer's vision. A shadow. It darted over the greater circle's lip, rushing at him in an all-out sprint. He had enough time to register the blade in its hand before it swung. He got mid-way through casting another half-ward before he abandoned it and leapt away. Cold steel bit into his arm and pain seared from shoulder to elbow.

White hair flashed within a dark cloak. For a moment, Archer thought it was Hane, only to have the shadow resolve in the rune light. This face was older, grime covered from weeks of travel. And furious.

The brother.

"Darrin!" Hane's cry of delight reached Archer's ears before the sword swung at him again. He weaved around it, sending off a striking cast in response—but Darrin was too close. He lashed out with a knee, driving it into Archer's stomach and threw the cast off course.

Kratting Wildners. Archer spun away. In his mind, a rune spasmed. Then another. He risked a glance to his sixteen-point ward. The girl and the ursa heaved at the barrier from either side—the girl in, the bear out. The circle gave a wobble.

What in the abyss is she? He sidestepped another swing, swung his dagger up, parrying a stabbing blow to his chest. The blades screeched, sound piercing in Archer's ears. Vibrations ran down the hilt and into his fingers.

Darrin's expression flickered, as if surprised. A smug smile pulled at Archer's mouth.

"You don't get on the Council of Seven without Order training boy," he said and, seeing an opportunity, he straightened. "Take your brother and leave. I won't stop you."

"And Lyss?" His eyes darted behind Archer. "The rarkyn?"

Even as he spoke, one of the runes in the sixteen-point circle collapsed. The ward's resonance slipped from Archer's mind and he grappled after it, pushing power at it. But it was too late. The ward had fallen, like water seeping through soil. Cobwebs of its power hung in his head. The girl let out a cry of triumph as the ward dissolved; her feet thumped across the grass, skirting the edge of the twenty-four-point circle, sprinting for Hane. Free at last. Archer clenched his one good fist. *Damn them.*

"The rarkyn is mine," he spat. And where the rarkyn went, so did the girl. He left it unsaid, but the mask came down once more and Darrin was on the attack. Swing, parry, thrust, Archer got lost in the movements. Duck, dodge, slice the dagger, cast again. His wooden hand drove into Darrin's ribs like a cudgel—until his power over the rarkyn's binding snagged. He parried a blow with his dagger, colliding metals shrieking, and focused inward.

The rarkyn's power was eating away the bindings. *No you don't.* Archer flooded Aether into the spell. The rarkyn let out a hiss, scrunched its face—and drew harder. Archer's hold on the binding wavered. He reached for the well inside him, drew it up and slammed it into the spell. The binding flared white and the aetherling screeched. Tykee's eyes flared wide, and he glared at Archer, enraged. Solid black rings split its irises. Archer's lips curled into a grin. Fever. At last. *I haven't even begun the summons.* Yet, as he watched, the rings vanished, ebbing back to the red and silver glare as if they'd never been. *Gods curse it.*

Darrin's sword sliced at him. Archer dodged, then bounded away; Darrin following. He cast a strike spell and heard it clang off Darrin's blade as the boy thrust it up before him. *Of course his sword is kratting 'graved.*

Again, the rarkyn's binding tremored. Archer didn't look this time, instead he fed power into it, swearing under his breath. He needed to conserve his strength, yet at this rate he was going to burn through his reserves before he could begin the real summons, rarkyn blood or not. He needed to end it. Quickly.

He searched the circle.

"Keep going Darrin, it's working," the girl shouted. She stood at the edge of the twenty-four-point circle, one shoulder propped under a sagging Hane. Next to her, the bear dug furiously at the ward, claws raking earth and runes—to no success. Archer barely noticed. Instead, he gawked at the girl. Something was wrong with her eyes.

Rings. Archer froze. Of course. She was bonded to the rarkyn; shared Aether with it. "Abyss damn."

Darrin's boot sank into his chest, sending him sprawling. He rolled and came up, snapping out a strike and stepped—

A hand closed around his ankle, just above the boot, hooking him still. Talons sank into his skin and pain prickled up his leg. Archer looked down. The rarkyn had weakened the binding enough to move, enough to belly crawl through the dirt to latch one hand around Archer's foot. A maniacal grin—all teeth and pink gum—split its face.

Darrin closed in. Archer swore. He twisted, ankle popping in the rarkyn's grip, and lunged around the thrusting blade, slicing his dagger upward. Darrin broke off his attack and jerked backwards. Archer's dagger nicked his nose. The Wildner let out a grunt, staggered, and pressed a hand to his face. Blood gushed down his cheeks. Archer brought the hilt of the dagger down over the boy's temple. He folded, crumpling to the ground like an empty sack.

Don't get up. Archer thought at the Wildner. Darrin didn't stir. He lay in the grass, chest rising and falling, his face a bloody mess. The rest of him was still. Out cold.

Archer released a long breath and tried to move away. His foot snagged against the rarkyn's hold. The broken bones throbbed. He gritted his teeth and sent a pulse of power down to the binding spell. The rarkyn grunted, but clung on, talons tight as a vice.

His twenty-four-point ward crackled, shuddered, and the barrier warped and rippled as they dissipated the force of an impact. Archer raised his head. The girl rammed the barrier of the circle again, the ward distorting as her shoulder slammed into it and she bounced away again. Beside her, Hane sat, arms wrapped around himself, ogling at her.

Was she getting stronger?

Lyss backed up again to make another charge. Archer reached into his well, began to draw on it. The power died inside him. One moment it was a furnace, hot and sweltering, the next it slid away. Heat drained from him, spiraling out of his reach. He gasped. *No.*

No, it wasn't spiraling—it was being *sucked.*

He rounded on the rarkyn and the talons about his ankle. *Gods cursed aetherling.* His boot hit its chin, snapping its head back. It made no noise this time, but its defiant grip tightened around Archer's ankle—and *pulled* harder. The well inside him spluttered, the heat doused as it drew the magic from him. If it went out—

If this is how it must play out, so be it.

He lifted his dagger, aiming for the rarkyn's abdomen, just below the ribs, right where he'd seen the spears of the Myron guards sink in all those years before.

The ward shuddered again. Then cracked. At the edge of his vision, the girl thrust her arm through a weakened section of the ward, then worked her body through as if squeezing through a gap.

"Rark!" she shouted. "Rark, let go."

Archer drove the dagger home.

Surprise flashed across the aetherling's features. Its grip slackened around Archer's foot. He wrenched the blade free, feeling it grind against bone and muscle.

"I'm sorry, Tykee."

The rarkyn's hand quested to the wound, pressing against it before holding bloody fingers up to its gaze. It coughed. Blood splattered the grass. *Must have hit an air sac.* Archer stumbled back, ankle throbbing, and the sword wound to his arm beginning to sting. *Not much time. Get out of the circle.*

He lifted the bloody dagger. Red ran down the shaft, dripping over his knuckles, thick and pungent. For a moment he stared at it, then at the black throbbing tendrils in his skin, frozen in indecision. Drink this and there may be no going back.

If it works, it will be worth it. It will all be worth it. The pain, the fear, the doubt. He had to try—or else become just another mancer broken under the wheel of empire. *I will not yield.*

Archer opened his mouth and licked his tongue down the blade. Heat ran into his throat, burning as he swallowed. It was like drinking forge water, and for an anxious heartbeat he waited, half expecting his heart to seize. Moments passed, and then the furnace roared back to life, flooding warmth through Archer's body. The pain in his arm deadened; the bones in his ankle ground back together. A barking laugh rose inside him. The gods were looking down upon him this day, and he was coming for their dominion.

Watch out Baer. I am one step closer to your Hall.

He limped to the edge of the ward. The girl was hunched over the runes, half in, half out of the ward, arms cradling her belly.

Archer grabbed the neck of her coat, and in one sharp pull, dragged her in, across the threshold—*into* his twenty-four-point circle. The motion jerked her alert and she twitched under his grip. She lashed out with a fist, bunched knuckles glancing his ribs as he dropped her in the dirt. She staggered to her feet, wheezing and clutching one arm around her stomach.

"Why?" she asked.

"There is someone I must save," Archer replied and stepped over the runes—*out* of the twenty-four-point ward as she rushed at him. A pulse of power mended the weakened runes and the girl smacked into the edge. She pounded on the barrier. Archer ignored her, firing off a strike spell at the ursa as the bear came charging around the circle. It struck in the flank and the bear's foreleg gave way under it, toppling it to the ground.

Archer visualized the runes in his mind, reached for his power, and brought a fresh ward to life around him, interlocking with the side of the twenty-four-pointer like a bulbous offshoot. For a moment he held his breath, heart racing as he waited for the complexity of the twenty-four points of the first ward and the eighteen of the new circle to overwhelm him. His well of power held.

How many nights had he rehearsed this moment?

Rehearsed and failed and rehearsed again. Rehearsed until the circles filled his dreams; until he knew every line and mark as if he were engraving it into his soul. He scanned the circles: the rarkyn lay motionless at the heart of it all, blood puddled about it. Everything was in place. He drew in a breath and pushed all other thoughts aside.

It was just him, the runes, and the summons.

Archer reached deep inside himself, summoning every ounce of power, and began.

CHAPTER THIRTY-NINE

Her skin, her muscles, her bones. And the wound. It seared in Rark's belly—and through him to her. Archer's dagger had sliced in, gouging flesh and arteries. She'd felt its tooth prick the back of her spine, then the pain hit. Small at first, a drawing out of the tide before the wave swept in. Rark had tried to shove her hugrokar away. But Lyss had stood there numbly, not quite believing it, and the wave had caught her up and snarled their minds into a knotted mess.

Gone was the hot ache of the Aether. Now she was on fire. Burning with the taste of blood in her mouth.

Run, Rark's thought brushed her.

With an effort, she pulled her scrambled hugrokar in and forced it into a fist. The double senses eased; the taste of blood faded, but this time it was different. Where her hugrokar had once balled tight, shielded like a nut in a shell, now a part of its husk had been ripped away. Through the crack, sensations poured in. The pain remained, and the fear gnawing in her gut and—she paused—regret, sadness, and something else. Another presence lurking at the edge of her thoughts; uncoiling its limbs, prowling out from its dark corner to peer through the crack. Something she didn't want to name. A shiver rose up her scalp. Lyss gritted her teeth. *Not yet.*

I am not running, she sent.

Run. Rark's voice grew stronger in her head, almost angry. *Ginndir are coming.*

Ginndir. The word stopped her still. A memory of a smoke-filled tent and Iga sitting opposite her, puffing away at her pipe, wafted through her mind.

"They will eat anything in their path. Aetherling, mancer, it doesn't matter." Hairs prickled down her arms. *Flesh-eaters.*

A pulse of Aether ran through the circle, flaring the runes white, illuminating the grass and fields like a bolt of lightning. The pressure of its power boiled against her skin, and her skin drank it in, filling her limbs then her head with a hot buzzing as if she were a steaming kettle in a hearth. Locked in his own protective ward, Archer stood, arms out flung, face still in concentration as the fingers of his right hand worked: *Ansu, raido, hagalaz.* Lyss recognized three runes, but the rest were an incoherent jumble.

Run. Rark's voice drifted to her, barely audible over the hive in her ears. His presence shrank, dwindling like a flame at the end of its wick —then vanished.

"Rark!" She staggered forward. Her legs were heavy, ungainly, as if they weren't hers. Her boots squelched into blood-churned mud. Clutching her abdomen, she sank down next to the rarkyn. The binding was close to failing, several of its tendrils already missing. Lyss grabbed the thickest part of the spell, dug her nails into the tendrils—not feeling the burn—and pulled. The casting gave like dry twigs, snapping away and dissolving in her hands.

Don't be dead.

She shook Rark's shoulder and jerked her hand away. He was hot. Almost too hot to touch. Lyss pushed him onto his side and caught a flash of silver iris.

"Rark!" She slapped his cheek. His eyelids fluttered open for a heartbeat, one brilliant silver orb staring up at her, a thick, black ring dancing within it. A flicker through hugrokar. Lyss snatched after it, grasping the mind before it sank away again.

Stay awake Rark!

The buzzing in her head mounted. Around her, the Aether pulsated, pressed in; just as she had pressed against Archer's wards. Pressed to breaking point. Realization drained through her. *He means to break the divide. He* wants *Rark to fall.*

She had no idea how to stop it. She shook Rark again. If she could get him out of the circle, if she could find a way to break the giant ward, then maybe—

Another giddying pulse; another prickling down her neck that turned Lyss' bowels to water. *Not yet,* she willed it.

Somewhere beyond, on the other side of the veil that split the worlds, something shifted. Lyss felt it like a rock dropping into her gut. Paces away, a shadow breached the grass as if were the sea and the shadow a sea serpent from Hreogan legend. Its form was too deep to make out clearly but for a roping body and spike-tipped spine. It ducked down again, scattering ripples through the grass as it went, as if the earth were water. *Ginndir.*

"Hane, Brin!" she screamed, straining her eyes to the blurred figures hovering at the circle's edge. "Get away, don't come in!"

A groan sounded in her ears. Lyss spun, gaze landing on the semi-conscious figure in the grass, white hair whipping in breeze, sword forgotten beside him. Darrin. The Eder Wildner twitched and lifted a hand to his face, gingerly feeling the wound to his nose. Lyss' gut knotted like a rope, heart rising into her throat. Not here. He should not be here.

"Darrin get up, get out!"

She stumbled over to him, grabbed his tunic and hauled him up not knowing whether to punch him or hug him. The Wildner blinked at her, swaying on the spot, struggling to focus. *Why didn't you just stay at home?*

"Lyss?" he asked.

"Hurry, he's summoning the ginndir."

Darrin stared down at her, gaze locking onto hers. Fear flashed across his face.

"Lyss, your eyes. There are rings—"

"Not now. You have to get out." Lyss scooped up his sword, hooked one arm under his shoulder, and pulled him along. He resisted, but she was stronger. She hauled him up, half-dragging, half-carrying him towards the edge of the ward.

"Lyss, stop, I can walk."

Lyss released her hold and let him stand. Out of the corner of her eye, two more colossal shadows rippled through the Otherworld's shallows, circling like sharks. The Aether gave a shudder and Lyss sucked in a breath as it pressed in on her, hot and thick as soup. A wisp of smoke coiled around her ankles. Lyss stared at it. *No, not smoke. Aether.* She glanced up. The world had taken on a misty sheen. She stood quivering, attention turning inwards, seeking out hugrokar. Rark was still there, just.

Darrin's hand found hers, grazed and bloody. Lyss caught the whiff of sweat as he drew close and searched her face. His forehead creased. "You're not alright."

She pushed the hilt of his sword at him. "Get to—"

Across the link, Rark's control broke. The pressure building under her skin rushed out, channeling back across the bond. Rark's mind fell away. A boom split the air. Then a hiss. A wave of hot mist enveloped them. The force of it knocked Lyss off her feet and, next to her, Darrin thudded to the earth.

"Get out!" she screamed, just as a howl of a ginndir pierced the night—a deep throbbing roar that vibrated through her chest.

Lyss rolled to her feet, fumbling for her sword. The mist settled, pooling out from the heart of the ward to swirl around her shins. Beside her, Darrin scrambled up, elbow over his nose and mouth as he coughed.

"What is this?" he asked, kicking at the mist around his feet to try and clear it.

"Aether." A tingle rushed up Lyss' spine and she spun, catching the shape as it flickered through the smoke. "It's not safe here." She tracked the mist to the edge of the ward where it buffeted the rim like water against a sea wall.

She reached her hugrokar out, groping blindly after the presence that was suddenly not there. *Rark!* No answer. Another gut-shuddering howl. A high-pitched cackle answered it. Then a shrill whistling from somewhere further off. Lyss swallowed and clenched her hands around her sword. Darrin's back pressed against hers and he shifted, bringing his sword up before him.

"Don't stay, Darrin."

"I'm staying."

Lyss snuck a glance over a shoulder. His jaw was set, gaze fixed out over the mist lapping at their knees. No changing his mind.

A shape rose out of the haze and sharpened into a six-legged ginndir. A human-like torso with long spidery limbs arched from it, plated like a crab. Aether ran off its carapace back. A drumming whickered from deep in its chest. It reared up, its two front-most limbs poised to strike.

With a nod to Darrin, Lyss launched into the fray, blade whirring. Her sword sank into a leg and she sawed it deeper. Beside her, Darrin axed his sword into the ginndir's abdomen. A head twisted round at them on a long neck, with silver irises in bulbous black eyes. So very human—and so very not. Lyss wrenched her blade free, and swung again, driving her sword into the belly of the beast, gutting it from navel to chin. Silver blood and white entrails slopped down her tunic, scalding her arms. The ginndir shrieked, listed, and crashed face down in the mist, legs askew.

"Lyss, look out!" Darrin's shout pulled her up. Another ginndir loomed over them—all jaws and no head. Eel like, but for the callous growths stuck to its side like barnacles. At its tail end, the body tapered away, white and worm-like, reminding Lyss of the intestines she'd seen in Matter's Emporium. The eater coiled itself and lashed. She swore and snapped her sword up to meet it.

A gray paw intercepted, black claws gouging into barnacle skin, and then Brin was standing before her, bear skin rippling on her back. Lyss blinked. Her friend's form was wrong. The ursa's shape was human— probably just enough to get through the ward—but fur ran down her torso, thickening towards her limbs where her hands and feet curled into giant paws. And she was huge; at least half her normal height again.

"I got this," Brin said, her voice gruff as she spoke through long incisors.

"I told you to stay outside. You need to guard Hane."

Brin grinned at her. "I was never one for listening. Besides,"—she pointed a clawed finger outside the circle—"I set him a task."

Lyss followed her finger. Outside the circle, Hane scrabbled in the dirt, knife digging lines into the grass.

"I told him to make the strongest damn ward he's ever made in his life." Her grin faded as she took in the mist creeping up around her waist. "We might need it." With that, she spun on the ginndir, bellowed and lashed a fist into the creature's body. Gobs of saliva flung through the air and the eater rounded on Brin—Lyss forgotten.

"By Sepp," Darrin muttered, watching them trade blows; a battle between giants.

With a roar the ursa broke the ginndir's jaw. The aetherling writhed, thrashing in the mist. Brin lifted a heel over its head and stomped, ending the creature with a wet, splintering thud. The bear-kin rounded on them. "Get to Hane, Ursa says more are coming!"

A clacking sounded above Lyss' head. Hot breath rolled against her back. A colossal plated body arched out of the mist, a giant centipede with spines along its vertebrae the length of Lyss' arm. A pair of mandibles snapped at one end. Four black eyes, irises the size of geis coins lined the creature's jaw. *Shit.* Her stance was wrong. Sword in the wrong position.

The aetherling lunged. Lyss glimpsed serrated spines along its back. Someone screamed her name. The mandibles opened above her, ready to pulp her skull to splinters. *Helpless.* The dark rose inside her, glee spreading her lips.

And swallowed her.

Lyss' vision dimmed, dropping away into gray. *No.* She rallied against the sinking sensation as it pried control away from her. Her feet shifted of their own accord, fingers honing together. *No!* She imagined sinking nails into the walls of her tunnelling vision and clawing, hand over hand, upwards.

Not yet. I will not go yet.

She bit down on her tongue. Pain bloomed in her mouth. Her head cleared, vision sharpened, color returning. She shouldered up and out, tearing off the cloud settling across her mind and, with a scream, came back to herself.

The mandibles clacked above her.

"I am not helpless!" she roared.

The Aether around her waist *surged,* shot up, and thickened over her head; mist *coalescing* into…into a barrier. A shield!

The ginndir's jaw met the Aether-shield, as if it were a solid wall. Its body arched, mandibles snapping inches from her face, straining against mist.

Sepp be. Lyss reached out. The mist shifted, a fresh sliver breaking free of the Aether-shield to return her touch. *What the 'byss?* Lyss sucked in a breath and the tendril of the mist came in with it, warming her lungs.

"Lyss!" Darrin raced to her side, grabbed her arm, and hauled her away from the shield and ginndir still straining in it.

"It protected me," Lyss said, numbly.

"Brin says there's more, we have to move." He pulled her along, striking out for the edge of the circle. Brin waded up behind them, mist rolling off her chest as if she were the figurehead of a ship. Beyond her, the centipede ginndir jerked free from Lyss' mist shield.

"Brin, run!" Lyss screamed at her.

Brin didn't look, instead she leapt, legs pumping through the fog. The ginndir arched up, roared, and thundered after them; tens upon tens of legs stamping into the earth as it raced after them. Lyss pushed Darrin on.

Run, run, run!

A clap of something not quite thunder echoed from deeper in the ward. The sound of tearing followed, reverberating through the air like ripping fabric magnified one hundred-fold. Around Lyss' waist, the Aether-mist shifted. It pulled at her hips, soft at first, then built into an urgent tug. She squinted at the circle's edge. Close as they were, the lines and runes were almost impossible to make out under the fog.

"There!" Brin shouted. Lyss followed her finger. A shadow, presumably Hane, scurried in the distance. Then Lyss' gaze landed on a figure standing in the dais of another circle, arms out before him, as if conducting an orchestra, the glowing runes of a ward diffused in the mist. Archer. His personal ward was smaller, just eighteen rune points, its lines interlocking with the larger twenty-four-point ward. And he was laughing. Full, head-thrown-back bellowing laughter.

"They're coming, Elena," he cried. "Hold on. They're coming."

Another rip, another shudder. The current intensified. Brin spun, grabbed Lyss and Darrin's arms, and dragged them along. A roar at their backs signaled the ginndir gaining ground.

Lyss' hugrokar twanged. She glanced back, just in time to see a shadow drop out of the sky and bury its talons into one of the centipede's eyes. *Rark.* Still alive. Still fighting. The ginndir shrieked, snaking its head, throwing Rark first one way, then the other. The rarkyn dug at the creature's eyes, burying his talons deeper. If those mandibles caught him...

Get out of there, Rark! she called, but his mind was underwater. *Sepp damn it.* Lyss hesitated a moment more, then spat a curse and twisted free of Brin's hold. "Keep going," she said as Brin jerked to a stop, pulling a huffing Darrin up on her heel. Lyss gestured at the edge of twenty-four-point ward and Hane's shadow scrabbling beyond it. "Go. Get out and stay there." She looked back at the ginndir and Rark clinging to it. "I know what to do."

"But—" Darrin began.

Lyss set her jaw. "I can't leave him like that, Darrin. I won't."

Brin turned her gray eyes on Lyss, then at the bucking ginndir. She gave a curt nod. "Be careful."

Lyss took a breath, steeled herself, and turned back into the mist.

"What, no—*Lyss!*" Darrin shouted, then, "Let go!" as Brin dragged him off.

Lyss blocked her ears to his calling. The mist buffeted around her chest, threatening to pull her under. If she fell, she would not get up again. Across the mist, Rark punched his talons into the cavity of the ginndir's eyes. The creature tossed its head, gnashed its mandibles and screamed; a crisp squeal on the edge of Lyss' hearing. She broke into a run. Mist dragged at her legs.

"Get out of my way," she snarled at it. To her surprise, it obeyed, clearing a path for her. Her strides lengthened. In six steps she was bearing down on her quarry. Lyss reached for the Aether in her muscles, felt it ignite, and sprang.

She hit the ginndir's head square on. Her free hand scrabbled for a grip, a scale, an ear, anything. Her fingers closed about one of the razor spines and pain stabbed through her palm as it cut in. Across hugrokar, the rarkyn flinched.

Rark. She pushed her mind close but was met with a wall of rage. *Rark!*

No good. *One thing at a time.*

She kicked her boots into the ginndir's plated side, trying to find a toehold. A spitting hiss and a grating of talons came from the ginndir's other flank. *Rark.* She caught a hold, dug her feet in and pushed up, and found what she was hunting for.

Those coin-like eyes. Four of them lined in a row, obsidian pits in swirling silver wells. Lyss unsheathed her sword, and the irises swiveled onto her. Fear clenched her gut. *Now, do it now.* She plunged the blade in. It pierced through the third eye in the row with a squelch, sinking halfway up the blade.

The ginndir screamed and jerked. Lyss scrabbled for a hold on the creature's neck. Her hand closed around another spine and it cut deep. She grunted. *Ignore it. Hold on. Fight. Finish it.* She kicked, aiming her heel for the pommel of her sword buried in the ginndir's eye. Her aim was true. The blade stabbed down. Deep. Through the sole of her boot, Lyss felt a heartbeat of resistance, before a dull, muffled crack issued from the ginndir's skull. A shriek warbled up its throat. It slumped, body crashing through the mist with her atop it. With a meaty thud, it hit the earth, the impact jolting her spine.

Silence.

The fog pressed against her, caressing her skin. Under her, the ginndir shivered, twitched, and stilled. Lyss held her breath, heart slowing in her chest, then released her lungs and eased off the creature's back. A foot to its head and she wrenched her sword free.

The fog pulled at her hair, sending strands into knots and buffeting her braid. An itching tingle in her hands made her look down. The torn skin on her palms were scabbing over. Lyss palmed her sword. *Worry about it later.* She searched the mist. No sign of the runes. She swallowed. *Calm down, it's a damn circle. Start walking and you'll reach the edge.*

A growl jerked her sword up to a shadow. It moved toward her in an all too familiar lope.

"Rark." She dipped her sword, relief filling her.

The rarkyn burst through the mist, talons aimed at her head.

CHAPTER FORTY

scrunched, lips drawn back, teeth bared, the wound in his belly crusted in dry blood. And his eyes: they were *both* silver. Silver with a thick, black ring in each iris, dividing it into two concentric circles. *Ginndir eyes.* He swept in, talons lashing. Lyss parried, left, right, left, saw an opening and planted her boot into the rarkyn's chest, driving him back. His giant wings unfurled, stroked down, and swept him away, vanishing into shadow as he dove into the Otherworld.

Lyss groped her mind after him—feeling the bond constrict as he reached their limit. She drew her mind closer, closer again, so close their hugrokars began to mesh. She slammed her mind against his, *pushing* just like he'd scolded her for doing weeks before.

Rark! WAKE UP.

A twitch. A moment of lucidity, a flash of something—fear, dread—before his mind fuzzed over again. No good. She needed more, something to shock him out of it. She stopped. That was it.

Lyss sucked in a breath and seethed the Aether in. Just as Rark had taught. *Hope your kratting ready for this.*

She sensed him circling back, returning for a second round. *Make it quick, before another ginndir came along, and then get out of the ward.*

If you can even get out. She shoved the doubt away.

Rark lunged out of the mist, talons extended for her neck. Lyss smacked his hand away with the broadside of her blade; seethed in a last dreg of Aether.

Do or die.

She gathered the power inside her and *pushed.* Everything went into it. The Aether gala roared out of her, buffeting the mist like a gale. It hit Rark head on. He flinched, as if he'd come too close to an open flame, feathers turning on end. The cobwebs around his hugrokar parted and Lyss took her chance. She plunged in, relaxed her hugrokar and reached everything out to the scrambled mind at the other end. Her thoughts enveloped his, hugged him tight—a shield before the Fever caught him up again.

Her senses reeled. Blood and Aether filled her nostrils, burned in her lungs, throbbed in her bones. She flexed her fingers, lifting them before her face. They were long and taloned. Fine feathers on her arms ruffled in the Aether's current. *Like wind over water,* she thought dumbly. Pain throbbed in her gut and she winced.

Reythr cursed mancer.

The thought made her pause, but she wasn't sure why. The ward gave an audible shudder, then another crackle.

The tear's growing larger.

Instinct pulled her gaze down. Horror blossomed inside her. The mist still swirled around her feet, but now she saw beyond it. Into the Deep. The abyss. It was like standing on a mirror. Under her feet, the world inverted. Instead of rock and soil, it became air. A vortex of thick Aether churned below her: a whirlpool waiting to swallow them. Within it, shapes circled. Shapes of all kinds, some small, others mountainous, all spiraling upwards to the crack above them, like insects to a flame.

Oh Sepp.

The words jarred inside her. No, that wasn't right. *Not right.* With a gasp, Lyss' mind jerked loose from the rarkyn's, her awareness snapping back to her own body.

Rark's mind slammed against her hugrokar. Enraged, but sharp and clear.

Rark, stop, it's me!

Recognition rocked through her, and Lyss pulled her mind away a little more. Rark blinked, his right eye fading back to its usual red.

"Lyss?"

"Still here, still alive. Let's get the krat out of here." She wiped her sword on the leg of her trousers and sheathed it. Streaks of silver seeped into the fabric of her pants in large wet blotches. Rark's nostrils flared, taking in the scent.

Ginndir blood.

The thought flashed through Lyss' head. She retreated from Rark's mind a little more. The fuzziness returned and the rarkyn swayed, clutching one hand to his temple. Lyss tightened her hold on him again, visualizing the husk of a shell, only this time with the rarkyn inside it with her. The pressure built in her skull; the ache in her gut returned.

"How are you—" Rark started.

"I don't know," Lyss swallowed and massaged her head. "But I can't keep it up for long."

The mist rippled again. Rark's eyes darted down, paused, panic lancing through him. He vaulted forward and wrapped one arm about Lyss' middle. With a lung-crushing lurch, he sprang, wings flaring open, beating hard as he lifted into the air.

A heartbeat later, a rumbling crack shot through the fog. Below, the earth bucked and rippled; water on a choppy sea. The Aether boiled, surging upwards like steam from a pot. It buffeted Lyss in Rark's grip. She wheezed in a breath.

Higher, higher, higher. Rark's single-minded thought pounded through her.

Higher from what?

The Deep, he answered before Lyss had a chance to actually ask. She peered into the whirling maelstrom below. A pair of jaws pushed up, breaching the mist like the open maw of a whale.

Oh gods. "Move Rark, move!"

"You think?" the rarkyn screeched back.

The jaws rose; two mountains lifting out of a sea. Rising into Terresmir. The skin was rough and ragged, the color of moss and lichen. In each lip, long pointed teeth the size of trees grew. The black hole of its gullet opened under them, and it was gaining on them.

"Higher Rark!" Lyss screamed. A downbeat soared them up, then Rark banked and Lyss felt the cold singe of galdar along one wing. The top of Archer's ward. The barrier quavered as they swooped under it, then warped as the mist hit and pushed against it.

Light flared from below: a green flash as twenty-four runes gained fresh power. *Archer.* The ward steadied. At the heart of the circle, the jaw's ascent slowed, reaching an apex. They hung in the air. Seconds ground by. At last, with a crackling, scraping groan, they drew down, closing about the dead centipede ginndir. The last Lyss saw of the crea-ture was its tail sliding down the titan's throat. Then the maw snapped shut and sank out of view. The mist surged into the vacuum with a clap of thunder.

Cold sweat slicked Lyss' face. Her heart thudded in time with the aching wound in Rark's belly. *Madness,* she thought, head feeling like it had been stuffed with wool. *I'm going mad.*

Not yet. Rark nudged her hugrokar, drawing her attention to the cold burn around her wrist as he pumped his wings. Lyss glanced down. Iga's last rune still glowed, holding on despite everything. *Oh Iga.* She clutched her hand to her chest and Rark swooped lower, drop-ping feet at a time as the mist pulled them first one way, then the other.

It's circling back. Lyss looked up to find Rark staring down at the spiraling mist. *His runes won't hold it a second time.*

Archer.

Rage boiled in her at the thought, not all of it all hers. She didn't care. *If I live through this,* she swore and reined in her thoughts as they fuzzed. Live first, deal with Archer later. In the air, Rark pitched side-ways, banking hard and Lyss' stomach sunk into her bladder as she swung in his grip. The cold pressure of a ward washed over her again. The edge, it must be.

Panic twisted through Rark's hugrokar and he banked, following the circle's edge. *We're trapped.*

Lyss ground her teeth. Her thoughts were fuzzing again. She shook her head. Focus. *Wait for that…behemoth to break it.*

Rark's belly knotted. *That only works if it doesn't eat us first.*

You got a better idea? His responding silence told her everything. *Get ready…I'm counting on—*

"Lyss!" A shout made them both look down. Faint shadows waved at them though the mist. "I see them! Lyss!"

The current swept her and Rark past and she lost sight of them. Rark banked, pivoting in the air and fought back against the mist. He dropped feet at a time, wings flaring with every stomach-churning dip.

"There!" someone yelled. *Hane.* "Throw it!"

A rope smacked across Rark's chest. Rark's free hand closed around it and he forced it into Lyss' grip. Leather, she realized as she took it, spotting the clean cut through the twisted hide. A faint jangle of metal on metal sounded from the edge of the mist. Horse bridle. Hope flared inside her. She wound the hide around her wrists, over and over. Sepp pray it held.

"Pull!" someone else shouted. *Darrin.*

Lyss' arm snapped taut, jarring everything from wrist to shoulder. Beside her, Rark's tail feathers twitched, following the direction of the line, wings pumping. They surged through the mist. At the edge of the barrier, the Aether parted and the three of them stood there.

Darrin: leather rope wrapped around his hands, half his body extended out over the runes.

Brin: in full bear form, teeth clamped around Darrin's belt, paws pressed against the twenty-four-point ward for leverage. Hane stood beside her, one hand clenched around Darrin's belt, the other pressed over a set of inactive runes under their feet, ready to cast. They were all there.

With a grunt of effort, Rark pumped his wings. They smacked against the ward and he dug one set of talons into it. Cold shot up Lyss' arm as her own outstretched hand met the barrier and she tried to find a hold. The ward shimmered under her touch, a kaleidoscope of color before her eyes.

A hand fell around her wrist, clamping down like a vice. Lyss jerked her head up and found herself nose to nose with Darrin.

"Grab hold!" he shouted.

Lyss locked her hand around his forearm and he pulled—only to find the ward resist as it encountered her skin.

Below, the Aether shivered. A giddying pulse ran through Lyss' head. Rark tensed, digging the talons of his feet and hands into the ward, ignoring the cold screaming up his limbs.

It's coming. Hold your breath.

A deafening crack ripped the air. Lyss glanced behind, just as the mountainous jaws breached upwards again. This time they kept coming. A gush of hot Aether-filled breath pushed the mist back, and the maw crashed into the top of the rune-ward. Power poured from the heart of the ward underneath—raw, undiluted Aether. *True Aether. The Otherworld.*

The way was open.

Terror grabbed at Lyss' chest, catching her heart and clobbering it against her ribs. The Otherworld plumed from the center of the ward. Seeping outward, thick and black. It rolled toward them in a turbulent wave that sucked up the mist in its path.

Within the plume, the titan's body pushed upwards, tearing through the jagged rent. A chorus of yips and cries issued from beside it, and shapes spiraled out of the tear. More ginndir.

Dread numbed Lyss' core.

Reythr, it's a swarm. Rark's thought shivered through her, turning her hairs on end.

The ginndir slammed into the top of the barrier next to the nose of the titan and set upon it. The ward hummed like a drum as they pressed, pushed, clawed and bit. The runes flared, and a weak pulse ran up the barrier, pushing them back for a heartbeat before they fell on it again.

"Fool," Rark hissed.

Lyss rounded on Hane. The boy was staring up at the titan and the monsters buzzing around it, mouth agog, face bone white. "Hane! Activate the circle!" she shouted. At his name Hane started, gaze snapping to hers.

"Do it now!"

"No!" Darrin shouted, squeezing her wrist tighter.

Lyss bared her teeth and looked past him, meeting Hane's stare. *"Now,* or it will swallow you all."

The boy gulped, eyes darting to Darrin once, then he pushed his hand into the earth. The circle ignited around him and a fresh wave of cold pressed against Lyss' skin.

"Darrin let me go."

"I won't." He gritted his teeth, tightened his grip on her wrist and wound the leather bridle about his free hand. Brin rumbled a warning from around his belt, legs braced for purchase against the new circle.

The Otherworld wave rolled closer, cresting higher as it drew in the mist.

Lyss reached up, digging her fingers under Darrin's, but he refused to budge. "Darrin!"

"I'm not letting—"

The wave hit. Lyss had enough time to gasp a breath before the heat seared through her, tingling her muscles as it wrapped around her body. Like a giant hand, it plucked her up in its current and *pulled.*

Somewhere on the other side of the twenty-four-point ward, a rune wavered, then cracked. The barrier slumped, flickered, and Lyss thought she heard a scream over the clamor of ginndir. The circle collapsed. Panic jolted across hugrokar as Rark's hold was swept away. He tumbled; his talons dug into Lyss' leg. She grimaced, gritted her teeth. *Kratting rarkyn.*

A creak of leather snapped Lyss' attention back to Darrin. Brin's teeth were tearing through his belt. The ursa's neck and shoulders bunched and she hauled back, paws scrabbling against Hane's circle.

We'll never get inside. The cold realization dawned on Lyss as the Otherworld dragged on her limbs. *Not now.* She began working at Darrin's fingers again, desperation growing as he clung on.

"You idiot, let go!" she screamed at him, then coughed as Aether burned down her throat.

It happened in slow motion. With a pop, his belt snapped, springing free from his tunic. Behind, Brin lunged after him, teeth closing on air.

With their last tether to Terresmir gone, the Otherworld closed about them, Aether dragging Lyss and Rark in—taking Darrin with them.

Fresh heat battered Lyss' body, snarling her up like a leaf in a gale. Her sense of the world vanished. Nothing but a searing hot that tossed her about in its grip. Her head throbbed; ears rang.

"Hold on to me!" she shouted, clutching Darrin's forearms. Between her blurred vision and roaring ears, she could barely make him out, but Darrin's hands locked tighter around her wrists. Together they tumbled, Aether spinning them in its torrent.

A taloned hand wrapped around her ankle, steadying them. *Rark.* He wheeled above, wings fighting the current. For a moment they made headway, to where Lyss couldn't say, before the Aether released a gust, slamming him into them and sending them into a sickening spiral.

Lyss' ears popped. *We're falling deeper.* Like a fish caught in a net; dragged inexorably towards that smiling crack between the worlds. Rark's talons bit into her ankle, drawing blood. She barely noticed. The pressure mounted in her head, as if her brain might knuckle its way out from between her eyes.

A stomach-dropping jolt knocked one of Darrin's hands out of her grip. Lyss clawed after him.

"Stay with me!" She dug her nails into his remaining hand, and he fluttered at the end of her grip; a kite in a storm. The Wildner's face was white, eyes wide, lips blue.

Sepp, he's holding his breath.

A pain on her wrist flared under Darrin's hold. Iga's rune. *No, not now.* She reached for Darrin's flailing hand, his fingers rasped against hers for a heartbeat, then they were ripped away again. The rune around her wrist tingled. Her head spun. Lungs burned. *Focus Lyss.*

With a hiss she felt rather than heard, the rune fizzled, then snuffed out, like a wet finger to a candle flame. Vanished. Her last defense against the blood pact. It was over. Her mind was at its mercy. *Helpless.* Something shifted and shivered awake inside her; uncoiled from its cave. It rose up her spine, forcing its way into her head, and clouded her vision to gray shadow. Her heart leapt into her mouth.

Fight it. Rark's thought sliced through her daze. Sharp and clear, as if he'd spoken it inches from her ear. *Don't become its plaything.*

A violent cough sounded in her ears. *Darrin! Oh Sepp, Darrin is drowning.* He'd pressed his free hand over his mouth. Behind his fingers, he gasped, gagging as the Aether hit his lungs.

"Don't breathe it, Darrin!" She wrapped both hands around his remaining wrist, but her grip began to slide.

"Lyss," he wheezed and reached. Wet fingers clasped her own, smearing thick, oily marks over her knuckles. Her heart gave a twist. She blinked hard to clear her vision, just enough to see him. Dark tendrils worked down Darrin's throat, across his chin and jaw. His lips were black, a trickle of dark oozed from the corner of his mouth. Like tar.

"Lyss," he croaked again. "I'm sorry." He sucked in another breath and fell into a fit of coughing, spraying the dark substance across her face and arms.

"Be quiet Darrin! Just hold on." *Rark!* But the rarkyn was tumbling.

She was tumbling.

Darrin's hand slipped, sliding from her grasp. Lyss threw herself forward, catching the edge of his sleeve. He lurched in the air, Aether whipping his hair as it roared past. He looked up at her—and smiled.

"I—"

Threads snapped. A soft gasp. The weight in Lyss' grip released.

Darrin was ripped away. For a breath, his pale face shone up at her in the black. The dark swallowed him. Gone. Lost to the Aether.

Forever.

CHAPTER FORTY-ONE

Archer tasted blood. Not the searing hot rarkyn forge water, but a warm metallic lapping in the back of his throat. He gritted his teeth and swallowed. Inside him, his Aether reserves unwound, like the windlass of a ship dropping its anchor into the depths. It had started off like a dream, all that power coiled inside him. But as he'd poured one sliver, then another into the ward, it'd unraveled. Now it was in freefall.

You always knew it would be hard, he reasoned and tried to ignore the steady knock against his masterpiece—his twenty-four-point circle. The ginndir swarm pressed against the barrier; teeth, claws and bodies all pushing. *So many.*

"A little more Elena," he whispered. "They will come soon. They have to."

The giant ward shuddered, runes at their breaking point. Archer dug into his reserves, channeling the magic into the circle and it flared. His relief turned into a stomach-clenching chill as he reached for more but found nothing. End of the rope.

"Come on damn you!" he shouted at the Aether. "Show your face!"

As if in answer, the darkness released a thundering crack. Archer's eyes bulged as the pressure on his ward increased tenfold. He strained his fingers, throwing everything he had into the circle. The runes of his own eighteen-pointer dimmed as he stripped away its power and fed it to the greater ward. *Hold it, Markides, hold it!*

A rumbling groan vibrated through his chest. The awe-shattering power entered the circle long before he saw it. Horror trickled up his legs. It was back.

The titan was back.

And it had brought company.

It rose, dwarfing the ginndir buzzing around it. They looked like bees swarming around a hive; the titan their queen. The peak of the beast pricked the top of his ward. The magic spasmed and warped.

"Not yet!" Archer closed his eyes, scraped every ounce of power he could find and thrust it into the runes. Pain burned through his fingers and toes, lancing up his extremities. His breath caught. Heart lurching, stopping, then stumbling on again. His eyes popped open.

That was it, he was done. There was nothing left. He'd used every drop of Aether in him.

Should have taken more blood.

The black veins twisted along his arms, writhing up, racing toward his heart. Above, the titan's nose kissed the barrier. The ward shattered. Its top split open and Aether spewed out, like one of the burning mountains of Eyos.

His knees hit the ground, hope eroding as the great ward died over his head. *Elena.* He would never see her again. And she would never laugh. Never eat and drink again at Eventide. Never smile.

"Why didn't you come?" he asked the tumbling Aether. "All I had was a question. One question."

His numb hand rummaged inside his coat, pulling out his journal. All that research. Years of attempts. Worthless. If only he'd had a name. He threw it aside and his gaze slid to Hane. The boy was screaming inside his own circle, the ursa the only thing holding him back from flinging himself over the runes and into the Otherworld.

Run boy. He lifted a hand, clenching his teeth as he pressed a thumb to the eighteen-point ward carved into his wooden palm. Nothing happened. No magic. No power. It was Isaac all over again. Elena all over again. He'd failed. His runes had failed. His daughter would never walk this world again. *Sepp curse this earth.* He crawled over the grass. Hand over hand, until he reached the boy's circle. He pressed his black-veined hand to the tip of one rune. One last ward. *Run boy, survive.* Archer drew on the only magic he had left.

Life.

Pain burned through him. Squeezed at his chest. He closed his eyes and gave himself over. The runes flared. Brilliant, blinding.

It's done.

His vision dimmed. His heart slowed. At his back, something unearthly howled.

Live, he thought—just as a ginndir's jaws ripped into him.

CHAPTER FORTY-TWO

Hasek was running by the time he reached the city walls. He pounded over the cobbled bridge of the southern gate, skidding to a stop as he spied two guards nestled under the arch, helmets together, muttering. One abruptly threw his head back and released a deep belly chortle. It cut off when the guard's attention landed on Hasek.

"What in Sepp's name are you doing getting in so late? The party has already started," he said as Hasek stopped before them and bent over, hands on his knees, wheezing.

"Close the gate."

"What?"

"*Close the gate!* Hurry, before it hits."

The guards took in his red cloak, exchanged a look, then one stepped forward and a plated mitt thumped onto Hasek's shoulder. A wisp of gray beard entered the corner of his vision as the guard leaned close.

"Are you all right, sir?"

"No, I won't be all right until you close the Sepp damn gates!" Hasek straightened, digging through his pockets until his hand closed around the silver brooch. It gleamed dull in the torch-light, unpolished for years. It'd been a long time since it'd last seen the light of day. The Conclave's crown and scepter imprint flickered in the guard's torch light. He turned it over, revealing a second insignia on the brooch's back. A rose and crown. *To think I almost threw it away.* Brennus had counselled him not to. He thrust it at the guard's chest. "By the Order of the Crown, I command you to close this city."

"We can't do that, it's winter festival. The gates—" the guard's companion began until his fellow nudged him and showed him the back of the brooch.

"Rose Brigade," he muttered. "Do as he says."

The companion, a fellow at least twice Hasek's age with a muscular width that only came from years tending a blacksmith's hammer, blanched. "Yes sir." He gave a short, awkward salute, as if unused to the gesture, and scurried off into the guardhouse.

The first guard handed the brooch back to Hasek. He was older still, with a white beard and deep lines on his brow, but his eyes were sharp. "All the gates, sir?"

"All of them."

The white beard twitched as the guard mulled a moment. "I'll take you to Officer Marsh."

Marsh turned out to be a middle-aged guard patrolling the top of the wall, leading a squadron of four. When White Beard introduced Hasek and his request, the officer's gray-flecked eyebrows shot up.

"What about the people? We can't sleep them all within the walls," he said.

Hasek checked his impatience. "They'll make do," he said. The words came out clipped and angry anyway. "Just get it done. Rouse all your guards. I don't care if they're half drunk, get them on the walls."

Marsh blinked at him, then squared his shoulders. "Listen here, what is all this about—"

Hasek muttered an oath and worked four runes through his fingers, casting the spell out beyond the battlements. Six paces from the edge of the wall, the air blurred, as if a clouded piece of glass had been drawn over it before snapping into sharp focus. Hasek snapped a finger upright, adjusting the angle of the casting. Joint gasps sounded from White Beard and Marsh's men as the casting magnified the southern fields. Hanging in the air, a dark substance roiled and billowed in a mancer's circle, strange shadows swimming and darting within it.

"Sepp be, what is it?"

"An Aether storm. And those—" Hasek twizzled his fingers, amplifying the magnification to land on a grotesque fish-like, tentacled quadruped pressed against the edge of the ward "—those are flesh eaters."

Marsh's mouth worked into a thin, colorless line, and he glanced from the sight to the dancing lights of the streets inside Torin's walls.

"Sepp be," White Beard muttered, staring at the spell.

A cracking clap sounded in the distance, and Hasek flicked the magnification out again. With a slow sinking horror, he watched a monstrous maw rise out of the swirling sea. Its teeth whooshed shut, scraping against the barrier. For a moment the ward held—then popped like a bubble. A keening of cries and caws reached them on the wind as the black mist rushed out, rolling and bubbling over the land like a flood.

"Man the walls," Marsh whispered, staring at the scene in a slow-rising horror before his training kicked in. He rounded on his squadron, voice booming against the battlements, "Get every fighter up here!"

His men scattered, bumping against each other as they raced away. Two took the stairs down to the street, the other two sprinted along the battlements.

"And rune-workers," Hasek shouted after their retreating backs. "As many as you can find. I don't care what kind of galdar they work. Bring them here." He glanced across the city, taking in the lights dancing on the keep's walls from the bonfires below.

"What about the civilians?" White Beard asked, as if reading Hasek's mind.

Marsh pulled his eyes away from Hasek's casting. "The castle," he said after a moment. "Usher them inside and barricade the Keep doors."

"Lord Karel will not approve."

"I will deal with my uncle later."

The old guard bowed his head. "Consider it done," he said, and with a nod to Hasek, departed.

"Do you have city wards?" Hasek asked Marsh.

"Old ones; 'graved above each gate. They've not been used since my grandfather's day."

Below, a gate closed with an unmistakable *whoosh-thud* followed by the clunk of a timber dropping into place behind it. *At least something is going right.* Hasek rubbed his chest, insides aching. The strain of Naqamal's summoning was beginning to wear through the last of his reserves. *A little longer.*

"You've got mancers in the city guard?" he asked.

"A few, yes."

"Put your strongest on the wards, space the rest along the battlements with instructions to fortify the barrier where they can."

Marsh nodded and then cast Hasek a look, eyes lingering on his travel worn cloak, more brown than red now. "What is your name, soldier?"

"Hasek, Corporal Hasek. Rose Brigade." The name of his old squadron tasted bitter on his tongue, but the lie was done. He had to see it through.

Surprise darted across the guard's features, then buried itself again and the man held out his hand. "You could have run for the hills, instead you came to warn us. Not many men would do that."

Hasek took it, feeling uneasy. "Don't thank me yet."

"If not now, when?" Marsh's gaze slid back to Hasek's casting. "We might not make it through the night." A low rumbling groan echoed from the fields. As if in answer, a bell tolled from within the city. The music stopped, the last note dying out on the breeze.

"I suppose it's too much to hope for backup?"

Hasek worked his mouth open. "It's a day away at least."

"Hold the wall for a day," Marsh stood taut in his boots, eyes fixed on the black wave rolling towards the city. "Against that."

Hasek nodded.

Marsh gripped the edge of the battlement, fingertips turning white against the smooth stone. Hasek thought he saw a tremor in the man's arms, but then the guard shifted, straightened, and his jaw lifted, as if he'd made his decision. "Then for one day we will hold this wall."

CHAPTER FORTY-THREE

LYSS SCREAMED. DARRIN WAS GONE. *Gone.* HER DARRIN. A flash of pain around her ankle, and Rark's talons ripped away. Alone in the Otherworld. Blood throbbed in her ears, down her jaw and into her teeth. Everything was burning. Inside and out. The Aether lashed; bucked and pulled; tumbling her in its maelstrom.

Over it all, Lyss' skin prickled. Dread clogged her throat. *No.* Inside, her monster shifted, bloodlust and glee rising in a wave. Gooseflesh washed over her; terror turning her arms weak. *Not yet. Go back.*

The darkness rose. A shadow in her mind's eye. Monstrous. She imagined it on four-legs as it circled. Form shifting and sliding, snapping at her heels. She bit back a sob, and deep-down rage flared. *You swore you'd not cry again. Swore on—*

A blistering wave of Aether rocked her, tangling her mind like a spiderweb in a hurricane. Her thoughts twisted, fraying until, with one last gust, they broke.

Her mind unhinged; senses flung into the wind, unfurling and stretching.

Aether poured in. Her vision shifted.

With a gnash of pincers, she hammered her head against a small glowing circle. *Meat. Fresh meat.* It was so close, yet she could not get at it. She bellowed her frustration, battered the ward again. Inside, Terresmiran creatures huddled together, a boy and a bear, their Aether

346

glowing like coals at their cores. The boy's green; the bear's a blue-gray yellow.

Brin. Hane. Her senses lurched.

Agony erupted through her temples, all the way to her horns. The Aether spun her in its grip, tumbling her over and over, chaffing away everything she knew—wearing her down like a river rock. The current tore through her feathers, plucking her like a pheasant. *Too deep. Can't see. Current too strong.* She was falling. Again. And she would not be so lucky to escape this time. This time she'd become bones in the abyss—or something worse.

Rark! Lyss clawed after his hugrokar, but his mind was faint. Her senses warped again, and he was snatched away.

Now she raced toward a white-walled city in a throng of twisted limbs and jumbled body parts. Her six-limbed body undulated over the land, claws raking the earth. *Flesh. Flesh within.* Hooting and keening rose from within the horde and she gnashed her teeth in anticipation of the prey awaiting her. *Flesh.*

Her senses hopped again. Folding into—

Stillness.

The torrent in her head turned millpond. Lyss blinked, opening her eyes. Dark all around, water under her feet; a silent pool in a void. She frowned. This was not how she imagined madness would go.

The sound of feet pattered across the water. Lyss' hairs prickled, and with a shiver rolling down her spine, she turned.

A shape stood on the water. Not four-legged as she'd imagined, but two. A human shape. Feminine even. Lyss knew it for what it was: her shadow. Her madness. Come to claim her at last.

Fight it. She was not sure if the thought was her own or Rark's or perhaps even an old memory of Fa. Maybe all three. She swallowed. How did you fight a shadow? You couldn't beat off madness with a sword. There were no runes left to stop it taking over.

Lyss picked her way closer, half expecting it to lunge for her, forcing her to...what? Run? Run where? Stomach writhing, she closed the gap, closer, then closer again, until they were a foot apart. So close Lyss could have touched it.

As if in response to the thought, the shadow shifted, a hand extending for her. Lyss vaulted back, heart cracking into her ribs. *Run. Get away,* her instincts screamed. She held her ground.

The figure shifted again, and a face appeared: narrow chin, a mess of dark hair, high cheekbones, and hard eyes that burrowed into Lyss. Her face. It puckered its eyebrows, pursed its lips, as if testing out her range of expressions. Her double's mouth cracked into a too-wide grin, and feelings flashed through her. Glee. Delight. Anticipation. She felt it gathering its strength and her hairs rose again.

This time, the shadow lunged.

Lyss yelled and plunged backward, tripping on her own feet. The shadow fell on her, shadow-hands prying at her face, forcing her mouth open. *No. Go back!* Lyss willed at it. The madness didn't listen. It clawed at her lips: rage, grief, and desire from her shadow crashed through her head. Lyss' vision swam, ears rang. She heaved against its chest, trying to push it off and away, but her fingers sank into it as if it were fog, like the Aether. The shadow pressed down on her, pushing tendrils of itself into her ears, up her nose, smothering her. *Gods, Sepp, Fa, help me.* It was winning. There was no way to fight it. No runes to stop it. It would take over. Wear her skin like a dress.

Elation. Joy. The monster's emotions surged through her. Lyss reached inside the fog of its chest, fingers searching for a heart, a hold, anything to push the creature off. Nothing. The shadow drew her close, arms wrapping over her head, fingers picking at the corners of her mouth as it hunted for a way in. Lyss writhed; punched and kicked. Her hands and feet met air. *Kratting damn you.* She bundled her hugrokar into a ball and swung it at the shadow like a club. The mind magic struck out, and instead of resistance, the madness' mind—if she could call it that—opened itself to her.

Hunger. Rage. Grief. Desire. Survive. Live. Not helpless. Not helpless. Live. Live. Live.

Lyss sucked in a breath and wrenched her hugrokar away. *Sepp be.* She blinked at her fists lodged the shadow's body. The fog of its chest was warm, so much like the Aether. No, not *like* the Aether. It *was* the Aether. Was that it? Was that what this was? Was her madness really magic? Her thoughts spun. Was this what had thrown up the shield of Aether to save her from the ginndir? Had driven its hand into the shuck's chest? Crushed a soldier's skull to stop her seeing a death that reminded her of Fa's? Lyss stared at it, the fight in her draining away.

Gods and ginndir, had it been protecting her all this time? Growing in strength every time she drew on the Aether, until it found itself pressing up against the runes Iga had sown to contain it like the bars of a too-small cage?

Understanding rippled through Lyss and Archer's words came back to her. *She's more aetherling than human now.* The mancer had been more right than he'd ever known. She peered into the shadow's face; her face.

"I see you," she told it. She relaxed her fists in its chest. "I *see* you." The shadow mirrored her, fingers easing around her neck.

"You're me," Lyss said. "My magic." Not rarkyn magic, not galdar, but something else, something that had been growing inside her, fighting desperately to survive. Or perhaps it had always been there, and the pact had simply woken it up.

They—*she* couldn't continue like this. She couldn't keep it at arm's length. It was part of her now, as much as her arms and legs. She couldn't fight it or lock it away. This was not a monster she could vanquish.

Lyss looked at her shadow-self. It quivered above her, as if sensing her train of thought and maybe it did. It no longer pushed or probed to be let in—or was it out?—and Lyss caught a flash of something new from it. *Hope. Life. Live?*

Madness. Monster. All this time, that was how she'd thought of it. A shadow to be feared. Yet not all monsters needed to be. Rark had shown her that. What was it he'd said? Fight what you can change, accept what you cannot?

It was time to accept.

Time to become the monster.

Lyss lifted her hands and drew her other self in, embracing it like a child. Then she opened her mouth, drew in a breath and *seethed.*

Warmth rushed into her. Glee spreading through her chest, down her arms. For a heartbeat, her limbs twitched as her magic settled in, plucking and pulling her muscles like ghostly fingers testing her strings.

The dark of the Stillness eased and muted colors flashed through the dim. Subtle blues, reds, oranges and, there, a flicker of pink. The water under her feet captured the patterns and reflected them back. Together they gaped.

Beautiful. In that moment of shared thought, something clicked, like a key sliding into a lock and turning. She and her magic became one.

CHAPTER FORTY-FOUR

She stood in the Stillness, skin tingling. Inside her, the magic flexed like a phantom limb as keenly as if it were the muscles of her own right hand. She stretched her fingers, feeling the magic surge up to her skin, ready. Willing. *This will take some getting used to.*

"Good, very good." A voice issued from the Stillness. It was light, but the words dropped into her like an anchor. The Otherworld shifted and for the first time she caught a sense of…her stomach clenched, *something* coiled around her. She extended her mind out and it ran against a presence in every direction—it was wrapped around her, shielding her from the storm outside. And it was enormous. Heavy beyond her ability to measure, a mass she couldn't grasp, the same way an ant couldn't comprehend a mountain.

"Tell me your name."

Not a question. An order.

She gaped, mouth dry. "My name…" she floundered. *Her name.* What had she called herself again? "We are…" No, that wasn't right. "I am…" she began again. Then it was there, as if it had never left. "Lyss." She wrapped the knowledge about her like a blanket. *Lyss, my name is Lyss.*

A face materialized in the air opposite her. Porcelain-smooth features, high cheeks and a narrow jaw. Two white stag horns bloomed from its temples like snow-frosted branches. The face hung there, bodiless in the Aether; open eyes hollows to the swirling color beyond.

Like a mask, Lyss thought. Only its features were too precise, from the fine hairs of its eyebrows to the full lips. Nothing of it moved, as if the mind behind it was waiting to see if she'd say more. When she did not, the head finally dipped. "Very well." Lyss couldn't shake the feeling she'd passed a test, whatever it was.

The Otherworld shifted again, and a swirl of fog gusted into the Stillness, as if a window had been thrown open to a storm and then slammed shut again. A familiar shape tumbled through the mist, landing in the water.

"Rark!"

The rarkyn didn't move. Lyss crouched, shook a shoulder. Unconscious. Her hands brushed against something wet in his feathers and she caught the whiff of blood. His wound had reopened.

"He will live," the mask said.

It was right. Lyss' fingers found the injury in Rark's belly and felt flesh already knitting shut. The weight of the mask's presence washed over her again, and she sensed it studying her. She stiffened.

"Who—what are you? Where are we?"

A translucent hand shimmered to life in the air. The limb twisted, stretching and rippling into an arm. A set of shoulders followed, then a neck, until a full bodice cloaked in a deep green robe stood under the mask's glow. It tucked its hands into its sleeves.

"One question at a time," it bade.

Lyss hesitated, staring at the hem of the aetherling's robe as it floated in the dark. *No feet.* As she thought it, a pair of pale toes appeared, poking out from under the robe. Her gaze snapped up to the mask. "What are you?"

The head of branches cocked. "Need you ask?"

A chill twisted in her stomach and the word came out in a whisper, "Eternal." She swallowed. She'd thought they were a myth.

"Not a myth."

Hairs rose down Lyss' arms, the sensation slithering into her legs with a cold flush of adrenaline. Her new magic twisted inside her, anxious and afraid. *Be careful,* it warned. Lyss hugged herself. "You're reading my thoughts."

"I am reading your cues. Your thoughts are your own."

Lyss shivered and instinctively reached for her wrist before remembering the runes were gone. She stretched out her hugrokar to nudge

Rark instead. His mind flickered with a brief flash of pain under her ribs, then ebbed away.

Still bonded.

"Where is this?"

"You are inside me. I am sheltering you from the storm."

Her gut folded on itself. Gods and ginndir, she was in an Eternal's stomach.

"We do not have bodies, not as you think of them. Relax, I have not eaten you."

Lyss' belly folded a second time. She didn't care what the Eternal said, it was near enough to mind reading. And was it her, or did it sound amused? The antlered head nodded to Rark. "Once your bond-partner wakes, I'll return you to Terresmir."

Lyss stared at the mask. "You know about our pact?"

"I can sense it. Down here it shines like a thread spun from your Terresmiran sun." The mask drew close, and again she felt those sightless eyes drinking her in. "Though I believe the bond you share is just the start of what I sense. Yours is a curious magic."

Lyss' heart leapt, and she tripped over her tongue to get the next words out. "You've seen something like it before?" *Were their others like her? Like them?*

"Something similar. A long time ago."

And? Lyss wanted to ask but held her tongue. Better not to bait an aetherling such as this. The Eternal sensed her question anyway.

"He died," it said.

Lyss swallowed, her magic pooling into her muscles as her heart quickened. *Easy,* she bade it, took a breath and steadied her nerves. "How?"

"Lost control." The mask motioned to Rark. "Similar to your friend here. Only your predecessor didn't fall into the abyss, the magic tore him apart." The antlers titled and those eyes bored into her again. "In that sense, you are similar." The edge of its mouth quirked, the first hint of an expression Lyss had seen from the aetherling. "You make a good pairing. Shame you want it gone."

Lyss' insides crawled. Definitely mind reading, she didn't care what it said. "Can you undo it?"

"No." The Eternal's tone cut through the air like a blade.

The hope died in her chest. "I'll go mad," she said without thinking.

This time the Eternal laughed, and the mouth of its mask curled into a closed-lipped grin. "You've crossed that threshold already, don't you think?" Something in those hollow eyes gave a knowing glint and Lyss understood. If she were to have gone mad, it would have happened when her magic tried to overcome her. If she'd denied it and tried to batter it down, she would have lost herself. She knew that now. Had she not accepted it, the magic would have slipped inside her like a haunting and turned her into its puppet. She shivered at the thought and glanced down at Rark.

"I promised him we'd be free," she said.

"Perhaps one day you will be. But not now." The mask drew closer. "Now you need each other. You may have already guessed, but you are not like other humans, Lyss. The Otherworld is not lethal to you— though it should be."

A black-blooded face reared up through Lyss' thoughts, screaming as the Aether closed in around him. *Oh gods, Darrin.* Guilt crashed over her and snagged the breath in her lungs. She blinked back tears. *You selfish krat.* The words stung inside her. *Worried about madness? At least you're alive.*

"As far as madness goes, all you have to fear is your bond-partner working the Aether too-hard and falling into Fever." The Eternal's mask tilted to Rark, listening. Lyss sensed a faint stirring on the edge of her hugrokar. "I believe he's got a better handle on it now."

Lyss barely heard the Eternal. Her thoughts were filled with Darrin's desperate hold around her wrists. How he'd clawed at her skin, veins throbbing in his face. What had he tried to say before he'd been torn away?

"As for other concerns, there is one. You may have tamed your magic, for now, but you've far from mastered it. If you do not learn how to control it, it will consume you. Tear you apart. As it did your predecessor."

The Eternal's words brought Lyss back to herself with an unpleasant turning in her gut. *Tear apart?* She swallowed. "How do I learn control?"

The robe under the mask shifted, and a glowing hand pointed down at Rark. "Your pact-partner is a good start. In that regard, his magic is similar to yours. He can teach you the basics."

"What of the rest? Who will teach me?"

"Another witch, of course."

"But all the witches are dead."

"One lives. Buried in Illredus. There you will find answers."

Illredus. All roads lead there. First Loric, then their sought-after cure, and now a teacher to help her master this strange new power inside her. *What is it about that city?* What answers would she find there? She scowled. *Wouldn't kill it to be a little more specific.* She considered probing further, but something in the way the Eternal had spoken told her it had said all it would on the matter.

A dull roar from above turned her head upward; a faint tremor rippled through the stillness. Beyond, the Otherworld stormed, colors churning together into a muddy brown. Shapes bobbed and dove within. Darrin was in there, somewhere. His black-veined face flashed through her mind's eye again. So pale. Aether burrowing into him like woodworms through a log. She'd betrayed him, lured him in and let him die. What would she tell Hane?

"Why did you save us?" The words were thick in her mouth.

The Eternal's horned head bowed towards Rark, expression softening as it took in the aetherling. "This is not the first time I've pulled this one out of the depths on my watch—though he doesn't remember it. You could say I've grown a little fond of him." The white face turned back to Lyss and its smile grew. "And *you.* You fascinate me."

An uncomfortable creep worked its way up Lyss' limbs as the Eternal gave her another one of its penetrating stares. Above, another grinding roar sounded, and Lyss craned her neck, squinting up at a speck of light shining overhead like a single star in a night sky. The tear.

"Is there any way to stop the storm?" she asked.

The horned head followed her gaze. "I will close the breach."

"What about the ginndir?"

"Those trapped on Terresmir will slowly die."

The memory of a white-walled fortress flashed through Lyss' head and the echo of hunger that went with it. *Torin.* Her gut clenched. "How slowly?"

"It depends on how much Aether they drew in before they crossed the threshold onto Terresmir. Some in a few turnings, others will take cycles."

Years? "That's too late!" Lyss thought of the dancing crowds in the square. Of the fiddlers and the merchants in their stalls. They wouldn't stand a chance. Their lives would be choked out as surely as—she veered her mind away.

"Is there nothing you can do?"

"The blood call was strong," the Eternal said. "They are hungry. It has been a long time since they've tasted Terresmir flesh."

"Then use blood to call back," came a rasp from their feet. Lyss looked down, just as Rark's hugrokar unfurled across her senses. The glow of the mask brightened, the darkness took on shades of grays and browns, and the scent of dry blood filled her nose as Rark sat up. She tried to draw away, to deaden the sensation, only to find she couldn't— their hugrokars were meshed into a woven lattice, threads thick and strong. A quiver in her gut signaled Rark, realizing the same thing. His eyes flickered to her, then to the Eternal as he rose to his feet, wincing as the healing wounds pulled taut. A shiver bristled through his feathers.

"Blood brought them," he said after a moment. His gaze fixed on the white face. "Blood can draw them back."

"Rark, you're hardly standing, you can't—"

The rarkyn shook his head. "Not me." He jabbed a talon at the mask. "*It.*"

If the Eternal was perturbed by the claw in its face, it gave no sign. "An Eternal's blood will not do. I am of the Aether, like them."

Lyss thought her hope had already gone, but the Eternal's words crunched in her chest, twisting in the cavity where hope had been. Darrin's drowning face floated up through her thoughts. She pressed a fist to her bosom and rubbed, swallowing hard. *No more,* she thought. *I don't want to see any more.*

Beside her, Rark shifted under the mask's empty gaze. "Use my—"

"Your blood may have summoned them here, but the scent of the city has them riled. It will not be enough to turn them back." The head of branches turned, and the white face's glow washed over Lyss. "But yours might."

She blinked, heart thudding into the base of her spine. "Mine?"

"You are different." The mask came close with a motion that glided rather than stepped. The Eternal drew in a long breath and a tendril of mist near Lyss' heart coiled up its nose, as it if were sampling the aroma of a steaming cook pot. Gooseflesh crawled over her belly.

"Your blood is…exotic," the Eternal said. "It's not quite aetherling, but not quite of Terresmir either." It circled, green robe rippling like flexing muscle. Lyss fought the urge to cringe. If the Eternal wanted to eat her, it would have done so already. Next to her, the feathers down Rark's spine ruffled on end and his tail twitched.

"A delicacy," the Eternal said as it finished its lap. "Perhaps enough to entice the ginndir back."

Lyss moved her tongue around her mouth, working up enough moisture to wet her throat. Her pulse drummed a swift staccato in her ears. "I'll do it."

Rark spun on her, eyes flashing as the anger flared through hugrokar. "Lyss, think first—"

"How much blood?" Lyss asked.

The Eternal's face was still as stone, glowing features giving nothing away. "Ginndir have good noses," it said at last. "A few drops is all it will take."

Rark's scowl eased with a trickle of relief. Lyss clasped the hilt of her blade. "Then let's do it." She readjusted her clammy hand on the leather grip and pulled.

"Wait." The Eternal's fingers pressed into the back of her hand, jerking her draw to a stop. Her sword eased back into its sheath with a click. "A few drops yes, but you have to break through their blood frenzy first."

"How does she do that?" Rark demanded.

The Eternal's sightless eyes didn't leave Lyss' face. "You will have to get close. Close enough to divert their attention. It will be dangerous, and once they have your scent, they won't forget it." Its head swiveled to Rark and his unease rose over hugrokar as the Eternal's gaze lingered on him. "You'll need help to outrun them."

A nervous twang ran through them both, and Lyss was not sure if it had come from her or Rark. At her back, she could feel Rark's feathers rising again. To her surprise, he rallied against it and straightened with a nod. "She'll have it."

"You don't have to risk—"

His mismatched gaze turned on her. "Ginndir have a taste for my kind already. If the city falls, where do you think they'll go next?"

The wilds. Lyss thought. *To wherever the Aether is thickest on Terresmir. To where the rarkyns are.*

"Besides," he tilted his head, his own horns listing sideways in a movement eerily similar to the Eternal's. "Can you promise I won't die if the ginndir eat you?"

"I die, you die." Lyss recalled the words Rark had spoken in Iga's circle all those weeks ago. It felt like years. Back then she'd not known whether to believe him or not. Even now she wasn't sure—and, she

realized with a jolt, neither was he. When he sensed her come to that conclusion, his teeth flashed into a smirk.

"I will carry you," he said. He ruffled open his wings, and Lyss sucked in a breath as the motion set off an echo of aches through her back and belly. In a blink, the Eternal was beside him, a thin white hand pressing on his shoulder.

"Save your strength," it said. A hot, itching tingle smarted down Lyss' side. A squawk worked up Rark's throat, and he tried to pull away from the Eternal's touch. The slender fingers clamped down.

"A bit of mending. You'll need it."

As Lyss looked, the healing wound in Rark's abdomen began to worm, flesh stitching together, scabbing, ridging into livid scars. Fine white feathers sprouted over them. The ache in Lyss' gut eased and Rark let out a breath and rolled his shoulders, wings ruffling on his back. The Eternal released him.

"Get ready. I will bear you both to the breach," it said. "From there you must make your own way. It will not take long to heal the tear, so do not dally. I will keep it open as long as I can."

"Thank you," Lyss began, then stopped when she realized the Eternal had never given her its name. "Who are you?"

A smile. "I have many names. But for you, I'll answer to Tinashe." The horned head turned upward, toward the jagged tear, star-like in the darkness above them. "Use it wisely."

Tinashe shifted, and a luminous hand extended to them, palm out, inviting. Lyss and Rark exchanged a glance. Rark gave a shrug and took it, talons wrapping the Eternal's dainty hand, dwarfing it like a child's. He crouched, opening his wings and offering his back to Lyss. She clambered on, tucking her knees just under the crook of each wing and they closed around her, cocooning her in. Not knowing what to do with her hands, she buried them into the thick mane of feathers that ran over Rark's shoulders, clasping them into tufts. Once settled she nodded to Tinashe.

The green robe shimmered, deepening into shadow as the air about them uncoiled, as if a great body had been nestled around them. A warm wind whipped her hair, buffeted her torn and bloody tunic as thick, murky tendrils swept over them. *The Aether.*

The shadow unfolded around them, stretching open like a pair of wings. With one almighty down stroke, they swept upwards. Joints popped down Rark's spine, his stretching muscles burning through his arm and into Lyss as Tinashe pulled them towards the grinning gap.

They gathered speed. Hurling up, mist streaking past, and still Tinashe drew them on. *It means to slingshot us out,* Lyss realized and her stomach churned into a ball.

The tear loomed above them, a crescent shaped sun behind a storm of mist.

"Be ready," Tinashe's voice reached them.

Rark's wings ruffled open and Lyss' heart smacked into her ribs as she slid backwards. An elbow locked around one knee, catching her.

Hold on, Rark sent. *Fall and you squash like a berry.*

Lyss stifled the choke in her throat and buried her fingers deeper into his feathers. *Don't drop me.*

She wasn't sure, but she could have sworn she felt a flicker of amusement. It was gone as quickly as it had come as she sensed Tinashe's grip slacken about Rark's wrist. The shadow surrounding them fell away. The Aether thundered in her ears.

"Go," Tinashe called behind them.

Rark's wings unfurled to their fullest extent, snapping wide, flight feathers flaring. The Aether caught them and spurred them higher, further, whipping Lyss' hair free from her face. A laugh bubbled up inside her. *This is madness. Utter madness.* She bit her lip before it spilled out in a scream and leaned her hugrokar close. *Any last words in case we die?*

I should have asked for three rabbits.

Together they plunged into the mist.

CHAPTER FORTY-FIVE

Corporal Hasek paced the top of the battlements, listening to the Aether crackle against the city wards. Inside, the dim glow of runes lit the grim faces of men and women as they stood at their stations, hands pressed to the smooth wall of their city. Many wore the green garb of the Torin guard, but many more were dressed in the color-streaked tunics and skirts of winter festival, necks and wrists still adorned in wreaths of braided ribbon and yellow winter poppies.

Less common, but nonetheless present, were those in servant's garb —cooks, stable hands, even a ragged beggar—who had answered the call.

Few cities can boast that kind of loyalty, Hasek thought. Though not all had been eager. A few folk had fled to the north gate, battering it with fists and household items—chairs, even a heavy oak table turned battle-ram—and nearly overwhelming the guard there until reinforcements arrived and sent them packing back to the Keep.

As Officer Marsh had predicted, Lord Karel had not approved of Hasek's decision. Less than an hour after the officer had ordered the Keep opened, the old lord had come storming up to the battlements, wine thick on his breath and cheeks ruddy. His thin white hair was wispy atop his wrinkled forehead, as if he'd been roused from bed— which, Hasek considered, he probably had. Upon seeing Marsh directing a band of the guard to bolster the western gate, Karel had marched straight up to him, hissing like an angry cat.

"Why in Sepp's kratting name is my courtyard full of—" At that moment, an aetherling had slammed into the ancient ward, sending ripples of green sparks across the barrier, along with a show of teeth and claw. Three paces down the battlement, one of the guards buckled, hands slipping from the stone as he slumped, Aether reserves spent. The barrier above them shivered as the ward's power redistributed itself. A heartbeat later, an old hawkish man dressed in a farmer's tunic and trousers stepped from a queue of townsfolk, pursed his lips, and pressed his hands against the stone. The runes atop the battlement flared again, and power flowed into the ward once more.

Lord Karel gawped, mouth turning into a perfect circle.

"What in Sepp's name—" he started and as Hasek opened his mouth to answer, Marsh shot him a warning look before snapping his heels together and giving the man a short, stiff bow.

"We are under siege Lord Karel," he said.

"I can well see that, nephew!" the lord spat. "By whom?" He glanced at the roiling cloud. "By what?"

Marsh dipped his head a little lower. "The Otherworld, m'lord."

Not the answer he'd been expecting, Karel's jaw worked a moment, his reddened cheeks paling. "Baer's mercy," he muttered at last. He took in the ward again, and then the rows of townsfolk dispersed every twenty paces along the wall, runes glowing under the warders' fingers. "How did this happen?"

Marsh exchanged a look with Hasek, who cleared his throat. "It came from beyond the southern gate. I believe it's the result of a summoning gone wrong."

Lord Karel's pale, wrinkled face had swung on him. "Who are you?"

"This is Corporal Hasek," Marsh said. "Rose Brigade. It was he who warned us the Aether storm was coming."

Lord Karel's eyes narrowed. "Pray tell, how did you come to know of it?"

Marsh's mouth drew into a thin line. "This is not the time to cast blame, uncle. The runes are old, and our warders spread thin." He'd gestured down the battlements, just as another of the guard collapsed and a fresh guard stepped in to take her place.

Hasek placed a hand on Marsh's arm. "It's alright officer, I will answer the lord's question." He turned on Lord Karel. "The summoner is an old mancer with a grudge. I've been tracking him through the mountains."

As he spoke, another aetherling barreled into the ward, a long-bodied thing with six legs and a plated tail bearing a pincer at its end. Its teeth sank into the barrier, scraping across the magic before they lodged and held the creature close. A purple tongue lathered against the ward and Hasek and the warders of Torin stared into a gaping gullet.

A shiver rose through Hasek, and he fought not to show it. Beside him, Marsh looked almost green, while Lord Karel blanched, a tremor passing over his shoulders.

"We need casters," Marsh said. "The wards will not hold if they're set on like that."

He'd not directed the point to anyone, but Karel turned, swallowed and motioned to the Keep. "Use my personal guard."

Marsh blinked at the old lord, eyebrows rising. "My lord—"

Karel drew himself up, clenching his shaking hands. "I'll not be the reason Torin falls." He strode toward the wall. "If we are to fall, I fall fighting—not cowering in my chambers."

With that, he lifted his hand, flexed his gnarled fingers and a green bolt arced through the air. It struck the aetherling suckered on the side of the ward, cracking teeth and bone, and sent the creature back into the mist.

If only that had been the end of it, Hasek thought as he clung to the wall, huffing as he gathered his shrinking pool of Aether to cast another spell into the horde. In the five hours that had passed, the ginndir had swarmed the ward like flies around a honey pot. They pressed on the barrier in the hundreds, big and small, their weight sending ripples of green across the shield.

We can't hold for much longer.

Ahead of him, a section of the barrier buckled. A long, serrated limb pierced through, snapping over the heads of the warders like a whip, sending them diving to the flagstones. Hasek leapt forward, reached for his dwindling Aether and sent out a casting. The spell sliced through the air, joining two others as it smacked into the limb. Their combined power severed it in a crunch of breaking carapace. The limb flopped, dropping into the waste at the bottom of the wall where the ward met the earth, smearing the ground in its silver juices.

"Hold the ward!" he shouted, turning on the warder responsible for the section. At the wall's rune point, a girl, no more than fourteen, gritted her teeth and pressed her white fingers harder into the stone. Sweat ran down her cheeks and neck, soaking through her maid's frock. No one stood behind her to take her place. The row of warder reserves was empty.

Hasek swung about, the call for reinforcements dying halfway out his mouth. It was the same at the other rune points.

The ward bucked again as another point failed, then another; power shimmering as it worked and reworked itself.

"Take their places, take their places!" Karel's voice cried from far down the battlements. A volley of arrows sluiced across the gap, passing through the ward before burying into the ginndir. A few of the monsters fell away, but most of the arrows went unnoticed.

Hasek squeezed out another spell, this one fizzling and dying before it even met the ward—and the power holding Naqamal to Terresmir quivered. The shuck must have reached Brennus by now, surely. Not that it would make much difference. Torin would fall long before help could reach them.

"Damn it," he muttered. It had been a long shot, and they'd all known it.

A gasp sounded from behind him and Hasek spun in time to see the maid-girl slump at the rune point. Hasek lunged, catching her before her unconscious body cracked against the stones. Above them, the ward shuddered, snapping smaller again. A howl rose from the ginndir beyond as they swarmed in, stopping short mere feet over their heads.

Curse it! Curse them all—

A bellow throbbed through the air, scattering Hasek's thoughts to the wind. The sound hummed in his head as if his skull were the flute of a ringing bell. Cries erupted down the battlements and he craned his head up. Dread hit him like a kick in the stomach.

A head the size of the Keep itself rose out of the smoke—mouth ajar like a jagged mountain range. It surged up, high over the barrier, a colossal neck arching behind it, angling the titan's maw like a serpent about to strike.

Gods have mercy.

Hasek laid the girl on the flagstones and pressed his hands out to the rune point. The rough graving scraped under his fingers and he pushed everything he had into it. A brief snag at his core and Naqamal's summons came undone as he diverted all his energy into the ward.

The barrier sprang into shape above him. The wall of ginndir fell back, waiting for the titan to make the killing blow.

Shouts echoed up the battlements. Hasek glanced over, half expecting to see warders fleeing their posts, but instead they were pointing. He followed their fingers, catching sight of a shadow as it streaked past, banked into the darkness, then loomed close once more. It looked like—he stopped, recognizing the shape a heartbeat before it came into focus.

Rarkyn. On its back: *the* girl. *Lyss.* Sword raised, eyes ablaze, she raked the blade across the backs of the ginndir, its honed edge biting into their flesh as if it were butter. Howls erupted in their wake and the pressure on the ward eased.

In a streak of steel and feather they swept over Hasek's position, so close the rarkyn's red eye swiveled and locked onto him as they past. On its back, the girl's skin glowed green in the rune-light, one eye a blood-red mirror of the rarkyn's; her pupil a pin prick in her fear. Still, she rode on, fingers clenched into the rarkyn's feathers. Her blade swung behind the rarkyn's beating wings, then swung again, edge nicking the bodies of the ginndir below. The aetherlings spun from the ward, arms, legs, pincers, and claws snatching for them, but closing only on air as the rarkyn whisked past, slipping and sliding like a shadow under candlelight.

Hasek tracked them upwards, high over the curve of the ward, straight for the titan poised over the barrier, neck still arched. They leveled out before its mountain of a head, the rarkyn's wings spreading wide as they glided. The titan's eyes, easily the size of one of Torin's gates, followed them. Hasek squinted, watched the girl straighten, twist her blade in her grip and slice it down the back of one forearm. Then she switched grips, repeating the move on her other arm. The titan's nostrils twitched, its cavernous jaw opening to allow a river of a tongue to taste the air.

"Sepp be."

Hasek turned to find Officer Marsh beside him, face pale and cheeks sunken from a night of working galdar, his drawn sword lax at his side as he watched the pair above.

"Don't question it, just look," Hasek said, nodding to the ginndir beyond his rune point. In a slow slink, they were clambering over one another; clawing higher on the walls of the ward, intent no longer inward but up.

"Is it me, or is the storm thinning?" Marsh asked. Hasek peered at the swirling smoke and mist. The officer was right. Where the Aether had tumbled and boiled, it now settled into a flowing haze. Utter darkness had ebbed, giving way to a faint red and gold hue in the east.

Sunrise.

Another head-swimming roar hummed the air, snapping Hasek's attention up as pebbles danced at his feet. The titan was on the move. Its head swung after the girl and the rarkyn as they banked and dove. One breath, two heartbeats, and a chorus of ginndir howls reached their ears. Louder, and louder again until the clamor merged into one long, pulsating roar. In a blur, the rarkyn swept past, wings beating hard. Hasek caught the flash of the girl, sword raised, blood slicked across her arms and tangled braid streaming out behind her, before they were gone. Lost behind a stampede of twisting bodies following in their wake.

Above them, ginndir abandoned their assault on the ward, joining the throng in whoops and screeches. Through the thick of bodies, Hasek glimpsed the rarkyn wheel south, sweeping through the lilac sky. The girl's sword flashed, fending off first one beast, then another when they got too close.

The pressure on the ward fell away, and the barrier swelled and stretched, as if shrugging off a heavy yoke. Hasek looked down the wall, searching the other rune points—the men and women were pale, slumped on the wall for support, but they all held.

"Where is she taking them?" Marsh asked. Hasek glanced up. The girl and the rarkyn were little more than a blot in the sky. Head of a horde of ginndir. They swept across the Torin plains, the girl like a mancer-general of old, leading her parade of monsters to battle as they chased the retreating fog, heading for the dark mist hanging low on the southern fields.

They dove into the cloud to a mind-numbing roar. At their backs, the titan ginndir rose above the horde, twisting its gargantuan head and dove in after. In its wake, a long ridge of spines, as tall as the Keep's towers, cut through the monster parade, rippling the beasts like flotsam on the sea. Ginndir poured in after, their dark shapes writhing over one another as they fought to follow.

"Right back into the breach," Hasek said, shaking his head, not quite able to believe their luck.

Under their watch, the parade dwindled, their shapes growing indistinct in the mist. Their howls turned to an echo on the wind, until there were no howls at all. No shapes to dread. Hasek blinked, making out the brown grasses and ravaged fences of the Torin plains. The sky brightened, and he spotted white clouds on the horizon.

In the distance, the Aether dissipated, burning off like a true fog. For a heartbeat, the grass plains warped, shivering as reality folded back into place, settling as the curtain of the Otherworld drew shut.

CHAPTER FORTY-SIX

Skaar dove through the tear, the breath of the ginndir hot on his tail feathers. He could almost taste their hunger.

Reythr, this is a ridiculously bad idea.

A twitch of his tail sent him banking, darting deeper into the furnace. The girl twisted, knees digging into his ribs as she tensed, lashing her blade. The metallic smell of her blood filled his nose, sweet like honey and rusted nails, before it was lost in the molten scent of ginndir blood. Something brushed the end of his tail. A heavy thud of a maw snapped shut at his back and Skaar's gut shriveled to the size of an acorn. *Close.* He seethed the Aether in, its heat radiating down his wings, and surged forward.

Still the ginndir followed, streaming behind them in a long arcing tail—the Otherworld's tear a shrinking star behind them. At its head, the titan swam, every huff of its humid Aether breath on his heels, sending Skaar's heart thumping. The girl twisted again, squinting through the churning smoke.

They're through, she sent, sensing the question rise in him before he could put words to it. Behind them, there was a rumble, as if mountains were on the move before an echoing crack of thunder. *Tinashe.* Skaar's ears popped, and the Aether bucked as if a giant boulder had been dropped into it. He clamped his arms tight around Lyss' knees, tucking his wings close.

Hold on.

The wave hit them, flooding Skaar's bones in heat, pitching them deeper. Behind, the parade broke apart, shadows tumbling past them like hail as they were flung into the Otherworld's underbelly. Skaar snapped his wings open, muscles pulling and stretching. The girl hissed, spitting out a curse that was lost to the current as Skaar grit his teeth and fought the Aether's pull.

Too deep. Too deep.

The pressure built in their skulls.

Skaar strained, flinging his senses out, probing the currents about them, searching for one that felt light and quick; one that would guide them back to the shallows.

Too—

"There," the girl's sword thrust out before his gaze, level with his ear, blade pointing up and a half-hand to his right. As her voice rang into the depths, she added: *That way.*

Skaar hesitated, sensing her certainty. How could she possibly know?

Trust me. Lyss urged.

A heartbeat of doubt. *Reythr be damned then.* He pushed back the creeping haze, seethed Aether in afresh, and swooped forward. He hit the current, felt the indeterminable pull at his core and spread his wings, coasting on its power, one with the Aether's flow. *No ripples.* Wonder bloomed inside him. This feeling. He knew this. He remembered riding Fengar's tail on it, mind nestled in the pack's hugrokar, safe from the Otherworld's delirium: *rasvenger* in the truest sense. True Aether flight.

The deep black shifted to muted browns and grays, the pressure in his head easing. Ahead, a speck winked into sight; a silver eye glinting in the distance. Shadows wrapped around them, a familiar dark against the dimness. It fastened around his limbs, seizing his wings. Lyss yelped and Skaar's heart vaulted into his throat, and together they were plucked out of the current like a fish under a hawk's talons.

"Not too fast or far, young ones." The words filled the Aether around them, the familiar voice echoing in Skaar's ears. "Dangers await on that tide."

"Tinashe," Lyss breathed, shoulders unknotting.

Before them the Aether condensed, tendrils surging together, coalescing into a familiar hollow-eyed face. "It is I."

"Did it work?" Skaar asked.

A smile, a slight nod of horns. "It did."

"And Torin?" Lyss asked.

"Safe."

Lyss released a sigh. "Good. That's good." Grief twinged inside her, laced with guilt and again Skaar tried to pull away, only to find the magic that bound their minds tight refused to let go. He turned his thoughts to other matters, casting his senses out and finding Terresmir and its Aether-sodden fields at its edge.

"We can find our way back from here," he said with a small ruffle of his wings as he dangled in the shadow's grip like an overripe fruit.

The Eternal's hold eased and a pressure fell underneath his feet: an echo of Terresmir earth. He stumbled, straightened, and released his hold around Lyss' knees to let her slip from his back.

"You have not asked your question," the mask said.

Skaar frowned, then turned as the spark of hope rose across hugrokar. Lyss swallowed hard, fingers knotting together before her.

"Is it true you can revive the dead?"

"The dead are for Baer to keep. It was decided long ago."

Lyss nodded, and where Skaar expected disappointment, he saw acceptance. Fresh grief and guilt welled up over hugrokar like a bubbling spring. Lyss' jaw tightened and her hands fisted together, turning white at the knuckles. Tentatively, he reached out across hugrokar, resting his presence on the edge of her thoughts like a comforting hand on a shoulder. Her breath shuddered, mist swirling into her where it should have killed her, and she nodded again.

An echo rolled up from the deep, a long, dim cry that shivered in Skaar's bones. *Ginndir.*

"You should not linger here long," Tinashe said. "The ginndir have your scent now."

Even as she spoke, the shadows shifted in the deep beyond. Soon he'd see them—and they him. He held out a hand to Lyss. She rubbed a blood-caked palm against her brow, smearing the grit on her face, then took it.

"Thank you, Tinashe," she said.

The horned head flitted close, mouth a finger's breadth from her ear. Skaar ears popped again, and he saw the Eternal's lips move, but heard no sound. Across hugrokar, surprise flickered, and Lyss' eyes widened, darting to the glowing face, then to Skaar. The Eternal pulled away and gave Lyss a nod.

"My luck to you," the Eternal said. It turned to Skaar. "This is the last time I rescue you from the Deep, little Unluck."

Skaar's breath caught, feathers rising down his neck and shoulders. *That name.* A slow grin spread across the Eternal's face before it inclined its head and washed away—like silt sinking in water. The shadows dissolved around them, and the Aether tickled the edge of Skaar's thoughts. Time to go.

"Brace yourself," he warned Lyss. "We've been in the Otherworld a while. It might be a shock."

The girl had enough time to frown before he reached for Terresmir, spread his wings and surged back to the plane of earth and sun.

CHAPTER FORTY-SEVEN

Lyss woke to soft feathers pressed against her cheek.
A headache pounded behind her brow. Her muscles were cold and stiff;
her lungs raw, as if she'd run for a day and a night without stopping.
She was moving, a gentle rock from side to side, as someone carried her
on their back. *Rark.* She groaned, cracking open her eyes. A feathered
shoulder and folded wing nestled her in. Beyond it, brown fields and a
dazzling blue sky.

Welcome back. Rark's voice sounded in her head.

What happened? She cast her mind back. Heat, warmth, Aether, an
odd twisting, folding sensation in her stomach before cold. So much
cold. It had been like falling into a frigid pond: the heat stripped away
from her in an icy blast. The air…it had been so *light.* Thin. She'd
gulped in breaths, not able to draw in enough. Panic, then darkness had
overcome her.

You passed out when we hit Terresmir. A silver eye glanced over her, a
faint trace of a dark ring still in its iris. *I did warn you.*

A breeze rustled the grass and Lyss shivered, skin prickling. Without
thinking, she reached out, groping for the dregs of the Aether in
Terresmir; for the warmth she sensed pooled in the trampled earth. Her
hugrokar lurched as Rark pulled on the pact, scattering her thoughts
like a flock of birds.

Enough Aether for today, he said. He tightened his wings around her and kept walking.

Lyss coughed, tongue dry and chalky in her mouth. *Perhaps you're right.* She lifted her head and gazed out at the road they were following. It cut through the pasture, following a toppled fence. Ahead, two lone trees dotted the horizon, branches stripped bare, twigs forking up to the heavens.

"Where are we?" Her voice left her in a rasp.

"On Torin's road." Rark shifted his head and Lyss made out the glint of white walls in the distance. She scanned the sky, spotted the sun in the east and orientated herself. Still south of the city, but miles away.

"Sepp, we got blown quite off course."

Rark shrugged a shoulder. "Happens."

They walked on in silence and Rark's strides, twice that of any human, swallowed the distance. Tucked between the warmth of his wings, Lyss' eyes drew shut, exhaustion seeping through her limbs, turning them heavy. Gods, she hoped Hane and Brin made it through okay.

Illredus. There you will find answers. Tinashe's whispered words came back to her, and Lyss recalled the unearthly Stillness the Eternal had created with a shiver. The magic inside her flexed, twitching up like an overeager child, ready to reach out and grab whatever it could. *No.* Lyss forced it down and the power squirmed inside her, setting her muscles tingling.

It will tear you apart. Lyss sucked in a breath. *Learn control.* Find a witch buried in Illredus. What had Tinashe meant by that?

Under her, Rark's pace slowed, a nervous flicker rising over hugrokar. His tail twitched at his feet. Lyss pried her eyes open again, rubbed the crusted grit away and spotted the reason for his uncertainty. A dead rune point smoldered in the grass at the side of the road, wardlines arcing off into the field. In the distance, the remnants of a camp were strewn. Torn packs, fragments of bedrolls, the coals of the fire scattered and cold. Lyss' gut pooled into her feet.

Brin. Hane. Her heart climbed her throat. Moment of truth.

"Let me down, Rark."

The rarkyn released her, and she slid onto wobbly legs, heart in her mouth. Not them too.

Black lips, white face, choking. *Not that.* She wrenched her thoughts aside, filling her lungs with cold Terresmiran air.

Her toe caught on a log in the grass. She tripped, cursed, and made to kick it away, then pulled her blow short. *That's no log.* It was a boot. Within it, the fleshy remains of a foot and severed tibia. Panic stabbed at her gut, wrenching over on itself as if whisked by a hook. *Gods no.* Frantic, she searched the grass and saw Rark standing over a lump of cloth, hugrokar still.

"Is it…" she choked, hurrying to him.

Rark didn't reply. Instead, he stared down, expression unreadable.

Archer.

Not much was left of him. A cloak shredded where ginndir teeth had hewn through it, a belt buckle, a few gnawed bones. And one wooden hand, runes blackened in the grain.

Rark sank into a crouch, pressing the tips of his talons together under his chin.

"I thought I'd be happy to see this." His words came more fluently, without his usual stilting accent, "But all I feel is pity." He reached over, touched the false hand and muttered a string of rarkyn tongue under his breath.

Go, be with them in his hall. Lyss blinked as the meaning filtered through to her. Her muscles tightened. The pact. Stronger again.

Beneath the pile of cloth and bone, the grass was drying a sticky dark brown. Around it, the mancer's ward was scuffed and battered, runes cold. Lyss eyes roved the earth: not a wink of magic left. Her gaze stopped on a tattered leather notebook resting in a tuft of brown stalks. It lay face down, trodden and trampled in the muck. She picked it up, dusted it off and flipped through it.

Pages and pages of words. She paused at one entry.

Dear Elena,

A journal? She skipped further along, finding diagrams at the back. Circles, runes sketched in ink, charcoal—whatever, it seemed, the mancer could get his hands on. She stopped on one page, recognizing the circle drawn on it, or at least—she counted, totaling the points at eighteen—a circle very close to the summoning Archer had used the night before. In its corner, scrawling letters read:

Broke through at points six and eight. Still not enough to hold him. No ginndir. No sighting.

How many times had he worked that summons on Rark? Her skin crawled. How many times had he been forced into Fever to bring forth the ginndir?

"You bastard," she whispered, glancing back at the mancer and the rarkyn brooding over him. A new thought occurred to her. Had forcing Fever upon Rark over and over been the cause of the pact? She looked down at her hands, down at the dry blood flaking from her fingers.

Or was it something else?

"Sometimes the Aether has a will of its own." Iga's words came to her again, along with the memory of the Aether's smoky tendrils holding back those giant pincers, *shielding* her.

Sepp, what are we? What am I?

Monster, whispered something in the back of her mind. *Murderer.*

Lyss shoved the thoughts down. *Go away.*

With a shiver she folded the notebook shut, wrapped its tattered string around it and tucked it inside her tunic. Better that no one else find it.

Across hugrokar, Rark's ears twitched, perking forward to the drum of hoofbeats. His back stiffened, wings ruffling open to a half hang, dread seeping over the link, turning the muscles in Lyss' shoulders taut.

Less than a hundred paces up the road, a squad of six riders cantered, silver mail glinting over dark green jerkins. Torin guard. They were coming straight for them.

Shit.

She glanced at Rark. "Rasvenger?" she asked.

A slight shake of his head. "Ginndir are still about." His feet shifted, padding back a half step. He looked at the sky.

"Don't, they'll shoot you down in a heartbeat," she warned, stepping between him and the approaching squad, spine tingling as an echo of feathers rose along it.

At least it's not the Order. The thought died inside her as the wind caught the cloak of the second rider, lifting it in the breeze. *Red.*

Cold drained through her legs. Her hand shifted to her sword and she stepped into a crouch, squinting at the other riders. She relaxed a little. Just one Red. Her gaze drifted to Archer's body. He'd shown them what one Red could do. A flash of panic rose inside her. She beat it down. *Focus. Remember the dance.* Yet even as she tried, her muscles ached, her lungs stung, and her limbs felt heavy, as if she waded through mud.

I don't know if I have it in me for another fight.

Nor I. Rark's thought was strained, and she sensed the fear warring inside him. It fired up his legs and across his wings, screaming at him to run. To his credit, he never moved. Prickling pain stung her hands as his talons dug into his palms when the squad neared, pulling up fifteen paces away beside the broken circle.

In a blink, four crossbows were up and locked on them. Lyss stepped into a battle stance, grip tightening about her sword. Blade against bolts. Terrible odds.

"Ursa's tears, you made it back!"

Lyss blinked as a familiar figure stepped out from behind the rump of the last horse and rushed toward them. Two giant paws slung over a set of shoulders crashed into her, a rough arm gathering her up in a hug that crunched her ribs. Behind her, Rark grimaced, teeth flashing for an instant before Brin released her.

"You were magnificent!" she said, and before Rark could move she'd swept forward, one arm wrapping around his middle in a spine-popping squeeze. "Both of you."

The rarkyn's tail flared, astonishment rocking through hugrokar. His talons hovered above Brin's head a moment, before one hand relaxed onto the shoulder of the bear skin and gave it an awkward pat. Across the field, the riders eased their bows, their aim dropping away to the earth though the weapons stayed drawn, ready to snap up again.

Lyss stared at the woman. "You survived," she said, dumbly. "I thought you dead for sure."

Brin stepped back. Her right arm was in a sling, and she was bare-foot, trouser-less with a green cloak secured tight around her middle with a belt on its smallest hole. A glance at the guards saw the head of the squadron was minus a cloak and belt. "Your Wildner friend really pulled out all the stops," Brin said, beaming, "strongest damn ward I've ever seen."

A soft step followed by a scuff of boots made Lyss turn. Hane had slid off the back of a horse and was heading for them. To Lyss' surprise, the Red soldier was two-steps behind, sandy-haired and with the beginnings of a scraggly red beard on his chin. His face, all knitted eyebrows and querying blue eyes, was strangely familiar, but she couldn't place it. Her gaze flicked back to Hane.

Where the soldier's face was anxious, the boy's was drawn and still. *Odd.* Hane looked smaller and thinner than Lyss remembered. Clothes scuffed and torn, grit on his cheeks.

Haggard, Lyss thought, taking in the deep circles and blood-shot eyes. As if he'd been awake for days. She searched the edge of the twenty-four-point circle and spied the remnants of Hane's own ward still whole on the earth.

Incredible, after all that. She looked at the boy. Familiar features, so much like Darrin's. Her breath grew short, vision hazing again—not the Aether this time, just hot human tears. *How am I supposed to tell him?* She bit her lip, took a breath and forced a smile. "That's a circle to make Iga proud, Hane."

Hane's gaze slid past her, searching over her shoulder. When he saw nothing—*no one*—the light died, his pale blue eyes turning to ice.

"He's not coming, is he?"

Behind him, the Red's face fell.

Lyss' throat closed. She shook her head, and in that moment, reality came crashing down on her shoulders. Words lodged in her larynx like splintered rafters. Her breath shuddered through in a whistling sob. She pressed her hands to her mouth and doubled over, tasting spit and snot and tears.

And blood.

Hane sagged, staring at the withered grass, saying nothing, doing nothing. Lyss forced herself forward.

"I'm sorry, Hane." Her voice was thick and slurred. She reached for him. "I'm so, so sorry."

Hane jerked away from her reach, rising to his feet. "Don't touch me," he spat. "Don't *ever* touch me." His stare burned into her, angry, accusing. "How...how could you let him die? He *loved* you, and you left him for the ginndir!"

"That's enough," Brin said, stepping between them as Lyss spoke, "Hane—"

The youth's eyes flashed, his anger searing Lyss worse than any galdar spell. His hands curled into white-knuckled fists. "It's your fault. You and that gods-cursed rarkyn."

"Hane stop—" Brin warned.

"I will *not!*"

The boy's fingers were up and shaping the rune in a blink. Aether surged inside him, and a bolt of green sprang from his fingertips, slamming into Brin. It hit the ursa in the chest and thudded her flat into the grass with an "*oof.*"

"Don't you move." Hane's hand swung to Rark as he started forward. The rarkyn fell still, a hiss rising in his throat, tail fanning.

No Rark, Lyss sent as the squad's crossbows rose.

Hane shuffled back, and for the first time, Lyss saw the wobble in his chin, the shake in his hand, the sharp rise and fall of his chest as he panted. That last spell had cost him. Yet, when the Wildner's gaze locked onto hers, it was steady and cold as the grave.

A gloved hand fell over the boy's shoulder. "That's enough, lad." Lyss blinked as the Red stepped between them and pushed Hane's outstretched arm down. "I know it hurts, but you'll regret this later."

"Get off me!" Hane snarled, pulling free of the soldier's grip. He shot Lyss a look of poison.

"I will *never* forgive you."

With that, her last tie to Darrin, her last friend of the Eder Wildner turned, shouldered past the soldier and left her.

She stared after him. Numb.

"Is it true?" the Red asked, and as Lyss tore her gaze away from Hane's back and took in his earnest face, she recognized him.

"You. You're the summoner from Ira Garrison."

The Red's head inclined. "Corporal Hasek." His eyes fixed on her. "Is it true?" he asked again.

Lyss pressed her lips together to stop the quiver and nodded.

The soldier's shoulders slackened, and he turned to watch Hane as the youth passed the horses, heading for the white walls of Torin in the distance. "I am sorry to hear that. Had I known bringing Darrin here would kill him, I would never have done it. He was a good man. Better than most."

A pressure rose in Lyss' chest, like one of Brin's hugs. Only worse. "Are you going to arrest us?"

Beside her, Brin drew in a sharp breath, rising under her bear skin. "*Lyss!*" she hissed.

Hasek's gaze came back to them, darted down to her sword, then at Rark hovering behind her. His lips pursed.

"You'll go straight to the gibbets of Nilos," he said. A chill frosted Lyss' gut, forking down her legs. "You murdered a Red, burned down a garrison, and you're wielding a magic far beyond the Conclave's permit," he continued, and glanced to Archer's body. "Whether directly or indirectly, you've also killed one of the Empire's mancers."

Rage flared inside Lyss. A snarl burst past Rark's lips and the rarkyn took a pace toward them. The crossbows snapped back up. One bolt on her, three on Rark and one even on Brin.

Hasek's gloved hand shot out. "Do not shoot!" he roared, gaze never leaving Lyss. Behind, the guard held position, fingers on the triggers.

"He brought that on himself," Lyss said, forcing her voice calm, even though she wanted to scream it.

"Let me finish," Hasek said. "As far as the Empire is concerned, you are an outlaw and a criminal." He held up a hand as Lyss opened her mouth. "However," he went on, "you saved a lot of people today." His arm swept out, indicating the silver haired Torin guard and his horse, the same horse Brin had leapt from. "Officer Marsh there and his men, his lord uncle too; the city herself. And me."

He paused to let his words sink in. Lyss cleared her throat, mouth dry as sand.

"You won't arrest us?"

Hasek gave a tired smile. "A life for a life," he said. He dug his thumbs into his sword belt, and straightened, face turning a little brighter. "Besides, my orders were not to arrest you. In fact, they explicitly said to keep well away." His attention shifted to Rark, taking in the rarkyn's full height and half-spread wings. "I don't much fancy my chances for trying either."

Smug satisfaction welled up over hugrokar at that.

"You have my thanks," the Red said. "The Empire might see you as an outlaw, but to these people you are a hero."

Lyss gave the crossbows a pointed look.

"Although a somewhat terrifying one," he amended, returning Lyss' look, then directing it at Rark. "Can't blame them for being skittish."

He peeled off his gloves and held out his hand to her. Lyss stared at it, astonished. Slowly, she took it, the soldier's skin warm against her own. At her touch, the Aether inside him stirred, simmering up and seething into her. The Red made no sign he'd noticed. Lyss jerked her hand away, clenching her fist into a ball.

Hasek raised a questioning eyebrow but let the incident slide. "While I'm not sure if Torin's hospitality will extend to allowing a rarkyn inside its walls, I heard you were headed to Illredus," he said. "Perhaps we can offer aid as a way of thanks, though I suggest we do it quickly."

Brin pushed forward. "Well, now you mention it, there is a boat we need to catch."

CHAPTER FORTY-EIGHT

Is it cold in Baer's hall, Elena? Warm? Do they treat you well?

I am so tired. Tired of the road. Tired of Tykee glowering at me from his pen. Tired of failure. Every night the circles break. I try over and over, night after night, until even Tykee's blood sustains me no more. Then I sleep, and I dream.

I am tired of the dreams. Horrible dreams. An effect from Tykee's blood I'm sure. Where his mind forgets, his blood remembers. And there is so much blood.

May the Gods forgive me for what I have done to this creature. For what I have made him. But I would do it again, Elena, if it meant I could bring you back. Again and again.

A ginndir got through last night. Ate my horse whole before I could force it back. And still I have had no sighting. Perhaps a circle and a few drops of blood is not enough. Perhaps the Aether demands more, perhaps it demands it all. But dare I risk everything in one last attempt?

Not yet. Not until I master the circle. Not until I know for sure it will work.

There isn't far to go now. We're at the Northern foothills. On the other side of these mountains lie the Ice Steppes and the Khanate of Galieva. A small kingdom. Their khanate are but a few thousand, their lands half the size of Eyos, yet by all accounts, they are a fierce people—both in love and war. I'm sure you'll fit right in. With them, you'll be safe and far from the Empire's reach.

Do you hear my prayers, Elena? Do these words drift to you as you sleep? Do you still think of me, or does memory decay in Baer's hall? Six years is a long time coming. It may be a longer time still.

If you hear this—hear me—I ask one thing.
Pray for me.

LYSS SHUT THE DIARY, LEATHER COVER CREAKING AS SHE wrapped the binding back around it.

"He was a very sad man," she said.

Across the dock, Brin lifted her head, pulling her gaze away from the school of fish circling a pylon.

"The mancer?" she guessed.

Lyss nodded, leaning back on a set of empty crates to take in the pink peaks of the clouds in the late afternoon sky. If an untrained eye were to look, they might see a large shadow drifting in looping arcs over the pier, but the dockworkers coming and going from the *Nishant* seemed oblivious.

"All he wanted was for his daughter to live," she said. *Love. He did it all for love.* Even then, he had still failed. She flexed the leather journal in her grip, listening to the paper crackle inside, thoughts turning to Fa. Those days on the road, his childish glee when they sparred, the glint in his eye that meant he'd concocted a game for her to unravel.

The sword swinging down.

Her breath caught in her throat, then eased past her lips in a long, low hush. For the first time she could remember, the rage felt less. After the loss and destruction Archer had caused, she had no more anger to give. Not right now. She rubbed her chest. Her scar was cold and silent.

Perhaps she was tired too.

But she'd made a promise. To Fa. To herself. And she'd damn well stick to it.

Brin came over, scratching at the bandages on her slinged arm, fresh wrapped that morning by one of Torin's healers.

"Be gentle with it," the woman had instructed, but Lyss doubted the ursa would heed the advice. The wrappings were scuffed and torn already.

Brin stared down at the journal in Lyss' hand. "I can understand where he was coming from," she said. "To have Nina back would be…" she trailed off, then sighed.

Lyss nodded. "As can I."

The chill of the giant maw breaching through to Terresmir rose in her thoughts again. Once more she glimpsed the people on the walls of Torin, eyes upturned at the beast, faces white in terror. Her skin tingled at the memory of the grip ripped away from hers.

Darrin.

Her fingers clenched around the diary.

Such a cost. Her gaze fell on the walls, towering up behind the dockyards, beyond them she listened to the telltale sound of wedding bells. It was the fourth serenade that afternoon. After staring into the face of death, it seemed the Torin folk were living with new fervor. *At least one good thing came out of it.* She wanted to smile, to show the world she was fine—would be fine. But somewhere between her mind and her mouth, the thought lodged, lost its power, and faded to nothing.

At an approaching boot-step, she looked up. Corporal Hasek came along the pier, two laden packs in his arms. Lyss stood to meet him as he set them down beside Brin.

"There's two weeks of food and supplies for each of you in here," he said. "As well as an extra set of clothes."

Lyss glanced down at her fresh tunic and coat. "You've already done more than enough," she said. And he had. The *Nishant* had been one of the few vessels in the docks at the time of the storm. Most of its crew had been in the city celebrating winter festival, but her captain, first mate, and four hands had been caught beyond the walls. Apart from one ruddy smear on the northern dock, there was no sign left of them.

With Hasek's help, the second mate, now Captain, had replaced the crew he'd lost and was preparing the ship for sail as if the ginndir still hounded his heels.

"One more thing," Hasek said. He reached up, undid the cloak from his shoulders, bundled it up and held it out to her.

"I can't take that, to impersonate a soldier is—" Lyss cut off her protest as Hasek raised an eyebrow.

"Criminal?" he asked, with the hint of a smirk on his face. At Lyss' steely silence he went on. "Banditry is rife in the south, but no one dares to assault members of the Order."

Unless you're me. Lyss hesitated.

"If you don't want it, I'll take it," Brin said, rolling her shoulder under the bear skin. "Ursa might be too warm in Illredus."

Lyss gave a huff and held out her hands. "Alright."

Hasek dropped the cloak into them. "This too," he added, placing a silver brooch on top of it. It bore an emblem of a scepter and crown. Lyss' mouth dropped open.

"This is a mancer's brooch." She ran her fingers over the embossed ridges of the design. How she'd longed for the day when she might gain one. She had never expected it to happen quite like this.

"Markides doesn't need it," Hasek said. He leaned in. "It might help you avoid having to set fire to any more garrisons."

Lyss stared at the silver brooch in her palm. A slow, cold burn seeped through her skin from the metal. "Thank you," she said. She cleared her throat. "The man I killed in Bardas Post. Do you know his name?"

Hasek paused, then, "Claud Yannis."

"And his family?"

"A wife and two daughters I heard."

Lyss nodded, internalizing it, setting it to memory. "I will make it right."

Hasek's voice was light, warning. "I don't know if you can."

Her insides twisted, and she clutched the brooch to her chest, waiting for her nerves to settle. She took a breath and asked the question.

"How is Hane?"

The soldier shrugged one armored shoulder. "Sad, angry, not talking much," he said. "As expected."

Pressure returned around her ribs, building into a slow, sickening squeeze. "I couldn't just—"

"He needs time, and I have already explained why it's best you don't linger here."

Lyss' jaw snapped shut. "Right," she said through her teeth. *The Order were coming.* A sliver of panic stabbed through her again, as it had when Hasek had broken the news outside Torin's gate. Across hugrokar, Rark frowned, banked and turned back towards the city.

It's fine, she assured.

A bell clanged from the *Nishant,* the new captain ringing it from beside the wheel. Ship hands scurried over the deck.

"That's us," Brin said, scooping up one of the packs and heading toward the gangplank.

Lyss fixed her gaze on the Red. "You'll take care of him?" she asked.

Hasek nodded. "You have my word."

"You'll get him home?"

"I'll take him to where he needs to be."

Lyss paused, brow furrowing, then nodded. *Good enough.* "Thank you, Corporal."

"Lyss," Brin called, waving from the stern of the ship. "The boat's going to leave without us. Hurry up."

Lyss picked up her own pack and dashed up the plank. Two ship hands pulled it in behind her with a clatter of wood on wood. Brin cupped her hands to her mouth, leaned out over the rail and shouted at the sky. "Hoi rarkyn, we're leaving!"

Someone huffed behind them. "I can see that."

Brin cocked her head and Lyss turned, finding the rarkyn standing on the deck, wings settling shut on his back. He stepped around a deckhand as the man rushed to remove a tether to the dock. The hand didn't so much as blink at him.

"Is it safe to be back in the Otherworld yet?" Lyss asked.

"So long as it's shallow." His gaze drifted to his feet. "And I don't stay long."

He came to stand next to her and Brin, watching the dockworkers reel in the lines as the *Nishant* pulled away from the pier.

Brin squinted, searching the air where Lyss looked. She sighed. "Well thanks to Hasek, we have a private bunkroom to hide you in, rarkyn."

Rark cast her a look over one shoulder, red eye blurring into the colors of the sunset. He quirked a lip.

"I have a name you know, ursa."

Lyss pursed her lips. "I've been thinking about that. Rark is a little, well, obvious. Maybe we can come up with something better."

The rarkyn was silent a long moment. "How about Skaar?" he said at last.

Lyss tilted her head, considering. "It's okay, I guess."

The bear skin head see-sawed from side to side as Brin mulled. "I don't know, it's a bit…guttural."

"Shame." Rark scratched his chin. "Because it *is* my name."

Lyss stopped her inspection of the Torin River bank and looked directly at him. "You're true name?"

He nodded. "Skaar Valke."

Brin sighed. "I was going to call you Fred." She frowned. "I thought names have power over aetherlings."

"They do."

"Then why tell us?" Lyss asked.

A smirk. "Because you couldn't summon a circle between you, *and* you'd have to know my other four names first."

Brin gaped. "You have *six* names?"

Skaar shrugged. "All the harder for mancers to learn."

Lyss held out her hand. "Well, Skaar, I think we got off to a bit of a bad start," she said. "My name's Lyss Rhyos. What say we put this bloody business behind us and find a way to break this pact?"

The rarkyn gave her one of his too-wide smiles, showing far more teeth than any human ever could. The Aether shifted, and his talons pricked her hand as they closed around it.

"Good tides to you, Lyss," he said. "And yes, I couldn't agree more."

EPILOGUE

Lieutenant Regis Eugenia Leandre took in the white walls from atop her kardunn. Very white and very much *not* under siege —aetherlings or otherwise.

Sergeant Prateus Hecaelon lobbed spit into the grass edging Torin's north gate and shifted the double axe on his back. "I told you sir, the man is a liar," he said.

Leandre's gaze drifted to him. "I'll remind my sergeant to hold his tongue, and his spittle, when in the presence of civilians."

Opposite them, the two city guards on gate duty snatched a glance between them, then at the lines of the battalion on their doorstep.

"Apologies milady," Hecaelon said. Leandre's eyes hardened, black pupils shrinking to pinpricks. Beneath his cropped beard, the sergeant's face blanched. "Sir," he amended.

One of the guards cleared his throat, palming the ledger in his hands. "Your name m—sir?"

"Brennus would not send us here without cause," Leandre said to her sergeant. Her attention shifted to the Torin folk. "We are the Rose—"

"Crown's Brigade," the guard's companion breathed, quivering like a startled gutter rat.

"I am Lieutenant Regis Leandre," she continued. "We received word there was an incident with a summoning."

At the guard's blank looks, Sergeant Hecaelon added, "Aetherlings spilling forth from the Otherworld."

"Oh," the guard's face brightened. "*That.*" His chest swelled, and he swept a hand to the walls. "As you can see, we held them off."

Eugenia Leandre was not easily taken by surprise, but there, at the gate of Torin, she blinked. Once.

"You turned away a horde of ginndir?" she asked.

"Aye we did. Thanks to Officer Marsh and Corporal Hasek."

His companion pushed forward, eyes dancing. "And the—"

"*Hasek.* I knew it," Hecaelon interrupted, then fell silent as Leandre's hand snapped up.

"Your last warning Sergeant," she said. "Speak out of turn again and you will cease to speak at all."

Hecaelon's jaw clunked shut, sweat prickling across his forehead. Leandre turned back to the guards.

"Corporal Hasek is here?" she asked.

"*Was* here, sir." The guard shifted, pointing to the north-west. "He left not long after the witch did. Seemed like he was in a hurry. Took a young Wildner boy with him, sir."

A thrill tingled down Leandre's spine. *Witch?* She slid off the back of her kardunn. Perhaps not a wasted trip after all. She glided over to the two guards, quieter than a blade through snow. Her red eyes narrowed.

"Tell me more."

ACKNOWLEDGMENTS

This book took a long time to write. When I cast back through my files, the earliest, almost unrecognisable, grain of this story came into existence sometime in 2006. As is the case with any 16-year love/hate, on-again off-again project, numerous people deserve a massive thank you for helping me get it across the finish line.

First, a big thank you to my editor Cindy Kilbourne for plucking this story out of the submission pile and championing it with The Parliament House. Also to Alyssa, Malorie and Megan for their keen eyes during the line edits and proofs. To Shayne and Kolarp Em for the amazing cover. The energy and time the Parliament House team have put into this story has been nothing short of phenomenal.

To Mom, thank you for spotting something awry in the story's timeline and painstakingly plotting out every mention of time passing so I could iron out the kinks. To Dad, for reading one of my early unpublished short stories and immediately seeking me out to simply say "wow". That encouragement made me realise I might be okay at this writing thing.

A special mention goes out to my grandmother, Rae, who read and reread countless drafts of this story in its 16 year incubation, along with just about everything else I've written. Except for the horror stories. Note to younger self: do not send Nanna horror.

To my beta readers Marjan, Robinne, Kay, Rich, Kirsten, Suzzane, and Jan, I cannot begin to convey how much your insights shaped the Lyss and Skaar's journey into what it is today.

To the North Shore Writers Group headed by Tim Owen, without you I wouldn't have dug this book out of the drawer and finished it. Your enthusiasm and calls of "is it finished yet?!" at our meetings lit a fire under me. Another shout out is also due to the Litopia Writers'

Colony for their feedback and comradery through the querying and submission stages.

An enormous thank you to my husband, Anthony, for plying me with a steady stream of tea, coffee and chocolate, for giving me the time and space to write when I needed it, and for always being there when I start making mountains out of molehills. You are my rock.

And lastly, thank you, reader, for taking a chance on this tale of mine. With so many fantastic stories available, I'm honoured you chose to spend your time with Lyss and Skaar.

ABOUT THE AUTHOR

Nikky Lee is an award-winning author who grew up as a barefoot 90s kid in Perth, Western Australia on Whadjuk Noongar Country. She now lives in Aotearoa New Zealand with a husband, a dog and a couch potato cat. In her free time she writes speculative fiction, often burning the candle at both ends to explore fantastic worlds, mine asteroids and meet wizards. She's had over two dozen stories published in magazines, anthologies and on radio.

Author Website

LYSS AND SKAAR STILL NEED YOU

Did you enjoy The Rarkyn's Familiar? *Reviews keep books alive . . .*

Lyss and Skaar need your help!
Help them by leaving your review on either GoodReads or the digital storefront of
your choosing. They thank you!

9 781956 136180